TERROR TALES OF CHAOS

TERROR TALES OF CHAOS

Edited by

PAUL FINCH

First published in 2025 by Telos Publishing,
139 Whitstable Road, Canterbury, Kent CT2 8EQ,
United Kingdom.

www.telos.co.uk

ISBN: 978-1-84583-249-0 (paperback)
ISBN: 978-1-84583-250-6 (limited hardback)

Telos Publishing Ltd values feedback. Please e-mail any
comments you might have about this book to:
feedback@telos.co.uk

British Library Cataloguing in Publication Data.
A catalogue record for this book is available from the
British Library.

CONTENTS

DRAUGR
Keris McDonald

Greenland, 10th Century

Thorbjorg Lítilvölva dies in my arms while I sleep, because I wake to find her already chilling under the reindeer-skin blanket. For a moment I struggle to extricate my limbs; I sleep with my own wrapped tight around hers, as it is my duty to stop her struggling out of bed as well as to keep her warm. Now her arms and legs are stiffening, and warmth lingers only in her torso. Her skinny thighs are locked tight around my leg and the yellow claw of her hand is knotted in my shift.

I wonder if she fought her death, and if I just slept through it. My dreams were full of salt waves and terror, like every night.

Freeing one hand from her armpit, I touch her face and try to close her jaw, but it is set hard in the silent, slack-jawed howl she has worn for days. A last condemnation, her bile spat from beyond death. Her skin feels like wax. I remember wax, from back when I was a girl. Long ago, there were bees and the honey they made and the flowers they fed on, in lush meadows. Flowers do grow here on the edge of the world, during the brief summer – harebells and yellow poppies and the white tufts of bog-cotton – but there are no honeybees. Just biting mosquitoes and flies everywhere, drawn by the smell of sheep and cowshit and old woman. At least Thorbjorg no longer breathes her foul breath into my face.

I'm aware of a cold swamp of piss spreading from under her bony thigh.

Lifting my head from her shoulder, I try to find my bearings. My breath steams in the sliver of light that creeps in through the wooden shutter over our bed. Behind me, the sounds from

7

beyond the bed-curtain are muffled. Someone still snores nearby – that will be Einar, Thorbjorg's eldest son, who holds this steading. A woman's voice mutters, without passion or energy to it. But the few remaining cattle are awake in their byre beyond the head of the bed, lowing with that despairing hunger that we've tried to ignore for weeks. Soon someone will fling them a few handfuls of hay from the dwindled heap in the loft above their stall. Not enough to satisfy their pains, but enough to quiet them for a while. There is not enough hay left – I've heard the talk. Perhaps, now Thorbjorg is dead, Einar will sacrifice a beast in her honour and the family will eat tough, wasted beef for a week. The slaves will get bone broth to damp their gritty barley-bread, and the other cows will have enough to eat for a few more days. Perhaps spring will come before they all starve, and the men will carry the little black cattle out on poles to crop the first grass, if they are too weak to walk out of the dung piled belly-high in their stall.

That is the gamble the family must make with winter every year; how many cows can we keep alive until spring? Every surviving beast drops another, restoring the herd after the November cull. One is always sacrificed to their god Freyr, to remind him of his duties. There's a little milk then; some cheese, curdled in the bag of the calf's stomach and hung to smoke over the fire. Officially the family are baptised Christian, but we are ten days sail from the bishop in Eystribygð, and what does Christ our Lord know about farming, they ask themselves.

Our bull sees most of his children castrated and slaughtered; no wonder he has a wicked temper. He is Einar's pride and joy, but he knocked Einar's youngest against the wall last year and trampled his leg, breaking it below the knee. Do we kill the bull, and hope for a strong bull-calf to replace him? If we kill the oxen, then what's left to draw the plough when the ground thaws?

I am trying not to think about Thorbjorg, I realise.

Rolf, the boy with the broken leg, is calling for his mother. Solveig shushes him quickly before Einar awakes. I think the lad's leg was set badly and pains him more than it should. I almost laughed when I saw the bull swing about and bat the boy to the ground, but I hid my expression. They would have beaten me if they'd seen that smile, and perhaps worse if they'd suspected me of cursing the lad. I am already tainted by my closeness to Thorbjorg. And my face, of course.

I must decide what to do. Her eyes are sunken back in their hollows, the lids only half-closed. Cautiously I press one fingertip beneath the lid, against that icy blue iris I know so well, but she does not start or wince as I rub the jelly gently. It feels like the cap of a withered mushroom, not even wet any longer. Just cold.

My heart sinks, and I feel fear steal in. When I withdraw my finger it leaves a gap beneath the loose lid, and I imagine Thorbjorg is peering out of it at me.

'I'm sorry, mistress,' I whisper. 'I had to be sure. Forgive me.'

But she won't forgive me. She is of the old, red gods – a *seidr*-witch once renowned across this land – and forgiveness is not in their nature. She used to strike me across the head with her weaving shuttle when she had the strength, and curse me when she grew too weak. She's barely been out of this bed for three months, and I am the one who kept her there. For the last of those months she's only been able to eat slips of frozen snow I've gathered from the herb-beds, and I've rubbed a little mutton fat over her black and cracked lips. She is ancient, a relic of pagan times. Old, old, old … and yet still it took her so long to die, even without food and water. Withered like a stick, cold like a wyrm. I wonder where all the piss has come from. Has she been storing it, like Kvasir's golden mead? If I drink it, will I gain the gift of poetry? If I cut out her black heart and roast it, will I know the language of birds?

For days and days it has been like she was already dead, but had not stopped moving. Skull-faced, slack-jawed, groaning – a *draugr*, in the language of these Northmen. I can't think of the right word in my mother's tongue, if there is one. It's too long ago, and I was too young. I've forgotten much.

Slowly I ease myself up onto my bony arse, shivering as the

cold laps around me. We are a long way from the hearth fire here. We were supposed to keep each other warm under the skins; that was my job. The only thing I was good for – keeping her warm and keeping her quiet.

My stomach aches, no more optimistic than the poor cows. I can feel the cavernous hollow in my guts. Should I shout for help? Maybe I should just lie down again next to the corpse, savouring the warmth while it lasts. It's the second-best bed in the house, after all; I'll never sleep so well again.

I don't like to think of what will happen to me now. Better to lie on the sodden sheepskins and pretend nothing has changed, it seems to me.

The sound of human movement nearby saves me from my shivering indecision. Lifting the bed-curtain, I look across the narrow passageway to where Solveig is climbing out of her own bed, carefully holding a stone lamp. The little flame dances in the darkness. Einar's wife is wrapped in her beautiful white bear-fur with the straps and ivory buckles, but her face is grey and pinched. She never was heavy-set and this winter has turned her to a tall scarecrow of a woman, and her yellow hair to the colour of ash. She meets my gaze.

'She's dead,' I say. Then think to add, 'Mistress.'

Her mouth sets to a hard line. Racking back both curtains, she advances to glare down at us both, the corpse and the slave in bed together. My hair has mostly escaped its bonds in the night and I try to tidy it back, as if that would fix anything, but she more interested in Thorbjorg, laying one hand on her throat to check for a pulse and then pulling back the sewn skins to get a proper look at the body. She sees then the hand knotted in my shift at my thigh, and tries to lift it free, but Thorbjorg's fingers are set hard around the bunched linen and resist her prising.

'Einar,' she calls over her shoulder. 'Your mother.'

Einar is a big man with quick fists, a father to sons and lord of this farm, but he's always been nervous of his mother. She's a *seidr*-witch, after all. It doesn't pay to cross a witch. He's grown more fearful as she approached death, I think, seeing the skull rise under her yellowing skin. He hasn't looked in on her in days.

'God's balls,' I hear him mutter as he rolls from his warm bed.

I cross my arms over my breasts, really shivering now.

For a moment he is silent as he contemplates his mother, then he crosses himself. 'May she rest in peace,' he manages. There is no point hoping that her soul is winging its way to Heaven, or that Christ will be waiting to receive her.

Solveig nods, leaning wearily against a bedpost. I can smell the hot walrus-blubber in the lamp and it makes my stomach growl.

'What's she doing there?' he asks Solveig, pointing at Thorbjorg's hand.

'I don't know. She won't let go. You try for yourself.'

Einar shakes his head and crosses himself again. 'Get her sorted,' he grunts. 'It's women's work.'

Preparations are made for Thorbjorg's disposal. I overhear some of the discussion, as I help prepare her body. There is no question of a Christian burial in the churchyard; she refused conversion all her days, scorning the White Christ. The ground is too hard to dig, and we could never waste the little wood we have on a funeral pyre. A barrow of earth and stones, they say, like the old days in Iceland and Norway. That might soothe her. Somewhere far away from the steading, on a barren headland.

But right now even the rocks are hidden by snow, or covered in ice as hard as any mortar.

There is no question of her staying on the farmstead while we wait for spring. The prospect of her prowling about the steading, her face turned blue by frost and rot, clawing at the shutters and knocking at the doors, is too much for anyone to bear.

There are other mutterings too, and sidelong glances cast at me. 'She wants to keep the thrall,' they whisper.

They daren't risk snapping her fingers, so they cut my shift to free me. Then we wash her and dress her, slicing the seams to force her rigid joints into tight sleeves. We lay her out in her best woollen gown, then I open the chest where her regalia was laid reverently aside, and we dress her in her lambskin hood, black outside and white-lined; her catskin gloves, and her boots with the pewter tassels. We thread her precious glass beads about her throat, and clasp her wrists with bracelets; Solveig, from her own store, pins a fine broach set with amber to her mother-in-law's shoulder; an offering that says *Let this be enough. No need to come back for more.* We also tie her ankles together with walrus-hide thongs to impede her walking, and hide little crosses of twigs and straw in her clothes. We work slowly, thralls and freewomen alike, slowed by winter weakness. Every time Solveig pauses for breath she kisses the little silver cross that hangs around her neck. Last of all we wrap the old woman in her blue witch's cloak and lay her upon a pallet to be carried out.

Upon her sunken breast Solveig lays a pair of iron shears that are supposed to stop her rising. I shudder, tasting the memory of blood in the back of my throat.

In the meantime, the men strip and dismantle the carved bed on which she lay, gather up her loom and her distaff and her clothes, and carry everything out of the longhouse, under Solveig's direction. And the work of the farmstead goes on, and strips of precious seal meat are added to the bones in the pot for the midday meal, and snow is brought in buckets to make water, and peat is piled on the fire to cook the broth. Einar's sons are sent off to the nearest farms with the news. There are plans made, but I'm not privy to them. I am only a thrall.

The preparations are done well before the end of the short day, and the whole farmstead – family and free churls and slaves – wrap up in their outdoor clothes and gather round the bier as Thorbjorg is carried feet-first out of the house, her face covered with a cloth so that she can't see her way back inside. I tie a strip of cloth around my own face, not to hide the ruination but for warmth. Einar prepares to lead the burial procession to wherever it is that they have chosen.

'Not you,' he says abruptly to me. 'Stay here and tend the

fire.'

It's the best job I've ever been given – to simply sit by the fire – and I'm confused and relieved in equal measure. Though it's not snowing, who would want to go outside if they had a choice? I turn back indoors and find myself a seat on a low stool, wondering at my luck. I don't think I've ever been alone in the longhouse. I look up into the rafters where the smoke makes opaque the rays of light creeping in under the turf roof. I walk warily around, run my fingers through the thick wolfskin on Einar's chair, test with my back the hard benches that line the length of the hall (I like Thorbjorg's straw and fleece mattress better, and miss it already). Finally, I break and drink two bowls of broth from the slurry remaining at the bottom of the cauldron, using my fingers to press out the remaining soft tissue from all the boiled up spinal bones that have been rattling round in there for a week. I know I will be beaten once Solveig notices they've been picked clean, but I can't stop myself eating. It's more meat than I've consumed in months. I'm nearly sick.

The light is dimming when they come back for me; two churls with dripping noses and frost in their moustaches. 'Come on now, you,' says one, Ola.

I cringe back, remembering what happened the last time I went outside with him, but he gestures impatiently. 'They are waiting for you.'

My stomach contracts around the greasy broth, and seems to freeze there, like Thorbjorg's cold claw is gripping it. 'What for?'

'Want me to hit you?' he answers, raising a mittened fist. 'Out, now.' But when I gather my cloak and hood and duck out under the stone lintel both he and Vili step back away from me, as if I'm unclean as well as ugly. The cold air outside burns like fire through my face, across cheeks and up into my forehead. They point me up the track, then follow at my back.

Why send two men to fetch me?

Einarshof sits on a low saddle between two inlets of the Vestribygð fjord. We are the last farm strung out along this valley, and we make our way not down the main track toward the other steadings and the little church to the south, but along the lesser-used track to the nearest bay. It is late afternoon, the weather dry but chill, the breeze biting at my face inside my hood. Under my feet the trampled grey slush crunches and snaps. If the two churls are talking behind my back, I can't hear it.

The walk does not take so long, and – fuelled by my illicit feast – I even find it warming, my fingers starting to tingle. My thoughts race.

Do they think I'm a witch too? They can't! I'm a good Christian! My people have been for centuries! I know nothing about their vile seidr-*magic, I never helped Thorbjorg or learned her songs or cast the bones or looked into the flames with her. She hated me!*

I start muttering the Lord's Prayer as I walk. I am still praying as we reached the little beach where everyone is waiting.

This far from the open sea there is no tide to speak of and the beach is nothing more than a sliver of grey and ashy sand under the surrounding hills. Great chunks of mushy ice choke the inlet, and to escape this the fishing boats have all been drawn up onto the land for winter and turned belly up, ready for re-caulking when the ice slips its grip. The people of Einarshof, along with others I vaguely recognise as families from farms nearby, wait in huddles on the foreshore. A wrack-fire of old seaweed is burning with an evil smell and green-edged flames. There's no priest. There's nothing Christian about this funeral, I intuit.

Einar and his eldest son, Njal, move forward to meet me. Njal has an axe at his belt and a sealskin bag in his hands, the fur silvery in the last light of the day. Despite the caul of cloud overhead, the southern horizon is bright, a lurid orange sunset streaked with grey. The breeze is bitter enough to bring tears to my eyes.

'Medb,' says Einar, smiling. 'Good girl.' It is the first time he has ever said anything remotely approving to me.

I look around for Solveig, and for Thorbjorg. The living woman stands with others near the fire, and as I catch her eye she ducks her head and crosses herself. The dead one is propped up in her rebuilt bed, near an upturned boat that stands a little apart from the rest. A low wall of slushy ice has been piled in an ellipse around the bed, setting it apart.

'Good girl,' Einar says, coming forward to take both my hands in his. 'She wanted you to go with her.'

Something is yanked down roughly over my head from behind, as Einar's hands tighten to pin me in place. Then the stinking darkness is split by a bolt of white light and I fall out of consciousness.

The insistent prod of a foot in my side rouses me. 'Get up,' says a voice, faint and muffled.

I can't breathe properly. I haul at the skin bag still hooding me, gasping for air. My hair is stuck to the inside of the bag with my blood and it hurts, but I have to get it off. Yet the darkness is no less complete when I finally succeed.

'Lazy girl,' says the voice. It's Thorbjorg's, which it can't be. 'Wake up!'

'Shut up!' I mumble, because I must be dreaming. Under my hands I can feel the dense, stiff pelt of a reindeer-skin blanket. 'You're dead.'

'And you need to come with me, Medb.'

My head is throbbing with pain. I stretch out a hand blindly to my left, encountering a familiar carving in wood; the footboard of her bed. I'm lying across the foot of the bed, at her feet. In the dark. It must be the middle of the night.

'You can go to Hel on your own, mistress,' I tell her, and casting an arm back I manage to snag the whole coverlet and draw it over me, cocooning me in the dense pelt. 'I want to sleep.'

The dream of Thorbjorg fades – or at any rate I don't hear her voice again before I slide back into dreamless night.

The next time I wake there is light. Faint, very cold light, in a narrow strip somewhere above me. I look at it for a while as it comes into focus, and I decide that it is the wrong shape, in the wrong orientation, to be the gap in the shutter over the bed. And there is another line of light, further off and lower down. I'm perplexed.

Slowly I raise my head to look around me. My head throbs. The dried blood on my scalp itches, tugging the skin where my hair sticks to it. 'Shit,' I whisper to myself.

It takes a long time for my eyes to adjust to the shadowy space I'm in. The roof is low, and the strips of light are horizontal gaps between overlapping planks, where the wood has shrunk in the winter winds and the old caulking has fallen out. The inside of an upturned boat, I think; only just deep-bellied enough to enclose the carved bed, even with all the seat-planks taken out. When I sit, I can stretch up a hand and touch the central keel.

'Awake again?' says Thorbjorg.

One glance over my shoulder and I'm off the bed, practically banging my head off the roof as I back off down the length of the boat. She is propped up at the head of the bed, wrapped in her blue cloak, watching me.

I trip over something bulky and sit down hard onto what feels like a wooden serving platter and pile of bowls. This cramped space is piled with stuff. All sorts of stuff.

Grave gifts.

I'm inside her barrow.

She grins, amused, as I flail around looking for a door, scrabbling against the planks overhead, screaming for help. There is no answer. I pause for breath and realise I can barely hear the wind wuthering outside.

'They can't hear you,' she points out. Her eyes have withered back completely in their sockets now, nothing but darkness under the drooping lids. 'And if they could, they wouldn't save you, would they? Einar put you here himself.'

That shocks me into silence. I skate my palms down across the overlapping wood. A boat. A *ferje*, small and deep-bellied, the kind used for fishing in the inlet. Clinker-built and iron-riveted. Mast unstepped. Flipped upside down.

One eye on the dead woman, I dig at the floor where wood should meet sand, but the whole thing has been footed on ice that has melted and re-frozen, and all I do it tear my nails. I cast around for something to dig with and find, in the half-dark, a stone lamp, a dough trough, then something hairy – a haunch of beef, the skin still part-on and the flesh frozen solid.

Recognition makes my stomach clench.

'Have you calmed down yet?' Thorbjorg enquires.

I shake my head.

'I imagine you thought you were rid of me. How disappointed you must be.'

'You … got your voice back, mistress.'

'The dead can speak, girl. They never stop speaking, that's the truth. It's only the living who can't hear.'

I try to lick my cracked lips, but my tongue is too dry to help. 'Why are we in a boat?' I ask, picturing us sailing upside down under a frozen sea.

She shrugs. 'We sail for Nastrond, the Corpse Shore.'

'No, no, no. *I'm* not dead.'

'You should be. That was the point. You are my faithful bondmaid. You are supposed to accompany me, girl.'

'To Hel?'

The pale light picks out the white hair framing her skull. 'To the field of Folkvangr, where Freya reigns. The Queen of all *seidr*-witches waits by the doors of her hall Sessrumnir, with a horn of ale, to welcome me.'

'Then go.' *Please go.*

'Alone? I can hardly arrive without a thrall to serve me.'

I laugh, bitterly. 'I've had enough serving you and your family. You think I'm going to do it for eternity?'

With a hiss she scuttles forward, spider-like, to the foot of the bed, reaching for me with her bony arms. I've no weapon, but there's a lamp to hand and I swing it, smacking her in the face with the heavy stone dish even as her fingers scrabble at my clothes. Her jaw breaks with a crack, hanging half-off, and she shrinks back.

'Look what you've done,' she says peevishly. Her voice seems unimpeded by the loss of tongue and teeth and lips. But she retreats back to the head of the bed.

'You go where you want – *I* am going to Heaven,' I pant.

For a while we sit glaring at each other.

'The boat,' I say at last, thinking aloud. 'We are under a boat, not a barrow. They have not buried you – I can still see light. And they need the boat. This is good strong wood. No one can afford to give up a good boat like this to the dead.'

'So?'

'So they are storing you for winter, like a side of smoked mutton. Come spring, when the ground thaws, they'll need the boat and they will come back to bury you properly.'

'What then? What happens to you?'

'I don't know.' Half-spun ideas twirl on the spindle of my mind. Demanding to see the bishop. Pretending to have risen from the dead, like Lazarus, like the Sleepers of Ephesus. I could become a nun in Eystribygð. An anchoress. The first saint of Grœnland.

'And you think you will live that long? Spring is months away.'

I look around my prison. 'I'll live.'

There is flint and a curved steel striker and a tiny pair of scissors in Thorbjorg's box of belongings, so I use my own greasy hair for tow, kindling a brief and stinking flame long enough to light a lamp. The warm flame is so bright it hurts my eyes at first. But by its light I make an inventory of my mistress' grave goods.

A bed, most obviously. It fills most of the barrow-space. A straw mattress, topped by five sheepskins. A thick reindeer-skin coverlet above. It's no sauna, but I am wearing thick clothing and I will not freeze to death.

A dead woman, in the bed. Her clothes, her belt with a walrus-ivory buckle, her brooch and beads.

Her wooden *seidr*-staff, worn short by use and now no taller than a child, but still with a brass top in which are set green sea-stones.

A pouch of hemp-seeds, so old they are falling to dust. I haven't seen hemp growing since Iceland.

A chest, pegged, no hinges. Flint, steel, charred linen scraps for lighting a fire. Three spindles with carved stone whorls. A net full of greasy fleece, ready to spin. Paired carding combs. A set of bone needles. A loom, with stone weights, hung with a half-woven length of woollen wadmal. Scissors no longer than my finger, for trimming thread or fingernails.

Three lamps carved from soft soapstone, with wicks of twisted moss, filled with walrus tallow. Those will burn dry long before spring. Or I could eat the tallow.

A bone hair comb. I remember hours sitting with Thorbjorg, combing out her long grey tresses, searching out the lice and throwing them in the lamp-flame to pop and fizz. The combing soothed her when she grew fractious.

Two antler spoons, three wooden dishes, a bread-trough, and a drinking horn of small size.

A set of bone dice.

A silk headscarf. I draw it wonderingly through my fingers, distracted for a moment by the sheen of the fine cloth under the flickering lamp. It must have travelled from France to Iceland, and before that from even further afield.

A copper ring.

A single dried fish. All they would spare from the diminishing store; it is almost impossible to get out to sea in the winter months.

Two puppies from Einar's own bitch-hound's litter, their throats cut. I doubt they would have survived past weaning anyway. They are frozen to the sand.

The skinny little carcass of a barn cat.

A haunch of beef.

A fine white fox-pelt, soft as cloud.

So, I conclude... almost no iron. What has happened to the shears? I could have made use of those, I tell myself bitterly. The family are being practical, even as they spare all they can for the funeral gifts. There is no smelting to be done in this settlement. So they have left me nothing that I can use to smash through the planks or dig my way out. I sit below the foot of the bed, rocking back and forth. It is hard to think when I'm so hungry.

'You owe me, girl,' says Thorbjorg. 'You should show some gratitude.'

'For what?' I am using the scissor blade to shave off a frozen strip of beef, which I pass through the lamp flame until it sputters.

'I took you away from shovelling cowshit and wringing laundry, remember.'

I give her a sour look, remembering feeding her and lifting her to the piss-bucket and changing her soiled clothes as she smacked me around the head and pulled my hair and berated me. The old woman is a lot easier to reason with now she is dead. 'I did plenty of your laundry.'

The taste of the meat, charred yet still half-frozen, is delectable; it transports me. I picture feasts of roast oxen and golden mead, shining lamps and golden harps, like in the old sagas. Is that the afterlife she is offering me? The boasting and bellowing of drunken men and the constant scurrying to fill trenchers and pour more ale?

'Didn't I save you from the dirty hands of churls?' she asks, as if reading my thoughts. 'You were safe with me, weren't you?'

The taste of beef turns to mud on my tongue. She has a point. Even my ruined face had not kept all the men away; slaves are not fussy. But being her thrall had worked like a spell of protection. 'You were a bit late,' I mutter, looking at the floor. 'I'd already buried two children.'

'Oh, listen to you. I laid six of my own to rest. Life is hard. You are not a child, to cry that it is unfair.'

'You didn't have to strangle yours,' I point out, 'to save them from … this life.'

She snorts. 'And what palace did you come from? What

garden of the gods that was so much better?'

'I don't remember.'

'Don't remember?' she mocks.

I'm defiant. 'I don't remember what it was called. I was too young when I was stolen. It was warmer, I remember that. Green, wet winters, with no snow. It was beautiful.' Songbirds and meadows full of flowers. Bees.

'So bitter? We didn't rob you from your paradise. We are not slave-takers.'

'You bought me from the thieves.' I swallow the taste of burning. She cannot imagine the depths of my hatred, the burning bile I feel for every one of them. 'You brought me to this frozen shit-pit at the end of the world. So don't imagine I'll follow you anywhere else.'

I huddle at the bottom of the bed, Thorbjorg at the top. In the dark of the night I wake from a dull doze to find her on top of me, her bony hands locked about my throat, her skull-face flaring with a blue phosphorescent glow. I scrabble wildly at her, sticking my fingers into eye sockets that are all but empty, before wrenching at her dangling jaw hard enough to rip it off her face. She's not heavy. Strange, that – the *draugr* are notoriously strong, and too heavy for an ox to drag across a field. But I club at her with that ugly weapon, hook a knee up into her stomach, and thrust hard enough to send her sprawling backward.

Then I scream. The wail solidifies into drawn-out 'Fuck you!'

She makes a gurgling noise of disbelief. She's torn scratches in my neck, but they aren't deep enough to bleed.

'I will snap your arms out of their sockets if you touch me again,' I tell her, trying to hide the quiver in my voice.

Muttering to herself, she cedes me some peace for the night.

I use her spindle to dig at the ice foundations of the wall. I don't make much headway, but I scrape together enough chips to wet my tongue. I'm always thirsty, and always hungry. I need to eke out the cow haunch until spring – along with the cat and the dogs, in all likelihood. It's hard not to cut slice after slice of frozen beef.

I employ the little iron scissors in picking at the caulk where I can reach it, admitting a sliver more light and air on the landward side of the hull. On the seaward side the wind has blocked all gaps with a thick layer of frozen rime.

Thorbjorg gibbers on her bed, not always lucid. I think she is trying to enspell me.

'Stop that,' I tell her, irritated. 'It doesn't work on the baptised.'

'What do you think I'm trying to do to you?'

'How should I know? You're the witch.'

She giggles. 'That's not what was said over the ale-cups. *There are two witches in Einarshof;* that's what people said.'

'I'm not a witch.'

'No? Why did they put a bag over your head then, if not to take your power?'

I reach up and touch the dried old cut on my scalp. I'd thought maybe they felt guilty for their pagan rites. Hadn't wanted to look me in the eye. 'If I had any power, would I be a thrall?' I ask, but it comes out less scornful and more plaintive than I intend.

'Let me tell you a secret, girl. The root of all magic is *fear*. Fear of the dark. Fear of death. Fear of becoming *nithing*. Fear of helplessness. Fear of the unknown. They fear you. Claim that.'

I'm incredulous 'Fear *me?*'

'Your face. The ugliness of it.'

I can't help a bark of laughter. The exhalation whistles through the exposed pit of my nasal passages. 'Your grandson did that to me, remember? And laughed at me ever after.'

She cocks her knob of a head on its spindle spine. 'Njal may have laughed. But underneath, he noticed every time he saw your death's head, watching him. You are a horror, girl. A *sceadugenga*, walking the night. You look more like a corpse than I do.'

'Not any more.'

For a moment she is silent. When she stops talking, she's so still – no breath, no twitching of her fingers – that it's like I'd only ever imagined her moving. Then she asks, curiously, 'What did you do, to make him take the shears to your face?'

'I didn't do anything.'

'Oh come. You pissed him off.'

'I asked him what he thought Our Lord would say to him when we both stood before the Seat of Judgment. When I could accuse him.'

'There you go. Fear.'

My laugh is like a cat spitting up a hairball. 'Pretty shitty magic, that hurts me more than him.'

'A strong spell. But you need to learn to grip the hilt, not the blade.'

I flick a well-chewed cat bone at her. She cackles to herself.

'Medb, what do think your Lord Jesus will say to you about your two murdered babies?' When I don't answer, she adds slyly, 'I don't think you want to go to Heaven, child. Consider your other options.'

My hands tremble with the cold. My fingernails are loosening, I note. 'And I don't think you know the way to Freya's hall, old woman. I think all this saying you are waiting for me is nothing more than an excuse. Maybe there isn't a way left open any more. Maybe our Lord shut it down when he descended into Hel to save his saints.'

She hisses. 'I need you to sing the songs.'

'The songs?'

'The *varðlokur*, the songs that let me open the doors and call the spirits.'

'I don't know those songs. I'm a Christian. I don't think anyone knows those songs anymore. It's all old and forgotten.'

She shakes her head, and suddenly I find myself giggling.

'You're stuck here, old woman. Not a *seidr*-witch, not even a *draugr*. You are nothing but a *haugbui*, sitting over your treasures in your barrow. Trapped forever.'

Thorbjorg goes still and silent.

But I've had enough. Enough of her taunting and her nagging. I rise and loom over her where she sits in bed, seizing her frozen body and pulling it from the nest of skins. She doesn't fight me; she seems frail now, weighing no more than a child. Certainly, less than the children I carried out behind the midden heap and buried under the corner of the manure pile, in the only ground warm and deep enough to receive them. 'I don't want to hear another word,' I whisper to the bobbing skull, before I fling her whole corpse sideways against the wall.

Climbing into the dint she left in the bed, I pull the skins up around me, smiling triumphantly as I claim my spoils. I hear Thorbjorg scuttling around the walls like a rat for a little while, whimpering to herself, but I'm not afraid of her anymore. And where there is no fear, there is no magic. Eventually even those small noises stop.

Day follows day follows day, each an infinitesimal moment longer than the last. I eat the cat and the puppies and the fish. The dogs are still milky, the cod rank and stinking. The cat tastes the worst, but I still crack its spindly bones in my teeth and suck out the marrow.

I am pared thin, skin and bone myself. My belly is a hollow sack pulled up under my ribs. I press my face to the gaps in boat wall, trying to tell if it is spring yet. I can't see anything but the thinnest chink of sky, but sometimes the light out there is so bright compared to that in here that I'm blinded and have to retreat to the shadows. The lamps have long since burned out, but my eyes have grown used to the half-light of the barrow under the boat.

I hear gulls sometimes.

The ice foundations melt and reset. The boat sinks lower, until I can't stand anything like upright, but must move about hunched. My fingernails have split to the quicks. Even my bowels will no longer move, which is a pity, because at least I've had my own shit to eat until now. I'm so hungry, all the time. It is the last thing that will remain of me, I think; the hunger.

There is nothing left to eat. Not a morsel.

How long before Einar comes with his men to reclaim his fishing boat?

There's a fly. It wakes me from my doze in the foetid nest of Thorbjorg's bed, by circling around near my head. Eventually it lands on my temple, and I start awake, sending it into another droning flight.

I mean, who can sleep through that?

Fully awake, I realise that there are several flies, and I struggle through my stupor to work out the significance. If there are flies then it must be warm outside. Bare earth. Sheepshit not covered in snow or frozen solid. It must be spring, then.

'Do you hear that, old woman?' I ask, my voice a whisper. I have to clear my dry throat several times to get any words out at all. But she doesn't answer. She's refusing to talk to me now that I've picked her bones clean and licked the frozen marrow from the inside grooves of her thighbones.

Well then, let the flies have what's left of her. She's no loss.

Rising, I grab her staff from where it's propped at the bedhead and slither down onto the floor. The sand is no longer frozen hard. There is no ice left under the gunwale of the boat. The wooden rim has settled at last to the beach, leaving gaps here and there where the ground isn't level. There's night air blowing underneath, and when I press my face to the rift I smell fresh air only a little tainted with seaweed.

Using the end of the staff, I start to dig away the grey sand. It's slow work though, and in the confined area between hull and bed, the staff is awkward, so after I've made a start on the pit I discard the wooden tool and resort to using my hands. The last of my fingernails slough off, but the bones underneath are stronger, points hard as iron, and I work quicker now. It's remarkably easy, and I wonder why I haven't tried this before. It doesn't take long before I've excavated a trench that I can wriggle all the way through, out into the night.

The sky is clear, the wind mild. Though there is no moon, the panoply of stars is too bright for me to look up at, illuminating the low hills behind the beach and the soft waves lapping the shoreline, and the track to Einarshof.

It smells wonderful out here.

I ought to take the chance to stand upright and stretch for the first time in months, but I find it easier to stay hunched now, even when I start to lope up the track. The night air feels fresh and damp on the gash in my head, ticklish-cool on the inside of my all-but-empty skull. I can smell woodsmoke now, so someone must have made it through winter. I can smell cows and human sweat and the stink of the latrine. I can smell sticky sweat, men and women, peat-ash and fleeces and a small boy asleep in his bed. The thought of all that soft, succulent flesh makes my mouth water, and I drop to all fours the better to run, my iron-clawed hands and feet scoring the earth with each loping stride.

I'm *ravenous*.

GOLEM

In its purest sense, the word 'chaos' refers to the formless matter at the dawn of creation, when nothing of the universe we know today existed. A contemporary meaning is anarchy or mayhem, in other words a state wherein all recognisable order has been dispensed with. An agent of chaos, therefore, is someone, or something that, while not necessarily the cause or perpetrator of this most destructive of events, is integral to its continuation and embodies it in every sense.

A monster, for example.

Monsters – most commonly perceived as unique creatures, often murderous, grotesque and terrifying, and innately amoral – feature in all the mythologies of the world. Invariably, they dwell outside the natural law, obeying no rules but their own, and wreaking such unimaginable havoc and pain that their very existence is considered inimical to human survival. They are the very definition of chaotic beings. And yet monsters can also have a role to play in our world. It's astonishing how, as horrific and uncontrollable as they often are, monsters' mere presence in our folklore can be instructive or metaphorical.

There is surely no better illustration of this than the legendary golem.

Many people today assume they know what the golem is, probably without understanding much about its background. Ask the average person, and they will likely describe it as a hulking, misshapen figure created from clay, dirt, rock, iron, ice or any other inanimate material of solid enough consistency to hold itself together when the mysterious words have been spoken and the figure has come to life. In short, to many, the golem is a crude statue given a form of animation through magical incantation.

That is the gist of it in the post Dungeons & Dragons era (the fantasy game in which golems featured regularly), but in the original tales there is much more to consider. First of all – and be under no illusion about this – the golem, as an entity, is supposed to be real.

The most famous account of all concerns the infamous Golem of Prague.

When the Holy Roman Emperor, Rudolf II, who ruled from 1552-1612, ordered a violent pogrom against the Jewish community of Prague, the capital of Bohemia, one Judah Loew ben Bezalel, the senior rabbi in the city, and a revered Talmudic teacher, went to desperate lengths to protect his people. Initially, he sought to negotiate with the emperor himself, but by now the blood libel had been invoked, and all across the capital, rioters were targeting Jewish homes and businesses. Jews were losing everything and even being murdered, so Rabbi Loew turned to ancient occultic magic, gathering mud from the banks of the River Vltava and forming it into an immense and grotesque humanoid shape. Carving the word 'אֱמֶת' ('emet', meaning 'truth'), onto the figure's forehead and inserting a shem, or scroll bearing the true name of God, into its mouth, a cabalistic ritual was then performed, and the golem was brought to life. Named Yoselle, it was tasked with defending the Jews of Prague, which it did to great effect, terrorising the antisemitic mobs who up until then had been coming nightly with clubs and torches, and using incredible strength and ferocity to vanquish any who challenged it.

Every Friday evening, Rabbi Loew removed the shem so that the golem could rest on the Sabbath as was appropriate in Jewish law. On one occasion, however, after the golem had successfully defended the Jewish community for almost ten years, the rabbi was unable to deactivate it in time, and, required to function against the will of God, the monster lost its mind, commencing a wild and uncoordinated attack on the whole population of the city, which saw it destroy buildings and brutally slaughter both Gentile and Jew alike, leaving hundreds of innocents torn apart in the blood-spattered streets. And it didn't just employ overwhelming physical strength to perform these heinous acts. The golem called Yoselle was invulnerable to all weapons and also said to have wielded cabalistic powers of its own, including the ability to walk invisible among its enemies and even to raise the dead, which sewed new horror and chaos.

As you can imagine, this made it a formidable opponent for Rabbi Loew, but somehow – it is never explained how – he managed to overpower his creation and by altering the word 'אֱמֶת' to 'מֶת' ('emet' to 'mavet', meaning 'death'), he reduced the golem to an image of clay and nothing more. Wrapping the lifeless relic in a Jewish prayer shawl, Rabbi Loew locked it in an attic in the synagogue and passed instructions that no one was to go up there. However, there are two addenda to the story. Several years later, one Rabbi Landau ventured up to the attic, intent on reanimating the horror, but outside the door became too terrified of what lay beyond it to go further, while as recently as the 20th Century, a rumour spread that the golem had been woken and sent on one last mission, to eliminate a prominent local Nazi, whose assassination, whether the golem was responsible or not, is certainly said to have happened.

There are many other golems in Jewish tradition, dating far back into antiquity. (At the dawn of mankind, you may recall, Adam himself was formed from clay, and therefore, possibly, the world's first golem). Interestingly, not all of these beings were as violent as the Golem of Prague. In most cases they were used as simple servants, messengers or labourers, and, unlike Yoselle, they nearly always collapsed into dust once the shem was removed.

But is there any truth in these prolific tales?

The story of the Golem of Prague in particular comes to us from many different sources, several of them claiming to be eyewitness testimonies, but it's been pointed out that most of them, though written down by Jewish scholars, were also written originally in German and are untraceable beyond the early 19th Century, a time when the study and collation of German fairy tales was very popular, which suggests they might have been fanciful inventions. Even the work of David Gans, a Jewish historian of the 16th Century, who thoroughly documented the visit of Rabbi Loew to the court of Rudolf II, says nothing about his supposed creation of the Golem of Prague, while Rabbi Loew himself made no mention of it in his own writings. It's also the case that, when the Prague synagogue, which had become old and unstable, was rebuilt in 1883, no body of any sort was discovered in the attic, though rumours were already circulating by then that Yoselle's remains had been secretly removed to a nearby cemetery.

However, other earlier golems are referenced in Jewish manuscripts, including several from the 11th and 12th centuries, and one from the 17th, the Golem of Chelm, in Poland, which was allegedly the creation of one Rabbi Eliyahu, who used it to perform menial tasks rather than for defence, and eyewitness sightings of which were also referenced in Christian records.

Certain groups within the Jewish faith firmly believe the golem to be a real entity, a gift from God. Others consider it to be a 'wish fulfilment' folktale. To start with, this latter group argues, it is not sinful to summon the golem. The golem has no will of its own, and therefore no soul and thus no harm is done by enslaving it. In addition, though it is considered wrong in Judaism to use sorcery, the golem is animated by the power of God, which means it is miraculous rather than magical. All of that makes it a far more appealing notion. But more appealing still is the golem's role as a defender or avenger, or both, of the Jewish people.

The Jews have been persecuted throughout history, particularly since the Roman-Jewish war of the 130s AD, which led to their ejection from their homeland. From then on, the scattered nature of their communities and the enduring myth that it was the Jews who crucified Christ, when in fact it was the Romans, made them easy scapegoats for many of societies' problems and the recipient of much unjustified hatred and violence. Even Britain, where so many Jews sought refuge in the years leading up to World War Two, was a hotbed of antisemitism in the Middle Ages. The idea that by praying to the true God, a monstrous thing could be invoked, which would retaliate against the aggressors tenfold, would understandably win the favour of any Jew who'd suffered or lived in fear.

That said, the specific message of the Golem of Prague is equally clear, and it differs somewhat: be wary of using extraordinary powers against even a genuine avowed enemy, for such powers are the province of God alone, and if you lose control of them, there's no guarantee they won't fall on you instead.

OGRE
Stephen Volk

I am broken. Again.

I feel it building up inside like a train coming down the track. The black in my head blocking my sinuses and the veins like thick tar. The trigger is the ludicrous shitshow of it. The orange one throwing Sharpies to the faithful after signing each executive order, the way Tom Jones used to toss ladies' panties to the crowd.

I squint at the insane spectacle of him punching the air to a gay anthem pumped out by some geriatric has-beens, as if the rest of it wasn't certifiable enough, the Indian chief milking the crowd as the felon dad-dances. My head pounds furnace-hot at the obnoxious sight of tech billionaires, all trying to out-Lex Luthor each other by kissing the ring. All so desperate to be in his gang. But don't we all want to be in some gang or other at some time? To be liked? To be wanted? To be loved?

Behind the corner shop is a no-go zone, but the shop isn't. I'm sent there for eggs and bread on a twice-weekly basis, and that's where I see them lurking. Jimmer, Short Fred, Elwyn Frond and Sam Jacobs. I ignore them, hoping they won't speak to me as they roam the shelves but they observe me for a while, then line up to buy cans of Coke and Fanta and Kit-Kats. They say they're going up the woods to play, and that is tantamount to an invitation.

We trudge up to Lion's Rock, the crag which overlooks what is now the bypass, and take the unpaved road next to Lan Farm into fields that don't exist anymore. I swish at ferns with a snapped-off branch, and that's when Jimmer asks if I want to be in their gang.

I nod.

He says if I do, I'll have to pass a test.

I shrug my shoulders, faking a don't-care response. Secretly hoping it doesn't involve showing my willy to a girl, which is the rumour going round school. I notice Sam Jacobs grinning and scratching his groin. Always something of an infestation about Sam Jacobs at the best of times.

'You have to go into The Cave and touch the back wall,' announces Jimmer (called that to differentiate him from another Jim, Jim Langham). He wears a denim jacket with patches sewn on. One a stars and stripes doing a two-fingered salute.

'It's a test of fear.'

'I'm not afraid.'

'You will be,' says Sam Jacobs. 'It's dark!'

'So?'

I wonder if I've laid the bravado on a bit thick, so tone it down and ask where it is, this Cave?

'Up the quarry.'

I know where they're talking about. It's situated alongside a rugged, rocky lane which provides a horse-shoe-shaped shortcut that means, upon leaving my front door, I can avoid crossing several busy roads, traffic-wise. On the minus side, there's nothing of interest to see that way except the back doors to some of my schoolmates' gardens and a patch of open concrete where neighbours park their cars. The rocky surface underfoot makes it seem abandoned and desolate, probably because of the coating of stone dust. It never occurs to me that there is a connection to the sheer cliff of bare rock I walk past almost every lunchtime. And it never occurs to me to look close enough to notice a cave in that rock face till now, when I see it.

With various gestures, they urge me to step closer, so I do.

I hear Jimmer hook the ring pull from his Coke can.

'Go on!'

'I will, I will! How far is it? The wall?'

'Only about twenty feet.'

'In the dark,' adds Sam Jacobs.

'I don't care,' I say back. 'That's easy.'

After all, how hard can it be? Walking, no, running into the dark for a few short seconds? Reaching out, touching a hard, wet – slimy possibly – stone wall? It'll be like going to the dentist. Get it over quickly. Like peeling off a plaster.

I step warily inside and it's refrigerator cold. The sunlight behind me is more or less instantly blocked out. My moving silhouette projected in front of me. I hear my gang shuffling their feet and muttering, but far away. It's like I'm a deep sea diver and they're safely on the boat, giggling.

I hear my own echoing feet scuffing the ground.

Holding my breath, I run to the far wall and slap it with the flat of my hand. I look at it and a flickering glow is cast upon my skin and the rough surface surrounding my fingers. I turn to run out again as fast as possible, but when I turn my head my eyes are caught by what I see around the corner in a deeper part of the cave at right angles to where I've come in.

Sticks of a campfire blacken, balled newspapers aflame. News print curling to ash. A pile of rags sits cross-legged, warming hands as grubby as gravedigger's gloves. I know for sure he hasn't cut his hair for as long as I've been alive. The carpet of beard is streaked silver and verdigris, matted with grot and grime like the underside of a rotting barge. I can't hear the boys from behind the shop anymore. Just the sound as he runs a can opener around the rim of a can. I'm frozen in every sense as he hooks out chunks of dark brown meat with two long-nailed fingers and presses them through the wound of his lips. I see pustules and scabs on his cheeks and forehead but the tramp's eyes are pure.

He sees me and I wonder how he will react. Much as I try to control my bladder. Much as I try to move my feet. Much as I try to move my legs, I can't.

He laughs, mouth wide open, and I see blood on his teeth and gums surrounded by the wild bush of his thick beard and moustache. He sounds like a creaking gate.

He dribbles gobbets of blood down his front, looking down at the mess, mystified yet not displeased, as a child might be at its first soiled bib. Then his head lunges forward in a storkish jerk and he lapses into guttural croaking. His fingers claw at his blood-sodden shirt. The buttons pop, the shirt comes apart, then, as I'm watching, so does he.

The stain becomes a cavity. The fleshy absence of a molar or a wisdom tooth extracted. I don't know if it's mental association but I get the smell of the dentist. And something is pressing through, akin to the kernel of a peach when you turn the half inside-out. The dark globe, I see, is covered in hair – a boy's hair. A little boy the same age as me, whose knobbly-jointed fingers crack open the tramp's thorax and, wiggling narrow shoulders, crawls out as if extracting himself from a drain, one knee at a time, one slippery foot at a time, onto the hoarded detritus of the old man's lair.

He teeters in front of me, naked, knock-kneed, shivering from head to crimson toe, hands slicking back his wet, clotted hair, wiping blood from his eyes as if he's just climbed out of a swimming pool.

That is the moment I am broken.

They're already gone by the time I run out, and I feel desperate and alone. I don't look back and don't go back. Ever.

The next day, in school, I grab Jimmer by the shoulder and I show him my hand, and tell him I touched the wall like he asked me to. I ask them why they ran away. Jimmer calls me stupid. He says they never did. 'We stayed there the whole time. We were waiting for you.' I feel a temperature build up inside and I tell him he's a liar. Jimmer bounces the ball a few times. They go away to play soccer and don't ask me to go with them.

From that moment I know I can't ever describe to them what happened in The Cave because they'll never believe me, and neither will anybody else. And if they did listen they'd think I was mad and lock me away, so I keep the memory in a little box inside, and sometimes I don't open that box and sometimes I do. If I graze my knee or bite my tongue and get the sensation of saltiness and wetness, it returns. The flickering sight of the old tramp and the little boy covered in blood emerging out of him.

Not long afterwards I move up to the big school, which is in the modern building next to juniors, so I am twelve. It's an old-fashioned Boys' Grammar and the Head (who we call 'Birdy' because he has dentures that cause him to whistle) has delusions of running a public school fiefdom, with teachers in black gowns and a Tuck Shop. The prefects have a ritual on the first day of shoving the heads of new boys into sinks full of water. I'm terrified of the prospect, so, instead of hiding, which would be sensible, I walk into the lion's den with my hands in my pockets to get it over with as quickly as possible. It's more shocking and violent than I anticipate. I'm convinced the kid holding my neck is going to hold me down forever and I'll never get my breath and I'll drown, but he lets go and at least it is done. The fear is out of the way, and that's the main thing.

My dad is one of the science masters in the same school, which people think is a joke or awkward but to me it isn't anything. I know there is no chance of preferential treatment, in fact, more likely the reverse. True to expectations, he ignores me, an absolute concerted act which he maintains for five years, which is no surprise to me as he more or less does the same thing at home. He teaches biology but I never see him exhibit a fragment of interest in the subject. He tells us how to cut up a rat as part of the syllabus. It is all about learning things parrot fashion to pass exams and I stay away as often as I can, though I don't go up the woods or Lion's Rock. I go to the precinct where the winos and drug addicts hang out. I get threatened with exclusion which embarrasses him no end but I don't care.

I'm well rid of Jimmer, Short Fred, Elwyn Frond, and that lot, who've all gone to 'Alcatraz' on the other side of the bypass, but one day in December of that first term we are introduced to a new boy who's joining our class.

He stands at the front next to Mr Hoyle who puts a hand on his shoulder as he talks. The boy wears a neat uniform that's slightly too big for him and a centre-parting at a time when centre-partings are chronically uncool. I can see from my desk at the back of the class he has a slight shade of bum fluff on his top lip but not enough to shave yet. I squint to get a better look as he shuffles from foot to foot, embarrassed at being the centre of attention. We are given his name and told he comes from Haverfordwest.

I go to the toilets and try to throw up but I can't. I stay there till one of the teachers comes to get me. I say I'm not feeling well and want to go home, but I know I can't stay home forever. I'll have to face him sooner or later, and I do, managing to do so without any eye contact and avoiding sitting next to him when we change classrooms, like when we decamp to the art room or science lab, for instance. I see the other boys being friendly and chatting to him good-naturedly as they heat test tubes on Bunsen burners, but I keep my head down, happy to give him a wide berth. I don't want him to be my friend. I don't want anything to do with him.

Because I recognise something in that bum fluff and the slicky hair and those dark plugs of eyes and thick lips and narrow shoulders, and the way he is looking at me, pretending that I mean nothing to him. And maybe I don't, but I know for a fact he is the thing that crawled out of the old tramp's body in that cave when I was little. He might look like a boy, but he isn't one. The rest of them might fall for it, but I don't.

He has a plastic comb in the breast pocket of his school uniform jacket. Sometimes I watch him as he uses it to scrape back his locks. His eyebrows are thick for a twelve-year-old. His eyes never crinkle in crow's feet when he smiles and when he does it's as if he is assessing the other person for a misdemeanour.

Sometimes in lessons the teachers tell him to wake up and sometimes in the playground I see him talking to himself, his lips moving. Not in thought or concentration but in conversation with someone or something invisible to the eye. Often, peering over my exercise book, I see a bubble of foam at the corners of his mouth. Perhaps it is medication of some kind. Perhaps it isn't.

One evening to my alarm he rings our door bell and asks if I can come out to play. He uses the word 'play' which is a bit young when applied to children of our age. I'm terrified my mother will ask him in but luckily she says it's dark already and her son is in for the night and he should go home and get a good night's sleep as it's school tomorrow. He doesn't reply and I hear the front door close.

We return to school after Christmas and there's a funny atmosphere at assembly and 'Birdy' tells us we are all to go home, our parents have been informed, but he doesn't say informed of what. I walk back via the quarry and I hear the whine of police sirens on the air, which is unusual. My dad is at home which is unusual too, and he and my mam know something but they aren't saying, which makes me annoyed and grumpy.

His name isn't over the front pages at first.

It begins with news that a boy and girl from what we called the 'Small School' have gone missing and my mam is really upset and I ask her why because she doesn't even know the family. She tells me to be quiet, which is the most she has raised her voice, ever.

They find the bodies in the woods a few days later, covered in a blanket of branches cut from the nearby tree. It isn't far from a pond I'd visit to catch frog spawn and newts. The five-year-old boy is found with twenty-six puncture marks in his chest and face, made, it turns out, with the same pen knife that cut off the branches. A branch from the same tree is stuck into the wound in the skull of the little girl and two yellow school pencils are inserted into her eyes.

The boy from Haverfordwest is spotted by a man walking his dog. He's sitting high up in the tree, stark naked. The police find his clothes bunched up and used as pillows for the bodies. I read this later. Much later. You know how it is. It all comes out in dribs and drabs. . . Journalism. Rumour. Stories. Television.

We never see him again, school-wise. Not surprisingly. He disappears as unexpectedly as he'd arrived.

The tabloids, predictably, go into overdrive with the usual

gutter press hyperbole.

MONSTER.

EVIL.

I don't know if they've done any research on the subject but I'm pretty sure those two words must sell more newspapers than anything else in the English language.

The reporters outside school torment us kids with questions. What was he like? Did you know he was mad? Soon it's them ringing our doorbell. In the end 'Birdy' has to give them a stiff warning, telling them his pupils are traumatised enough. Requesting a respectful distance, to which they grudgingly comply.

Psychologists from the Department of Education ask me to tell them about my feelings. How can I talk about my feelings when what I really know to be true is bottled up inside me unable to get out? I can't. So it just sits there inside me. A sore that is untreated and suppurating.

Anyway, by the natural order of things, in time, the circus leaves town. Once the legal process in underway and the vultures and jackals are unable to give details of the accused for fear of contempt of court, it goes insanely and uncomfortably quiet. The news cycle moves on. But I can't move on. I'm in limbo. Nothing is resolved for me. The murky water is churned up and will never settle or be clear.

All I have is the pictures. The headlines. But most of all I have the memory of a boy my age combing back his oil slick hair in the front row of class while the geography teacher drones on.

All I have is the image of the cracked lips mutely moving in the drizzle at playtime and the thing made of scarlet jelly tearing itself, throbbing, into this world in the spitting firelight of The Cave.

I leave school with a paltry few GCSEs. English, RI, I forget what else. Not enough to impress any decent employer. Not one with any sense anyhow, and it doesn't bother me since any job I do go for, the bosses seem like absolute wankers.

I end up with a broom in my hand working long hours for a builder's merchants. If I'm a good boy they let me sit at the till and fry my brains that way, by dealing with customers who are invariably a pain in the arse and require a certain subservience as part of the deal, so stuff that. Then money goes missing, no fault of my own, but who gets the blame? Yours truly. The nitwits tell me to clear my desk – *what desk?* – and I'm happy to get out, back to the ranks of the unemployed at twenty-seven. My parents pay what is due to stop it going to court. I say I wanted to fight it, but my dad tells me to stop being an idiot. I say there was an accounting discrepancy. He repeats the two words and laughs. *Accounting discrepancy!*

He remembers all the times I said I was revising for exams and instead of getting my head down, I'd sneak out of the French windows of the middle room and run down the precinct to hang out with my glue-sniffing pals. Since then he's harboured the unwavering belief I'm incapable of applying myself to anything worthwhile and I'm unlikely to do so in the foreseeable future.

I make tea in an architect's office where the loudest and most interesting thing is the clock ticking. The PA, Tina, can't stand it either. She's leaving to do teacher training and, half out of the door, says to me, why don't you do the same?

Not a bad idea, so I ask my dad if he thinks I have what it takes. For a fleeting moment I wonder if he'll well up sentimentally at the thought of his son going into his chosen profession, but he doesn't. He doesn't say he thinks I'll be good, as a normal father might. The most he says is I should give it a go and find out. I could see in his face he anticipated the usual disaster. Thanks, Dad.

Meanwhile, on the positive side, my relationship with Gaynor is on solid ground, and with the stability of a regular income, our marriage is, too.

Then I find out she's been seeing another feller, and has been, from the day we got back from honeymoon. This I know because he was decorating our house while we were away. Nice bloke. Reliable bloke. Hard working. Grease under his fingers from fiddling about with engines, even when he's in a morning suit. Oh yeah. At the wedding; of course he was. Friend of the family. Lot of money in MOTs, evidently. I mean – what is she thinking? Two kids, five and three, and another on the way, is what. I see her in the town centre or on the escalator at Sainsbury's, showing off her bump in a floral dress and flip-flops. The penguin waddle. Like a fucking queen.

Worst is, I can't even avoid her as she hasn't moved away and I can't afford to, so that's a kick in the teeth. I've always hated her smug family behaving like they're royalty. Looking down their noses at me like it was all my fault. How'd they work that out? Anyway, I don't go up that way if I can help it. I skirt around that part of own at all costs.

No, believe me. I do my best to keep indoors and keep to my own company nowadays, as you can imagine. A teacher's workload is knackering and so is dealing with ten year olds all day. Mind you the parents are worse. So when I get in it's a Chinese or a microwave meal on a tray and a Stallone or Bruce Willis, and I'm lucky if I'm awake by the time the end credits roll.

I think sometimes: *Everything changes but nothing changes.*

There are bungalows built in the quarry where they used to park cars. The woods where we used to play as kids was levelled years ago. It's become a pricey estate of executive homes you buy off-plan.

The only constant is the fear and anger. That doesn't go away.

The Cave doesn't go away.

The rock I carry in my chest is as heavy as it ever was and sometimes it burns like a meteorite, like the centre of the fucking Earth, and I try to cool it down with booze, anaesthetise myself with a dram or a bottle, but it's all still there, just with added fog, with added pain. Everything else in my life around it is numbed but the sick part is still sharply focused.

Irradicable. Fucking immortal.

And now I've seen him.

The boy from Haverfordwest.

I've seen him again.

Behind the checkout when I'm buying a toothpaste at Boots.

I look up as he bleeps it.

I stare at him as he tells me what it costs. My jaw must be hanging open slightly making me look like a mental defective because he says the price a second time. A pain slashes across my chest. I think I'm having a heart attack.

He's changed his appearance. He looks different, but he would. It's twenty-five years fucking later. He's done his time. He's out on suspension. What do they call it? On licence, whatever the fuck that is. He's not on an ankle tag, obviously. He's free.

He holds out a hand. I see tattoos on his forearm. An eagle. The eye of Horus. Egyptian. And on the side of his neck, a heart. He's skinnier. Skinnier than I'd expect. Heroin skinny. So what? I know it's him, behind the Frank Zappa moustache and beard. I see through the mask of passing years. I'd know him bloody anywhere.

I say card. I say the word 'Card'. I'm paying with card. I pay with my credit card. It's him.

He asks if I want a receipt. I shake my head. I say no, then I say yes. He tells me to have a nice day. He smiles, but there are no crinkles at the corners of his eyes.

I turn away. I put the receipt in my wallet. I leave.

I am broken.

I switch off the TV coverage. The memory of it echoes. *USA. USA. USA.* The baying morons are gone but what fills the void? He does.

The boy no longer a boy. What is he? A visitation is what.

He has grown up. Sprouted. Not that he looks an ounce heavier than he did at twelve. I think of him squatting bollock-naked in that tree, looking down at his dirty work. I'm sure I recall that he'd pissed on the corpses from on high. My anger builds. It has to have somewhere to go. I have somewhere to go, and I know it.

My white-knuckled hands don't stay on the arm of the chair. I'm up on my feet and pacing. I upturn my glass on the draining board. I've sank a bottle of red and now it's my third Bell's and if I could wring the bottle and lick the inside I would.

My eyes are prickling. Fuck it, let's go, before they defocus completely and I pass out. Come on, shit for brains, I tell myself, there's work to do. I put on the mud-encrusted hoodie I use when I go running and a Barbour coat over that. Jeans replace the tartan house pants. I sit on the stairs and knot the laces of my Caterpillar boots.

There is no alternative. That has become clear to me.

Something must be done. Someone has to do it, and that someone has to be me.

From under the awning over a restaurant in the market place I watch the interior glow of Boots the Chemist as the last of the customers leave and a pudgy bottle-blonde manageress bolts the doors top and bottom. I'm no longer on fags but discover I need one more than ever. Perhaps I'll afford myself the luxury of a cigar when I get home after the deed is done, though that seems far too celebratory and I'll probably opt for a sleeping pill.

A couple stumble out of the Regis, all groping and shag-nasty. Her half out of her crop top. You can see where her night is heading.

The pockets of my Barbour bulge heavily. In one I carry a diamond-shaped carbon steel trowel, newly acquired from B&Q. The other is weighed down with a claw-headed hammer. In a plastic bag – a *Bag For Life*, ironically so called – I carry a small axe I use to chop and split logs for my wood-burner and a bread knife taken from my kitchen drawer. Fucking wedding present.

I indulge in another Polo mint as I watch him leaving the

shop, waving goodbye to his friends and colleagues cheerily as he shrugs on a lemon yellow anorak. They call him a first name I don't recognise. But I recognise him all right.

MONSTER.

EVIL.

I have no idea where he lives so I follow him blind, hanging back like they do in the movies to avoid detection, but he never looks back, not even once, and never pauses in his steady pace, hands in pockets, skinny legs in skinny black jeans, turning left at the bus station car park, through the tunnel under the railway line, sucking a vape, puffing a trailing white cloud and taking the streets I know from my childhood, towards the estate and school and home.

In the pitch black outside the solace of street lighting he takes to the rocky horse-shoe road I used to take walking home from the Grammar. The surface still hasn't acquired the dignity of tarmac and I think a fair few cars opting for this route will have suffered tyre damage over the years. The nameless road must have its scalps.

I follow him to the quarry. He turns off where the three identical bungalows have been built. Not a single light is on inside them and they look uninhabited except that when he walks up the narrow alley between them, lined by wire fencing, a dog starts barking. I can't tell where the dog is or who owns it. The thing sounds unhinged.

The man I'm following disappears into the darkness but, of course, he hasn't disappeared at all.

My stomach tightens as if a fist has gripped it and twisted.

The Cave is still there, black and prehistoric as ever. You'd think they would have bricked it up by now. Filled it in, especially since they were building the new houses. But no. What stopped them? What hold did it have over them? What did they consider fitting about its continued presence?

It strikes me for the first time the aperture is like a sightless eye with a heavy lid.

This time, when I step inside, the flickering glow from around the corner is not the warm orange of flames but an almost iridescent blue. The soles of my boots crunch under my weight. I dread to think what it is I'm treading on. My phone affords me a flashlight. It illuminates broken glass and small bones. Feathers and beaks are scattered, mixed with nails and eyelashes covering a floor of patterned linoleum. A breed of panda acquired from a service station lies face down, eviscerated of its cheap foam innards. In place of the campfire, this time, a small portable TV screen is showing the inauguration. *USA. USA. USA.* The tramp is on his knees, cradling on his lap the thin man I've been following, making the image of a perfect Renaissance pietà. The younger man's anorak is ripped and he wears no jeans any more. His pale, bare legs show patches of hair. One arm hangs listlessly. His mouth is attached to the old man's left nipple which he is sucking voraciously.

My feet snag on a tangle of newspaper. I look down and see the arm of a baby, wrapped up like fish and chips.

'I kept some for you,' says the old tramp. Blood on his grinning teeth.

The teeth are what I hit first, after dropping my phone. I don't know how the axe gets in my hand but it does. It rises and falls effortlessly, and the long-haired head is cleft like a log, the contents not spilling yet so the necessity is for the addition of blows. I sink the hefty blade into both shoulders, hearing the collarbone crack, once, twice. The neck I hack at like a lumberjack, right and left. The jaw, with the flapping wings of a beard, hangs off. I hack again with the claw-headed hammer. I don't stop hacking. I thrash with the pointed trowel and the bread knife. His organs cascade out. The tunnel, that maw, is opened and the younger man escapes into it. Down the rabbit hole.

I try to grab him by the ankles but it's as difficult as grabbing soap. He kicks at me and his filthy feet vanish. I'm not going to let him get way. I hear the bad boys giggling. My bloodstained weapons clatter onto the floor of the cave. I plunge my arms into the fetid morass. The gore takes my head and shoulders, I enter it, I'm drowning in it, I'm grasping and pulling and choking and thrashing and clawing. I'm swimming and I have no breath. Skin pulsates and puckers all around me, holding me like a sheath. I have to escape. I see a hole. I paw and squelch towards it.

I crawl out of the red mud. The butcher's shop fills my mouth.

I feel the cold air of The Cave.

I am twelve years old and naked. One knee before the other, one foot before the other, I step out. I rise.

I rub the ruby clots from my eyes.

The old man sinks his fangs into the umbilical and shakes his head like a terrier with a rat. When it is broken, he slurps it into his mouth like a dangling string of spaghetti, grimy fingers poking the ragged end into his bulging cheeks. He shows me the trophy of his bloodstained teeth as if for inspection.

As my eyes focus, I see the imprint of a hand on the cave wall. It is red and it is mine.

I cough up a bolus of flesh that uncorks my throat.

I pluck the snail trail of dried phlegm from my weeny foreskin. Afterbirth slides down my leg. I step over it towards the dim pall of the light from one of the bungalows. I can smell the bathroom – all toothpaste, bubble bath, and suppositories.

My nipples harden. My dentition needs a place to call its own.

I've got an appetite.

My Dad knows. The Cave knows. The Wheel turns and is complete.

I shall clothe myself in baggy leisurewear replete with logos.

All will be well.

All will be good.

I shall have no rest, but I'll not hunger while someone's on the bone.

And if they ask who I am, I'll say I come from Haverfordwest.

LAMIA

In the year 1909, English artist, John William Waterhouse, produced a hauntingly eerie painting. It depicted a beautiful young woman, half-clad, sitting alongside a woodland pool as though admiring her reflection, while heaped on her knee, as if it had just been shed, was a mass of ornately patterned snakeskin. The painting was called Lamia, *and it drew on a myth which from the earliest days right up to medieval times had unnerved primitive communities across the western world.*

The story isn't quite so well known in Europe today, with the possible exception of in Greece, wherein the Lamia originated as a mythical entity and where it is still used as a bogey-woman figure with which to cow petulant children. Of course, when it comes to perverse monstrosities, the canon of Greek mythology is bulging at the seams. Every kind of ghastly monster lurks there. Yet the story of the Lamia is perhaps unusual in that there is no natural ending to it. The Lamia is never recorded as having been slain by a hero or having learned the error of her ways. If anything, one tale tells how she was actually spared when a hero had her at sword-point, which according to students of the Greek mythos, means that the Lamia, cursed with immortality, is still wandering the world today (maybe doing evil, maybe not – who knows?).

If nothing else, the Lamia's basic nature and appearance are well-known to scholars.

Most of those who've heard of her will be aware that she is half-snake and half woman, (though some offshoot myths, rather curiously, describe her as having foul-smelling testicles!), and that her sole purpose for existing is the killing of human children, which she prefers to tear from the bellies of their mothers before they are even born. It's a horrific concept, of course, but as with so many Greek legends, there is much meaning behind the violence and gore.

To start with, is it 'the Lamia' as in a kind of monster, or is it 'Lamia', as in a single individual? The truth, if we can use that term, is now long lost. The origin story has become muddied beyond comprehension by innumerable retellings, translations and fictionalisations.

In a nutshell, the basic tenets of the legend hold that the Lamia was once Lamia, the Queen of Libya, and a dazzling beauty who was also famous for her intellect and wit. Her people were said to have been so happy under her rule that they wished she could reign forever. Confusingly, Queen Lamia was said to have eyes 'as blue as the sea' and hair 'as red as fire', which is difficult to compute when you consider that in classical times, 'Libya' was a term used in reference to all the lands west of the Nile, which obviously were occupied by Saharan peoples. But back to the story: Lamia was so delectable that, once again, Zeus, the King of the Gods, and the king of seducers, descended from Olympus to have his way with her. Strangely, on this occasion, it is said that Zeus was overtaken by love rather than mere lust. Either way, and as these stories so often go, Zeus's wife, Hera, the Goddess of Marriage among other things, was so enraged that she attacked the Libyan queen, rendering her eyeless and at the same time striking down all her children. So angered was Hera that even Zeus was subdued. Accordingly, instead of restoring the stricken woman to the happy state she'd been in before, he merely restored her eyes; the children he would not replace.

This wasn't enough for Queen Lamia, who quite simply went mad, ordering the destruction of all the children in her kingdom and then sending her armies to invade neighbouring lands and wreak the same carnage there.

A ruler once known for her wisdom and beneficence had overnight become an unstoppable, raging hag, whose grief-fuelled hatred was so intense and whose crimes and atrocities so numerous and despicable that they slowly affected her physically, transforming her from the most handsome of women into a horrific beast. This doesn't explain how an entire tribe of such monsters were shortly afterwards said to have exploded out of ancient Libya, though they nevertheless are reported to have followed in the footsteps of their former queen, who, now having become a monster, had abandoned her throne and people, and was busy cutting her own bloody swathe through the infants of the world.

So go the ancient stories, and it wasn't just the Greeks who believed in them. The existence of the Lamia as a genuine, living predator was affirmed by later intellectuals. Isidore, the 7th Century Archbishop of Seville, and Hincmar, the 9th Century Archbishop of Reims, were among several senior churchmen who wrote that the 'lamiae' were genuine monstrous beings, and an all-too-real supernatural threat to mankind.

That said, the moral behind the story is not difficult to discern either.

In similar fashion to the legend of Medusa, who in punishment for being raped by Poseidon, was turned by Athena into the Gorgon (another monster with serpentine characteristics), it clearly paid Lamia poorly to be a scarlet woman, though in modern times the interpretation is of course different: namely that the so-called heroic age treated women very badly, not just viewing their rape with neither outrage nor even sympathy, but then reviling them afterwards as if they were some kind of aberration. The key difference between the two stories is that, while Medusa took her vengeance out on everyone (though mostly men, as it was mostly men who came to kill her) by turning them to stone, the Lamia embarked on a trail of infanticide, picking on the most innocent in society.

If that seems like a distinctly unmotherly revenge, it's not impossible that, back in the deep mists of time, it was a coded reflection on the multitudes of children born of rape thanks to the endless conquests of warlords and their vast armies.

Despite these complexities of origin, over the following centuries the Lamia slowly morphed into a more easily understood being.

At one point she was allegedly sent by Apollo to destroy the city of Argos, and so already had become a celestial weapon rather than a lamenting demigod, rather like Cetus, the sea-dragon, whom Poseidon sent to vanquish the kingdom of Ethiopia, or the gigantic Nemean Lion, sent by Hera to ravage the land of Nemea (modern day Corinthia).

As early as the 1st Century AD, the Lamia's not uncommon appearance in works of Greek and Roman fiction saw a melding of the original creature with the more familiar vampire, succubus or siren, the once grief-stricken mother now a sexually enticing stalker and murderess of lusty young men. Hence the suggestive image painted by John William Waterhouse, among numerous others.

Hence similar depictions of the Lamia throughout humanity's creative history, from bestiaries, poems and horror novels to prog rock maestros Genesis's seminal 1974 album, The Lamb Lies Down on Broadway.

Why could this be?

Is it human nature to bring sex into everything?

Or is the original concept simply too disturbing: that Lamia was a demented, mutated monstrosity hellbent on slaying and devouring our children?

REDCAP
Christopher Harman

After his interview at *Parklands Academy for Girls,* Ryder went through the front gates, crossed the quiet cul de sac and entered Atavan Park. He took the path past the tennis courts to the beech-lined avenue running alongside the wide river. In the distance was the Riverside Café, mostly glass under the single slope of roof. A mile further on was the hazy huddle of the drab estate from where he'd set out ninety minutes earlier from the house he was renting after his recent move. It was midday and he was hungry.

In the café he ate and waited for Miss Cadley's call. Framed in the tall windows the great amphitheatre of grass rose to bushes and trees overlooked by tall imposing Georgian residences at this southern boundary of the city. Miss Cadley's questions and his answers kept flashing in his head. She'd finally looked engaged on reaching the 'interests' section of his application form. 'Creative writing, I see. Anything published?' Her pleasant enquiry froze on her face at 'Short stories mainly.' 'Novel?' she'd said with a hopeful shake-nod of her head. 'Who knows.' This said with a shrug, modestly, tantalisingly, while thinking hell would freeze over first. 'Well good luck with that,' she said, quickly proceeding to ask if he'd any questions and receiving the answer, 'No thanks, I haven't.'

Deciding to kill more time in the park he left the café. A few yards short of the railway bridge over the river he took the path that rose as it wound through rhododendrons and stands of silver birch. A line of imported rock features towered on his left, at once decorative and serving to support a high bank of earth and scrub. Where the path levelled off before heading to the park's main gates there was a rock slab twice his height with uneven notches along the top suggestive of castellation. Stooping through the opening that previous one time, he'd entered a roofless dirt-floored area of a few square yards. With an inclination now to go inside, he felt a faint irritation that someone had pre-empted him. Furring soporifically in his head, a preoccupied humming was dispelled abruptly by a cracking as of a pet dog gnawing a bone, and could well have been that. Conjecture vanished as his phone ring-tone sounded sooner than he'd expected.

Miss Cadley offered him the caretaker's post in the bland congenial voice of officialdom and he acted pleasure in his acceptance. He agreed to start on Monday afternoon.

In the pub that evening Iris turned the celebration into a second interview. 'Nervous? No way!' He hadn't cared enough to be. Yes, he'd mentioned bleeding a radiator, his IKEA bookshelf construction. What about his sideline? 'What, the writing?' He shrugged, admitted 'It may have helped.' Iris had advised beforehand that he'd be a fool not to mention it. 'I'm convinced amateur dramatics got me into hospital admin.' She added primly, confident in her assertion, 'They like you to have a hinterland.' 'You don't need a hinterland to unblock a toilet,' Ryder said. He was glad when talk turned to her upcoming appearance with the Harrowby Players in *Haggardly Hotel* at the Trade Hall Theatre.

Over the weekend he couldn't concentrate on *Bad Fairies* as a regular paid work loomed. The editor had invited him, as a not unknown quantity, to submit a story and the theme had a fairly wide remit. A few ideas scribbled into the A4 pad bought for the purpose looked like graffiti. The *Academy* buildings had auditioned as a setting when he'd first approached them a week ago, the differently pitched roofs looking over each at this possible interloper. Madeline, the statuesque head girl, had given him a tour. With pupils in classes the corridors had been empty but for someone intermittently evident from his or her sharp tapping steps. The sense of being monitored within hearing distance only passed when Ryder entered the echoing din of girls in the acre-sized swimming pool.

Sunday, and faint nausea like when he was a kid the day before a new term. His final hours of freedom on Monday morning felt anything but free. Ideas for *Bad Fairies* teased and giggled behind murky hedges.

He walked through the leafy clamour of the park and was entering Miss Cadley's upper floor office at close to two pm. A large-framed woman in a chiffon blouse, she was sitting behind a huge presidential desk. There was an ash-floored fireplace to one side, it was that kind of school.

'Leave the door,' she said, smiling past him as knocking steps approached in the corridor. At the rap on the open door, Ryder turned, dropped his line of sight to a red cap and the small pasty face under it; eyes were shadowed under the peak pulled low. A jockey-sized man in his checked shirt, braces holding up 'gorblimey' trousers and yes, wooden clogs that had made the impacts.

'Ah, Red,' Miss Cadley said. 'This is Rodney Ryder, your other half.' A little frown at Ryder. 'Rodney's a mouthful. Rod?' There was probably some law about caretakers having single syllable names.

'Why not?' he said, amenable. *Rod the caretaker, Rodney the writer.*

'Red and Rod,' she said, tickled then instantly serious. 'Anyway, Red will show you the ropes.' Then Ryder was to return to her office for more form filling tying him into the establishment.

As Ryder followed Red down the stairs the two pm bell went off like an alarm – violent, implacable, shocking every organ in his body, obscuring whatever Red had started to say. The corridors and staircases magnified the chatter and laughter of hordes of girls. They disappeared behind doors and quiet resumed but for Red's tapping steps as he pointed out fire extinguishers and emergency doors.

'Been here long, Red?' Ryder ventured. 'Red' felt fictitious: was there some connection with his crimson head gear?

'Longer.' A low voice; a faint Scottish burr.

In the main entrance hall, Red drew Ryder's attention to the burglar alarm box, a defibrillator, the cleaners' store cupboard. Then he led the way to another door where he entered a number into a keypad.

Inside, steps descended into an extensive gloom insufficiently lit by a single bare bulb. Ryder thought of those huge shapeless basements at the bottom of stone steps in old Universal horror films. Mould on exposed red brick, and it was soot-blackened in places. An aperture contained the opening of a dumb-waiter. Further dim spaces had metal shelving for books, and deeper shelves for anything else. There was a flock of cream-coloured computers hairy with cables. The iron block of a boiler grumbled a welcome.

Red clicked a wall switch and another bulb lit what had been a dim right-angle of brick courses; it was lined by worktops, high wall cupboards, a fridge. Placing a hand on the back of a battered armchair Red said, 'This is mine.' Which presumably meant the facing red plastic stack chair would be Ryder's. There was a footstool before the armchair. The worktop had a kettle, toaster, microwave, sink with taps and a draining board.

'Home from Home,' Ryder quipped, thinking of Mole's underground quarters in *The Wind in the Willows*. There were two metal lockers, one above the other; they appeared to be empty from what he could see through the partially open doors.

'Our orders,' Red said, looking towards an ancient school desk on which a computer screen glowed with a password scotch-taped to the top. A glance revealed messages, 'Red, can you…' 'Leaking tap in science room 3, Red, if you could…'

Red led him up the steps again, and into the brightness of the entrance hall. In the depths of his reflection in the polished floor the man's cap glowed like a coal. He went out of the main doors onto the forecourt, then was through the main gates and gone, his day presumably done. Charming, Ryder thought. An inauspicious start to their working relationship but with he and

Red covering afternoons and mornings respectively they would meet, if at all, only at the cross-over. Ryder decided that would suit him just fine.

After a further discussion with Miss Cadley, she took him to the teachers' staffroom. They were standing and sitting, younger ones looking barely older than the sixth-form, others, more stricken in years, lined and crumpled.

'This is Rod, everybody, caretaker mark-two,' she announced into an instant silence. *Rod Everybody*, Ryder thought. And did 'mark two' mean in terms of being successor to the previous fellow or second-in-command to Red from now on? Murmurs welcomed him. While Miss Cadley took a breath before some announcements just for the teachers, an iron-haired bloke muttered close by, 'Hope you last longer than Ken.'

In the entrance hall Ryder said, 'Ken couldn't take the pace, could he?' Either Miss Cadley didn't catch his jokey tone or was pointedly ignoring it. 'They weren't getting along. Red's rather taciturn but he gets the job done. Ken had a drink problem. He didn't turn up one day.' She added airily, 'The police were involved for a time. He was designated a missing person. That was the last we heard of him. Unfortunate, but these things happen.'

The next day, Ryder checked the job list on the computer in the basement. There was a message from Miss Cadley herself. *'Rod, can you see me about Friday night's disco?'*

In her office she said it was for the 'lower school' and admitted it was 'throwing you in at the deep end but it shouldn't present any problems.'

'I won't be spinning discs, will I?'

Miss Cadley didn't seem open to banter. 'You'll open the building, help the DJ set up. We had gatecrashers last year but Red dealt with them.' How? Ryder wondered, from the righteous relish in her voice.

Friday came and Ryder hadn't seen Red at all in the interim. He assisted the DJ to set up speakers and coloured spotlights in the assembly hall. The boys and girls entered, accompanied by teachers and volunteer parents. Ryder felt invisible in his regulation blue house-coat. Finally he could lock the school's main doors and close the inner ones on the assembly hall.

Ryder had eighty minutes to himself. He could ignore jobs that would take him too far from the disco. Sitting in the admin-reception office by the entrance doors, he could hear the DJ welcome everyone in his amplified voice. Ryder took a sheet from the photocopier and played with the idea of a teacher with wings pressing out the back of his suit. The fellow flew off as disco hits took Ryder back decades. He was fully into the present some time later as a squeeze box wheezed against a rhythmic sequence of penetrating knocks. He crossed to the assembly hall, pushed a leaf of the double-doors inward a few inches.

Within the encirclement of crowding youthful bodies clapping to the beat, the cap, bobbing like a balloon on a string, glowed an intense red under the single spotlight. One dancer – Red, his clogs tapping in a rapid rhythm to the sprightly folk tune, now on flutes and fiddles. Bemused, Ryder moved to get a better view over the head of a shorter kid. Red wouldn't notice, not that it would matter if he did, as he was looking downwards at his deft toe-and-heel clog-work, thumbs tucked behind his braces. With a quickening of the music, his short legs were close to a blur.

It was with a succession of repeated chords and sharp stamps of Red's clogs, that the music ceased. The rhythmic clapping collapsed into frenzy of applause and there were piping cheers. Almost without a break came a new recording, the Bee Gees and *Stayin' Alive;* the boys and girls drifted apart leaving Red nowhere to be seen, and Ryder, back in the admin office, didn't see him for the rest of the evening.

The following Monday Miss Cadley came into the top floor library as Ryder was showing roofers where a ceiling leakage had occurred over the weekend. A morning closure had been arranged for repairs. Miss Cadley and Ryder left and with no indication that she was going to refer to Friday and question or thank him in regard to the evening, he said, 'The disco seemed to go well.'

'So I hear. It's so good to get the boys and girls meeting each other.' She stared ahead, not engaging, her court shoes hitting the floor smartly.

'I was surprised to see Red there,' Ryder said, persisting. Over the weekend, thoughts of Red had intruded, his tapping clogs and red cap scotching the ideas trying to take shape for *Bad Fairies.*

'Oh, he's always popping up outside his contracted hours. He's totally dedicated to the school.' She added, maybe pointedly, 'He's no clock watcher.'

Ryder had to walk fast to keep up with her and the time left to probe was diminishing. He said, 'But the clog-dancing –' playing surprised and charmed by the loveable eccentricity of Red's solo turn. 'And the kids loved it, clapping away. I mean, he's no slouch.'

'He certainly isn't.' A sidelong disapproving glance, as if the mere word 'slouch' in a discussion pertaining to Red offended. As he was thinking how to frame another question, she filled the hiatus. 'He was in a dance troop known as *The Cappers.* This was before your time in the Seventies. They were quite the thing, even came top in a TV talent show called *Opportunity Knocks.* They toured, mainly in the north. Played in town at the Trade Hall Theatre. That was when it was a venue getting big acts like *The Kinks.* Anyway, Red decided to settle down here and get a proper job.' A wry glance at Ryder who gamely said, 'Ah', getting the parallel and not showing his displeasure at it.

That evening only a few tables were occupied in the Riverside Café. Ryder ate and stared through the floor-to-ceiling windows. A wraith of mist crawled on the river. Over the clotted darkness of trees and massive crouching blurs of rhododendrons, the blue-black sky had a single star winking between ghosts of silvery cloud.

A jogger powered down a lamp-lit path; on a farther

dimmer one there was a brief fiery speckling. Another, then another: Ryder realised they corresponded to steps. Someone in iron-shod footwear was striking sparks. Hob-nailed boots? Motionless now, an upright shadow. Perhaps someone was taking in the view down to the beech avenue and the river, some wavelets bloody from the sunset. Perhaps the café and its few occupants were in their sights?

Down the slope from the figure, a cluster of movements. Slender forms, slim-necked grazers on delicate legs. Deer, enchanting. At a neighbouring table a man and woman had noticed. She said the deer came over the river on the pedestrian bridge by the tennis courts, from fields and woods south of the city. The animals' heads were up now, alert.

The sparks again, in a rapid one-two, one-two until they left the path. A rapidity to the dense shadow converging on the deer as they scattered. Not all. Two darknesses became one in a tumble, spindly legs kicking at air, before the greater blackness of bushes took them both. Ryder wanted to share his astonishment but the couple at the next table were disagreeing on some other topic. As he was leaving, the girl at the counter was removing cakes from the glass display. He outlined what he'd seen and she looked out through the big windows. Bordering the grey slopes of grass the lamplit sections of the paths stood out against the trees and black clumps of the bushes.

'I'll mention it to the grounds people. They come in here. Someone's dog wandered off the other week and was found in bloody bits up by the rocks. I reckon it's one of them dangerous dogs off the estate the other side of the railway bridge.'

Where *I* live – for the time being at least, Ryder thought.

The following afternoon, an odour of toast and the scraping of a knife slowed Ryder's descent down the steps of the basement to a stop. Facing away at the worktop Red broke off spreading margarine from a tub and inserted a fresh bread slice into the toaster. He took an unlabelled jar down from the cupboard, dipped the knife and covered the first slice with jam. That done, Red sat in the armchair and ate.

With Red's clogged feet up on the footstool, Ryder noted metal set into the wooden soles at the heels and toes ends; that accounted for the penetrating sounds of the impacts when he walked. Would they strike sparks? Ryder recalled the stroller in the park the previous evening.

As Red chewed, crumbs cascaded. Why didn't he use a plate? He should know better than anyone that stray food would attract vermin, particularly in this underworld. Ryder envied the teachers with their bright, windowed staffroom, which by some unwritten rule of the educational caste system caretakers appeared to be barred from, except when cleaning it.

'Overtime?' he said, by way of a greeting, continuing down the steps, resenting Red's presence. A look was Red's answer as he turned towards Ryder. With the bulb's light directly overhead, Red's eyes were obscured in the cap peak's shadow.

Ryder made himself a mug of tea and fished a couple of *Gypsy Creams* from the packet he'd brought in on his second day. He sat in the plastic stack chair.

'Impressed by your turn at the school disco.' He couldn't help sounding ingratiating, like a weedy kid with the school bully. Red fed the last of his toast into his mouth, chewed then wiped his lips with a small ugly hand. He stood, faced Ryder, hands behind his braces, his eyes tiny glints in the cap peak shadow. Red standing was a mere head or so taller than Ryder sitting and he felt intimidated.

'*Opportunity Knocks,* eh?' he said, pushing on. Mentioning that moment of glory might break the ice.

'Oh, I can *dance,*' Red said, in a tone suggesting it was one of his more minor accomplishments.

With a metallic rasp the toaster ejected a slice and it flew high. Ryder's heart leapt, his mug slopped. Red extended a hand back over his left shoulder and with little more than a token turn of his head caught the slice on its descent.

He turned fully to the worktop. The knife scraped.

'This is for you.' He faced Ryder again, in one hand a plate with the toast, the butter all but smothered in red jam. Jam on the blade of the knife in his other hand. The dirty faded-yellow handle could have been ivory and had curious arabesques cut into it.

A dispassionate observer might have thought the plated toast in one hand and the knife in the other were a choice Ryder was being presented with. He took the plate, couldn't help but hesitate.

'It's jam,' Red said.

Ryder said through a weak laugh, 'I didn't think it was tomato sauce,' though it could well have been from its matt texture. He nibbled at a corner and apparently satisfied Red headed for the stairs, was up them and gone. Ryder spat out toast into his hand, disposed of it and the rest in the pedal bin.

There was material for a story here, dammit, but in months, years from now, in another time and place.

Later, as he entered admin-reception to hand in his overtime form for disco night, the clangorous three-thirty bell sounded. The entrance hall filled with young voices. As girls swarmed at the gates, parents manoeuvred their cars on the road. A single-decker bus lumbered up.

A rude rasping horn fanfare had Ruth the admin secretary and Monica her assistant standing to stare out of the window.

Ruth tutted, arms folded under her ample bosom. Monica sucked in her cheeks as the young man unfolded from a white open-topped sports car sliced vertically by the railings. He wore sunglasses, his black hair back-combed. A slash of white teeth in his grin as Madeline approached, tall, auburn hair catching the breeze, her gait queenly, taking what was her due. He stood straight and like a chauffeur opened the passenger door for her. With both seated inside, the car blew a raspberry at the dowdier vehicles shunting back and forth and zoomed effortlessly away and out of sight.

The show over, Ruth and Monica sat down again at their desks. 'She could do so much better,' Ruth said with a breezy despair. 'Yes, she could have her pick of hedge-fund managers in a few years,' Monica said, viciously sharpening a pencil over the wastepaper basket. 'A car like that and you're not doing so badly,' Ryder chipped in, fighting a curdling of envy.

'You think?' Monica said, extending her disapproval to Ryder now. 'He's doing very *badly* to afford a car like that, you ask Red. He knows. Madeline's been warned by Miss Cadley but you know what they're like at that age.'

Probably rebelling against her wholesome head-girl image, Ryder thought but kept to himself.

Starting work the next afternoon he found a message on the basement computer from Miss Cadley requesting a meeting in her office. Ryder felt a pulse of foreboding. Was he already judged to be failing? Had there been some complaint? Was Red finding fault? Only yesterday as he'd been washing a well-aimed smear of seagull shit off a window of the art block, he'd spied Red, outside his contracted hours, staring from the far side of the sports field. And at Ryder himself, he'd been sure of it, the chap's large green polythene refuse bag, like a wordless cartoon thought bubble, angrily restless in the breeze.

'Sit down,' Miss Cadley said, writing some note onto a pad as Ryder entered. After a moment she laid down her fountain pen.

'Your writing ...' Jesus, had she read some of it? 'Word has spread.' Staring, waiting for him to be pleased, realising she waited in vain. 'The thing is, we have a sixth-form writing group – they call themselves the *Scribblers*. I think they might benefit from somebody who's been at the coal-face, as it were.' Ryder hadn't bargained for this and 'been' made him bridle. 'Could you meet them?' Miss Cadley continued, 'A one-off, I suggest. Half-an-hour should do it,' she said, adding to the injury, as if that duration should cover the extent of his know-how. 'It's very informal. They mostly eat, drink and chatter.' This was endearing to judge from her wistful far-away look. Back to business, she informed him they met once a fortnight in the sixth-form common room.

'Yes, why not,' Ryder said, with a grim grin of acquiescence.

'I'm sure I can find a window in my busy schedule.'

His waggishness didn't appear to register as her expression turned whimsical. 'It's funny, two caretakers each with a hidden talent.'

'Red's isn't so hidden,' Ryder said.

'Nor should yours be,' she said, with a teacherly forthright tapping of her finger on the desk blotter. Her confidence didn't convince: he doubted she'd read a word he'd written.

'Do they know the kind of thing you do?' Iris asked him on the phone that evening.

'The kind of stuff I do doesn't matter. I'll just go into the blood, sweat and tears of it all.' 'Blood'; that reminded him of the film they'd seen at the Odeon the other week. He'd hoped she'd appreciate the finer points, the acting, the striking visuals of the auteur director trying his hand at horror. But she'd squealed and covered her eyes at the gore.

'Blood sweat and tears? You said you only do three hours a day!' Encouraging as ever. He could foresee a time for Iris to go the way of the others he'd met on that dating app.

The next day he had settled himself at a table in the sixth-form common room before the *Scribblers* trooped in like a delegation, armed to his consternation with folders and ring-binders. He resisted a gentlemanly impulse to stand.

'You come bearing gifts,' he said, an awkward line he'd put a red pen through in a story. Some nervous giggles. Ryder felt horribly exposed. Two girls went and busied themselves in the tiny kitchen at the end of the room. A girl with flat hair and granny glasses brought things to order, rapping a spoon on the table.

'We are honoured to welcome Mr Rod Ryder in his capacity as published author. Now, er, *Rod*, what's your thing?'

'Well, it's not clog-dancing.' No reaction at all in their faces, just waiting for the interesting stuff. He hurried on, needing to be serious, and upfront straight away. 'I veer towards the supernatural.'

'Do you believe in all that stuff?' a ponytailed girl asked, as if it were at all relevant.

'Not till I started working here,' he said, flippant. 'All these old complicated buildings with their shadowy corners and long echoey corridors and creaking staircases.' That was met with non-committal smirks. An odour of toast brought Red uncomfortably to mind.

'Have you written a novel?' a stocky, firm-jawed girl in Doc Martens said, throwing down a challenge. The two girls came in with trays laden with mugs and plates, a coffee pot and a platter loaded with toast.

'No, my subject matter requires a briefer treatment. I'm wary of the –' He eyed the thick batch of sheets bulldog-clipped before the stocky girl: she placed a protective hand over them. '– the over-extended narrative.'

The girl stared severely into his tawdry inadequate soul. He cracked a grin to suggest he was only stirring things for debate; his ploy working he took a back seat, drank from his coffee mug and declined the toast when it was offered. Minutes later they were reading extracts from their work when granny-glasses girl broke in to ask Ryder if he was currently working on anything.

That was easy. *Bad Fairies* had one or two of the girls sitting up from their slouches.

'I'm at the ideas stage,' he said, his fingertips joined together, professorial. 'I've not found a suitable one yet, but when I do I'll let it mature in my mind first, like a fine artisan cheese. Only then –' The suddenness of his utterance made a girl jump in her chair, 'Will I begin to write sentences – oh …' He'd been enjoying himself.

A small girl stood in the open door into the corridor; a serious sixth-former seen through the wrong end of a telescope.

'Miss Chisolm wants you in the gym. It's urgent.' She had been turning away even as she spoke. Ryder felt a little deflated at the premature end to the session. With the *Scribblers* literally his followers, he left the common room, apprehensive at whatever was going to be required of him.

A hush in the gym despite the numbers. Girls in leggings and leotards ignored the gym mats, the vaulting box, the balancing benches, as they stared up at the rock-climbing wall.

A shape fluttered at the corner of the ceiling, a good forty feet high. It was a pigeon, not far from a window open on the hinge at its base.

Tall, athletic, curly-haired Miss Chisolm, in her red tracksuit, was pushing through the girls, some of whom now noticed him.

'Can you do something, Rod? One of our girls has a bird phobia.' Ryder noted a huddle around a tear-stained girl seated on a gym bench.

Ryder's thoughts scrambled. Even if he'd put on one of the safety harnesses available and had the expertise to undertake the climb, the upper edge of the rock climbing wall was five feet short of the ceiling. Under a pressure of expectation, words struggled out of his mouth. 'It must have got through that open window. Give it time and it will fly out again.'

'We can't wait for that,' Miss Chisolm asserted. The *Scribblers'* faces were deadly serious as they wondered how the writer would rise to this stern test.

'Maybe bird-seed or an air-rifle ...' Ryder was saying faintly, just as a collective sigh of relief turned into a hubbub of excitement. Miss Chisolm turned away and Ryder saw the reason, thought, *I don't believe it.*

Though he was redundant, virtually invisible, relief vied with humiliation at the sight of Red, hands on hips, staring up the rock climbing wall, then climbing, eschewing the safety harness, his hands and over-large bare feet deftly coordinating as they found the multi-coloured protrusions. His clogs were neatly side-by-side on the floor, not so the cap, as ever on his head. He was rapid, almost monkey-like.

Eyelids half lowered, Miss Chisolm said, 'Oh *Red*,' breathily through parted lips. She lifted an eyebrow at Ryder. 'You can always rely on Red.'

Supremely confident, Red had arrived at the top of the rock climbing wall where there was some kind of ledge. He worked his way along it until he was a few feet from the pigeon. Towards his outstretched arm the bird flapped, as if sensing rescue – and with not an instant to react before Red's hand grasped it. Now Red, moving sideways, came to the open window. He blocked the view of the bird; there was a moment in which Ryder wondered if it was struggling against the freedom Red was offering it. But then his arms jerked and the window banged shut.

Red descended as fast and easily as he had climbed. There were cheers, whistles, applause, which Ryder joined in half-heartedly, not wanting to appear a conspicuous exception to anyone deigning to take him into consideration. The *Scribblers* nodded at each other solemnly, as if they would have expected no less from Red.

His own height from the floor, Red jumped backwards, implausibly landing his feet directly into his waiting clogs. No doffing of his cap to accompany his deep formal bow acknowledging the audience. Standing straight again he pinched at his lips and they lengthened from the corners into a grin as he brandished a feather for all to see. The girls laughed and clapped again.

That evening, Ryder helped Iris with some of her scenes in the murder mystery *Haggardly Hotel.* They took a break and she imparted some hospital gossip about a surgeon bloodily botching an operation. Ryder mentioned Red for the first time, the clog-dancing, *The Cappers*, his long ago appearance at the Trade Hall Theatre. 'You can run it by Roland. He's been with *Harrowby Players* forever,' Iris said. He had risen from humble stage-hand to his current post as artistic director. 'You'll see him at the first night party. You're invited by the way.'

'Can I enter your lair?'

It was Madeline, pattering down the steps, interrupting his afternoon fifteen minutes of dunking *Hobnobs* into his mug of builders' tea. Were pupils even allowed down here? She was carrying a ring-binder.

'It's not mine alone,' Ryder said, rising from the ugly comfy armchair to stand, as if she were a visiting school governor.

She caught on, 'Oh. Red. He's not here is he?' Lightly spoken but she glanced as if Red might be watching, fused into the red-brick courses.

'You never know with Red.' She'd made him unexpectedly uneasy. He cast a rueful glance at the armchair he'd rebelliously sat in.

'Have you got a minute?' she said, without invitation sitting in the plastic stack chair. Ryder had no choice but to sit in Red's armchair again and listen to what she looked set on saying.

'I hear you're a writer.' Frank, business-like.

Ryder braced. 'One writes, that would be more accurate.' Mentioning the matter on his application was having unforeseen consequences. It was going to sit on his back like a succubus.

'I'm into it too.' Spoken like a desperate confession, as if with this revelation he'd leap up into her arms, two sufferers in a common cause.

'I had a face-to-face with the *Scribblers* the other day. I didn't notice you there.' Coolly direct, his tone expecting some explanation.

'I used to go,' she said, defensively. 'But they're just playing at it. I'm serious. I've been working on some ideas for a novel. I've even written some scenes.' She tapped the ring-binder that now troubled him. 'I'm dying to get properly started but I've got exams next spring and then there's my responsibilities as head girl. Then I'll be at uni.'

'Of course,' Ryder said, approving of the excuses. He wondered where that flash young chap in the sporty car came in all this. Maybe he was another hobby, as ephemeral as the writing might turn out to be.

'So I've had some thoughts about *Bad Fairies*,' she said, startling him. She tapped the ring-binder. 'Somebody said you're struggling for an idea, stuck, lacking inspiration.'

'Would that be one of the *Scribblers*?'

Her buoyant look of affirmation faded.

'I'm not 'stuck'. It's early days. It's a matter of finding a good idea and letting it mature like a –'

'– like a fine artisan cheese?' she said, eagerly, sitting forward, eyes gleaming. 'God, that's brilliant.'

That placated him a little. The *Scribblers* must have been impressed by that nugget of writerly wisdom, and it *was* a fitting analogy for his working method.

'Thoughts, you say?' he said, watching as she opened the ring-binder.

'Redcap.' She looked at him, letting that sink in before continuing.

'Recap?' he jested.

'*No*, Redcap.' A fondly admonishing expression. She might have been thinking, *You men.* 'You must have heard of it in your line of work. It's a kind of wicked gnome. Wears a …' A gesture over her head.

'A cap, yes. Of course, I've *heard* of redcaps, who hasn't?' Decidedly no expert, he went on in his expert voice. 'A kind of mytho-legendary brand. And of course there are garden gnomes. There's Enid Blyton's Big Ears. The common denominator is the red cap –'

'– I've done some research.' She read aloud from a sheet in her binder, and Ryder learned things: the redcap was a brutal dwarfish creature in Scottish Borders legend; it skulked around battlefields, seeking spilled blood. Elsewhere it just killed, mopped up blood with its cap and thus sustained its existence. Ryder thought that as the basis for a story a redcap had its limitations. But there was a more pressing issue. He raised a finger.

'A certain school caretaker known for wearing a cap that happens to be red has nothing to do with this?'

'Of course not!' Her protest and irritated frown undermined her denial. 'Red's just a little old caretaker man and former clog-dancer who wears a red cap as a sentimental reminder of his dancing days.' Madeline had a certain authority in the way she spoke; he foresaw her running some organisation, maybe even this school, post Miss Cadley.

Ryder reflected that if he ever did write a story about a redcap, he wouldn't like the fact to get back to Red. But this lively debate was fun. 'So what thoughts did you have for a redcap story?'

She rolled her eyes. 'Oh, where to start! I've had tons of ideas.'

That's more than he would have were he to put his mind to the matter. A blood-thirsty and/or murderous pixie-type horror is at work in the city, what then?

The pc pinged with a new email and Ryder got up to read it.

'Someone's been sick in the theatre. I'll have to clean-up. We'll continue this another time if you like.'

She did like that, her smile said as much.

The day after he had lunch in the Riverside café. Above the slope of the vast grass sward a long hatchback vehicle was intermittently visible between trees and bushes as it moved along the path from the main gates of the park. Ryder glimpsed busy figures close to where he judged the castle-shaped rock to be. A thin length of white was suspended between trees, a loose end rippling. Someone entering the café said a body had been found. Ryder left and followed the path up the upper edge of the park.

As he came in sight of the rock facade with the rough battlement crenulations, a uniformed officer stooped to enter through the opening. Onlookers were gathered at police tape. Ryder had to take to the open grass until he could get back onto an upper path and head onwards to the school.

It was old news by the time he entered the admin office to put in an order for *Shake-and-Vac*. He learned that in a special assembly Miss Cadley had instructed pupils not to enter the park at lunchtimes until further notice. A cross country run had been cancelled.

'It's not the first. There have been three murders there in my time,' Ruth said.

Ryder got to work, replaced two strip lights, bled a radiator, set up tables and chairs in the assembly hall for an inter-school chess congress at four.

After the event, he set about locking the building up and noticed a light on in the admin office. He went inside where Ruth didn't interrupt her keying words onto a spreadsheet on her screen to say, 'It's that young man Madeline was involved with. Some drugs deal gone wrong they're saying.'

Ryder was shocked; Madeline had kept dangerous company, maybe unknowingly. Schoolwork, writing, Redcap would be far from her thoughts.

The next day the murder came closer. He found some excuse in the afternoon to enter the admin office, as had a number of teachers to judge from their guilty looks. Feeling it necessary to keep Ryder in the picture Ruth spoke low, with exaggerated lip movements. 'Red's been interviewed by the police.'

Ryder's immediate thought was that capable of clog-dancing, was Red capable of murder?

'Is that 'helping them with their enquiries'?' He laughed edgily and people looked away.

'Red can help them if anyone can.' Staring hard at Ryder, Monica said, 'The park's his back yard. He has a flat in one of those big posh houses overlooking it. He loves to stroll there. He doesn't miss much.'

The teachers' rumbles sounded like agreement on her latter point.

The following day Miss Cadley rang him at nine-thirty.

She replied to his initial short 'Hello' with 'Is that you Rod?'

'I hope so,' he said, absurdly.

'You sounded like Red for a minute there, but he's on my mind at the moment.' She prattled on, 'Can you come in early, Rod. Red's not turned up for work today, and it's not like him.'

Ryder agreed promptly, Miss Cadley thanked him and the call was over. There had been no mention of Red's police interview, as if it were too delicate a matter to bring up even with his opposite number though she would have to at some point. Surely everyone was bound to view Red's absence as incriminating.

Working that day, Ryder was given to understand that Madeline was another absentee. Ruth needed no prompting when he went into admin to empty the wastepaper bin later.

'Madeline's been in here in bits. Miss Cadley drove her home. Of course we all knew getting mixed up with that ne'er-do-well would end in tears – but not like this!'

That evening was the first night of *Haggardly Hotel*. In the opening scene in the games room, a woman's body was found with a knife protruding from its back. The snow-bound stock characters came and went, amongst them a spiv, a vicar, an overbearing businessman and a precise and fussy retired detective. In her role as mousey companion to a wealthy dowager, Iris's voice was forced and shrill. Ryder found the actress playing the femme fatale more compelling in appearance and in her caramel warm tones.

At the backstage party, Ryder found Iris and said, like an actor himself, 'Darling you were wonderful'. With snakes of white hair dangling over the collar of his black polo-neck sweater, Roland the director called for attention and gave a congratulatory speech, then there was drinking, chatter and mingling.

Iris dragged Ryder into Roland's temporarily empty orbit. Ryder had something astute and complementary in mind but before he could say anything Roland said to Iris, 'When is this author chappie going to write us a play, eh? Something spooky?'

'I'm working on him,' Iris said. Not recalling her doing so, Ryder put on a playful coy look as if it might be only a matter of time before he put pen to paper. With Iris being pulled away by a chatty woman who had played the stabbed corpse in the first scene and later a sinister nun, Ryder could question Roland.

'Iris tells me you're writing a history of the Trade Hall Theatre?'

'Oh that,' Roland said, as if weary of the fact even as he welcomed the inquiry. 'Yes, I'm gathering memories and material, and there's a frightening amount.'

'Anything on *The Cappers*? They were clog-dancers. Back in the Seventies.'

'*Cappers.*' He scrunched his mouth trying to recall. 'I've a misty recollection. Not everything will make the cut. Clog-dancing. Hmm. Hardly sets the blood racing.'

'One of *The Cappers* was a chap named Red.'

Roland grinned and raised a hand at someone, though Ryder couldn't tell who when he twisted around.

'I can't remember all the names of the cast these days,' Roland said. He tapped Ryder's shoulder, preparing to move on. 'Nice to meet you.'

Ryder persisted. 'He's still around. I work with him in fact. At Parklands Academy.'

Roland seemed to be covering his shock. '*Teaching*?'

'No, our official titles are 'Custodians of the Premises', caretakers, if you like.' To emphasise it wasn't his main occupation in life Ryder felt it necessary to add, 'Part-time. We both are.'

'But aren't we all part-timers, in a sense?' Roland let out a hard nervous bark of laughter. Glancing anxiously for someone else to talk to, he cried out 'Colin!' and hooked his arm around the actor who had played the handsome spiv. 'This is one spot-welder with the world at his feet. He has an audition for a TV drama next week. He'll get the part.' *Who knows*? in Colin's raised palms and meekly tilted head. Roland gave a theatrical sigh. 'In the meantime, some of us, Rod, it is Rod isn't it? – must continue to take the King's Shilling.' Roland and Colin drifted off, chuckling and glad-handing.

Ryder mingled; accepting several glasses of wine he felt less like a trespasser. Later he shared a taxi with Iris, both of them sloshed. He escorted Iris into her block of flats. Inside she was giggly and useless; both flopped onto the king-sized bed. He couldn't sleep as she alternately snored and mumbled lines from the play. The Bakelite ringtone of her phone didn't wake her. He went around the bed, saw 'Roland Devine' on the screen.

'Sorry, Iris is asleep,' Ryder said, a thud of foreboding in his chest.

'It's you I want to talk to,' Roland said, confirming what Ryder had suspected.

Ryder took the phone into the living room. 'Yes?'

'This "Red". If he's the same fellow, you need to watch him. How long has he been at the school?'

'Since the Seventies.'

An audible gasp down the line.

'And he *is* the same chap,' Ryder said. 'I've even seen him clog-dance in front of the kids. He's a mainstay at the school, popular.'

'Of course I remember him.' Roland sounded assertive yet anxious. 'His final appearance in clogs was with us – after that he vanished. He wasn't missed by his colleagues. He'd only been with the troop a few months. I first saw them in a telly special from Castle Kirkbride, this big outdoor entertainment venue on the Scottish borders. Turns out that's when he first joined them. He somehow inveigled himself into the group on stage in the midst of a performance. He was an instant hit. *The Cappers'* manager kept him on. There would have been an outcry if he hadn't. The reviews were over the top: 'There's a new star in the clog-dancing firmament, and his name is …' 'I have seen the future of clog-dancing and its colour is –'

'– Red?'

Roland's breaths sounded asthmatic. 'The audiences loved him, their faces – almost mesmerised. Not so his fellow cloggers. I mean he could dance the socks off them. In fact he was so brilliant it was weird, you might say uncanny. Talk about first amongst equals! His bright red cap made everyone else's look dim. I heard there was something more than resentment and mere jealousy amongst his fellow dancers. I saw him backstage. He'd watch the comings and goings, saying little unless asked. And that face, pasty, urchin-like, old and young at the same time, little snitch of a nose. You could never quite see his eyes with them shadowed by the peak of his cap. A new clogger taken on teased him for apparently never removing it, when off duty so to speak, and I was given to understand that whatever Red said in reply turned the fellow pale and he resigned the same night. Red never appeared for the final night with us, or anywhere else. He's never shown his face back here and I don't want that to change. You got that?'

Forestalling any reply Roland rang off.

Ryder looked up Castle Kildare on his phone. It had plenty of history, much of it violent. A ghost in the apparel of a soldier was said to walk on the ramparts: nothing new there, Ryder thought. 'Like a number of other castles with bloody histories Kirkbride has its reports of a redcap, a gnomish supernatural being, lurking in the aftermath of battles and supping on the blood of the dead and wounded.' Ryder guessed that not many respectable castles would be without one. He'd resist the notion of such a supernatural being straying from folklore into real life. Red might be a taciturn eccentric, and maybe much worse than that, but he was also human.

The next morning Ryder was taking his tea-break in the basement when the door opened at the top of the steps. Not Madeline, not remotely. A man with grizzled thinning hair and a lined face, probably younger than the age he looked.

'Mr Ryder? Detective Inspector Toomey. You'll have heard we're investigating the death of the young man in the park?'

Ryder said yes and indicated the red plastic stack chair. The inspector sat, drew a notebook from the pocket of his thick grey overcoat. Sitting in the armchair, Ryder steeled himself for another kind of interview.

'As you probably know we're trying to trace your other half, Robin Redman.'

Ryder was startled, and then reasoned that he shouldn't be. Red's surname had never been offered by anyone, nor had he asked for it. Red was a suitable shorthand for Redman and it tied in conveniently with his former red-capped persona as one of *The Cappers*.

'Is anything the matter, Mr Ryder?'

Ryder admitted he'd never known Red's full name and Toomey considered that for a moment.

'Noticed any change in his behaviour recently?'

'No. He struck me as ... eccentric from the start, not that I saw him much with us working different hours. We've barely spoken.'

Toomey was pointing at the lockers. 'Which one of those is yours?' Ryder said the closed top one. Underneath, Red's was open an inch. Toomey pulled it wide. 'Hmm, empty. We've visited his flat. Mountains of unopened mail in the porch. Bare boards inside. No food in the cupboards. It looks unlived-in.' His stare was either to unsettle him into saying more, or he was taking time to formulate a question towards the same end. Finally, pocketing his notebook, his pale blue eyes still intent on Ryder, he thanked him, handed him a card and said to call if anything else should come to mind.

After he'd gone, Ryder reheated his coffee in the microwave. Red seemed not merely gone, but as unreal as any in Ryder's personal pantheon of weird and frightening beings from fiction and film. Staring into a peripheral gloom of the basement, he was aware of a patch of redness. He got up, paced closer and the redness took a sharper outline.

It was Red's cap. He picked it up. He couldn't picture Red not wearing it, try as he might, as if it was part of the essence of him. Had he inadvertently left it in an extreme hurry to get away from the school, get away from Harrowby?

The door of the basement was opening again. Like the TV Columbo, it would be Toomey again, about to say, 'Just one more thing, Mr Ryder'. Seeing the cap he'd think Ryder had been withholding evidence. Ryder threw the cap into an empty cardboard box in a soft wall of them.

'Rod?' It was Madeline, unsure, maybe with the first name. To Ryder if felt like a promotion.

'You're back,' Ryder said, relief surging through him as he stepped out into the light.

'Yes,' she said, through a sigh. They stood a moment. What now? he thought, and why was she here anyway? She must have more on her mind than he had.

'I did some writing last night.'

Some distraction from her troubles, he supposed, though she'd be better off reading. 'Can I show you some of it?' she asked.

'Of course you can.' And there was no way he could avoid the issue. 'I'm sorry to hear about –'

'Oh, that, yes.' *Oh that*; it seemed callous, but maybe compartmentalising the murder of her friend, the horror of it, was a coping mechanism. 'I bet they think Red did it. He was a little sneak, but not a murderer.'

'Sneak?'

'Have you seen that little rock castle thing in the park?'

Ryder said he had.

'We were in there, me and … Having a smoke. Red came in, stared, and walked out again. That's how Miss Cadley found out.' Madeline was getting upset.

Ryder raised a hand. 'That's all water under the bridge.' A cliché to smooth the waters. There was no need for her to go on though he was fascinated and would have drank in more details. 'Run something by me when it suits, the writing I mean,' he said, his voice in an inviting lilt.

'Today?' Eyelids batting with appeal.

Ryder coughed, his instinct to put off. 'I'm working for two at the moment and I've a few jobs to do first, but how about when everyone's gone? About four o'clock in the sixth-form common room?'

She had a lovely smile. She left.

He had a flickering strip light to sort out, a leaking tap. He noticed a garden waste bag was floating around the hockey field and went to pick it up. Close to four he went to the basement. He plucked the cap out from the piled cardboard boxes. This would prove to Madeline that the little man wouldn't be back other than in handcuffs at Harrowby police station. He wouldn't be coming back here for his damned cap, that was for certain. Nor for the clogs that Ryder had spied behind the boiler.

Ryder felt liberated, like a new man. He got to the sixth-form common room five minutes before Madeline. He went into the kitchenette. He heard her bustle in and called out 'Hi.' She said the same back and he heard the click of a ring binder, a sheet removed.

'Before we start,' he said. 'I suggest a bite to eat. What about you? And tea? Coffee?'

A shuffle of papers. 'Er tea,' she said absently, adding, 'Please.' Polite girl.

'There's bread here. Fancy a piece of toast?'

'That'd be good,' she said.

He slotted two slices into the toaster.

He took the cap out of the pocket of his house-coat. This would reassure her that Red wouldn't be coming back. And wearing it would put the pint-sized bad joke that was Red in his place. And give Madeline something to smile at. As would the clogs he'd put on earlier.

On his head, the cap fitted like a dream.

She said, 'Got anywhere with your story for *Bad Fairies*?'

'No, but I feel something is there, waiting to come through.'

'You could always go with the redcap thing, now that Red has gone. I was thinking – the story wouldn't have to be set in a school. What if he gets a job in a hospital? He's a porter, cheerful, helpful. And has access to people and medical blood products of course.' It was good that her imagination was at play.

'Redcap needs fresh blood.' Had he read it somewhere to sound so assured on the matter? 'But that's great. There would be hundreds of people in all those wards and private rooms, operating theatres, stores. He'd have keys to everywhere. There he is, old Red, bless him.'

The bread slices flew out of the toaster, he caught them, one in each hand. Not pale, not a trace of burning, just nicely brown

– how he liked it. He found two plates and put a slice on each. With the splendid knife with its ornately carved bone or ivory handle, the one he'd fished out of the basement cutlery drawer, he positively plastered the slices with butter out of the fridge. Then he made two mugs of tea. He placed everything onto a tray.

He said, 'D'you know what? I feel this redcap idea is the way to go.'

'Great!' she said, sounding pleased.

A tinge of redness in his vision. He pulled the peak of the cap low. The red deepened. He felt a flush throughout his body, a bright, cruel and fierce energy. The cap was tight on his scalp. His clogs wanted to dance. He picked up the tray, placed it down again on the worktop.

'What about the title,' she said, as he took up the butter knife and went out into the common room where red light, like an intense invading sunset, stained everything. She was scribbling words onto a pink sheet. She said thoughtfully, 'I'd keep it simple. Why not just *Redcap*?'

She looked up. A smile amidst bones, flesh, nerve-endings, hair, skin and red, red blood. The smile vanished, leaving the rest.

'No,' he said, the iron-tipped heels and toes of his clogs sharply tapping him forward in a jaunty rhythm. 'Redcap's the writer.'

WENDIGO

The wendigo is probably one of the most westernised of all ancient mythological entities. Ask anyone today what they think the wendigo is and what it looks like, and they will likely describe a monster that roams the wild northern woods of Canada and the United States, vaguely humanoid in shape, but of towering height, covered in shaggy hair and with antlers on its head. In terms of its nature, it is completely malevolent, killing and eating anyone who crosses its path, destroying property and spreading disease and madness.

While the Algonquian peoples, from whose legends the wendigo first came to prominence, might recognise some of these traits, there are substantial differences too. To start with, the original wendigo, as indigenous North American groups like the Saulteaux, the Ojibwe and the Cree, knew it, never had antlers or any kind of horns. Neither was it a giant; nor was it covered in a pelt of fur. It could kill you, yes, or even possess you, and it was indeed a spreader of illness and madness, but it was a far more complicated creature than something that simply did evil for evil's sake. Among the native peoples of North America, the wendigo, in its normal form (because it was a shapeshifter and wielded powerful magic), was humanlike and mostly human-sized, but painfully thin, its bones protruding through dried-out flesh. The reason for this was that no matter how much it ate, it remained insatiably hungry and thus became a voracious consumer of human meat.

It was indeed a terrifying monster, but it owed little if anything to what we might call 'forest lore'. The Algonquian natives lived most of their lives in a forested landscape. Almost everything in their everyday experience was connected to the forest, and the wendigo was a resident there alongside them, not some patchwork representation of the forest itself. Our current 'New Age' interpretation of the wendigo as a symbol of woodland godliness, as so many mysterious horned beings are held to be in European myth, derives initially from Algernon Blackwood's 1910 novella, The

Wendigo, *and of course from multiple other fictional appearances in books, movies, TV shows and games.*

Of course, that isn't to say that the wendigo wasn't symbolic in its own way. It's entirely possible that in long-ago times, various Native American tribes held a firm belief that this was a genuine adversary whom you might encounter in the winter woods, and woe betide you if you did. But there were other native teachings too, in which the wendigo was a metaphorical being.

In a part of the world where very harsh winters were the norm, the wooded wilderness could be a brutal environment. Hunger was never far away, and in a realm where genuine predators like the wolf, the mountain lion and the grizzly bear were common, sometimes forcing hunting parties to stay indoors, there was always a danger that cannibalism might be a solution. In fact, certain North American folktales tell how men first became wendigos, because during lean times they gave up all their scruples and killed and ate their neighbours, literally changing into monsters before their families' eyes.

It's perhaps rather obvious when one considers it. Cannibalism as a response to winter-induced famine could wipe out small, scattered communities. The creation of a monster that embodied this horror should surely be no surprise. It might even explain the so-called 'Wendigo Psychosis', as first reported by Jesuit missionaries in eastern Canada in the 1660s, after they witnessed the capture and execution of several supposed wendigos, outcast native men who had been possessed by the monstrous spirit and subsequently went on killing sprees, afterwards eating the bodies of the slain.

While modern psychiatry refuses to accept that there was any such form of mental illness unique to this region, there were many reports later than the 1660s in which disturbed individuals were said to have behaved like crazed beasts in their pursuit of victims whom they intended to kill, mutilate and devour.

It's easy to see how such tales would also frighten the white settlers of that era.

Liver-Eating Johnson was a famous antihero of those days, a mountain man who avenged the murder of his Kootenai wife by killing, scalping and eating the livers of over 300 Crow tribesmen, and whose presence in the Montana territory was said to have intimidated both the natives and the pioneers from back East. Then of course there was the infamous tale of the Donner Party, a wagon train that became marooned in the snows of the Sierra Nevada during the winter of 1846/7, and who resorted to cannibalism. Rumours circled long afterwards that those members of the Donner Party who first turned to human meat had been inspired by the spirit of the wendigo.

In fact, many American mass murderers, both from past and present, have been mentioned in the same breath as that ancient forest demon. In 1879, Swift Runner, a Cree scout, who was hanged for the murder and consumption of his wife and children, actually claimed that the wendigo had been controlling him, while in today's world, press coverage has likened several serial killers to the wendigo. Jeffrey Dahmer, the 'Milwaukee Cannibal', for example, who slew and dismembered 17 men for the purposes of necrophilia and cannibalism, and Richard Chase, the so-called 'Sacramento Vampire', who drank the blood of his six known victims.

In modern times, there are few people of any race who believe in the existence of the wendigo, which in some ways is strange. After all, those great sweeps of trackless, thickly treed wilderness reputedly play host to all manner of other strange creatures, which are still gamely pursued by cryptozoologists: Bigfoot, the Dogman, the Goatman, the Skinwalker.

Is it that the wendigo is simply too archaic a concept? Or is it that the real meaning behind this monstrous stalker of forest and mountain is that gluttony and greed will lead only to destruction. Most First Nations people today rationalise it that way, as do many western folklorists. Taking more than you need in a land of scarcity could never end well.

It is certainly food for thought (no pun intended).

NEPHILIM
Reggie Oliver

Poor Professor Chambers! If it had not been for that shambles in the Middle East, he might well have been Sir Horace Chambers by now, but he personally must carry some responsibility for what happened. Like most brilliant men he had a stubborn conviction in his rightness about everything, an unwillingness to bow before the prevailing orthodoxy. Such integrity is, of course, admirable, but it can seem like arrogance; it can often *be* arrogance. As for me, I have learned to say the words: 'I may be mistaken, but ...' Call me a coward if you like, but that is one of the reasons why I am still here and Horace is not.

So let me begin by saying again: 'I may be mistaken ...' This is my account of what happened. You can believe it or not, as you like: I am not going to insist on it. We are told, after all, that we now belong to the 'post truth generation.' Everybody has their own truth which is just as valid, or invalid, as anyone else's. You could say that is regrettable, and I might agree with you. By this time, you may have concluded that I am a professional philosopher, and you would be right, up to a point of course.

Horace was not: he was an ancient historian, but when we first knew each other as undergraduates we were both studying the same course at Oxford, *Literae Humaniores*, which includes both ancient history and philosophy in its curriculum. He was a brilliant student, and though we both got firsts, his was generally regarded as the best of our year, and, as a result, he got an Oxford fellowship in his discipline quite some time before I did in mine.

There are, you may know, two kinds of ancient historian. There is the kind that stays at home, studies the texts in libraries and comes up with learned articles about whether Thucydides was right about Pericles's strategy in the Peloponnesian War; then there are those who, in the words of my old tutor George Cawkwell, 'like muckin' about with squeezes.' (A 'squeeze,' by the way, is a latex squeeze that you put over stones and tablets to catch the impress of the inscriptions upon them.) They are the ones who go out on archaeological digs to discover surprising things about how our ancient forbears lived. Horace was one of those.

He was a Middle Eastern specialist and, a couple of years ago now, he was involved in a dig in Israel at a location not far from that fateful border with Gaza. This was at a place called Negeb Zin near the ancient city of Eglon in the land that used to be known as Canaan. Israeli archaeologists had discovered a group of ancient Canaanite settlements up in the hills above the desert plain. Horace had been called out because he was the world expert on the ancient Canaanite language. That is to say, he was the only one who could claim to understand any of it from the few meagre inscriptions they had left behind on clay tablets, and these archaeologists had found a new cache of the said tablets at the site. It was, if you like that sort of thing, terribly exciting, and on his return, at the end of the summer vacation Horace told me all about it.

I was one of the few people, inside or outside his discipline, that he would confide in. The truth is, Horace didn't go in much for friends, but we went back quite a long way, to undergraduate days when he would occasionally allow himself to get drunk and be unguarded. The aloofness, the monomania, the intellectual arrogance, all the professional deformities of the stereotypical academic, came upon him gradually with his increasing reputation. He had not married, and, as far as I could tell, never showed the least interest in sex of any description. Only I was permitted to see the complicated vulnerable human being beneath his formidable intellectual carapace.

I won't tell the story, as he told it, at a series of meetings, sometimes at his college (St James's), sometimes at his rather bleak maisonette in Norham Gardens. That would be too long and tedious, and full of academic detail that even I found hard to follow or remember. I will just give you a summary of the relevant facts together with a few comments of his that stay in my mind.

The excavations at Negeb Zin had been going on for some three months before Horace joined them at the end of the Trinity term. The site had been only very recently discovered. A heavy rainstorm, rare in that desert region, had washed away part of a hillside to uncover what looked like a wall of cyclopean masonry standing proud on its heights. A geophysical survey revealed a chain of fortified settlements along a ridge of hills, together with what looked like a palace complex and, next to it, a large paved area or courtyard in the middle of which were the foundations of some kind of monument, possibly an altar. The clay tablets which Horace had been called upon to decipher were found in a small room in the palace complex adjoining the courtyard. They had survived reasonably intact because they had been baked hard (and black) in a fire.

I asked Horace what period he thought they dated from.

'Around 1100 BC.' (Horace always scorned the more politically correct BCE.) 'About the time of the Trojan War.' Again, this was typical Horace. He was convinced that all the myths and legends of the ancient world were firmly based on actual historical events.

'So did you manage to decipher the tablets?'

'A fair amount of them. They were nearly all rather boring palace records, of course: household accounts, you might say. You know the sort of thing: so many bushels of grain, so many cattle, so many slaves paid in tribute from various towns or cities to the king. So much gold paid to so and so, perhaps a priest of some kind. There seemed to be quite a lot of gold about, a surprising amount in fact. But there were some tablets which intrigued me, and they were the most difficult to make out because there were words and phrases in them that I had not come across before. But with a bit of cross-linguistic analysis and intelligent guesswork, I was able to make out some of them.'

'Well?'

'They were records of a series of payments made to a group of people called the Nef-el-lee-may. It's a syllabic script, you see, that I'm talking about, not like Hebrew, more resembling Linear B inscriptions on the tablets from Cnossos, and from about the same period, though the signs used were quite different. These Nefelime – I'll call them Nephilim for short from now on, for reasons I will make clear to you – were sometimes referred to as "great" or "great offspring" of someone or something called An-na-kee. Again, I will call this being Anak, for short, for reasons … etcetera. Anyway, these payments or tributes were never in gold or grain but always in livestock of some kind: cattle, sheep, horses, and – well – young children.'

'Children? Are you sure?'

'Oh, yes. Sometimes they were referred to as "coming from the breasts of their mothers", a rather graphic phrase, don't you think?'

There was a pause while he let this sink in.

He went on: 'But that was not all. In the courtyard, underneath the altar-like structure at its centre, we found an inscribed stone. It was made of a dark granite-like material, rather similar to that of the Rosetta Stone. Unfortunately, it was much worn away by exposure to the elements, unlike the tablets, and a good deal of it was in tiny bits. It was like a jigsaw puzzle with most of the pieces missing, but I was able to get the opening words of the inscription:

"To the Great Nephilim who fell from the sky."

'Then it got tricky. Among the fragments, I caught the words for "sacrifice" and "tribute" which seemed to be used interchangeably or together. Then the word "gold" came up a lot, and, once, the phrase "mighty gifts of gold". Finally, there was one word which occurred frequently, once in connection with the phrase "children coming from the breasts of their mothers", which I had met on the tablets. The word was "da-ma-ha-ma". Now I had never met this word in Canaanite before, but after a lot of puzzling I reckoned that it must have something to do with "blood". You see the Hebrew word for blood is "dam", and then there is the ancient Greek for blood, "haema" from which we get our word "haematology".'

'Yes. Thank you. I *am* familiar with Ancient Greek.'

'Okay, sorry, I was forgetting. You're supposed to be the Plato expert, aren't you? But of course, there is also the Arabic word "hamas" which means "strength". Hence... Well, never mind. That may be stretching it a bit far, but I reckon that this word "damahama" must mean something like "life-blood" or "blood strength", or possibly "strength through blood".'

Horace paused. We were at the time in the Senior Common Room of St James's. He went to the window and looked out onto the Fellow's Garden. It was late afternoon, but still light. A wind was blowing the first bronze autumn leaves onto the lawn. There was a distant look in his eyes as he stared down at this tranquil, slightly melancholy scene.

Then he turned back towards me. His mood had changed. He was suddenly animated again, but restless, troubled.

'But that was not all. About a fortnight after I had arrived the men started to dig in an area on the other side of the courtyard. There they found a number of cist graves. You know, like stone coffins or tombs.'

'Yes. I do know what a cist grave is.' I was beginning to find his condescension irritating: I often did.

'They were obviously the graves of high-status individuals, but there were no grave goods to speak of. Tomb robbers had stripped them out long ago, though there must have been some there originally because we found little flecks of gold among the bones. Of the tombs, two were quite extraordinary. In them we found the complete skeletons of two – "beings", I suppose, that's the only way I can describe them. They were humanoid in structure, but they were not human beings as we know them today. They were huge: about twelve feet in height, possibly more. They were giants.'

Horace looked at me intently. I think he was searching my face to see if he could detect any signs of incredulity. I kept my features as blank as I could.

'Go on.'

'I said they were humanoid, but there were differences from ordinary humans, quite apart from their sheer size which was, of course, the most striking thing about them. Their skulls were bigger in proportion to the rest of their bodies and the craniums extended further back than normal, a bit like some of those Egyptian heads you see. Then it was impossible to determine if they were male or female skeletons: there was no thick bony ridge on the brow line as in the male, and the jaw bones were fairly light. On the other hand, the narrower pelvis area, shorter torso and longer legs were more male in character. Another oddity was the greatly enlarged scapula bones, in other words the shoulder blades, to which were attached some curious bony extensions which looked to me like the beginnings of wings.'

'Wings? Are you sure?'

'Impossible to be certain. I only got the most cursory look.'

'Any indication as to how they died?'

'Not really. Both had sustained one or two bone fractures, but probably before death, rather than as a cause of it. This was not surprising because the bones seemed to be rather light and fragile for their size. The composition of their bones has not been chemically analysed.'

'Why the hell not?'

'I'm coming to that.'

What happened next was this. The very day after these sensational discoveries had been made, a company of Israeli soldiers turned up and told the archaeologists that they must vacate the site immediately, taking nothing but the bare minimum with them. Intelligence had been received that Hamas guerrillas were to make a raid in strength across the border from Gaza, and that the target was to be the excavations at Negeb Zin.

'Why there?' I asked.

'Some idiotic rubbish about the desecration of ancestral heritage apparently,' said Horace. 'You know what these people are like.' I didn't, and neither did he, for that matter, but I said nothing. 'I was for taking a risk and sticking it out for a few more days. We were at such a critical stage in the dig, but the army was insistent, and my colleagues from the Israeli Archaeological Institute all caved in immediately. We were just packed into the back of a lorry and carted off. I was barely allowed to take a change of clothes and a toothbrush, let alone a clay tablet, and of course removing the skeletons was out of the question. They just threw a few tarpaulins over them and that was that. It was quite clear that the army had zero interest in our finds.'

Horace told me that they were away for over a week, during which there had been, apparently, the mother of all battles over the heights of Negeb Zin. When the archaeologists were finally allowed to return to the site, they found it had been devastated. The great cyclopean walls had been blown to bits; the courtyard and the palace complex were covered in rubble; the clay tablets and the skeletons had completely disappeared.

When he told me the story of his return to Negeb Zin, we were in his cramped study in Norham Gardens. I don't think Horace could trust himself to talk about it anywhere but in the privacy of his own home. Even so, his narration was punctuated with long, frightening silences. His features went rigid. I have never seen anyone go white with anger, before but this was what Horace did.

'Bloody Hamas! Bloody Israelis! Bloody war!'

Stronger, cruder adjectives were simply not in Horace's vocabulary, but the fury was very real.

'Bloody Hamas! Bloody Israelis! Bloody war!'

He repeated this mantra several times as he stamped about the room. His rage was not directed against anyone in particular, so much as the fact that he had been deprived of a great archaeological discovery. The Israel-Palestine war with all its tragedy and suffering was nothing to him: it was just a gigantic, hideous obstacle standing in the way of his scholarly achievements.

Finally, he calmed down, and said: 'Luckily, I had taken a few photos with my digital camera. Do you know, the army even wanted me to hand that over to them, along with my notebooks? Security reasons, they said. Security? Rubbish. They were up to something, God knows what. But I managed to hide them. Told them a lot of guff about having thrown them away. Would you like to see the pictures?'

He went over to his desk, opened a drawer and pulled out four half plate colour photographs, printed on glossy paper. He laid them out neatly on the desk and stared at them for a long while before he allowed me near enough to see them properly.

'You're the first person I've shown them to,' he said.

For once, the build-up did not result in an anti-climax. The first picture showed a general view of the site of the cist graves. I saw several tombs crammed around two central ones which contained two skeletons, the heads of which possessed the elongated crania that Horace had described. The surrounding graves had skeletons which were less than half their size. They could, I suppose, have been the bones of children except that their skeletal structure was fully developed. The second picture showed a close-up of one of the big skeletons with an archaeologist standing beside it. From this, it was clear that we were seeing the bones of a gigantic creature. In the other pictures, measuring rods had been placed beside the corpses to confirm that they were both about twelve feet tall.

'You see?'

The only explanation I could think of was that Horace had been the victim of an elaborate hoax. It was just conceivable. Horace was not the easiest man to get along with; his arrogance and aloofness may have irked the Israelis so much that they had decided to play a trick on him. I kept this notion to myself. It was unlikely, of course: almost as unlikely as the idea that I was looking at the bones of real giants.

'It all ties in with the tablets and the inscriptions, you see,' said Horace, now wild with excitement. 'The Nephilim, the giants of the Old Testament. Then there is that passage in Numbers, when the Israelites are in Canaan. And the spies report back to Moses.' There was a Bible on his desk and he opened it at a marked page. 'Here we are. Chapter 13: verse

33: "And there we saw the giants, the sons of Anak, which come of the giants: and we were in our own sight as grasshoppers, and so we were in their sight." There you are. These are the great offspring of Anakee recorded in the tablets. The Nephilim who fell from the sky, the so-called fallen angels.

'Of course, there are other mythical stories of giants being cast out of heaven. Like the Titans, children of Uranos and Gaia and chucked down into Tartarus by Zeus and his chums. It's the same story again and again about outcast giants, some of them, like the Titan Prometheus, bringing forbidden knowledge and technology to men, like fire, or, in the case of Lucifer, the knowledge of Good and Evil. It's an account – I'm sure of it – of giant beings of superior intelligence coming from some other part of the cosmos.'

'Aren't we jumping to conclusions?'

'That's what science is about! Of course, all this would also be supported by Dawkins's theory.'

'Dawkins? You mean Richard Dawkins? *The God Delusion* Dawkins?'

'Yes. And Crick, the DNA man. You've heard of *Panspermia*, of course?'

'Yes, I know all about that.'

Typically, Horace went on to expound it, despite what I had said. In my experience other men are just as likely to be the victims of mansplainers as women. 'To account for the prohibitively long odds of life arising spontaneously on earth, the sudden leaps in evolution of the Cambrian Explosion and all that, Crick and Dawkins proposed that advanced intelligences from beyond Earth in the Cosmos came at intervals to "seed" new and more sophisticated forms of life, thus disposing of the problem of one in ten trillionth chances, the "intelligent design" wallahs, and all that God malarkey.'

'You do realise that *Panspermia* doesn't solve the problem, it just postpones it, kicks it into touch, or rather into outer space. Dawkins's ideas are based on a number of unsupported *a priori* assumptions.' I thought it was time I aired my philosophical credentials and gave Horace some of his own medicine.

Needless to say, he completely ignored me.

'These Nephilim come from somewhere in the Cosmos. They arrive here from outer space with advanced technology and probably precious metals to bribe the natives, hence the references to gold in the tablets. They are superior beings in every way, except perhaps that physically they are not well enough adapted to the earth's atmosphere. They seem to come from some smaller planet with a weaker gravitational pull: hence the wings, the less substantial bones, the fractures.'

'The need for human blood?'

'Possibly. Possibly,' Horace did not seem to regard this as a particularly important observation. 'The main thing is, we now have a substantial body of evidence to suggest that there were giant alien beings in Canaan three-thousand odd years ago.'

'Unfortunately, you tell me, most of the evidence has been destroyed.'

'But I have my notes. And the photographs.'

Three months later an article by Horace appeared in the *Journal of Archaeology*. Its title, 'Some Recent Excavations in Ancient Canaan', sounded innocent enough, but its conclusions, though couched in quite subtle and scholarly terms, were radical. The academic world has never been a hermetically sealed one; word got out and Horace's conjectures were soon all over the media, both computerised and printed.

Almost immediately Horace became the victim of scathing attacks, and not just from those qualified to make them. The photographs, which had been printed in the original article, were denounced as fakes, and reproduced many times on social media. Crude parodies of them were circulated on Facebook, Twitter (or whatever it now calls itself) and other platforms. Horace was utterly unprepared for the notoriety and abuse to which he was subjected. He did his best to defend himself, but his appeals to the Israeli archaeologists on the dig to back him up went unheeded. Were they silent of their own free will, or had they been silenced by the authorities? It has never been made clear.

As an example of the abuse he suffered, there was a headline in one of the British tabloids which read:

THE POTTY PROFESSOR WHO BELIEVES IN GIANTS FROM OUTER SPACE

On the morning of its appearance, a colleague had left the paper, open at the page where it featured, on the St James's Senior Common Room table. As soon as he saw it, Horace had snatched it up, bore it away, and, when we met that afternoon, his hand trembled as he passed it to me. Fortunately, I had already seen it, so I was able to hold back any involuntary laughter. From now on, I thought, Horace would be known throughout Oxford as 'the potty professor', but I kept this to myself. I had become his only confidant, and very nearly his only supporter.

And now we come to my more active role in this strange and terrible story. If anybody asks, I will have to admit that I am to blame for having introduced Horace to Sonia Gaill. It was all with the best of intentions of course, but the consequences were – Oh, just let me tell you.

Sonia Gaill was a postgraduate student and I was her supervisor for the doctoral thesis she was writing. The title, a snappy one I think you will agree, was *The Philosophical Implications of Chaos Theory*. I guided her to that, away from *Love and Strife in a Postmodern World* which was her rather sensationalist and downmarket choice. A Doctoral thesis is not the place for crude populism, I told her, and for once she bowed to my wisdom.

The burden of her thesis was that Chaos Theory, far from being a new concept, was in fact a very old one that had been anticipated by the Presocratics, in particular Empedocles. I won't go into the details: the Empedoclean concept of the opposing forces of Love and Strife directing the universe etcetera; you get the picture. I thought it was pretty good stuff, though I'm not necessarily saying I was wholly convinced by it. In any case, it was clever and wittily expressed. Sonia was a star pupil, as far as I was concerned, and there would have been a bright future ahead of her in academia, but for one thing: she was theatre mad.

You may call me prejudiced if you like, but I have seen many a promising intellect ruined by this passion for drama. Of course, I know that some Oxbridge alumni have gone on to very successful stage careers -what about, Peter Brook, you will ask, what about Peter Hall? – but there are many who get ensnared by the footlights, fail to produce their weekly essays, and don't get a decent degree, all for nothing.

Maybe Sonia Gaill will be one of those rare exceptions. Despite being President of OUDS (Oxford University Dramatic Society) in her final year, she managed a congratulatory first in her finals and had continued her involvement in student theatre as a postgraduate, without apparent detriment to her studies. She was – is – undoubtedly a brilliant young woman and, as if that weren't enough, she is also very beautiful, with long auburn hair and the features of a Raphael Madonna. If you met her for the first time walking down the High, or wandering in Port Meadow, you would never guess that her seraphic exterior conceals a steely intellect and a ruthless ambition.

At the end of each weekly session with her, usually held at my house on the Banbury Road, I would give her tea or, if we had run over our appointed time, a glass of sherry, and we would chat for a while about anything that was not to do with her studies. I enjoyed these little conversational moments but, usually, Sonia took the lead, shyness not being a failing of hers. However, on this particular day, towards the middle of the Trinity Term, she appeared to be rather more diffident than usual, so I made the opening remark.

'Are you involved in any theatricals this term?' I asked. She seemed to bridle slightly at my perhaps rather satirical tone.

'As a matter of fact, I am,' she said briskly. 'I'm directing the OUDS garden major this year.' That means she was directing the principal outdoor student production, an event usually held in one of the College gardens.

'Where?'

'New College.'

'A Shakespeare?'

'No. Milton. *Paradise Lost*.'

'I was under the impression that was an epic poem rather than a drama.' This time she took my irony rather more calmly.

'A friend and I are adapting it. Believe it or not, it works incredibly well as a play. The scenes in Hell (which Milton calls *Chaos*, incidentally), the whole Adam and Eve business. Satan is, of course, the real star of the show. Actually, Milton, in my opinion, was on the Devil's side, even if he didn't realise it –'

'I believe William Blake said something similar.' I could see my intervention did not please her but she pretended to ignore it.

'We're devising a lot of wizzy effects too; it'll be a sensation. As a matter of fact, I was going to ask you …' For the first time since I had known her, Sonia seemed almost hesitant.

'You want me to assist in some way?'

'Well, yes … No, not exactly, but … I gather you know the Potty Professor quite well.'

It was now my turn to be offended. 'Are you by any chance referring to Professor Chambers?'

'Yes, actually. Sorry. It just came out. Professor Chambers. You seem to be the only person in Oxford he is seen with, socially, I mean. Do you think you could introduce me to him?'

'May I ask why?'

'I want to consult him about something.'

'To do with *Paradise Lost*?'

She nodded. I agreed to make the introduction, and she seemed so overjoyed that I thought she was going to kiss me. I am glad she didn't. My wife is not a suspicious or jealous person, but I would have felt awkward about it, and she would have noticed.

The following day I approached Horace about a meeting with Sonia, to which he seemed surprisingly amenable. So they met, though what they discussed I did not find out till some time later. All I could get out of Sonia when we had our next session was that their meeting had gone well. I told my wife about this and said their association might be rather good for

Horace, given his present situation. She merely smiled and shook her head.

The weeks following were strange ones. I saw less of Horace, and when we did meet, he seemed more than usually distracted, but not as harassed as he had been. I liked to think this was the influence of Sonia. The weather that season was unusually hot and dry for Oxford, and then there was the so-called 'mystery of the Jericho babies'. It caused quite a scandal at the time.

Jericho had once been a poor and rather disreputable suburb of Oxford next to the canal. Its streets of small terraced houses are now occupied by students and young families from whom, in the latter part of May, five, some say six, babies were abducted. How or who performed these terrible acts has never been discovered. The police, as they used to say, 'remain baffled'.

I mention this perhaps only because one morning in early June, a week before the opening night of *Paradise Lost*, I picked up a copy of the *Oxford Mail*. The front page story was that the remains of one of the vanished babies had been found floating in the canal: it had been horribly mutilated and drained of blood. In the same paper, on one of the inside pages, I found an article which revealed exactly why Sonia had been so interested in meeting Horace. The headline read:

OXFORD DIRECTOR SEEKS ADVICE FROM
CONTROVERSIAL PROFESSOR OVER MAJOR NEW
PRODUCTION

The gist of it was that, in Sonia's version of Milton's epic, Satan and his fallen angels were in fact, as the Bible suggested, Nephilim, the giants of the Old Testament, and that the story of Adam and Eve was a mythical representation of the interaction between extra-terrestrial super-beings and humans. Professor Chambers, who had actually seen the skeletons of these creatures, and had speculated about them from the tablets, was being consulted on their look and exact proportions, so that giant puppets, twelve feet high, would be made to represent, as accurately as possible, the real Nephilim found at Negeb-Zin.

It was all nonsense, of course, just a clever publicity stunt devised by Sonia to attract as much attention as possible to her show, but it worked. However, it would not have worked nearly so well had not Sonia been a genuinely gifted director. My wife and I went to the first night.

There is a large stretch of lawn in New College gardens in the middle of which is what is known as The Mound, a little hillock covered in bushes and trees. Around one side a parabola of seats had been built on raised stands. The performance began rather later than is customary while there was still some light but the cloudless sky was beginning to turn a deep violet colour.

There is a rumble of drums. An actor, dressed as Milton, enters and points up into the sky above the mound and the audience sees a light, like a star shell, rising and then falling rapidly towards the trees. We hear a cracking sound like branches breaking and the trees on the summit of the mound are made to shake violently. It creates the extraordinary illusion of something huge crashing downwards towards the earth. A few moments later, a figure arises out of the bushes on the mound. It is twelve feet high and golden in colour, human in shape, naked but sexless with a great domed cranium surmounted by a mane of red orange and yellow fibre optic cables which gives the impression that it has a head of fiery hair. The eyes are oval surrounded by black lines of kohl, like those of a god in an Egyptian wall painting. The features are narrow and perfectly symmetrical. Dark purple wings sprout from its back. It is a giant effigy of a Nephilim, Milton's Satan, operated by two puppeteers in black who manage to make themselves almost completely invisible.

This *coup de theatre* was greeted by a spontaneous round of applause; then the actor playing Milton intoned the first lines –

Of man's first disobedience, and the fruit
Of that forbidden tree ...

– and so the drama of *Paradise Lost* began.

I won't describe the whole show. Milton purists, assuming such creatures exist, might have been horrified, but, if Sonia's *Paradise Lost* was misconceived, it was dazzlingly misconceived. The special effects were extraordinary, sometimes barely believable. To give you some idea, I will take you to the very end.

Adam and Eve have been tempted and have fallen. The angel Michael, also a giant puppet, similar in all respects to that of Satan, except that its wings are white, appears to escort the two mortals out of Eden. Holding a flaming sword in one hand – how was that achieved? – Michael drives them around The Mound and away from the audience's view.

As Adam and Eve disappear behind The Mound, the lights are suddenly directed upwards to its summit where the twelve-foot puppet of Satan Nephilim is seen. There is a roll of drums, a blare of trumpets as he raises his arms in triumph. A second or so later, from behind The Mound, a great spray of fireworks, a riot of green, gold, silver and scarlet incandescence, bursts upwards into the night sky. The fireworks fade, the lights go off and there is a silence.

Then, on that first night, there was a burst of applause and cheering from the audience. The next moment, they were on their feet stamping and shouting and clapping. Usually, I intensely dislike standing ovations in theatres. They seem to me self-conscious, as if the audience is congratulating itself on its superb taste in being there, but this was different. It was entirely spontaneous, and my wife and I were on our feet too, cheering and clapping with the rest.

The after-show party, to which we had been invited, took place in the Spooner Gallery in New College, a large, long room that looked out onto the now darkened gardens. Most of the guests were already there when we arrived. On one side of the room was a long table covered with a white cloth on which a great number of bottles and glasses had been set out. On it also was a vast metal cauldron into which bottles of gin, brandy, sparkling and still wine, fruit juice, and even Coca Cola had been indiscriminately poured. Slices of orange and lemon floated on its foam-flecked surface. A girl in a tight black dress with green hair who stood behind the table dipped a ladle into the cauldron and filled a glass for me. I asked her what the concoction was meant to be.

'I think it's a kind of fruit cup,' she said.

'*The fruit cup of that forbidden tree?*' I enquired.

She stared at me blankly as she handed me my glass. I sampled the potent, chaotic brew. It tasted horrible, like fizzy medicine.

The room was full of people who seemed to be enjoying the drink, but they were nearly all young. Some of the cast were still in costume, though Adam and Eve had changed out of their body stockings. A mood of exultant gaiety prevailed. At the end of the room stood Sonia, her face flushed, surrounded by important-looking people. My wife was able to identify a well-known drama critic, a prominent theatrical producer, even a recently knighted actor. When Sonia saw us, she smiled and waved, but the wave was merely one of recognition, not an invitation for us to join her circle.

In an isolated corner of the room stood Horace a large half-drunk glass of the 'fruit cup' in his hand. He looked morose and was swaying slightly. He was alone and ignored, perhaps even shunned. We went over to join him. To raise his spirits, I made a rather inept remark about his deserving a share in the credit for a triumphantly successful show.

'Oh, do you think so? Well, no-one else has taken the trouble to congratulate me. And Sonia hasn't spoken to me since the dress rehearsal.'

'Have you two fallen out or something?'

'God, no! Nothing like that. But I just can't get near her, and after all I've done!'

I looked over towards Sonia and managed to catch her eye. She frowned, shook her head, then pointedly turned back to her crowd of admirers. It would have been no use taking Horace over to her; in any case, the fruit cup had done its work and he was already quite drunk. My wife and I escorted him from the room and put him in a taxi to take him to Norham Gardens.

It was a fortnight before Sonia came for her session with me as thesis supervisor. When it was time for tea at the end of our formal discussion, I congratulated her on *Paradise Lost* which had just come to the end of its sell-out run. She seemed oddly distrait.

'Yeah. Yeah. Thanks. It was a blast; it really was.' Then a hesitation. 'As a matter of fact ...' I knew at once this was a preliminary to her asking a favour. 'I was wondering if you might have a word with your friend Horace for me.'

'*Your* friend too, now, I hope.'

'Yeah, well ... He keeps trying to get in touch, wants to see me, wants me to go out with him. Well, I'm sorry, but I am incredibly busy just now. He's harassing me, and when I tell him I'm just not interested in ... you know, he gets all upset. Of course he was a big help, but that's over now.'

'He may be feeling undervalued ... that he was just used by you.'

'Yeah? So? People use each other. We all do; we wouldn't be able to exist if we didn't. That's life.'

I was tempted to offer a reasoned critique of her rather extreme brand of Utilitarianism, but I refrained. There is a time and a place for moral philosophy, and this was not it; but I agreed to 'have a word' with Horace.

'I am not going to go to the police or anything,' she said, 'but if he carries on like this there will be consequences. Tell him. I think he'll understand what I mean.'

I rang Horace the next day and gave him a summary of what Sonia had said. There was a silence.

'So, you've become Sonia's messenger boy now, have you?' he said eventually. I felt confused, ashamed, annoyed, and was about to hang up when he prevented me.

'All right! All right,' he said. 'Look, I've got to talk to someone. If you've nothing better to do, come and have dinner with me on high table at St James's this Friday.' It was not the most gracious of invitations, but I accepted it.

When I arrived at St James's that evening, it suddenly began to rain fiercely though it had been clear all day. The paving of the quadrangle glittered and sparkled in the sun which was westering in an unclouded quarter of the sky. The porter lent me an umbrella to make my way across the quad to the Senior Common Room where a pre-prandial Amontillado and, I hoped, Horace, would be waiting for me.

He was not there, but I was cordially welcomed by the other St James's dons. Lord Swinbrook, the Master of St James's, came over to speak to me, all genial condescension.

'Ah, Dr Smythe! I gather, you are the guest of our resident *giantologist*,' he said. The ponderous semi-joke was Swinbrook's speciality. 'He should be here presently. As a matter of fact –' I had begun to dread that meaningless little prelude. '– we at St James's are a little worried about the good professor. He seems out of sorts. Something is troubling him, and disruption appears to follow in his wake. Complaints about noise … A couple of days ago there was a fire in his rooms, the cause unexplained. It was soon put out, very little harm done, but all the same … I believe you are quite an intimate friend of his.'

'I wouldn't say …'

'Perhaps you're the one to have a word with him. Maybe he has been overworking. A sabbatical might be the thing to recommend. Perhaps –'

Just then Horace came into the Common Room. He was properly dressed for the occasion with a gown over his dinner jacket, but his black tie was askew and his hair was uncombed. He looked pleased – relieved perhaps might be a better word – to see me. We barely had time to exchange words before it was time to go into hall for dinner.

I was seated on high table facing down the hall at the long tables swarming with undergraduates. On my left sat Horace, another don was on my right. The noise coming up from the main body of the hall was considerable so conversation was not easy, but I tried to talk to Horace. His responses were perfunctory; he kept glancing around nervously, often upwards towards the great hammer-beamed roof of St James's hall.

'Looking for giants, eh, professor?' said the don sitting opposite us on one of these occasions. Horace did not respond, but stared back at him coldly.

Eventually I gave up trying to talk to Horace and turned to the man on my right who was, unfortunately, a young bio-chemistry don. He asked me if I was 'familiar with the works of Taylor Swift' and then went on to explain them to me in great detail. Strange conversations like this tend to be the rule rather than the exception on Oxford high tables.

At the end of the meal, Horace tugged at my sleeve and said: 'If you don't mind, we won't stay for coffee in the common room. Let's go for a walk. I can't talk to you here with all these people.'

The sky was clear and it was still light when we left the hall. At the college entrance, I handed back the umbrella to the Porter who glanced at Horace waiting for me impatiently outside the Porter's Lodge. There was a look of concern on the Porter's face.

'You'll see the Professor home safely, won't you, sir?' I nodded.

Horace and I left the college together. As we wandered rather aimlessly around Oxford in the twilight, Horace began to talk. He talked obsessively, unstoppably, about Sonia. He told me how brilliant she was, how beautiful, how … everything. He told me how well he thought they had got on, how helpful she had said he was at rehearsals; but then, once the play was on … nothing. She had totally blanked him. Why? What had gone wrong? Why?

I had no answer for him, but I don't think he was looking to me for one. I was just the sounding board.

In the course of our wanderings, we found ourselves at the gates of Christ Church Meadow. 'We'll go back this way,' said Horace, and we took the Broad Walk, the tree-lined path that goes past Christ Church College on its left, and through the Meadow until the River Cherwell is reached. Once beyond the gates, Horace paused and looked around him, intent and silent. There were very few people about, which seemed to be to his liking. Then, abruptly, he set off at a brisk pace along the Walk. As he did so, he began talking again in an urgent, confidential voice.

'You know the cliché: "seeing is believing". It's rubbish, of course. Seeing is not believing. As I know to my cost. No, the truth is: *believing is seeing*. You, as a philosopher must realise that.'

'Well, up to a point, I suppose –'

'The Nephilim are still here. That's the great secret Sonia helped me to discover, or I helped her. And just because we can't normally see them, it doesn't mean ... You see, they've *evolved*. As you'd expect after three-thousand years. When they first came here to our planet the sons of Anak were already highly developed beings –' I noticed that Horace now pronounced the name 'Anak' with a long second 'a', so that it sounded like 'Anark'. '– But they were ill-adapted physically to the earth. And now they *have* adapted. They're still here, and they can be contacted.'

This was sheer madness, but I decided to humour him. 'And have you ...? Contacted them?'

Horace stopped. We were about half way down the Broad Walk, with Merton Field and Deadman's Walk now to our left.

'No. Not exactly ... but I believe Sonia has.'

He spoke almost in a whisper, though there was no-one else anywhere near us. It had been a still evening, but suddenly a breeze sprang up. Horace looked round and upwards fearfully.

'What makes you think that?'

'I don't know! I don't know!' He sounded frantic. The wind was increasing. Horace looked up again and I had the impression of something dark passing over us. This startled him, and he began to run ahead of me along the Broad Walk.

The trees that lined the Walk quivered as if a giant hand were shaking them. It was only the wind of course. Something seemed to brush past me. Again, it was only the wind, but it felt like a presence which filled me with fear. Ahead, Horace was now running desperately. I called for him to stop but he only ran faster. Then something happened which I believe I saw but cannot really explain. The wind caught him up and launched him twenty, thirty feet into the air. It was as if he were being tossed up by a huge hand, like a ball before a giant tennis service. Above the wind, I heard a wail of terror. For a moment he seemed suspended high up in the air, then with a despairing scream he began to fall, spinning round as he did so like a leaf in a gale.

He fell, and as he tumbled towards the ground, his body caught a branch on one of the trees which lined the path. The branch, a big one, broke, and came whistling towards me driven by some kind of contrary wind in the storm. I took action to avoid being struck by it, so I did not see where Horace fell. The branch dropped to the ground in front of me, its main arm just missing my head, its leaves whipping my face. I felt as if I had been punished by the offended tree, but for what?

Then, as suddenly as it had come, the wind died. There was silence. Not a bird sang, no bus or car coming down St Aldate's behind me roared or hooted. All around was silence, stillness, the grey dusk of a summer evening. Just in front of me was the tree branch which had fallen across the Broad Walk. I stepped over it and saw Horace lying on the path about ten yards further on. His skull was split open; his body was utterly broken; he was dead.

When questioned later, I was very discreet and reticent about what I had experienced, and my interrogators – police, pathologists, coroners and the like – were as circumspect in their verdict about what I had told them. It was so totally baffling. Horace's corpse was smashed and bruised, but the strange thing was that they found so little blood, either outside his body on the Broad Walk, or within.

As I was waiting in the gathering dusk on Christ Church Meadow for the ambulance and the police to arrive, some lines of poetry had come into my head. They were not from Milton, but from a generation after by Alexander Pope who doubtless had *Paradise Lost* in mind when he wrote:

> *Lo! Thy dread empire, Chaos! is restored;*
> *Light dies before thy uncreating word;*
> *Thy hand, great Anarch! lets the curtain fall*

And universal darkness buries all.

Sonia completed her doctoral thesis, had her viva, and the dissertation has been accepted with no corrections. But, as I feared, she has forsaken academe for the bright lights of London's theatreland.

Only last month, Sonia Gaill's production of Marlowe's *Dr Faustus* opened at the National. It was rapturously received; the *Sunday Times* called it 'a revelation'. A colleague has told me that 'you have to fight to get tickets.' Not literally, I hope! As a matter of fact, Sonia emailed me only last week offering my wife and myself complimentary seats to the production.

I was tempted, naturally, but we will not be going.

GRENDEL

No list of chaos creatures could ever be complete without the inclusion of Grendel, the 'Marsh-Reiver', the 'Walker in the Dark', a being of utter and wanton destructiveness, and yet one who all the way through the 12-year reign of terror accredited to him is said to have been fully aware of the evil he was doing, and thus revelled in it all the more.

The legend of Beowulf and Grendel is well known across the western world. In Britain, it is related to youngsters almost as a rite of passage, though there is no obvious moral meaning, no hidden lessons to be learned, except those found traditionally in heroic Nordic fiction. But there is something about the characters involved, even the evil ones, like Grendel, that has made them hugely appealing both to tellers and consumers of fantastical stories for many centuries, and in Britain, in England especially, it carries extra resonance because of the vivid picture it paints of the Anglo-Saxon world, earls and thegns feasting riotously together in a fire-lit long-hall, presided over by a great warrior king, while beyond the bulwarks of his fortification lies an eerie land of wilderness and dark forest.

The story itself is relatively simple. It describes a successful but aged Danish king, Hrothgar of the Scyldings, who to celebrate his lifetime of victories, seeks out a remote corner of his kingdom in order to build a golden hall, which he calls Heorot. Once his new capital is completed, a great feast is held, Hrothgar, his wife, Queen Wealhtheow, and his many warriors eating, drinking and singing long into the night. All is well until the hubbub disturbs a mysterious being who dwells in the nearby marshes. We know him today as Grendel, which in Old English means 'Grinder' or 'Tearer'. Initially curious, having never heard song or laughter before, Grendel comes to investigate, and on seeing the Danes' joy, and realising to his despair that this is something he can never share, forces entry and brutally attacks the happy host, killing 30 warriors and desecrating their corpses by rending them to pieces and lapping up the blood.

Thus begins Hrothgar's 12-year nightmare, the monster returning to Heorot with every nightfall, killing anyone he finds there or encounters en route, vampirising and cannibalising their remains. The Danes are helpless to stop him. Ambushes are laid, armies lying in wait, but Grendel, protected by some magical charm that always turns blades away, destroys everyone sent against him.

The hall is eventually abandoned, Hrothgar's decimated court scattering across the land. However, news of the atrocities has now travelled, finally reaching the land of the Geats in modern day southern Sweden. They too are a Viking-like people, but not always friends with the Danes. However, on this occasion there is peace, and a Geatish warrior, Beowulf, son of Earl Ecgbeow and nephew to King Hygelac, one of Hrothgar's old allies, vows to take on the monster.

When he arrives in Denmark, he and his war-band are accommodated in the desolate shell that once was Heorot, and that first night, when Grendel returns, Beowulf springs upon him. Having heard that Grendel is protected against cold steel, Beowulf opts to fight the fiend bare-handed. An epic struggle ensues, at the end of which, Grendel, who has never met his match before and now is terrified, attempts to flee, only for Beowulf to rip his arm off at the shoulder. Mortally wounded, Grendel staggers back into the marshes.

In Heorot meanwhile, with the monster's arm now nailed to a high beam, Hrothgar and his people return and a great feast is held in Beowulf's honour. But that night, as everyone sleeps, another intruder slinks into the hall, snatching away Hrothgar's best friend, Aeschere, leaving a trail of blood back to the marshes, which, when Beowulf and his men follow it, finally leads them to Aeschere's torn-off head.

Terrified again, local people now admit that, sometimes, when Grendel was abroad in the night, he was seen in company with one other, a similar devil to himself yet female in shape. Realising that his work isn't done, but this time armed with the famous broadsword, Hrunting, Beowulf searches the marsh, finally locating an underwater cave, which he alone swims down to. Inside, it leads to a network of caverns, where treasure and weapons, clearly pillaged from those Grendel has slain, are lying in unused heaps. Grendel is also there but he is dead, having expired from the critical wound that Beowulf inflicted.

Unfortunately, someone else is there too: Grendel's mother.

Referred to as a merewif, or water hag, she is, if anything, an even more terrible opponent, and when Beowulf strikes her with Hrunting, the blade shatters. Realising that he's in deadly peril, Beowulf is hunted through the caves until he finds another sword, its blade inscribed with magical runes, which indicate that it was forged by the frost giants. Rejoining the fight with his new special weapon, the hero is victorious, hacking open the water hag's head, then needing to flee because the boiling black effluent that flows out is clearly poisonous.

Thus goes the story of Beowulf and Grendel. Most of us will be aware that it comes down to us as part of the epic Old English poem, Beowulf, original author unknown but believed to have been composed in the 10th Century, most likely as a Christianised version of a much earlier folktale.

But what was Grendel?

Strangely, given the horror he wreaked, the poem says little about his origins or even his form. Though he's referred to as 'a child of Cain', such a phrase would not be atypical of early Christian writing when describing a wicked individual, seeing as all evil was descended from Cain, the first murderer. We may assume that he is an anthropomorphic monster from the way he wrestles with Beowulf in man-to-man fashion, but hugely powerful and ferocious. One obvious conclusion is that Grendel was a troll or ogre, one of those hairy, malformed brutes, vast in size and savagery, who terrorised ancient northern communities, though Grendel is never specifically referred to as either, unlike for example, the main antagonists in the legends of Bragi Boddason and Jack the Giant Killer, which is curious.

Some scholars have proposed that Grendel was a human outcast, possibly an early type of berserker, one of that cult of Viking warriors who by donning wolf-fur, chanting to Odin and ingesting some form of drug, were transformed into raging homicidal maniacs. But this is unlikely for two reasons: firstly, when the poem was composed, the Anglo-Saxons were well aware of berserkers and had met them many times on the battlefield, so there is no obvious reason why Grendel wouldn't be referred to as such, and secondly, the poem labels him repeatedly as a demon or fiend, implying a satanic level of evil. Likewise, Grendel's mother, is described as a 'water hag', which in the Dark Ages is a reference to the pagan belief that ancient goddesses had once occupied springs and wells, and a clear suggestion that she and her offspring had supernatural prowess.

One other possibility is that Grendel was one of the sceudagenga, or shadow-forms said to have roamed the northern wilds, doing evil deeds in abundance. In an age before artificial light, the night, particularly in winter, was an especially frightening time, and the idea that Grendel was simply part of this, an unknowable, murderous shape that could steal upon you in an instant, would have been harrowing indeed.

One final question is whether there could be any truth in this tale?

Easy enough to dismiss as a simple myth, there are, nevertheless, strangely mundane, even realistic aspects to the story. Grendel dies after his battle with Beowulf rather than during it, and overall, Beowulf is unsuccessful in his main clash with the monster, failing to eliminate the threat entirely, thus enabling another opponent to continue the murder spree. Is it also significant that several characters in the Beowulf epic are known to have been real people? King Hrothgar, for example, appears in many sagas and historical records of the 6th Century, as does Beowulf's uncle, King Hygelac of the Geats. And then there is Heorot, the great hall, which has been tentatively located at Lejre, on the isle of Zealand, in eastern Denmark, a known seat of Scylding government in the 6th Century, and is still being excavated today.

Does this mean that Grendel also was real?

Who can say? But Lejre is close to many desolate places, where once there were deep woods, night-black marshes and a genuine air of foreboding.

POLYPHEMUS
Helen Grant

You can see the island from here, in all but the darkest, foggiest conditions. There is a stretch of water which is always restless but sometimes boils over into savage white foam, and beyond it a solid mass patched green and brown like a gigantic chunk of copper ore. It has a name, one I can't pronounce, and it used to be uninhabited.

Truthfully, it's pretty much impossible *not* to see the island. This place, built in the Sixties, has huge plate glass windows looking out onto it. Even when the clouds are low and rain is running down the windows you can still see its uncompromising bulk. Part of me would prefer not to see it, and sometimes I do forget it's there, for a little while. I get engrossed in my work, or what remains of it. It's been scaled back, obviously, but the project is still active. Time slips by and the island sinks down through the conscious layers of my mind until there is nothing but a vague feeling of unease underlying my thoughts.

Still, I'm not sure it would be a good thing to forget about the island's presence altogether, even if I could. Vigilance is required. There's one particular spot where the channel of water between here and there is at its narrowest, and that's where boats cross the strait. Well, it's where they *used* to cross the strait. On this side there's a small concrete jetty and a slipway. On the island there's a long section of flat rock with metal rings for mooring. There are never any boats moored up there. There's a large official notice on the mainland side warning people that there is strictly no access to the island. The word *DANGER* stands out in stark black letters on a toxic yellow ground. Trespassers would be foolhardy indeed to take a boat over there. All the same, that is the point where a crossing would be most feasible, and that is why the gaze slides back to it, every so often.

Used to cross the strait, did I say? *Never any boats moored up there?*

There's one there this morning.

I stand at the huge window with the component I was carrying in my hands. My fingers roam restlessly over it, unthinkingly testing its contours – the hard ridges, the truncated tail of electrical cord. My gaze never moves from that little blue and white craft tethered to the iron rings in the rock, rising and falling gently with the waves. There's nobody in it, nor is there anyone visible nearby. Self-evidently, however, someone must have gone over; the boat didn't get there by itself.

My mind leafs automatically through the possibilities. It can't be a fellow worker: I'm the only one left and if they sent anyone else, that person would come here, not head for the island. Anyone even remotely involved with the project would have more sense than that. Fishermen and land workers have no business on the island, and in spite of Scotland's lenient access laws I doubt they'd set foot on it. They wouldn't want to piss off the organisation that brought so much investment to the area.

Youngsters, I think, and that sort of makes sense. There's very little to do in this part of the world, and the devil makes work, as they say. The same exploratory instinct that impels them to break into abandoned factories and hospitals might encourage them to visit the island in spite of the warning sign. Or even *because of it.*

There's one other option, but I'm not even going to consider that.

Well, whoever sailed that boat over, they're nowhere near it now. Much of the east side of the island is visible from here, and there's no sign of anyone moving about on it. That means they've followed the track up and over to the other side of the island, the one hidden from the mainland.

It's an uphill slog, that track. You'd have to be very keen indeed to see what was on the other side, and once you had, you probably wouldn't be content to survey it at a distance. It's intriguing, after all – such a large building, all those brutal straight lines against a setting of softly blurring greens and browns. The small, high windows that give away nothing about what is inside. The motorised industrial strength steel shutter sealing the main doorway. Well, I assume the door is still sealed. I've never been back to look. Perhaps it lies open now, yawning darkly like the entrance to a cave, and exuding the musty scents of disuse and decay.

The place was state of the art when they built it. The ceilings were of necessity very high, and the brilliantly-lit interior gleamed with dazzling white tiles and highly polished metal. A temple to science, you might say. When I toured the facility for the first time Cathy accompanied me and I remember she gasped when she saw the biggest room. Of course, she didn't understand what she was seeing, and even when I tried to explain it in layman's terms she very soon gave up trying to follow. All the same, she was impressed; you couldn't not be. I certainly was, though my visible response was far more subdued. I've always been like that: reserved, keeping my feelings under the surface. Possibly that was why things went the way they did.

The building has living quarters too, of course, and those were the antithesis of the sterile laboratory environment. There were luxuriant thick carpets, large sofas in jewel colours, and soft elegant lighting. The bathrooms had onyx effect tiles, free standing tubs and underfloor heating. The kitchen was equipped with a gigantic cooking range and butler sinks. In addition there was extensive food storage, including enormous walk-in freezers, since it was neither desirable nor practical to travel to the nearest village for provisions. And there were bedrooms, with comfortable super king size beds. No expense spared – but then you expect that, when you ask people to cut themselves off from the world for most of the year.

My mind has wandered, thinking back to all this, but when I

snap back into focus everything is just the same: the blue and white boat gently rides the waves; the landscape is empty.

That boat is a problem, or if it isn't now, it will be. Oh, I suppose there's a chance whoever moored it there will complete an uneventful circuit of the island, then sail back over and go on their way, none the wiser. But I don't really think that will happen. More probably they will go to the building. And then … Well, they won't come back – but something else might.

There may be ways to prevent that eventuality. If I had another craft, I could sail over there myself, and tow that little boat back. I imagine myself standing on those damp grey rocks in the rain, with my hair plastered to my head, trying to undo knotted ropes while water ran down my cold face. I'd be working feverishly, turning every few seconds to see if anyone – any*thing* – was coming down that steep track. The thought makes me horribly queasy. But it's not even that simple. There are no boats on this side – you may be sure *that* was dealt with some time ago, when what remained of the project was relocated over here. They even removed the upturned rowing boat that had been mouldering away on the machair since before this facility was built. The *DANGER* sign was erected in a prominent position and then everybody left, except me.

Why didn't I go, when all the others did – even Cathy? I've asked myself that, often. The truth is, I was afraid this day would come, and I thought I could guard against it. Now I think perhaps I should have left when I could, and taken up a post far away. New Zealand, perhaps. Antarctica. Anywhere but here.

It started so well, that was the thing. The project was so advanced that most people would have thought of it as science fiction. It wouldn't just have made my career; I'd have been on the cover of magazines – nice gritty portrait shots of me looking fiercely intelligent in a lab coat, with maybe some dynamic wavy line effects to suggest the science in a user-friendly way. There'd have been headlines saying I'd made history, and transformed the future, and all the rest of it.

None of that has happened. As I said, the project is still

active, but that's mainly because of the slight hope that one day what's done might be undone – or at least, the funders could claim that we *tried*. Considering how enthusiastic they were about supporting the project in the beginning, they're now very, very focused on arse covering.

Truthfully, Cathy wasn't as keen on the whole thing as I was. She couldn't have found fault with the living arrangements, which were fantastically luxurious compared to the overpriced, grotty flat we'd been living in, but she thought she'd be bored, or lonely. I knew I wouldn't be either of those things. When I'm intellectually engaged with something, I don't really care where I am. It could be the centre of a city or the middle of a desert or hell, the face of the Moon. I see the work; that's what fills my mental horizon. Cathy's a lot more gregarious. In fact, people are what she loves. She was always out seeing this friend or that, playing tennis and going for coffee; she never got tired of listening to the trivia of other people's lives. When you think about it, it's surprising that we ever got together. But I loved her, I truly did. I still do, only like everything else it got messed up.

Anyway, just before we moved to the island, one of the other key personnel died suddenly, in a road accident. I knew him and his wife very well; I'd been looking forward to working with him. So suddenly we had to recruit again, and this time it was someone I'd never even met before. To be honest, if it had been down to me we wouldn't have picked him. Even if it had put the project back, I'd have waited for exactly the right person. But the funders were very keen.

Sam Thomson, that was his name. It's not a name you're likely to hear again soon, not if the funders can help it. He was a little younger than I am, but with an impressive string of letters after his name – something of a prodigy, in fact. If he hadn't chosen this project he'd probably be a professor by now. Anyway, he was highly intelligent and also intellectually creative – he could think outside the box, as they say. The ideal person for a research project like this. He was single, which struck me as potentially annoying, because if he felt the need for social contact he might be leaning on me and Cathy. He was also irritatingly good-looking, in a flashy sort of way – grin a bit too wide, very white teeth, that sort of thing. I was a little concerned that he might impose on Cathy – try to flirt with her or something. Some scientists do, you know – we don't have mechanical hearts beating away under our white coats. He looked just the sort. But when they met for the first time, he didn't try anything like that. In fact he seemed a bit subdued.

There were a couple of other staff, and that was it. Some of the work could be done remotely, and it wasn't the sort of project where you wanted extraneous people stumbling into the middle of things at inopportune moments. There were definite dangers.

We worked small scale at first: inanimate objects over short distances. It was not so much the unravelling that caused the difficulties as the ravelling at the other end. We had some success with simple geometric shapes made from a single elemental metal; it was easy to judge whether those had arrived in exactly the same form as they had departed. When they did, it was a huge triumph, and one which we celebrated very heartily; it had proved that the process worked, in a basic way. We opened a magnum of Champagne, I remember. Alcohol wasn't amongst the provisions supplied to the place; it wasn't outright forbidden but it was subtly discouraged, on the basis that it could become too much of a habit, out here with not much else to do. Sam had smuggled the bottle in, in expectation of celebrations. He was an optimist. We all drank rather a lot, and I awoke the following morning with a thumping headache, and blinked at the morning light like a mole. Cathy was in the kitchen when I staggered out. She said she'd passed out on one of the plush sofas, and slept there all night.

Next we tried sending a carrot through, and it came out looking weirdly corrugated. That set us back quite a bit, because we couldn't see any reason why that should have happened, not at first. We had to be sure of the process before we tried putting a live animal through, even something like a mollusc or a worm.

Anyway, the weeks passed and we kept on tinkering – calibrating, I should say – until eventually we got a carrot that looked completely normal, even when you put slices of it under the microscope. After that we tried other vegetables – potatoes, onions, a red pepper. All of them went through and came out seemingly perfect. We got a little drunk on success this time, I think (no Champagne required). Cathy came into the lab to see us transporting a head of romanesco broccoli across the room, which was an absurd item really with which to demonstrate a miraculous new technology, but it was the most complex vegetable shape we could think of. When it came out exactly as it was when it went in, Sam and Cathy were so excited they hugged each other.

I stood and looked at them for a second, and then Cathy let go of Sam, looking a little awkward, and came over and hugged me.

'Congratulations, darling,' she said into my ear.

I hugged her back, but it was about then that I began to wonder.

Once you have an idea like that in your head, it's difficult to *stop* wondering. I didn't say anything, but I found myself watching too. I can't say there was really anything untoward. If anything, Cathy seemed to avoid Sam when she could. If she came through into the working area to leave a cup of coffee on my desk and he was in there, or if she came into the living room in the evening and the pair of us were discussing how something had gone that day, she'd make herself scarce as soon as she could. But still … I wondered.

Once, Sam had a day off and proposed to walk around the island, which takes longer than you might think because the terrain is so rough, and there are few proper paths. At lunchtime, purely on a whim, I went back into the living quarters and Cathy wasn't there. That evening when I finished work I went back and there she was alright, fussing about in the kitchen. I went and leaned on the work surface, and said:

'I popped in at lunchtime but you weren't here.'

She paused just for an instant, with a pinch of herbs in her fingers. Then she said:

'I went out to get some sunshine. Didn't you look out the back?'

'No,' I said. It was perfectly true; I hadn't looked.

'Oh,' she said. 'Well, I was out there.'

She didn't look at me; she kept stirring the dinner, and I went off to have a shower.

A lot of time passed, and still we hung back from sending anything alive – in the animal sense – through the transporter. The funders were fairly patient, considering how much they'd invested, and they were also close-mouthed. If the project were fully successful, after all, it would be *huge* – like the invention of the wheel or something. Equally, it was critical that nobody else got a sniff of what we were up to until the thing was done and dusted, and patented too. So we stayed on our island, sending vegetables across the room and collecting them at the other end, and the seasons turned, and my gregarious wife, who'd been so concerned about the lack of company, was strangely silent on the subject of how dull it all was.

One evening, when we were having dinner together in the kitchen, I recall she paused with a forkful of pasta on the way to her mouth and said:

'Are you going to try with animals soon?'

I glanced at her. 'We're not ready.'

'But darling… You've been sending vegetables through it for months now, and they've all been fine. It must be time soon.'

This time I held her gaze. 'That's what Sam says.'

Was it my imagination, or did some tiny reaction cross her face, like a ripple? Then she shrugged

'Great minds, I suppose.'

'It's not up to Sam,' I said. 'He's not the lead researcher.'

She put down her fork. 'I've offended you, haven't I?'

'No,' I said stiffly.

She didn't seem to hear me. 'It's just … You know, some time you're going to have to make the leap of faith.'

Sam says that too. I didn't say that out loud.

'We're talking about living things,' I pointed out. 'If they come out scrambled … Well, it'd be inhumane.'

'It's not rabbits though, is it, darling? It's nematode worms.'

'Our treatment of animals should not depend on their cute factor,' I pointed out.

There was a long silence. Cathy coloured.

'Sorry,' she said in the end. 'I just … I just want you to have the success you're after, that's all.'

'I'll know when it's time,' I said.

We ate the rest of the meal without exchanging any more words. When she got up to clear the plates, I went back to the lab. It was well past working hours; I just wanted to think for a bit, without Cathy or Sam or anybody else around me.

The trouble was, Sam was probably right – Sam, who was constitutionally optimistic. We were going to have to make the leap sooner or later, and probably sooner. But I hated the fact that he was so much more prepared to take the leap than I was, and that made me resist it. Worse, he and Cathy seemed to be in league over the topic. I'd never caught them having a single conversation that didn't include me, and yet I couldn't help imagining it – covert meetings, words being exchanged that I wouldn't have wanted to hear. Before long he'd have talked her round completely, and she'd be despising me for not having the courage to take the next step. Despising me, and admiring him. It made me feel hot and cold to think about it.

A couple of days later I told Sam peremptorily that we'd be trying with nematode worms.

'Good,' he said.

It was hard to pick holes in a single word but I still managed to feel slighted; he'd pronounced on something I'd decided, as though I needed his approval.

I realised he was looking at me quizzically.

'Is everything alright?' he said.

'Of course it is,' I replied. 'We just need to make the leap of faith, you know?'

Anyway, we set everything up, and sent the worms through.

Then we went to the other end of the lab to see what had arrived. Part of me – the perennially pessimistic part – fully expected to find worm soup. But the tiny creatures were squirming away quite happily, blissfully unaware that they had made history.

'I knew it!' said Sam. 'I knew it, I knew it!'

In that moment I hated him.

Representatives from the funding organisation came, and watched another set of worms being transported across the lab. They were delighted.

'What else do you need?' asked one of them, a heavyset man with a politician's bluff tone.

I was ready for that question. 'More funds for a larger transporter. Eventually we'd like to try bigger mammals. A dog, maybe.'

'A dog?' The man turned to his colleague. 'A bit of a PR problem if it went wrong.'

'A sheep then,' I said. 'Or … I don't know, a cow.'

'A cow?' That got a chuckle. 'That's ambitious.'

'It's the same principle,' I pointed out, 'whether it's a worm or a heifer.'

'How about a crocodile? Nobody could say those are cute and cuddly.'

I forced myself to laugh. 'I still wouldn't want to scramble one. We won't send anything through until we're absolutely certain it's safe. I mean, ultimately, we want to create something people can use. So we have to be sure.'

'Alright,' he said eventually. 'You'll get the funds.'

After that there was a lot of back slapping and congratulation. Then the visitors went back down to the landing place to take their launch back to the mainland, and I accompanied them to the boat. A tall dark-haired guy called McQueen, like the film star, held back for a moment to speak to me. He was wearing a formal suit and tie, quite unsuitable attire for the Scottish weather, and the tie kept flapping about in the wind, like a snake.

'Great work with the worms,' he said.

I started to thank him but he just talked over me.

'When you get to the mammals, don't fuck it up,' he said. 'Like the man said, bad PR.'

Then he nodded, and went off to the boat.

'Thanks,' I said into thin air.

When I got back to the lab, the two lab assistants were cleaning up. There was no sign of Sam or Cathy.

In the end, there was only one really gruesome mistake, and that was a rat. Don't get me wrong: I like rats. They're intelligent little creatures, and cute in their way. It's always been a mystery to me that people love squirrels but think rats are disgusting. However, in PR terms the rat was less of a disaster than, say, a golden retriever would have been. It was still grim. The only consolation was that the rat was DOA. At least, I think so. It was difficult to tell when it first came through, but I gave it a shot to euthanise it, just to be sure.

We had to write up the rat incident, of course.

Sam said, 'I don't think we should tell Cathy about this.'

I paused. 'That's very thoughtful of you,' I said. I was looking at the screen where the cursor was blinking away at the end of an unfinished sentence about the rat, so I didn't look at him.

For a while, all of us were cast down by what had happened. Nobody likes to see anything die, even in pursuit of noble scientific objectives. Plus the words *When you get to the mammals, don't fuck it up* were still ringing in my ears, at least figuratively.

It also took a lot more time to work out what had gone wrong. There were so many factors it could have been: size, weight, structure, water content ... On bad days I wondered whether a mammal was just too bloody *complex* for the process. Worse, perhaps we were being dense, missing something obvious – and that raised the spectre of being overtaken by cleverer competitors.

At last, though, we cracked it. We sent another rat through, and this one arrived at the other end looking fine and dandy, with its little nose twitching.

That night we all celebrated again, in my and Cathy's living quarters. Another milestone achieved! There was no magnum of Champagne this time, but there were some bottles of wine left over from the funders' visit, so I opened those and dispensed the contents liberally.

I made a show of imbibing pretty heavily – just this once, release of tension, etc. etc. When the lab assistants had gone, I got up, tottered into the bedroom and slumped heavily onto the bed. I lay still, eyes closed, and waited.

It wasn't long before I heard Cathy's light footsteps approaching the door. They paused there, and I presumed she was looking in. Then I heard a second set of steps, a little heavier. Sam. The pair of them were standing there, watching me.

There was a rustle, which might have been him sliding an arm around her, or perhaps the pair of them embracing. Sam said something in a whisper, so low that I could hardly make any of it out. It might have been: *He's asleep. Come on.* Then there was a faint wet sound. A kiss.

Every muscle in my body was rigid by now. It took a supreme effort for me not to leap off the bed and punch Sam on the nose. But research scientists are used to playing the long game; he'd get his comeuppance soon enough, I thought.

I heard them move away after that, their footsteps stumbling a little, as if they were hopelessly entwined. They went out of our apartment, but Cathy didn't shut the door, probably thinking the sound might wake me. I heard them go down the hall, and then there was silence.

I left it five minutes, just to be sure they weren't coming back for anything, and then I got up and tiptoed down the hall after them. The door to Sam's quarters was ajar, so I flattened myself against the wall outside and listened.

It was a bitter thing to have my suspicions confirmed. I suppose part of me still hoped I'd been imagining it. But no; I heard murmurs and more of those disgusting wet noises, and then a rhythmic creaking began. It was absolutely distinctive. Eventually I risked a sidelong peep around the doorframe, and the pair of them were at it on the plush blue sofa. Cathy was *on top*, for God's sake. I ground my teeth so hard it was a wonder they didn't hear me.

Then I crept away, and got back onto the bed. When Cathy came in, very much later, I was genuinely asleep.

We kept the rat under observation for a month, and it seemed perfectly healthy, something which was later confirmed by an autopsy. By then we'd sent more rats through without any further mishaps, and the new, larger transporter had been commissioned, so we moved on to other, bigger animals. Rabbits, then a dog, which had to be brought in by boat.

I tried not to let Cathy see the dog, which was a handsome little beagle; I still cared about her, after all. It was Sam I hated. Unfortunately, however, she heard the dog barking when we brought it into the facility, and there was a storm of tears. She was thrilled when it went through the process unscathed, like the new rat and the rabbits had. I didn't remind her that it would have to be euthanised and autopsied later.

It was good to be able to tell the funders that we hadn't *fucked it up*, apart from the original rat.

All of this, of course, was working up to the day when a human being would go through the transporter.

There was a lot of debate about that, not just between us, but with the funding organisation. Various ideas were tossed about, like asking a long term prison resident to do it. That was never really going to take off though, because you could be sure that if it did go wrong, there'd be a huge court case, prisoner or not. I don't think there was really any doubt that one of the research team would eventually do it. I mean, Jonas Salk tested his polio vaccine on his own family, didn't he? Anyway, we weren't at that stage yet. Not quite.

About this time, I mentioned to Cathy that I was having

occasional palpitations. She seemed genuinely concerned, and asked me a lot of questions: did I have any pain, especially on the left hand side? Did I feel faint? Shouldn't I try to go for a medical? I played it down heroically. I said I was sorry I'd said anything, because I didn't want to worry her, and it wasn't really that bad, nor very often.

I knew she'd tell Sam. When you've lived with someone for years, you can love them desperately, but know all their weaknesses as well as their strengths. Cathy can't keep her mouth shut. She has to share pretty much everything.

I don't know why I'm thinking about all of this again now. Maybe it's because that was the tipping point: I went from wanting to do it to actively planning. That was a significant thing for me. I expect a lot of killers kid themselves that they're only thinking about it in a theoretical sort of way, right up to the moment when they shove somebody off a cliff edge or whack them with a blunt object. It's harder to look into your own soul and say: I am capable of this. I am going to do it.

It also sucked up a lot of mental energy. I had to make sure my behaviour towards Sam and Cathy didn't noticeably change. I've always been a little tetchy, so being wonderfully genial all of a sudden would have made them smell a big fat rat. I also took care to make my movements predictable, because walking in on them at this stage would have messed everything up. The oblivious middle-aged spouse, that was me.

Anyway, eventually we'd worked our way right up to primates, and once the autopsy on the chimps was done, we were back to the question of the first human test subject.

'It should be me, of course,' I said to Sam, in a brooking-no-nonsense voice. We were both in the lab at the time, rereading the results on the last chimp.

He was silent for a moment. 'Okay,' he said in the end. 'But you're the lead researcher …'

'Yes; so it should be me. I feel,' I said, looking at him over the top of my glasses, 'that I have earned my place in the history books.'

'Yes,' he said. 'But you'll have that anyway, won't you?

Since you led the whole project. And if something happened to you ...'

'Nothing will happen to me,' I said firmly. 'Every single one of the chimps was fine. In fact we haven't lost a test animal for months and months.'

'No, we haven't,' he said reluctantly.

'That settles it, then. I'll be the Jesse Lazear of transporting.'

'Jesse Lazear died,' he pointed out.

'Well, the Stubbins Ffirth then.'

Sam opened his mouth to object to that example too, but then he shut it again, doubtless thinking that he wasn't going to talk me round. And indeed he wasn't, not yet.

I knew he wouldn't let it lie, though. The mere fact that I had declared it was going to be me irked him. And that, I suppose, showed what kind of man he was. It wasn't enough that he was fucking my wife; he wanted the laurels for the entire project, too. When you think about it, he deserved what was coming.

The topic came up again a few days later, when Sam was having dinner with us. He and Cathy were fairly quiet that evening; I suppose it's hard to think of anything to say when you've got an illicit thing going and you're in the same room as the third person, who (you assume) doesn't know. I rambled on at some length about a previous project, and the others no doubt silently yearned for each other, although they were good at hiding it.

Then Cathy asked about the current project, and Sam said, 'We were discussing the next steps the other day,' and he looked at me.

'We're about ready for a human test subject,' I said. 'I was going to talk to you about that, actually. I think it ought to be me, as lead researcher.'

She stared at me. 'Isn't it ... dangerous?'

I shook my head. 'Absolutely not. All the primates came through without any problems at all – you know that. In the pink of health, in fact.'

Until we killed and dissected them.

'Anyway,' I added nobly, 'I wouldn't ask any of my staff to

121

do something I wouldn't do myself.'

Of course, Sam couldn't resist that.

'I know you wouldn't,' he said. 'But you don't *have* to ask anyone to do it. I'd be happy to volunteer.'

'You?' I said, pretending not to notice the look of horror on Cathy's face. 'No, no, Sam. There's no need for that. And anyway, you're quite as critical to the research as I am.'

'I thought you said it wasn't dangerous?' said Cathy.

'Well,' I said, and left an infinitesimal pause before I went on. 'It really isn't.'

'I don't think ...' began Cathy, and fell silent.

'Look,' I said, in a reassuring tone, 'We haven't decided anything for certain, not yet. And nobody is going through at all unless we are one hundred per cent sure it's safe. Don't worry about it.'

I knew she *would* worry about it, and Sam would continue to be heroic. More fool him.

When the time came, Sam and I agreed not to tell Cathy. She'd have been beside herself with nerves, which wouldn't have helped anyone, and it raised the possibility of hysterical interruptions.

Pretty much up to the last minute we were still discussing who was going to do it, with perfect sincerity on Sam's part. I always argued firmly in favour of myself. On the morning of the test, however, he came into the lab bright and early and found me leaning heavily on the work surface, breathing raggedly.

'Oh my God!' he said. 'What's wrong?'

I shook my head, as if to say, *give me a minute.*

He put a hand on my arm. 'Look, this is madness. You can't be the test subject. You're not well.'

'I can,' I gritted out. 'My project.'

'You'll still get the kudos.' He paused. 'I know about the palpitations. Cathy told me. She's worried about you. *I'm* worried about you. If it's your heart, who knows what the stress will do?'

'Don't care.'

'Even if you don't, think of the project! You can't be a test subject if you're already sick. It's not safe, and if something happens to you, how will we know whether it was the process or a pre-existing condition?'

There was a lot more along those lines. I valiantly resisted for a long time, but eventually allowed myself to be talked round. Oh, the disappointment! The regrets! But for the good of the project ...

As for Sam, he did his best to look completely neutral and professional, but he had to struggle not to smirk, thinking about the fame that was going to be his.

Well, we set everything up. There was a bit of paperwork first, because of the change of test subject; Sam had to sign a disclaimer, fill out various forms, etc. When all that was done, he had to strip off and get into the transporter.

While he was doing that, I called over one of the lab assistants, and told him to go and stand outside the door and ensure Cathy didn't try to come in. I sent the other one, a thin, pale, bespectacled girl who barely ever said anything, to monitor the chamber at the other end. Then I went over to speak to Sam.

'Nervous?' I said.

'Not remotely,' he said. Then: 'Bloody terrified actually.'

'It'll be fine,' I told him. 'You'll see.'

Even then, I could have changed my mind. I empathised with his feelings of terror – they were well justified. But seeing his nakedness made me think of ... that time. Him and Cathy. It made me angry all over again, in a cold, vengeful way.

I went back to the control panel and started the process, the unravelling. I could see Sam from there; his face was visible through the safety glass, looking tense and expectant.

It wasn't difficult to fuck it up a bit. A bit was enough, I reckoned; no need to turn the guy into meat slurry. A small error could be retrospectively concealed too, especially since the main expert apart from myself was currently being unravelled. I watched bright light bloom inside the chamber as Sam disintegrated.

For perhaps a second there was silence other than the hum of the machinery. Then there was a brief flash of light from the far chamber, followed by a dull meaty thud.

I saw the lab assistant flinch at the sound. Then she looked at the glass door of the chamber, stepped closer and looked again. Her jaw dropped. For an instant it just worked soundlessly, and then she began to scream, a staccato series of cries that worked its way up to a ragged crescendo.

I didn't have to pretend to look stunned; the shrieks were ear splitting.

'What's happened?' I shouted, jogging across the lab.

Abruptly she stopped screaming and stared at me, her eyes huge in a face that had drained of what little colour it had. Then she pressed both hands over her mouth and ran past me. She didn't make it to the bathroom; I heard vomit splatter onto the tiled floor.

Of course, I had to look.

It was hard to make sense of what I was seeing, because nothing is supposed to look like that. There was something – a limb, or maybe an organ – pressed against the glass panel, and it was far longer than any part of original Sam could have been, like an etiolated plant. Above it was a single huge, bulbous, glossy eye.

I swallowed, my mouth suddenly dry. I'd known it would be bad, but the reality was shocking. And I had ...

'No,' I said under my breath. 'It was an accident. An *accident.*'

I mean, it wasn't, but it had to be one from now on, as far as everyone else was concerned. And when I looked at what was left of Sam, I suddenly wanted to believe it myself – wanted it so hard that I almost did.

I knew I'd have to open the door. That was what you had to do in this situation – check for vital signs and all that, even when it was plainly hopeless. It took me a couple of attempts; I think part of Sam was pushed up against the mechanism. Then all at once it opened, and with a great slap something fell out, onto the floor.

It was the upper part of a body, unnaturally elongated and horribly thin. At the top was that enormous, wet-looking globular eye. The head was practically all eye, in fact – just one of them, with a ruff of spiky-looking lashes around the base of it. It hurt my brain to look at it; I thought I was going to vomit, like the lab assistant had.

This … *thing* … lay there on the clinical white tiles for several moments. Then it *moved*.

Sam wasn't dead.

Things are a little hazy after that. I remember screams, though I don't know whether they were mine or someone else's, and I remember flinging myself towards the door. I slipped on a pool of fluid and scrabbled like an animal on the floor. All I could think about was putting as much space as possible between myself and what I had done.

Behind me there were sounds. Thumps. Slapping sounds. The thing was trying to get up. I tried not to look – I really tried – but of course I did, and my God! It must have been at least eight feet tall. It lurched as it came on, and I heard glass breaking as a flailing limb swept across a work surface. The worst thing, the very worst thing, was that bulging, liquid eye at the top. I looked at that and thought I should go insane.

Then I was outside the lab, leaning on the closed door with all my weight, and Cathy was there, fighting with the male lab assistant because she'd heard the screams and come running and he wouldn't let her go in.

I grasped her by the upper arms.

'There's been an accident,' I said, and my lips were trembling. I was afraid I would burst out into manic laughter. 'But don't worry, darling, it wasn't me. It wasn't me.'

'Who was it?' she quavered, her eyes enormous.

'It was Sam,' I said, and then I couldn't help it; I laughed.

Cathy screamed, and then she fought me, but between us the lab assistant and I managed to haul her away from the door. She kept calling Sam's name.

'I'm here,' I told her. 'I'm fine, darling. It wasn't me.'
She looked at me as if she didn't know who I was.
'Sam,' she said. 'Oh God. Sam.'

The cleanup was expensive, even by the funders' standards. It might have been easier if Sam *had* died – but he hadn't, and he showed no sign of doing so. Euthanising him would have been murder, especially since we couldn't find out whether that was what he wanted. The funders might have been tempted to do it anyway, but there was the question of the witnesses: the lab assistants, and Cathy. Oh, and me, of course.

The lab assistants had signed NDAs when they came to work on the project, but they also got a substantial payoff each to keep their mouths shut. Cathy got a lengthy stay in a small, very exclusive sanatorium. I thought she'd come home when she got out, but she didn't. In fact she vanished. I have a suspicion she got a payoff too, because nothing has come out about what happened to Sam.

As for me, I got to keep running what was left of the project. No blame was attached to me – not overtly, anyway. Both Cathy and the lab assistants had heard me arguing forcefully that I should be the first human test subject, and the assistants had heard me reluctantly capitulating in the end on health grounds. Otherwise I would have been the one who got *fucked up*, not Sam. So now I'm in the second best facility, supposedly trying to find a way to *unfuck* Sam, and thereby covering the funders' arses.

What to do about Sam, that was the biggest headache. It wasn't as if we could take him to *hospital*, like we would have done if it were a regular industrial accident: what could the doctors possibly do for him? Only sedation, I suppose, and that would have to be constant and permanent. Because Sam is aggressive. You can't blame him, I guess, but it makes him impossibly dangerous to approach. In the time before we left the island, he tried repeatedly to attack us.

Well, not *us*. *Me*. I don't think that's accidental, either. Of course, who knows how much he understands of what happened? If his brain is as scrambled as the rest of him, maybe nothing. Or maybe he just remembers in some dim way that it was me who pushed the button, so to speak. Whatever the case, he definitely wants my blood. The handful of times the male lab assistant and I tried to go in and – I don't know, examine him, or try to communicate with him – he went for *me*, unerringly. He knows we're enemies, alright.

In the end it was decided that Sam would stay on the island – alone – for the foreseeable future, like some hideous Polyphemus. He'd have all the comforts of the living quarters, after all, though God only knows whether he cares about cosy beds and hot showers. They'd airdrop food supplies in, ensuring they were nutritious things that could be easily consumed without special preparation. And then we'd wait until I found a way to unfuck him, or he died, whichever was first. Meanwhile, all transport to the island was removed and the *DANGER* sign went up. No boats went there anymore.

Until today.

I'm still gazing at that little boat. Youngsters, probably, in which case they may never come back, or perhaps not be believed even if they do.

The other possibility is that it was Cathy who went over. She never actually saw Sam after it happened; maybe she has some misguided idea that love can solve everything, that it means you don't have to be afraid. If she thinks that, she has a surprise coming.

Whoever it was, they still aren't back; on all the visible part of the island nothing moves. I'll have to do something about the boat, but that will require some planning because there is no way to get over there from here. I turn away from the window, but the nape of my neck prickles, as though I can sense that someone – or something – is watching me.

Time slips away from me; it's getting dark and looking back over the day I can't think what I've achieved. I haven't put the lights on yet and my computer screen is a rectangle of white glare, a blank page waiting for me to type in words I don't have, for a report I can't compose. I should have transported things back and forth across the lab today, running over the old tests from the start, but I don't have the stomach for it; the thought of seeing a rat, or even a nematode worm, all scrambled up is too much.

Outside, it's a wild night. I don't have to look out of the window to know that. I can hear the rain pattering onto the glass, and the wind howling: a symphony of foul weather.

Above those sounds, I hear a thump.

I stand there, irresolute.

The wind, I think, but when I go over all the possibilities – an unlatched window swinging back and forth, a tree branch slapping the side of the building – none seems likely. Just as I am beginning to think it was my imagination, the sound comes again.

It's very definite. *Thump.*

It's coming from the south end of the building, where the main door is. If I didn't know better, I'd think it was someone knocking. Knocking *very* hard.

'You'll have the door down,' I murmur to myself. I make no move to go and see. When you live somewhere as remote as this, it's not a pleasant idea, to open the door after nightfall and peer out, straining to see who might be standing there in the dark.

The rain is very heavy, the squall working its way up to a storm. There is a flash of lightning, followed by the rumble of thunder. Then there is that *thump* again. Did I imagine it, or did I hear glass cracking this time?

I drift over to the window and press my face close to it. When the lightning comes again there is one instant of brilliant, almost dazzling illumination. Then the darkness closes in again and I hear the thunder, so close on the lightning that the storm must be overhead. In that one instant I could clearly see the strait, the island, and the rocks where the boat was moored. It was gone.

There is a crash: the main door. I tremble. I want to tell Sam: *It wasn't me. I didn't mean it. It was Nobody's fault.*

Instead, I stand there, paralysed, and wait for the Cyclops to come for me.

WEREWOLF

Even a man who is pure in heart,
And says his prayers by night,
May become a wolf when the wolfbane blooms,
And the moon is full and bright.

One of the most instantly recognisable monsters in the annals of human folklore is the werewolf. So much so that there are probably very few aspects of the beast that a general readership isn't already aware of. However, there are a couple of mysteries at the heart of the tale which bear some additional analysis.

Firstly, why is a wolf the most popular form into which lycanthropes allegedly transform?

Werewolf legends are common across the world. But they aren't always connected to wolves or wolflike behaviour. For example, in parts of eastern Russia and Asia, folktales describe were-tigers. Likewise, in Africa, there are traditions of were-leopards (from 1890 to roughly 1930, the murderous Leopard Society, though it comprised entirely human adversaries, drew much of its power and control from the ancient stories about were-leopards). In South America, there were tales of were-jaguars, and in the extreme north of Scandinavia, were-bears. In fact, the modern word 'berserk' derives from the Viking word 'berserker,' or 'bear-shirt,' an ancient term for a special breed of warriors who absorbed extra rage and strength from clothing made from charmed bear-fur, and who in the midst of battle, could transform into bears.

But for all this, the werewolf (or his anthropomorphic cousin, the wolfman) is by far the most popular of all these variations, which is maybe a little unusual, as wolves weren't to be found everywhere. One obvious explanation is the European factor, because it was in old Europe, much of which was heavily forested and broken up into remote communities, where of all Man's natural predators, wolves were the biggest threat. And of course, it was Europeans who went on to colonise much of North America, taking their folklore with them, leading in due course to a welter of werewolf fiction, not just in book and story form, but, most importantly of all when it came to making the werewolf a global phenomenon, the movies.

However, it can't be denied that the werewolf legend in itself dates back to the earliest times. The Navari were a Slavic tribe who in the early 1st Century were described by the Roman travel-writer, Pomponius Mela, as having the ability to change into wolflike creatures on certain days of the year. Similarly, in Greek mythology, Zeus is said to have created the world's first known werewolf by transforming the Arcadian king, Lycaon, into a savage brute as punishment for the murder of his own son. So, the idea that men could become wolves was reasonably popular long before the age of mass media.

The tradition grew apace in the Dark Ages and Middle Ages, a period during which the mere mention of the beast struck terror and fascination at all levels of society. Famous medieval werewolves allegedly include Bajan, Prince of Bulgaria, and semi-mythical 12th Century Breton nobleman, Bisclavret. It was also recorded that King Canute issued laws against werewolf transformations (in a casual fashion that indicates this event wasn't at all unusual in 11th Century England!). Even holy men got in on the act, the 4th Century's Saint Augustine of Hippo, whose writings were normally restrained and rational, railing against those men who shapeshift into wolves, while Gerald of Wales, a noted churchman of the 13th Century, gave detailed accounts of contacts made between Irish priests and the Wolves of Ossory, a well-known werewolf clan believed to live in the Irish kingdoms of Meath and Leinster.

Even as society advanced into the Renaissance and Early Modern Age, there was no slowdown in the reporting of werewolf incidents, a whole preponderance of werewolf hunts and trials resulting, particularly in France, the Netherlands, Germany and the Baltic states. In nearly all these sensational cases, detailed records were made, some of which make hair-raising reading today.

In 1651 in Idavere (modern-day Estonia), a suspect we know only as Hans the Werewolf confessed to having transformed regularly over a period of several years as a result of incantations worked on him by a mysterious 'man in black'. Likewise, in 1605 in

Maastricht, in the southeast Netherlands, one Henry Gardinn admitted to having been part of a pack of werewolves who tore a young child to pieces, explaining that the transformation was achieved through deliberate sorcery. Scarier still is the tale of the Beast of Gévaudan, which comes to us from relatively late in this era, the 1760s, and concerns a werewolf, or some similar ferocious beast, said to have depredated widely across the southern French province, killing over a hundred people and grievously injuring many more, most of the victims dying from having their throats torn out. Surviving witnesses described it as a very large wolf, but with unusual, manlike characteristics. The terror in this case only ended in 1767 when a hunter and expert marksman, Jean Chastel, shot it dead with bullets allegedly made from medals engraved with images of the Virgin Mary. (In this case, the creature's corpse, stuffed with straw, was supposedly sent to Versailles, so that King Louis XV could see it for himself, but in fact, one of the king's apothecaries was sent in his place, and on falling ill having merely smelled the foul remains, it was buried before it could cause harm to anyone else).

Perhaps more disturbing still, though, are those records of werewolf trials wherein a culprit was apprehended who later confessed to mass murder, but who denied that he was a werewolf, and yet where he was still convicted of transforming, the local authorities unable to believe that such horrors could be the work of ordinary Christian men.

The best examples of this include the case of Nicolas Damont, the infamous Werewolf of Châlons, who in 1598 was burned at the stake in the Champagne region of France, after he raped, murdered and cannibalised scores of children (in this case, the criminal appeared to compound his crimes by calling on Satan to save him as the flames devoured his writhing form). A similarly grim tale concerns Gilles Garnier, the Werewolf of Dole, again in eastern France, a vagrant said to have hunted, killed and eviscerated five children, and to have taken their meat home to share with his wife; Garnier was burned at the stake in 1574. Most bone-chilling of all is probably the case of Peter Stumpp, the Werewolf of Bedburg, in Germany, who died in 1589, having confessed to murdering and mutilating at least 12 women and children. Despite his denials that he was a werewolf, Stumpp was broken on the wheel first, and then burned. For good measure, his daughter and mistress, also suspected of involvement in his crimes, were burned alongside him.

If one wonders at the extreme cruelty of these punishments, one should also consider that some of these men at least were serial killers. But one also needs to free one's mind of any modern notion that werewolves were themselves unwilling victims.

In George Waggner's seminal horror movie of 1941, The Wolf Man, from which the opening verse to this article originates (as penned by screenwriter Kurt Siodmak) and in which so much 'werewolf lore' was established (the full moon transformation, for example, and the notion that a silver bullet is the only way to kill a werewolf), the hero, Laurence Talbot, played by Lon Chaney Jnr, reluctantly succumbs to lycanthropy after being bitten by another werewolf. Equally important in the genre was Hammer's 1961 The Curse of the Werewolf, in which Oliver Reed as the titular beast only becomes afflicted because he is born of an unwed mother at the toll of midnight on Christmas Eve.

But in olden times, when these horrific beings were held to be real, there was nothing innocent about them. Many men who became wolves were believed to have brought the transformation on themselves either through making a pact with the Devil, using a magical ointment created during a black magic ceremony, or through donning a wolfskin or wolf belt. The purpose was so that they might find a way to satisfy their unnatural craving for human flesh, and sometimes their unbridled lust for women because in a possible throwback to the days of the berserkers (or their wolf-skin clad allies, the ulfheðnar), many of the accused were also said to have raped their female victims before killing them (an even stronger indication, if one is needed, that many of these monsters were simple sex murderers).

There are other potential explanations for the werewolf terror in past centuries. Medical conditions like hypertrichosis, which causes excessive hair growth, is now fully understood, but it wasn't in the past. Also, in central Europe in the 15th, 16th and 17th Centuries, a succession of cool, wet summers led to the infection of wheat and other crops by a hallucinogenic fungus. This may explain, at least to some degree, why people might have behaved like weird human/animal hybrids or thought they had encountered such.

Whatever the explanation, the werewolf still looms large in our collective consciousness as one of the deadliest supernatural foes we could meet.

But just in case you're hanging all your hopes on that supernatural aspect of werewolfism – ie banking on it not being real – always remember that werewolf activity has continued to be reported well into the 21st Century. The so-called Beast of Bray Road in modern day Wisconsin, a bipedal wolflike thing, has been sighted many times by locals between 1936 and 2020, while 300 miles east, the Michigan Dogman, which is almost identical in terms of the descriptions given, continues to scare the occupants of rural settlements. In neither of those cases have there been reports of killings, at least not of humans, but if nothing else, werewolves are clever. They're likely to know that modern law-enforcement would track them down quickly. So, just because they aren't leaving bloody carnage in their wake, that doesn't mean they aren't still out there.

BAUK
Simon Clark

'You got us into this, Celeste. It's up to you to get us out of it!'

'And in one piece!'

'Not like poor Robyn!'

'The face in the window … look … that face in the window!'

And that was that. After the outburst of yelling, loud enough to rattle the mucky old windowpane, there was silence. The verbal discharge of terror had left us all drained. Five people, sitting on the long, dusty sofa, facing the chalet window, and we uttered nothing more for a long, long time, our frightened faces illuminated by candles burning in a candelabra that stood on a table.

Vince Miller, a red-bearded Irishman of fifty, clad in a massive white parka, had anxiously perched himself on the edge of that communist-era sofa, which might have once cushioned the backside of General Tito himself. Also on the sofa, Kurt Vorman, Norwegian, forty-seven, shaved head, beard trimmed with forensic precision; he was a factory engineer, a veteran of hundreds of wild camps in the great outdoors. Once, he'd casually shooed vicious leopards out of his tent in Kenya. Tonight, Kurt was scared to the bone. As was Celeste Mehmet. It was Celeste who had suggested the expedition to the abandoned ski resort. Celeste, thirties, a Chicago dentist, wore an exceptionally striking coat: it resembled the pelt of a snow fox with long strands of white fur. All synthetic, of course. She detested animal cruelty. Celeste's expression hinted she constantly made shrewd judgements of her surroundings and the people she surrounded herself with. Her athletic build had been adroitly sculpted by a passion for tennis. Swathes of black hair fell softly over her shoulders; her almond-shaped eyes enhanced by a dramatic application of eyeliner. Then there was thirty-nine-year-old Rick Fairburn, who looked like a rockstar – one with blond dreadlocks – he seemed to hear music whenever he walked, because he moved his feet to the rhythm of a pumping drumbeat. He taught history at an English high school and played bass guitar in a pub band.

And there was me, Tony Westkirk. I'm on the silver side of forty, currently between office jobs, since the demise of my place of employment – a plastics factory that once extruded flexible pipes for all your plumbing needs, great or small.

It was Rick who kept uttering the invitation to: 'Look at the face in the window …'

There was such a face. A face pressed up close to the glass. You see, the face was supported by a snowdrift that had piled up against the windowpane. But only a face. No head, no body. The face lacked eyes, and it had purple lips drawn into a death snarl. The stranger's face might have been there all winter. Preserved by subzero temperatures here on the mountain. Most certainly, the face belonged to another victim of the bear that prowled this forbidding hellhole. Frankly, we didn't know what to do next. We simply sat there. It occurred to me that if falling snowflakes covered the face, we would be set free of the gruesome relic's hypnotic spell, then we could talk again, and figure out some means of escape.

Before the peeled-off face was covered, however, the roar came again. That terrifying roar of the maneater.

The whimsically named Gone Out Adventure Directive (GOAD) had coalesced online around Celeste Mehmet. Swiftly, GOAD became a tight-knit group of thrill-seekers, who relished visiting out-of-the-way places scorned by most tourists. Hence, Celeste's suggestion to visit Serbia, a landlocked nation with a deeply troubled history (Nazi occupation in World War Two, followed by Communist dictatorship, followed by bloody conflict with Bosnia in the 1990s). There were six of us on this adventure to the Balkans. And we'd only been ensconced in our hotel for a day when Celeste gleefully told us she'd arranged a visit to the ski resort of Broz, standing at an elevation of fourteen-hundred metres on Mount Sorabi. Of course, when it comes to trips that Celeste organised, there are always the strangest of twists. Over shots of the local apricot brandy in the hotel bar, she sat there, long hair falling over bare shoulders, her brown eyes flashing with mischievous delight. 'Guess what,' she had purred, 'guess where we are going tomorrow?'

'Not another dental house of horror museum,' said Rick, nimbly referencing her profession as a dentist.

'No.' She smiled. 'We are visiting a ski resort.'

'We don't do skiing,' I pointed out.

'Tony, this is no ordinary ski resort. Back in the Communist era, it was the playground of party leaders. Its chalets can only be reached by cable car, and ...' That sense of mischief positively radiated from her. And was there a delicious hint that she planned something transgressive? Even criminal?

'And?' Kurt prompted.

She smiled over her brandy glass. 'The Broz Ski Resort has been abandoned since the civil war in the early Nineties.'

'That's typical of you.' Robyn grinned. 'You're taking us to a place of wretched desolation.'

'Hardly. The skiers may have gone, but the chalets are just like they were in 1992, with portraits of Marx, Trotsky and General Tito on the walls.'

I was suspicious of her motives. 'But there's got to be more than you showing us mothballed holiday chalets. It's not like you, Celeste, to visit some mundane destination.'

'Agreed.' The mischievous smile returned to her lips. 'The Broz Ski Resort is a forbidden place. We are not allowed there. Nobody but the caretaker is permitted to even ride the cable car up to the resort, let alone enter the chalets. You see, during the Balkan Wars, the resort was considered to be of strategic military importance. That's why hundreds of landmines were sown there.' Her unsettling laugh sent shivers down my spine. 'That's right, my lovely friends. We shall stroll through a minefield. Won't we have the time of our lives?'

Most clearly, the caretaker risked getting sacked; however, he had a low-paid job with a family to support. Therefore, upon being presented with a fistful of banknotes by Celeste, he rattled open the gates of the cable car station at the foot of the mountain. Already, nightfall loomed; moreover, it was cold enough to freeze the blood. With the cash securely zipped into his anorak pocket, the caretaker handed Celeste the skeleton key that would open all the chalet doors, then he pulled a lever to restore power to the cable car system before opening the doors to a box-shaped cable car with a cream-coloured roof and vibrant red body. All six of us were soon onboard. The caretaker then demonstrated how to operate the controls from inside the car – these were in a metal box affixed to an inner wall. They were simple enough. A blue button boosted the car upwards into the darkness above us. A yellow button would return the car to the base station. Simple.

'What could go wrong?' grinned Robyn.

Before the caretaker pulled the doors shut, sealing us into the car, he called out, 'Stay inside big chalet until darkness gone and all is light. Keep out of minefield. They big Commie Russian mines. Mines still go BOOM! Okay?'

We chorused back, 'Okay.'

Some of us waved at the caretaker as motors hummed, carrying the car upwards. And some of us stared up into the gloom while wondering if this thirty-minute journey to the bleakest of mountain summits was one of the most foolhardy things we'd ever done.

The snow had covered the peeled-off face. Out there, in the gloom, harsh winds carved rounded forms out of snowdrifts that, Celeste had observed, resembled Henry Moore's avant-garde sculptures. Rick declared that the bulbous protrusions of ice and snow reminded him of skulls – skulls with empty eye sockets beneath thick eye-ridges.

No, I didn't see the drifts as Moore's artwork or gruesome skulls. However, the thing is, this place does possess an eerie aura. Gigantic rocks were like fists that savagely punched upward into the sky. Grey cliffs that rose to the rear of the chalet could have been vast tombstones, set there by a deranged pagan god. Storm winds were the screams of the damned. Chalets, standing dark and bunker-like, could have been the lairs of vampires and werewolves. And there were the minefields. These were the size of tennis courts, situated about fifty paces from one another, enclosed by barbed wire fences. Warning signs in Serbian and English ordered people to stay back: KEEP OUT – LIVE MINES – DANGER OF DEATH. Agreed, most of the minefields were clearly marked. However, time and snowstorms had begun to erase some of the boundaries between land where it was safe to walk and areas where those lethal canisters were buried. Canisters that would explode, should a person unwittingly step on them. This terrain on the cold, dead mountain absolutely does have its own bleak aura, which has the power to reach into our brains and fill them with evil imagery. That aura breathes terrible truths into your ear – that it is dangerous for humans in this place. And we now knew the mountain to be haunted.

Haunted by a brute. One that had pounced on Robyn and torn him apart. See? There's the streak of blood where the monster dragged his bisected corpse toward the neighbouring chalet, then through a low-set door, leading into what was possibly a cellar.

'A bear.' Kurt trembled from head to toe. 'It must be a bear, mustn't it?'

'Bears don't have horns,' declared Rick. 'This animal has horns.'

'No,' snapped Vince. 'You're wrong. There weren't any horns.'

'What we must do now –' my heart thudded with a grave rhythm '– is get off this mountain, then tell the police that a bear killed our friend.'

'I saw horns,' insisted Rick. 'And the creature was so thin …

gaunt like a … like a dying man.' He covered his face with his hands and wept.

Nobody responded to what Rick had said. Celeste, meanwhile, had gone to the window, to gaze at the brutal terrain with a thoughtful expression on her face. Outside, the darkness was a strange one. Intensely black, yet the snow seemed to gleam with its own spectral glow, which revealed areas that were radiantly luminous.

I said, 'We need to go to the cable car. It will take us down the mountain. We'll be safe there.'

Celeste spoke with icy calm. 'However, we must go outdoors to reach the station. What if we meet the beast on the way? We don't have weapons.'

'Run.'

'Robyn was running,' Kurt pointed out. 'Poor guy still didn't stand a chance.'

'I'll hear his screams for the rest of my life.' Rick looked close to vomiting.

Vince was becoming doubtful. 'It *was* a bear, wasn't' it? I mean, it couldn't be anything else, could it?'

Kurt's eyes blazed with sudden savagery. 'That bear will stand on a landmine, blow itself to fuck! Mark my words, it will soon be in shitty little pieces!'

'I don't think so.' Celeste wore an odd, dreamy expression. 'The creature should have been blown up long ago. It knows where the mines are buried – it knows to avoid them.'

Rick's eyes bulged with terror. 'That's why it's not a fucking bear. Didn't you see the horns? Curving backwards, like horns on a fucking ram.' Rick's expression screamed out that sheer panic had overwhelmed him. 'I'm getting out of here!'

Before any of us could react, he sprinted for the door. Threads of blood red veins stood out against the whites of those bulging eyes as he ran. He began yelling, but there were no actual words – this was the disgorging of raw terror in a primal scream – the kind of scream his ancestors would have made before being torn apart by wolves in a prehistoric forest. He clawed at the door, pulling back bolts, dragging the door open, admitting a shrieking wind that blew out the candles, plunging us into the deepest gloom.

Celeste and I pounced on Rick, whereupon we succeeded in pulling him back from the yawning doorway that led out into a raging blizzard. And where that 'thing' might lurk.

'Rick, calm down,' I yelled as I held on tight.

Celeste tried to soothe him, stroking the side of his face. 'It's okay, it's okay.'

'It killed Robyn!' howled Rick. 'And it's going to kill us!'

I bellowed at Kurt and Vince, who did nothing other than stare at us, like they'd been stunned by a bolt of electricity: 'Don't just stand there! Shut the fucking door! We don't want that animal in here with us!'

The very real possibility of a raging beast lunging through the doorway did the trick. Both Vince and Kurt raced to the door, slammed it shut, before driving the bolts across.

Celeste shouted, 'We need to see! Light the candles!'

It took three of us to hold Rick down as he screamed, 'We'll be killed! That monster is going to eat us!'

Candles relit. Celeste staring out of the window. Kurt and Vince sitting on either side of Rick (poor, frightened out of his mind, Rick). They occupied the sofa that was probably the venue for much fucking back when Communist overlords ruled. Nobody talking. Everyone so tensed up I fully expected muscles to surrender to the strain of unbearable tension, and for snapping biceps and rupturing abdominal muscles to burst out from my friends' bodies. *Dear God … Anxiety and terror, conjuring horrible thoughts inside my aching skull.*

Then Rick muttered something that sent fresh shudders through my body. 'The monster took Robyn into the cellar beneath that chalet over there. What if the monster can get to us through the cellar under this building?' He pointed at the floor.

I pulled out my phone (not to make a call; no damn signal up here on this Godforsaken rock) and switched on the phone's flashlight. My friends turned their faces away from me, as if they suddenly hated me. *Maybe they will push me out through the door – a sacrifice to the beast?* I forced the paranoid notion back into the part of my brain from where it had so dangerously oozed. *These are my friends. Why am I thinking things like this? The light dazzled them, that's all.* I reasoned that the horrific situation was responsible for such wayward thoughts. *Pull yourself together. Do something constructive.*

Lowering the phone by my side, so it didn't dazzle everyone, I tried to muster a firm tone. 'I'll go down into the cellar and check that any outer doors are locked.'

They stared back at me. A couple gave small nods. If I'd expected volunteers to accompany me, I was going to be disappointed. Nevertheless, I headed into a hallway where I figured I might find the cellar entrance. No cellar door there, just doors that led to other rooms – a dining room, then a private cinema with rows of flip-down seats, then an office equipped with a huge desk where Communist chiefs signed death warrants, no doubt. Another door led into a kitchen. There, I found a door that, upon my opening it, revealed steps going down into utter darkness. The worse part of my discovery was the scrotum-shrivelling blast of cold air that roared up the stairwell. This was the cellar, alright. And someone had left the outside door open.

Okay, call it pride, but I couldn't return to the others with the admission I'd been too scared to enter the cellar. Even though the maneater might be down there, I descended the steps, shining the phone light ahead of me, killing darkness, revealing stone walls coated with ice. White clouds vented from my lips. My heart hammered. I wanted to scream. Not because I'd seen anything that might slaughter me, but screaming would feel good – screaming would release the tension that painfully twisted my muscles into knots.

Here, there were desks on which stood antique phone apparatus. A fax machine, covered in dust, had vomited waxy fax paper from an aperture in a long stream, downward onto the floor. It looked like a frozen waterfall. This was a bunker – it had to be. A refuge, in case this playground for the party elite was ever attacked. They could hunker down here and send fax messages to their generals: *Perfidious America has infiltrated our country with assassins.* What I saw next ripped any other thoughts from my skull. A steel door yawned open to reveal darkness, threaded with streaks of snowflakes.

'Close the door!' The command to myself echoed back from the walls.

The moment I reached that bullet-proof slab of a door, I began trying to get the thing shut, because the beast might suddenly lurch from the darkness. Even as I fought to close the door, I pictured claws ripping my face.

'C'mon, you fucker! Move!'

The door did not move.

Frantically, I checked the door. Had hinges rusted to the point of immovability? Had the door been locked open in some way? When I glanced downward, I finally understood. Snow had drifted against it. Not deep snow, but when I kicked the drift that held the door open, I realised it had frozen as hard as concrete. Immediately, I began looking for an axe or shovel I could use to clear the obstruction. Of course, there were no tools. What I noticed, however, were metal brackets that supported shelves of documents. The brackets were absurdly over-engineered chunks of ironmongery – something typical of Communist era factories, when even a humdrum item like a shelf bracket was produced with the same mindset as the factories that built hulking battle tanks. With a savage burst of strength, I grabbed hold of the iron bracket and succeeded in ripping the thing from the wall, cascading documents onto the floor, which in turn spilled out photographs of men and women hanging by their necks in prison courtyards.

A roar blasted through the doorway. *The monster is here …* I spun around, ready to fight the creature with the heavy bracket. My eyes watered, my heart all but detonated with terror inside my chest. I lunged forwards swinging the bracket, aiming for …

Aiming for what? There was nothing there. No tall creature with black fur and fangs. Storms winds had generated the roar I heard. That's all. Thereafter, I set to work. Gripping the bracket in two fists, I chopped at the ice that held the door open. My flesh quickly became fiery hot with exertion. Two minutes later and, thank God, the door was free. Now, it easily swung shut, allowing me to slide across three formidable bolts. Thirty years ago, that barrier would hold assassins at bay. Yet would it keep the creature out? Panting hard, I leaned back against the door and let the bracket fall from my trembling fingers. *You've done it,* I told myself. *You've locked the brute out.*

Then the change came.

Yes, it was cold inside the cellar. Frigid air tingling my skin. But the change that came brought with it a new kind of cold. Suddenly, the inside of my bones felt to be freezing. The blood in my heart painfully turned into what I can only compare to a thick, ice-cold slush, though this was an irrational comparison, I know. However, that's the frightening impression I had. *Heart attack.* That's what I thought was happening to me. *My heart is failing.* The cold invading the very core of my bones made them hurt so much. I clutched at my aching arms and chest in turn. And then something began to push from the other side of the door. The door moved inward by half a centimetre before the bolts prevented the door from opening any further. Metalwork creaked. Someone, or something, pushed so forcefully that the metal slab juddered. After that, a scraping sound. Claws against metal. Not frenzied clawing … surely, this was meant to torment me, the human being, on the other side of the door.

'You're not coming in.' Why I muttered those words I don't know. Maybe the sound of my voice would reassure me. 'Go away or … I'll kill you.'

Yeah, with what? Suddenly, the shelf bracket I'd used to chop the ice seemed a flimsy weapon. I closed my eyes. Did I imagine it, or could I hear the rasping breath of the beast on the other side of the door? What I did hear next was a sudden roar. My eyes snapped open.

The noise seemed to go beyond natural sounds I heard with my ears. The roar – and it definitely came from a beast – was as unpleasant as it was visceral. Something like the roar of a lion, yet more savage, more resonant with bloodlust. And now, flooding along every nerve, came a sense of absolute dread. That dread didn't come from my own fear, rather it seemed to be poured into my body from outside of me. I can only describe it as an infusion of dread from an external source. What I can say with absolute certainty is that the sense of dread paralysed me. Moving my arms became impossible. My jaw dropped open, leaving me with an idiot's slack mouth. I tried to retreat to the cellar steps. Couldn't. Couldn't even move my fucking feet. Darkness swirled into my brain ... it rode in on the back of the utter dread that flooded my nerves. I tried to shout ... couldn't. Tried to scream for help ... couldn't.

'I want to go to bed with you.'

Those impossible words from God knows who brought me out of the trance with a jolt. I could move again: the spell was broken.

There, approaching me, delicately placing one foot in front of the other, came Celeste. The white fur coat she wore appeared to give her a shimmering aura as the long hairs moved in the cold air. Her brown eyes fixed hard onto mine with a power that was nothing less than mesmerising.

'It's true,' Celeste purred. 'This vacation was going to be the one where I welcomed you into my bed.'

This absolutely wasn't the time for such a conversation. Therefore, I hissed, 'Celeste, we need to get out of here. That animal is on the other side of the door.'

'I hoped it would come to us.' She smiled again, red lips framing white teeth, the flash of her eyes transmitting undeniable glamour.

'You hoped it would come to us? Why on Earth would you hope for that?'

'To lure it in here – to trap it in the cellar. No, Tony, not to kill it. To keep it for ourselves.'

'You want to capture a bear. It killed Robyn!'

'Help me trap the creature. We will make a fortune.'

'Celeste. You're a dentist. Dentists are rolling in cash.'

'You can never be too rich.' She moved closer to me, until I could feel her warm breath on my face. 'My mother was rich when I was a little girl. We were secure in our big house. Then all her money vanished. I was too young to understand how that happened. What I did understand is that we had to live in a one room apartment in a festering slum. Many of our neighbours were the vilest kind of predators you could imagine. We heard every detail of their nasty lives through paper-thin walls. Therefore, you can never be too rich. Money brings safety.'

This woman bewildered me. I thought I knew her, but clearly not, and yet the powerful lure of her earlier statement about us sharing a bed had lit fires inside my heart – and somewhat further south inside my body than that.

'Celeste, how can a bear make you rich?'

'It's not a bear.'

'How so?'

'The creature,' she began in soft tones that were strangely enticing, 'is well known in Serbian folklore. It is known as a Bauk.'

'Mythical creatures don't kill people – they're not real. That fucking animal killed Robyn.'

'Creatures of myth and legend are memories of real animals. Memories that have been handed down through the centuries by our ancestors. Believe me, the Bauk is real –'

'What?' I interrupted with a snarl of contempt. 'Real? Like the Loch Ness Monster and unicorns and –'

'You saw it wasn't a bear.' This time she had interrupted me. 'We all knew that it was absolutely not a bear. Only Rick had the guts to describe it properly because you and the others daren't admit the evidence of your own eyes. We saw that it was a tall creature, gaunt as a starving man; that it walked on two legs. Yes, and it does have horns, backward curving horns, like those of a ram.'

'I went to school with a boy who had five fingers and a thumb on each hand. Six digits. Mutation shit happens.'

Celeste spoke calmly while looking in me in the eye with such an expression of sincerity on her face. 'I have spent a lot of time and money researching this example of cryptozoology.

There is ample evidence that the Bauk exists; however, when the Communists ruled this country, they brutally suppressed all evidence of the Bauk when citizens reported sightings. The Communists didn't want people to believe in the Bauk any more than they wanted people to believe in God. Tito yearned for a modern, secular state where its citizens were devoted to the socialist utopia.'

'It is a flesh and blood creature out there.'

'Perhaps it is,' she conceded. 'But that creature has a remarkable power. You felt it just moments ago. When I entered the cellar, I saw how you were leaning back against the door. You could not move. You experienced dread to such an intensity that you felt that you had been paralysed. I'm right, aren't I?'

Still, I tried to rationalise the horror monster away. 'No animal on Earth has the power to transmit bodily control instructions into another animal's nervous system, which restricts the movement of its limbs.'

'Don't be so sure about that, you handsome boy.' Flirtatious as ever. That's Celeste's way to control people. 'Once I was on a beach and saw dolphins hunting mackerel, just five metres away from me. Suddenly, I felt a distinct change inside my head. I'd been tensed up with worries about my dental practice. Times were hard, Tony. As I watched the dolphins splashing in the shallows, catching fish, I suddenly became calm. It was as if I'd been injected with a tranquiliser. All my worries vanished. I felt so relaxed. Later, I researched the dolphins' ability to transmit high-frequency clicks through water. This is their natural sonar that enables them to detect the fish they are hunting. What occurred to me is that the soundwaves also have the power to enter the nervous system of the fish and calm them to the point they become sluggish, which allows dolphins to catch their prey more easily. Those soundwaves the dolphins emitted reached me and dampened down my own nervous system. The Bauk has a similar power – maybe it's the soundwaves it emits when it roars, or maybe something else entirely – something that we have no knowledge of.'

Her calm tones seemingly had the power to reach deep into my own nervous system. Her assertion that a mythical creature actually existed was entirely believable. Besides, hadn't I seen the strangely elongated creature with my own eyes? Hadn't I seen the horns on its head for myself? The answer is a resounding 'yes'. As for its power to reach into the human brain. Hadn't I seen Robyn inexplicably slow from a run to a shambling walk when the creature pursued him? And hadn't I felt that intrusion of total dread when I had stood on the other side of the cellar door from the monster? Yes, I had. And it was such a strange sensation. I felt that malign intrusion passing through the layers of my skin, then penetrating the subcutaneous tissue before entering my flesh and blood and bones.

The Bauk was real. I couldn't deny its existence.

'You planned all this.' A sudden anger blazed inside of me. 'You tricked us into coming up here, knowing that this – this Bauk monster was living on the mountain.'

'I'm not a bad person, Tony. If any of you help me, I will share the millions that the Bauk will yield for us. My government will pay a king's ransom for a creature, which has the power to modulate human emotion. Think of the military applications. Enemy soldiers will flee in terror without firing a shot.'

'Celeste, it killed Robyn.'

'Nothing I can do will bring Robyn back.' She leaned closer to me to breathe these words into my face, 'Listen. I need your help. You go up the cellar steps and get ready to lock the door from the cellar into the kitchen. I'll open this door and –'

'No!'

'And let the creature in.'

'No, it'll kill you. Just like it killed Robyn.'

'I'll let it in, then slip out before it even knows I'm here, and before it can exert that influence on me. Then I close the door from the outside.' She gave an enticing smile. 'The Bauk will be trapped. We will become rich.'

'No, Celeste. That monster gets inside your head. You can't

move; you can hardly breathe. I refuse to help you.'

Celeste gave a heartfelt sigh of regret. 'Point taken. Okay, we stay here until it's safe to get off the mountain. According to legend, the Bauk is frightened of bright light. Daylight should be sufficient to drive it back into its cave or wherever it came from, then we head to the cable car station.' Celeste held out her hand, an invitation for me to walk ahead of her. 'We'll join the others. I've got something important to tell you all.'

I headed for the cellar steps, because even at that point I trusted her. When I heard the clank of steel, that's when I knew I had been utterly foolish to believe her sudden desire to get off this mountain at first light. Because Celeste hadn't followed me. Instead, she'd waited until I was sufficiently far enough away for me to stop her – that's when she'd seized her chance, disengaged the door bolts before swinging the door open. First to come roaring in were the brutal storm winds. A moment later, in *it* came. The creature. The Bauk. And it truly was a monster. Picture a stretched-out bear, seven feet tall, that walks on its hind legs. One with black fur, pale eyes – eyes that were almost completely white, apart from two black-as-night pupils that glared at us with total ferocity. Its face was similar to that of a bear yet flattened and therefore lacking a pointed nose. The jaws were not symmetrical. One side of the mouth curved upward, which gave the mouth a permanent snarl. The black horns that protruded from the sides of its skull glistened like they were wet. With the brute came a powerful odour, which I can only describe as wet mud from a stagnant ditch. At that moment, its jaws parted to reveal sharp, white teeth. The subsequent roar rebounded from the walls: the sound distorting and mutating into a frenzy of echoes, which mated with the original roar. The cacophony jabbed so fiercely into my skull I yelped in pain. Then the sound found the rivers of my heart and froze them – that's what it felt like. As if my heart had been replaced by a chunk of ice.

'You idiot,' I thundered at her. 'You fucking selfish idiot!'

She yelled back at me, 'Lock the cellar door. I'll close this one!'

And then Celeste's great, glorious plan fell apart. The moment the Bauk saw her, it lunged at her. Perhaps it had evolved to walk on four legs, not two, because that elongated body was so ungainly it blundered into a filing cabinet, causing the monstrosity to lose its balance, whereupon it dropped forwards onto all fours.

'Celeste!' I shouted. 'This way.'

Even then, at that moment of absolute crisis, I could tell that she considered trying to push by the monster to reach the outer door with the intention of closing it, to lock that thing inside the cellar. However, Celeste's confidence in her plans evaporated as the Bauk began to haul itself upright. If she ran for the door, she would be running into its arms that terminated in claws as sharp as zombie knives.

Celeste sprinted across the cellar toward me.

'Come on,' I shouted. 'I'll lock the door at the top of the steps!'

We ran up to the kitchen where I slammed the door shut. Yes, there was a lock. A good stout lock made of toughened steel.

But no key. There was no way of locking the door. And there was nothing I could see that would barricade it, either. The Bauk was free to come lurching into the chalet where it would dismember everyone there.

By now, I was grasping at any chance to save ourselves. 'We'll get the others. Then we run to the cable car while that fucking thing is finding its way out of the cellar.'

Celeste and I raced into the lounge where our friends sat on the sofa. They stared at us, their eyes huge and glittery with alarm. Clearly, they realised we'd just experienced one hell of a shock.

'It's in the chalet!' I yelled. 'Run!'

Celeste added with a full-blooded shout. 'We're going to the cable car!'

From the kitchen, the clatter of plates being swept off a worktop onto the floor. What followed the sound of breaking pottery was the roar of the monster. Before I'd even mentally processed what we were doing, we were outside, running as fast as we could, our feet exploding white shrouds as our boots smashed into snowdrifts. It was still night, the sky black. A blizzard began to assault the mountaintop, yet what struck us didn't feel like soft snowflakes – these flakes were hard and sharp, like splinters of glass. They stung our eyes to the point all we could see were blurred shapes of our surroundings.

There, ahead of us, the cable car station. When we'd arrived, it had only been a short walk to the chalet. Now, the station seemed far off, across deep snow that was increasingly difficult to traverse as we sank in it to the depth of our knees.

From behind us, the Bauk gave a massive bellow as it came lurching from the chalet on its hind legs. Instantly, it spotted us. The hunt was on. Its uncanny white eyes blazed with ferocity. And, relentlessly, it moved in that unsteady shamble toward us. I now understand that the Bauk radiated some strange power beyond the boundaries of its flesh. Somehow, its evil aura reached us – and that aura penetrated the brains of each and every one of us.

Rick's face was wet with tears. 'My legs … I can hardly move my legs.'

'It can do that to us.' My heart was pounding. 'Like paralysis.'

We had been running until the creature reached into our nervous system, where it exerted its power to slow the movement of our limbs. Yes, we were still moving forwards, but each of my feet felt like they weighed fifty pounds. My legs ached. My belly muscles hurt so much with the sheer exertion. Even my tongue felt strangely heavy in my mouth as I called out: 'Keep moving. Whoever … whoever reaches the cable … car first, open the doors … get ready to use the controls.'

Vince began to weep with despair. 'I can't go much further. I'm exhausted.'

Kurt pointed to his right. 'We don't have to follow the path. We can take a short cut, across that flat area.'

Celeste nodded. 'He's right. We'll reach the station quicker.'

A fresh surge of terror blasted through my veins. 'We can't!

Look at the sign … it's a bloody minefield.'

'It's okay.' A frantic hope transformed Rick's face into a grinning mask that was disturbing to see. 'The mines are old. They won't work. C'mon.'

Rick began to lope across undulating snow, lifting his feet absurdly high with every step, like he was taking part in a hurdles race.

'No,' I shouted, 'we must go around the minefield. Stick to the path we used earlier.'

'Fuck that!' shouted Kurt. 'That thing's getting closer.'

He was right. The Bauk was perhaps less than a hundred paces away. Though possessing an ungainly shuffle, it moved faster than us, especially now that it used its malign power to make our legs feel so incredibly heavy. Nevertheless, we followed Rick as he loped in that peculiar high-stepping way, like he didn't want his feet to linger too long on ground that played host to buried canisters of high explosive.

Despite it being night, the intense whiteness of the snow allowed us to see enough. The oblongs of the chalets were behind us. The bigger oblong of the cable car station squatted ahead of us. The car was inside, which meant we couldn't see it. However, I could make out the cables that would carry the car downwards – the cables standing out as dark threads against the snow-covered mountain across the valley.

This was a life-or-death journey across the snow. We moved like weary soldiers plodding across no-man's land of World War One. Each of us knew, we were in a killing zone. And that this was the dominion of apocalyptic danger – because a monster pursued us. Sharp-toothed, razor-clawed, hungry for the meat on our bones.

I pictured landmines, hanging in a brownish mist that was the soil beneath my feet. Indeed, I confess, my treacherous imagination had gone rogue again. In my mind's eye, the landmines were akin to rounded eggs. Instead of unborn birds, there was the slumbering yolk of explosive. The Bauk roared again – loud enough to dislodge a thick cap of white on a sloping chalet roof.

Whether it was exhaustion, or terror, or the malignant power of the Bauk, I don't know, but my mind seemed to detach itself from my brain. My mind soared high above me, becoming something akin to a drone that filmed our progress. There we were: Vince, Kurt, Celeste and myself, moving in a cluster. Rick was well ahead of us now, just thirty paces from the station. While pursuing us, the Bauk, leaving deep pawprints in the snow. Its breath gusted from its jaws in flashes of white vapour. It did not tire. Nor did it fear us. The thing was pure savagery contained within a pelt of black fur. Maybe I was preparing to die, for I no longer felt the sting of ice splinters driven on vicious storm winds. I didn't feel cold. I didn't feel panic. My friends were slowing down as exhaustion took its toll.

I asked myself these questions: *Which one of my friends will be caught first? Do I stop and try to save them from the creature? Or do I keep running to save my own skin?*

The explosion felt like some very strong individual had punched the side of my head. The flash dazzled me. There was a vile stench of burning. White hot pieces of metal from the mine casing moved so fast through the air they drew straight lines up into the darkness. I saw what remained of Kurt falling in steaming lumps onto the snow. Pieces of my friend formed a ring of wet body parts around a crater that had been created by the blast. *I wonder if the monster will stop to eat Kurt? That will buy us some time to escape.* Yes, a grotesquely selfish wish. But there you have it. When faced with trying to save our lives, we only think about ourselves.

Though I'd been partly deafened by the bang, I did hear Celeste shouting, 'Keep running! Nearly there!'

We survivors needed no further encouragement. We kept on running, though 'managing to achieve an exhausted shuffle' is a more accurate description. Rick had almost reached the station by now, despite moving slowly due to the inhibiting effects cast upon us by the Bauk. The Bauk, meanwhile, lurched past Kurt's bloody remains without even glancing at them. So much for pausing to eat.

Another deluge of thunder engulfed me. This time, I fell flat on my face into the snow. Instantly, I began grasping at my feet, because I truly believed I'd stood on a mine.

'One, two …' All my feet were there.

I struggled to lift my face out of the snow. My body felt so heavy I was sure I'd sink down into frozen muck beneath the layer of white, then keep sinking through bedrock. Celeste, having been knocked off her feet by the blast, managed to sit up. Blood trickled from her nose.

'Vince … Vince!'

Again, I'd been almost deafened by the sheer decibels generated by the exploding mine. Though I could make out that Celeste was shouting Vince's name.

Vince crawled toward me, his eyes locking onto mine, beseeching me to help him. Vince moved quickly, skittering over ripples of snow. He could move fast, you see, because the bottom half of him had gone. Consequently, he'd lost a considerable amount of body weight. Flesh, trailing from the point just below his navel, where he'd been cut in half by the exploding mine, formed things tantamount to nightmarish paintbrushes that were wet with blood. They painted crimson lines in the snow as he moved, rapid as a snake.

'Tony, help me,' cried Vince. 'Take my hands. Pull me to the station. Don't let that thing catch me!'

His eyes were as bright as lightbulbs as he gazed up into my face. All our years of friendship were contained in that bright-eyed look he gave me. I held out my hands to him, just as a parent holds out their hands to a child that has fallen and needs help to stand again.

And then the Bauk took him. For once, hunger overwhelmed its instinct to hunt. Reaching in through the sloppy wet wound that was the bottom of Vince's torso, it forced its paw up through Vince's stomach to reach what must have been the delicious morsel that was his still-beating heart. The monster pulled out Vince's heart, and took obvious pleasure in watching me as its teeth bit into the pulsating organ that jetted threads of blood from severed arteries.

As Vince's heart had been ripped from his body he'd

screamed. Yes, he was dead now. But his scream lived on as an echo, as it went shrieking and reverberating amongst the mountains.

The monster devouring my friend's warm and generous heart gave us enough time. Memories of what happened next come back to me as if they are nothing more than black and white photographs taken a hundred years ago.

An image of us running. Celeste and me. Into the station, into the cable car. Rick stands by the control panel. Slam go the doors! Shut against cold air and nightmare beast. The loud crank of cogs, the hum of electric motors, the car swaying as the station births its metal child into cold night air.

Far below, the town's lights are shining. We are clinging to one another, sobbing, telling each other everything is going to be alright. We are wailing the names of our friends who died tonight – though, in reality, we wail so loud, and with such tearful passion, because we are relieved it's them, not us, that died. God, or evolution, embedded a profoundly selfish gene into our flesh. *As long as it is me that survives, that's all that matters.*

Then fragmentary memories of the cable car gliding down through the soulless void, to convey us to the warmth of the hotel, where we reported the tragic events to visibly sceptical police officers, then the soothing blast of a hot shower to ease away pain from aching limbs ... and, later, many restorative glasses of brandy. After five hours sleep, tormented by awful dreams, I felt compelled to sit down in my hotel room and record what happened to us while it was still fresh in my mind. So, you have now read my story. Make of it what you will.

Police description of video footage presented to Coroner's hearing, Belgrade, 30/10/2025. Note: the events described hereafter occurred twenty-six hours after the return of Westkirk and his companions by cable car from the mountain top. It should be further noted that the CCTV camera develops a still undiagnosed technical fault at 06:48.

Footage reveals the following:-

CCTV – Camera 3 – Hotel Onyx – Lobby. Onscreen date and time: 10/02/2025. 06:46.

On camera are Hotel Manager: Marina Obrenovic, Receptionist: Jovan Haas. Hotel guests: Tony Westkirk, Richard Fairburn, Celeste Mehmet. A scene of frantic activity, suggestive of panicking individuals, either searching for an escape route from danger or for somewhere to hide. Apples and oranges from a bowl on the reception desk lie scattered across the floor.

Audio: Mehmet shouts: 'It's here! It must have followed us down from the mountain!'

The five victims run about the lobby at considerable speed. Suddenly, they slow their movements, as if overcome by some narcotic, until they either stand still or walk very slowly and with difficulty. Then, what appears to be a large bear enters the lobby.

Here, CCTV footage ends. The screen goes dark.

Audio: screams – just screams – then nothing more.

MANANANGGAL

In 1992, a story made its way into the Chicago Tribune *concerning some strange events during a local election in the Tondo district of Manila, in the Philippines. The newspaper reported that the election process had been disrupted by a widespread scare story in that part of the city, local people refusing to come out to vote, and locking their windows and barring their doors because, they said, a manananggal was hunting there.*

Filipino urban legend doesn't record the outcome of the election, but it does have plenty to say about the mysterious manananggal. But to understand the nature of this terrifying entity properly, and the impact it can still have in the modern world, we should first take a look at the history of horror movie making in the Philippines, the very first entry in which canon, way back in 1927, the work of one José Nepomuceno, was called Manananggal.

The film itself no longer exists. There is no script remaining, no written version of the storyline and apparently no living memory of it. The only existing clue to its contents comes from a single newspaper review from that same year, which compliments the filmmakers for their imagination and the startling visual effects they created with a small budget. However, the film was popular at the time, popular enough in the Philippines to spawn a homegrown horror film industry that has demonstrated astonishing longevity and created multiple hits like The Twilight People *(1972), and much more recently,* Feng Shui *(2004) and* Eerie *(2018). Part of this success owes to the style of Filipino horror cinema, which has produced successive movies notable for their immersive magic and mysticism. This is primarily because, while western horror filmmakers only seemed to discover 'folk horror' in the late 1960s, Filipino cinema commenced mining its own folklore back in 1927 with the aforementioned* Manananggal, *and it's a vast realm through which they have roamed ever since.*

So, what exactly is the manananggal?

MANANANGGAL

Given how many movies it has featured in, it's probably tempting to consider it the Philippines' trademark monster. Their own version of Romania's vampire, France's werewolf or the USA's bigfoot. But in actual fact, the manananggal isn't nearly so grand. It's only one example of an incredible range of devilish entities populating Filipino folklore, collectively known as the 'aswang'.

In its most straight-to-the-point sense, 'aswang' means 'evil creatures'. It's a general term for all manner of malevolent, supernatural beings. The tyanak, for example, which shapeshifts into a baby, lies in the jungle and cries, and when a rescuer arrives, resumes its monstrous shape, killing them and sucking their blood. Or the usikan: a witch or sorcerer, who can inflict damage and death through the simple use of words. Or the weredog, which does exactly what you'd expect it to do (though it doesn't transform into a pet, you can be sure of that). And then ... the manananggal.

To modern eyes at least, the manananggal must easily be among the ghastliest monsters still feared in the world today, an undeniable testament to the strength of Filipino folk belief. The Philippines, we should remember, was subjugated to Spanish colonial control for several hundred years, Roman Catholicism becoming a huge alternative to Taoism, and then, after World War Two, to a massive American presence, both of which influences have left that beautiful Asian archipelago steeped in western culture. The fact that the manananggal survived all that is impressive, all the more so when one learns how extreme a monster it is.

From the outset, it should be stated that the manananggal is a kind of vampire, but very different from the western variety. Often in western popular culture, we have smoothed out and even sanitised our most horrific stories. The werewolf, therefore, instead of a scheming, voracious killer, has become a sad, forlorn individual, appalled by the crimes he commits. The vampire, instead of a walking, blood-soaked corpse, is now a lonely, handsome aristocrat of the night. Even our female monsters have changed, from the cackling hags and beldams of the deep medieval forests to beautiful seductresses whom mortal men might even fall in love with. Not so the manananggal, though its female nature and the fact it can also appear beautiful are aspects of the monster that serve its predatory instinct well.

To start with, the manananggal is a product of the jungle. In all the folktales, the tangled Filipino rainforests are its abode and its birthplace. Thus, in primitive times, the manananggal would target isolated jungle villages, which it would simply traipse into in the guise of an unattached young woman, attractive of course, and looking for a home and a husband. Invariably some equally unattached village man, no doubt considering himself lucky, would oblige. This might be a young bachelor, but more likely would be a prosperous older man, perhaps a widower, as it would suit the manananggal best if it could locate a safe and secure home from which to operate and find respectability as the lady of a well-regarded house. Once the manananggal was implanted, it would commence trawling the surrounding villages for victims. Note, it would not prey upon its new family or their friends, as that would be too obvious. Besides, it almost never attacked male targets unless they were part of a newly-wedded couple, as its primary focus was on young women, preferably pregnant.

The manananggal's method of hunting was truly obscene. Once the household was asleep, it would slip quietly out and disappear into the jungle. There, it would find a secluded spot, possibly a cave, or a bower it had made out of undergrowth, or even a high perch, a branch or ledge perhaps, which it would be difficult for anyone else to ascend to.

Then … it would separate.

And that phrase, 'separate,' means exactly what it says.

The upper portion of the manananggal's body would detach from the lower portion, the legs, hips and sexual organs remaining where they were, upright but rigid, while the upper half of the monster would sprout a giant pair of bat wings and with ravels of hideous, ordure-dripping entrails dangling below it, take flight. The demonic thing would make no sound as it travelled through the darkness, save for the bony clicking of its wing joints. Once it had settled on its target, it would simply perch on the window or roof, and from its mouth extend a mosquito-like proboscis, which would lengthen as much as it needed to as it penetrated down through any chinks or faults in the building, finally piercing the swollen belly of the sleeping mother-to-be. The manananggal would then suck out anything vital: the unborn baby, the organs, the viscera, the blood of course, and all other life-giving fluids. If the victims were newly-weds, the same process would be repeated with the sleeping husband, the manananggal drinking him dry.

After that, it would take to the wing again (presumably considerably heavier), return to its motionless lower half, meld itself back into one, and return quietly to its husband's bed. Those it had feasted on meanwhile would be discovered in the morning, a dried-out, papery wreckage unrecognisable as anything human.

It should be pointed out that there are several other creatures of the dark in southeast Asian folklore, upper sections of which fly by night and vampirise their victims. The *ahp* of Cambodia, the *rokurokubi* of Japan, the *penanggal* of Malaysia and the *leyak* of Indonesia all possess similar qualities, and yet, for some reason, the manananggal remains the benchmark horror creature in the Philippines. But it doesn't really take a genius to work out why.

A monster that doesn't need to waylay you in some lonely spot, or break into your house, but instead sits unnoticed on your roof, and in the morning your lovely young wife has been reduced to a shrunken, mummified husk, is not to be taken lightly.

COCKATRICE
Sarah Singleton

1644

Viewed from the hills, the valley seems full of trees and in its acres of damp woods and brambly marsh you might still find a beaver's lodge. Travel down and see between the trees there are overgrown meadows and small barren fields which, not long ago, grew rich harvests of wheat, barley and peas. Closer to the village, the road widens. The surface is pocked and rutted by the hooves of horses and cartwheels. Over the bridge stands the market cross and public house, a smithy, the lock-up. In the upper room of an old house next to the church is a damp wood-panelled room where a man is writing. Infected with the apocalyptic fever of the age, he's haunted by visions of corruption and chaos and describes how the country is coming to pieces. The writer trims the end of his quill, dips it in ink and continues his tract. When the pamphlet is written and printed, it falls into the hands of John Philips, who will take it to the cottage in the woods he shares with his sister.

Hear me! I, Josiah Turner, second son of the preacher Thomas Turner, have listened to the voice of Our Lord in these times of the tribulations of the People of England. We are sorely tried, due to the wickedness of the people, the vain and murderous ambitions of those who set themselves in authority over us. And the Lord has turned his face from this Most Blessed of Kingdoms, has withdrawn his Grace, as the Once Great Men of this land, have resorted to fighting one against the other, and the People who should be as one family have turned into Monsters – far worse than beasts, for what beasts kill their brethren and starve their own children?

But the Lord has sent visions unto me, and I have

witnessed his Signs and Wonders. I have seen blood on the face of the moon. I have seen the handwriting of Our Lord inside the bark of trees, and angels rise from the water, their hands covering their faces. I have seen the Cockatrice strike with a glance and kill all living things – man and beast and the flowers and fruits of the fields.

My sister Agnes puts her hand on my arm and tells me she's heard enough. I place the pamphlet on the table. Above the text is an illustration: the design of a man with a wolf's head. He holds a sword in his hand upon which a baby is impaled. A devil dances at his feet. Above his head, two angels stare down, open-mouthed. The cockatrice – a beast with a cock's head and wings, and the body of a snake – is suspended in the air between them.

'These are truly the last days,' she says. Agnes is twenty-five but so thin and pinched, she looks like an old woman and is already a widow. Agnes is recovering from the bloody flux, which carried off her two-year-old son a few weeks ago. Food is hard to come by and of poor quality. Grief and illness have stripped away what little flesh, what little hope, she had left.

'The leaflets are all over the village, and further,' I say. 'Some were reading them. Others were using them to light their pipes. One man boasted he'd wipe his arse with it. But Mr Turner has his followers.'

She gives me a straight look. 'He draws too much attention. Be careful, brother. I do not want to lose you too.'

Our cottage is simple, with one room downstairs and a loft above with two beds. Agnes keeps the flagstones clean, and we have two wooden chairs left to us by our mother, who inherited them from her mother before her. Although modest, it always used to be a comfortable place – neatly thatched, a garden flourishing with fruit trees, vegetables and salads. My sister's husband owned a few acres: a patch of damp meadow and a piece of arable land, as well as a coppice wood and the cottage, and it is this piece of land I shall tend, in place of the husband who was killed by deserters from one of Parliament's armies.

The soldiers also trampled the garden and pulled apart the thatch at one end (they stole it for fuel, she says). The arable field is still unsown, growing over with weeds. Agnes no longer has a pig though it was the King's men who took that.

It is already August and she worries. What will we eat, over winter, if there's no harvest to take in, no pig to slaughter? She has repeated the question to me several times this afternoon.

Someone tries the cottage door. Finding it barred, the visitor knocks.

We glance at one another.

'Open it,' she says. 'Or they'll break it down.' This has happened before, I judge by the rough repair.

Two men are standing on our doorstep – one I know and one I have never seen before. The one I know is tall and well proportioned, with flaxen hair and a long brown coat. His companion is shorter, broad across the shoulders, with a black beard. I look back into the cottage, where Agnes stands, wringing her hands.

'Agnes, it's our brother.'

William pushes past me into the cottage and his companion follows. Will wraps his arms around me in a tight embrace.

'John!' he says, then proceeds to our sister, who shrinks away.

'Be gentle with her, Will.'

Agnes plucks the cloth of her apron and kneads it in her fingers. She looks from Will to the other man.

'I would not have recognised you Agnes,' Will says softly. 'It's been five years, but even so.'

Then he turns to me again. 'John – this is Henry Bridges. He and I travelled from London together. We had the carriage leave us on the highway and walked the last mile up through the wood. Like old times.'

How well-fleshed and well-dressed they are these visitors from London. Henry Bridges makes a stiff bow and raises his hat to our sister.

Behind his back, Agnes gives me another straight look.

I invite them to sit, and we converse about their journey and my brother's employment in London. Agnes begins to prepare a meal. She has a broth of pea soup warming over the fire and finds a meagre few leaves of spinach and sorrel, water cress and mint, which she finely chops.

'There's no bacon to be had,' she says, when she spoons the savoury mess into wooden bowls.

Our guests take the chairs and I sit on the bench while we eat. Agnes keeps her distance. The cottage door remains open. Afternoon sunlight catches the buckles of my brother's boots, the gold of his hair.

'Why are you here?' I say. 'How long are you staying?'

They exchange glances, my brother and Mr Bridges.

'Brother, I have explained that I serve the Parliamentarian cause,' Will says. 'It's upon that business that I've come. I want to find out the conditions for the people living here. I know the king's men have caused a great deal of hardship, and there is grief and discontent. I've been asked to collect intelligence from the people themselves. It is my root and origin in this district, it is you, my family, that make me the man to do it.'

'Well, you can see how our sister has suffered,' I say quietly. 'Her husband had no wish to be part of the war and was pressed into the army by the followers of Mr Cromwell, while last year's harvest and this year's pig were taken by the king's men. Irregular soldiers and deserters are causing misery. They are – both sides – plundering and despoiling the fields and farms. Hunger is everywhere.'

Mr Bridges glances at Agnes. Will looks a little guilty as though he is to blame.

'There is a cost to war,' he says. 'We've all paid a heavy price. And once we've won, order will be restored. You will be recompensed, Agnes.'

The words sound fine but I would say his voice is not entirely certain. Our sister shoots him another fierce glance, as though to ask if Parliament had the competence to replace her husband and child.

'You have the authority to say so?' I ask.

Just at that moment, a blackbird hops into the cottage

through the open door and perches on the threshold, turning its head to consider us. The light catches its bright beak and the golden ring around its eye. I have never seen such a blackbird so bold – it flies up to the table and is about to taste the remains of the broth in Mr Bridges bowl when Agnes steps forward and shoos it away.

My brother asks if they might stay for a couple of nights in the cottage while they carry out their business. They appreciate its discreet location. I look to Agnes and she nods.

Do we have any choice?

When she clears the bowls away, Mr Bridges spies the pamphlet written by second-son Josiah Turner and he begins to read it. I tell him the county is over-run with Levellers, Seekers and the rest, though Mr Turner seems intent on creating a sect of his own.

'And what is his particular view?' Mr Bridges asks, carelessly dropping the paper.

'He believes that if God is in all things, then God must be in all his creatures and indeed all living things, and so mankind must be mindful and remember he is neither better nor pre-eminent,' I say.

'Did God not give us stewardship of the Earth and the living things in it?'

'A steward is one who manages and takes care of others, for their benefit,' I respond. 'As creatures made in God's image we have greater responsibilities. It is against God's wishes for us to wantonly or cruelly destroy each other, or the land, or the creatures who share it with us.'

Mr Bridges sniffs. He says he's tired from the journey and will rest. Will and I go outside, into the garden.

Bees hover about the lavender. House martins swoop over our heads and up to their nests under the eaves. The shady woods echo with the music of turtle doves and song thrushes. Will seems troubled, sighing, rubbing the scrap of pale beard on his chin.

He asks how long I have been living with our sister and who it is I associate with in the village and in town. He wants to know how deep dissatisfaction runs, and whether it is the king's men or Parliament they hold responsible for their suffering. He asks for names, which I do not provide.

'Life has become very difficult for us,' I confide.

'I do understand the country hereabouts has been badly troubled by the civil wars,' Will says. He leans forward and lowers his voice – glancing from side to side, as though there might be listeners in the trees.

'We've heard rumours that the people here are in such discontent that they're organising their own militia,' he says.

'Is that so?' I try not to laugh but a snort escapes me. 'And how will they arm themselves? With pitchforks? Ah no. Even those have been taken.'

Will's head gives a contemptuous little shake. He wants me to take him seriously. 'They call themselves the Clubmen.' He has my pamphlet in his hand – I hadn't noticed he had picked it up.

'Do you think, John, this Josiah Turner might be one of them?' He is grasping at straws. I sense the weight of responsibility hanging over him, wonder who in Parliament has despatched him to return to his home county and entreat with his own people.

'Do you have any idea how many preachers there are? How many ranters and ravers? They sprout from the ground by the dozen.'

I suggest we go for a walk in the woods. After a while the sense of oppression hanging over him seems to fade.

We reminisce about our childhoods and he tells me stories of London life. It seems almost like old times. When we return to the cottage, Mr Bridges says he is still tired and perhaps a little feverish so he will stay in bed. He urges me to take Will to the public house in the village to better gauge the situation, so we leave him in the care of my sister.

Around a dozen men are drinking at The Angel when we arrive. It is a warm evening, the windows wide open. Swifts fly screeching circles over the village. The publican's dogs lie panting outside. The drinkers remember my brother and welcome him warmly, eager to know about his life in the city and the progress of the war between the king and Mr Cromwell. When he asks them about the influence of war on the West Country, the men are diffident. They are simple men: millers and weavers, ploughmen and shepherds, yeomen and labourers, masons and quarrymen. Privately I know that not one of those gathered here has been unaffected by the matter of His Majesty King Charles I and his argument with Parliament.

On a stool in front of the pub, an old man starts to sing a song. It's an adaptation of an old favourite, an ancient lament, except in his updated version the singer tells of a beautiful young woman who is raped by one of the king's soldiers and consequently drowns herself in a pond. The conversation in the public house dies away and everyone listens to the odd, melancholy sound of the old man's voice. Like a golden ribbon, the melody floats in through the open window and winds in circles over our heads, bringing us together in a moment of such shared love and deep sorrow that even old Jeffries, the miller, spills a tear, and the wasps seem to stop their business and the swifts pause in their endless flights...

The song ends. The dogs get up and shake. Someone suggests a song we can all sing, something ribald like *Watkin's Ale*. Everyone laughs. I turn to Will and tell him we should set off before it gets too dark and with a nod, a look and a goodbye to the men in the pub, I lead him out and along the road.

It is cool now. The sky is deep blue, the street softened by twilight. Here and there hot yellow light shines through a window. Smoke drifts from chimneys and a bat swoops down over our heads. As we walk out of the village, past the old Roman Bridge, Will seems agitated. He waves his hand in front of his face, which is sweaty and pale.

'Brother, are you sick?' I say.

I can't hear what he answers because his speech is mumbled and hard to understand. I quicken the pace, wanting to be out of the village as soon as possible.

'Did you drink too much?'

Will turns from me and seems to address someone to his

right, someone I cannot see.

'Who are you talking to, Will?'

'She is a beautiful woman, John. Slender and fair. But her eyes frighten me.'

'Which woman?'

'This woman,' he says, impatient, gesturing to the right.

'Describe her, Will. I can't see her.'

He looks at me as though I'm a lunatic and indeed at that moment a great silver moon rises up over the trees on the other side of the valley as we climb the hill out of the village.

'She's a dead woman, brother, but more beautiful than any I've seen. She's dressed in black and her hair is black and loose, and it looks drenched, as though she's walked out of deep water. And her skin is white and the moonlight makes it shine.'

I think of the woman in the song, who drowned herself, and the angels in Mr Turner's pamphlet, rising from water.

'What frightens you about her eyes?'

'Empty eyes,' he says. 'No colour. There's no soul inside her.' Will staggers and I catch him, hold him upright. Sweat drips from his forehead.

'My head aches,' he says. 'I have a fever.' He tries to sit down but I urge him on. We need to get into the wood and off the road.

Once in the trees, the darkness thickens. Twigs and branches pass the face of the moon.

'Is she still with us?' I say. Will rallies a little, pulls away from me to walk by himself. He still talks, but his voice is low and mumbling, obscuring the words. He sounds like a man speaking in his sleep.

'What are you talking about?'

'I asked her what manner of beast she carries,' he says. 'It is under her arm. I couldn't make out what it was. It has the scaled body of a dragon but the head of a cockerel, fine-feathered. It's gold and red, all aflame.'

Sweat drips from his face and even in the twilight I can see how wide and empty his own eyes are, as though the lids have been stretched back.

167

'The cockatrice,' I murmur. He too is remembering Josiah Turner's pamphlet: the beast that kills all.

'You can't see her?' His voice is soft, almost pitying.

'No,' I say. 'I can only see you.'

My brother stops and stares, his face filled with terrible doubt. He looks at me as though I'm a stranger, and then speaks again to the invisible other but his speech is slurred and garbled.

'My head hurts,' he says, pressing the palms of his hands to his temples. 'It feels like someone is knocking a nail into my skull.' He looks up at the tree tops, staggers in a circle, reeling and moaning.

'She says you've killed me, John. Oh John, my brother!'

His body shudders and the muscles in his face twitch and spasm, but he gathers himself together and runs at me, dagger drawn, and knocks me to the ground. He holds the weapon above my throat to stab but I have greater control of my faculties and overpower him, rolling him onto his back and then I push the point of the dagger deep into his neck instead.

It is horrible, the way the sharp blade slides into the living skin and meat of him, grazing the bones in his neck while his eyes are fixed on mine and blood wells up into his mouth and spills out, so much dark blood. He struggles and chokes, noises I will never forget, and the dying seems to go on for a long, long time. My brother.

Finally, he is still. The moon looms over us. When I look up, I think I see them, the beautiful woman and the cockatrice. I shake my head. No. Only shadows.

My hands are shaking, sticky with my brother's blood. There is blood is on my sleeves too. I drag the body behind a hawthorn, cover it with last year's fallen leaves and start running home. I know the woods so well I find my way easily, even in the dark.

Agnes runs out of the house.

'Is he dead?' I ask.

'Yes.'

'Our brother's in the wood. Bring the spade, and I will drag the body, and we'll bury them together.'

Agnes does as I tell her. It takes four hours to accomplish the burial of the two men to my satisfaction. While we are busy and afraid, the gravity of what we are doing is kept at a distance, but I dread the arrival of daylight. As we walk back to the cottage, I say to my sister:

'We had to do it, Agnes.'

She nods.

'They knew about us, the Clubmen. He needed proof, and names. Our brother was working against us. He would have betrayed us.'

'You don't need to explain,' she says. Her voice is flat and cold. Her husband, children, and now her brother are all dead.

Our country is the Devil's land. The civil wars have destroyed men and beasts, and the crops we grow to feed ourselves. We are turned upside down, brother against brother. We are tired of the ruination of our farms, of being pressed into their armies, of the rape of our wives and daughters, of the taxes, of hunger and fear and working for nothing. We are preparing to defend ourselves, to protect our place against them all. We could not let him inform against us.

But for all my arguments, it is the primal sin, brother against brother – the Curse of Cain, Cain the wanderer, cast out of home forever.

The Clubmen are safe for a little time but when the sun rises, I will be on the white road, heading north.

Agnes hides all day in the house with the door barricaded. She lies on the bed where lately Mr Bridges lay – alive, and then dead – and she stares into the rafters of the cottage, at the hanging bunches of herbs. She has been slack of late in her husbandry: the dried plants are wrapped in webs and covered with dust, a kingdom of spiders. A robin has penetrated the broken thatch over one of the eaves and is making its nest.

I kneel beside Agnes, invisible, my wings laid over my back. She lies so still, for so long, I fancy the whole house – stone, wood, thatch, lime wash – could slowly melt back into its constituent parts, into the forest, and she would lie there just the same – staring upwards, seemingly empty, an imperishable body without a soul.

A day passes, and then a night. The trees murmur in the wind. The birds go about their business. At mid-day, her focus sharpens and her gaze latches on to my face. She sees the cockatrice on the floor beside the bed – the beast that kills with a glance – man and beast, fruits and flowers. Now it pecks at the boards like any ordinary fowl.

'Who are you?' she says. 'Josiah Turner said he had seen Beasts standing on two legs, like Men, to prophecy the Last Days. So are you one of God's creatures, or of the Devil's party, my lady, come to take me to Hell?' Her voice is small, slightly querulous, as though she's ready for an argument, prepared to complain.

I shake my head and place the palm of my hand on her cheek. She feels cold, a resonant, ancient cold, like a stone.

'I killed my brother,' she says. 'Belladonna in his broth.'

I keep my hand on her forehead, till it starts to sweat. Eventually she sighs, sits up in bed and weeps: for the murder of her husband, the death of her child, the killing of one brother and the exile of another, for the ruination of the land and the months of hunger behind and yet to come. But not for her: an empty bowl stands on the table. She has eaten her last meal and summoned me: Belladonna; the beautiful woman.

'It will end eventually,' I say. 'The war.'

'But there'll be other wars, and more grief and more suffering, Lady Death. There's no end to it.'

Agnes brushes the hair from her face, gets off the bed and climbs down the ladder to the living room. She is struggling to stand but opens the door, letting in the late summer sunshine, and the blackbird hops in again looking at her sideways.

This is where Josiah Turner will find her, lying over the threshold, on his way back to the village with a new pamphlet.

TITANOBOA

Is it possible that colossal, man-eating serpents still exist in hidden corners of the world? Snakes of such immense size and ferocity that they could easily swallow a fully-grown human being alive, and maybe even a cow or a horse, and then digest said unfortunate creature over a period of days?

It needs to be acknowledged straight away that there aren't many places in the modern world that could genuinely be considered 'hidden'. In the 21st Century, our cameras have been near enough everywhere on land, and if any such species was ever identified, there'd be red flags planted all over that region. But if that's the case, how do we explain an event of 1959, when a Belgian military pilot, Colonel Remy Van Lierde, was flying in a helicopter across the Katanga region of the Belgian Congo, only to be leapt at by a huge, angry serpent, which he estimated to be at least 70 feet in length? Even a reputable war hero like Van Lierde would have been unlikely to persuade anyone on his own that this story was true, so it was fortunate for him that a companion flying with him managed to photograph the monster, an image that is still pored over by experts today, the majority remaining baffled about what kind of animal it portrays.

Equally intriguing is the more recent photographic evidence provided by Northern Irish father and son team, Mike and Greg Warner, who in 2009 captured still shots of a gigantic snake slithering across a forested waterway in the Napo region of the Amazon, the same area in fact where in 1906, Britain's celebrated explorer, Colonel Percy Fawcett, disappeared while also on the trail of an immense snake. The Warner beast's length was estimated at an incredible 120 feet.

There are of course large snakes around today that science has studied.

In eastern Asia, the king cobra, which is venomous and therefore especially deadly, has been known to reach 18 feet in length. The

African rock python, a constrictor, can grow up to 20 feet, the Sumatran reticulated python to 25 feet, and the infamous green (or 'giant') anaconda of the Amazon basin, up to 34 feet. Be under no illusion, any one of these creatures is large and powerful enough to easily kill and devour an adult human. So, in a way, scaly, carnivorous monsters do exist. But all of them fall a long way short of the Warners' 120-footer. Of course, back in the dim and distant past, it was a very different story.

The titanoboa, whose relics have mainly been found in the Central American region, could grow up to 70 feet in length and was almost certainly the apex predator of its day. According to the fossil record, it flourished during the Paleocene era, which ended about 56 million years ago, at which point it went extinct. Possibly because of its dramatic sounding name, which was coined at the Florida Museum of Natural History, the titanoboa has come to symbolise the gigantic prehistoric serpent genus that haunts the imaginations of fantasy, sci-fi and horror writers the world over. But it wasn't the only example of its kind. Gigantophis, which inhabited what is now the North African region, commonly grew up to 40 feet and only passed out of existence around 40 million years ago. Likewise, the recently discovered vasuki indicus, a former inhabitant of the Indian subcontinent, grew to around 50 feet, and lived until 34 million years ago.

But if the titanoboa and its brethren died out all these trillennia into the past, what's the explanation behind the plethora of mysterious sightings that now pepper the internet's paranormal channels? Apparently, it wasn't just the Warners or Colonel Van Lierde who've got up close and personal with a raging mass of scales, fangs and forked tongue.

A casual browse on YouTube will display all manner of bizarre imagery. Everything from an implausibly huge snake being ridden along a jungle river by laughing locals, to a less friendly specimen slowly winding itself around a four-wheel drive van and crushing it like an empty beer can. In this latter one, a man appears in the background, lending a perspective that indicates this particular serpent is perhaps 80 or 90 feet in length.

We all know of course that internet footage often comprises trickery. Sadly for genuine cryptid hunters, it's too easy these days to fabricate such things. Some of them are embarrassingly obvious, but others are so cleverly done that it is usually only diligent enquiry into the back-story that 'outs' them. But even in this age of sophisticated hoaxes, it is still possible to believe that the titanoboa, or some version of it, might well have lived past its evolutionary expiry date and even into the era when humans dwelled on Earth.

There have long been legends in the deepest parts of the Amazon of the Yacumama, or Mother of the Water, an aquatic serpent of such gargantuan size that it has assumed godlike status among local tribes. The Yacumama, it is said, is a voracious hunter and eater of human beings, and yes, according to the traditions of the rainforest, it – she! – still exists. The fact that this creature only surfaces very occasionally is usually given as the reason why scientific discovery has been kept at bay.

If the Yacumama isn't enough, there is similar, perhaps even more terrifying folklore to be found in South Africa, where the Grootslang supposedly inhabits the depths of the Richtersveld cave system. Again, the Grootslang is a gigantic snake, but in this case a subterranean entity, which only rarely visits the world above, though when it does, it depopulates whole villages, clears corrals of their livestock and generally razes local human society to the ground. Seeing as the Grootslang is described as having an elephant's head on a serpent body, it's easy to assume that it's entirely fictional, a chimera similar to those found in Greek mythology. But the deep caverns of the Richtersveld – scarily nicknamed 'the Bottomless Pit' and 'the Wonder Hole' – are real enough and said to be a natural reserve of diamonds. This has led many men to venture down there, only a few of whom have returned, which of course has only boosted the tale. One famous casualty was the British explorer, Peter Grayson, who disappeared in the area in 1917, and was openly spoken of as having been killed and eaten by the Grootslang.

It would be easy to dismiss such myths, which often come down to us from ancient tropical cultures where large, predatory snakes pose a very real danger to remote communities. It doesn't take a leap of imagination to consider that creatures of this sort have become deified as a means of fending them off. But more questions arise when similar myths emerge in lands where snakes and serpents are a rarity.

We know today that the venerable Nordic word 'wyrm' refers to a dragon. The great wyrm, Fáfnir, was typical of the breed, a clawed, winged firebreather who slept for centuries on his ill-gotten hoard of gold, occasionally taking flight to torment mankind. But equally there are more serpent-like monsters in Northern European legends. The mysterious lindwyrms, for example, were forest-dwelling dragons, but often described as limbless and slithering after their prey at breakneck speed, while Nidhogg and Jörmungandr were godlike serpents of impossible size, the latter of which would go on to poison the entire sea with his venom. One should also consider those many engravings on Viking monuments, depicting multiply coiled and intertwined creatures, clearly snakes or serpents that are many hundreds of feet in length.

Even in the Hebrew Bible and the Old Testament, the serpent is often a figure of cunning and wickedness, most famously in the Garden of Eden, where, it was responsible for the Fall of Man. Scholars are still divided about whether this particular serpent was under Satan's control, Satan himself, or a sly and sinister being in its own right, which afterwards received divine punishment when its limbs were removed. Either way you look at it, the destructive nature of the great serpent has long been at the front of Man's thinking.

In the modern world, we should be glad that monstrous snakes like titanoboa and gigantophis are nightmares from the past. But it's not impossible that our early ancestors weren't quite so lucky.

NIXIE
Lynda E Rucker

With a strained brightness that even she could hear in her own voice, Kat told people she was 'taking a gap year'. It sounded better than 'lost my job, and my husband, and my house'. It sounded whimsical. It sounded *you-go-girl*, which was the kind of thing people who thought that was still a current thing to say said to her. Kat hated it. Why was everything *girl*? Didn't she remember fighting in her twenties to be called a woman instead of a girl? *Slay qween* someone wrote on the photo she posted of herself on Facebook with the Eiffel Tower in the background, which mortified her further. Jesus, could these people hear themselves? Kat was pretty sure that if women her age – in their forties – were attempting to use a piece of what they thought was still youth slang, its shelf life was long past. She deleted the photo in embarrassment, and then she deleted her entire Facebook account. It was too full of pictures from her old life, anyway, and had depressed her every time she looked at it.

Divorce is so in *this year, have you been reading any of the memoirs?* another American tourist had enthused at her in Paris as Kat desperately tried to extricate herself from their shrill brittle middle-aged circle (*she* was middle-aged, and calling women things like *brittle* and *shrill* was sexist, she chastised herself) but one of the women handed her another glass of wine and she felt obliged to have 'just one more', as the woman urged, before making her unsteady way back to her hotel room. 'We've adopted you now so you won't be on your own!' one of the other women had gushed, and she'd had to skip breakfast and hide in her room till mid-morning to avoid being swept along on their expedition to Versailles. She found a cafe down the street from the hotel and tapped in 'divorce memoirs 2025' on her phone and got increasingly gloomy as she scrolled title after title about women who found the breakup of their marriage to be 'empowering'. After that, she steered clear of her fellow Americans as much as she could, going so far on one or two occasions as to pretend she didn't speak English. She even resurrected her college-era Russian in the face of one particularly persistent pair.

But it was hard, because there was so *much* to steer clear of, and she never knew what was going to strike her. In Paris, she'd cried on the Metro because they'd once ridden it together and never would again. In Barcelona, she'd cried on the beach because they'd never been there together and never would now. Music was the most dangerous of all. When it drifted over from a party in the flat next to the Airbnb she'd rented in London, she could still hear him singing to her over Jarvis Cocker's lyrics, changing the name from Deborah to hers: 'Your name was Katherine, Katherine.' Sitting outside a pub in Brighton, Lana Del Rey's crooning about summertime sadness drove her away entirely even though she'd just ordered a full pint. She bought a ticket for the Eurostar to Paris the next day in the hopes that at least the soundtrack wouldn't be in English any longer.

The fact was that Kat didn't want to take a gap year. She'd liked her marriage. She'd liked their little house. Okay, she hadn't liked her job, a boring admin position in the legal department of a shipping company, but it had paid the bills, which was good since her other job, writing a moderately successful cozy mystery series about a crime-solving librarian didn't. Oh, the books paid enough that she could take a year off without wiping *every* single cent of her savings out, if she was very careful, and spent much of the year in the cheaper corners of the world, but the truth was that you couldn't really live like a grownup if you were a full-time writer, not unless you were Stephen King or something. 'Starving artist' had never been high on Kat's list of lifestyles to pursue. She liked having a house and savings and going on vacations and being able to buy things she wanted without having to decide between doing that and paying a bill. Anyway, it turned out that her day job was as lukewarm about her as she was about it because when layoffs swept through the company, she'd been one of the first to be let go even though she'd been there for ages. The harder she tried not to remember the moment her boss had told her, the more vividly it replayed for her: *Monica, please. You can't dump me the same week my husband's dumping me.* Or maybe that humiliation was so bright in her memory because so much of what came after wasn't. Fuguelike weeks, lying awake in her sister's guest room staring at the ceiling. How easily a life came apart.

For the first time ever, she found herself wishing for the children she'd never had nor wanted. At least they would have been something to hold onto.

Somewhere during her fugue she thought of *Eat, Pray, Love,* a book she'd written a savage review of many years ago for some long-gone women's lifestyle site. Where do websites go when they die? *Dead links, that's my whole life now,* she thought, but she also thought about the book's heroine, whom she'd called 'irritating', gallivanting off in search of herself. *I could do that*, she thought. She wouldn't have any money by the time she got back – she'd have to move in with her sister for a while till she found a new job. Her old house was on the market, but who knew how long it would take to sell and for all the money to get distributed? He'd offered to be the one to move out and his efforts at being decent when he'd done something so indecent as leaving her infuriated her. She'd told him to keep the furniture, keep everything. She left the house with two suitcases. She couldn't bear to look at anything from the life they'd built together.

'Hell hath no fury,' her sister Beth said, and encouraged her to get drunk, get laid, get on Tinder. 'The best way to get over somebody is to get under someone else.'

'Ew,' Kat said. Beth had three boys under the age of twelve – Kat could never quite keep track of how old her nephews were – and Kat suspected that Beth secretly envied what she saw as Kat's new freedom. Beth and her husband didn't have sex anymore, she'd confided to Kat a few years ago, and Kat had said, 'Oh' because she didn't know what else to say and they never spoke of it again.

She'd lain awake all night thinking about running away, and the next morning, she looked up cheap flights to anywhere in Europe and found one to London in two weeks, booking it before she or anyone else could change her mind. 'You're doing what?' Beth said when Kat told her. 'That's insane.'

'No it isn't,' Kat said. 'I've been to Europe before, so it's not as unfamiliar as the rest of the world. I'll get my travelling legs under me there first and then move on.' Secretly, she hoped she'd be a different person by the time she came back. 'Anything could happen.'

'*Travelling legs*,' Beth said. '*Move on.* What are you even talking about? Move on where?'

Kat shrugged. 'Morocco. Thailand. Peru. Who knows?' She found she was actually enjoying the expression on Beth's face, and she hadn't enjoyed anything since her husband told her he was in love with someone else.

'That's crazy,' Beth said again. 'That's – that's not real life. That's the plot of a romcom. What are you going to live off of? You need to be looking for a job, not an escape route.' Then she got mad, and said that Kat was being irresponsible and she hoped that Kat didn't think she could just waltz back in after everything crashed and burned in a few weeks and start sleeping in their spare room again and Kat said good, I hate it here, like she was a teenager and Beth was their (difficult, long since deceased) mother, and that evening she packed up her things and moved to a shitty Airbnb and then to a slightly less shitty one and then a motel near the airport, and she ignored all the texts from Beth that said things like *I'm sorry, can we talk?* and then she was on the plane, gripping the armrests as it climbed into the air and a baby screamed in the seat behind her and she thought *I'll never hold my screaming baby on a plane,* an unwished-for life path that had nevertheless still been some kind of distant possibility until just a few months ago when her marriage ended with a bang, not a whimper, and the ground below fell away and she wished she could open her mouth and howl just like the baby was doing and then they were going up, up, up into the clouds, into the heavens, into a new life she didn't want but at least here everything was clear and simple and straightforward. All she had to do was keep moving.

But by the time she got to Berlin, all she wanted to do was stay still. She'd been travelling for two months by then (*only ten months to go*) and she was fed up with it. Fed up with other tourists, fed up with 'digital nomads' in coffee shops tapping away on their laptops (just as she was doing, because publishers' deadlines were like death and taxes and this was now her sole source of income), fed up with travel influencers striking awkward poses wearing impossible clothes at inconvenient locations shouting orders at hapless photographers. Fed up with hotels, hostels, Airbnbs and the regular kind of B&Bs. Fed up with feeling like she had to appear to be having fun. She'd heard Berliners were grumpy, and she was too, so it seemed like it might be a good fit.

In truth, she did want to go home. She was not turning into a different person, the type of person who reclaimed her life by doing something crazy like this, and she wouldn't be that person in a year, either. Beth had been right; this was a terrible idea, but it was all Beth's fault as well that she couldn't go home. No way was she going to let Beth be right.

Also, there wasn't any 'home' left to go to.

She'd booked an Airbnb outside the city. She was tired of cities too, but she felt like she couldn't leave Western Europe without seeing Berlin. The person she no longer believed she could turn into would not have skipped Berlin, but the person she was currently couldn't bear the thought of any of it. Kat was worried she'd made a mistake with her booking, though. The place she'd chosen turned out to be further out than she'd thought, past the reach of even the S-Bahn, the city's suburban train system. She'd had to go to the Hauptbahnhof and catch a regional train and from there switch to a bus and *then* walk for ten minutes. Her wheelie suitcase rattled behind her as she made her way up suburban streets that were not terribly different from those in her own neighbourhood. *Not my neighbourhood anymore,* she reminded herself, and felt a stab of something too big and painful to call homesickness, which was the kind of thing kids got when they went to summer camp or stayed overnight with a friend. What she had was more like *lifesickness*. When you missed everything, and knew you'd never get it back.

The room she'd rented was at the top of a three-story house. 'Tranquil cosy room in a family home on the outskirts of Berlin,' the listing had read. 'One lake down the street, another a few minutes' walk away.' Her host was a warm blonde-haired woman named Hannah, older than her but of otherwise indeterminate age, who spoke impeccable English and was not at all grumpy. 'I like mysteries,' she said as they exchanged pleasantries over a cup of tea. 'I'll read one of your books!' Kat assumed she was just being polite but the following day Hannah came home from work with a battered, dog-eared paperback of Kat's third novel, *A Woolf in the Fold*, that she'd picked up at an English language bookstore. Kat had titled each book in the series with a play on the name of a famous author, which she'd thought was a great idea when she started with *Death in the Dahl House* and had since come to regret now that she was up to book five. There just weren't that many homophonic author names. She had to bite back the urge to tell Hannah that she really had to read the first two books in the series to 'get' the third one and realised that she felt touched by Hannah's gesture; she then realised that *touched* was the first emotion she'd had toward someone that wasn't some variation on anger or frustration or annoyance or sorrow for a long time.

She'd booked for three weeks. It was more than three times longer than she'd stayed anywhere else, and she hoped she'd get her head together there. Her space at the top of the house was sparse but lovely. The desk where she would work on book five in her series sat before a window built into a sloping roof that looked out on a pristine green lawn. Beyond, Kat could see a lake, a still blue circle in the distance, looking more like a piece of abstract art than a natural body of water.

The following day, she took the bus and the train back into Berlin. She joined an ostensibly free walking tour – the guide shook them all down for tips at the end – that took them to the neoclassical splendour of the Brandenburg Gate, to the maze of concrete slabs that made up the Holocaust Memorial, to what was left of Checkpoint Charlie, now a fake re-creation next to a KFC. Kat remembered watching the Wall fall on TV as a kid, and her dad trying to explain its significance to her. 'We won,' he said, and she hadn't understood – won what? Her father had been a Vietnam vet, more out of her life than in it. He'd lived in Florida now for decades with a different wife and family and they rarely spoke. Still, she thought of him when she visited Mauerpark, once the no-man's-land where the Wall had divided the city, a place where people had once been shot dead trying to reach the West. There were graffiti artists out that day, doing a bit of inelegant tagging. Kat turned left and then right, looking all around as she tried to picture it as it had once been, imagining guard towers and barbed wire.

She couldn't. 'We won, Dad,' she said, as she touched the surface of the Wall. *Won what?* she thought again. She was surprised that the Wall felt so ordinary. This place had been a kind of portal once. If you managed to pass through from one side to the other, you moved from one world into another. Now it was all just part of the same world. There was concrete and scrubby stretches of grassland, people sunbathing, walking, cycling. She ought, she thought, to send her father a postcard, but she wasn't sure she had an address for him.

There, she thought on her way back out of the city, *I've seen Berlin* even though she knew that wasn't really the case at all, but the thought of making a second trip in, of following another careful itinerary, exhausted her. Her dreams that night were fitful, and full of music. Her husband had been in a band when she'd first met him. It seemed like everybody she knew had been, back then. Now he was a software engineer. Kat had sometimes thought that he quietly resented her for finding some small measure of success as a writer when his band had peaked with an undesirable slot at Bonnaroo and had broken up for good a few weeks later when the drummer got the bassist's girlfriend pregnant. She used to downplay her own work as a result. 'Oh, I just got lucky!' she would say – nothing about all the late nights and early mornings hunched over a keyboard, the five novels she wrote first before the sixth one, her 'first', the one that finally sold. *Maybe if I'd been a failure I'd still be married,* she mused.

She spent the day working on edits and accepted Hannah's invitation for a glass of wine that evening in the kitchen. She was surprised at how much she liked the woman, given that nearly everyone she'd met up to now had exasperated her to some degree. 'I forgot to tell you,' Hannah said as she went up to bed, 'I'll be away this weekend. You'll have the place to yourself until Sunday night!'

Kat dreamed about music again, this time a woman's haunting voice, laden with sorrow and longing. She woke with a start and lay there for several minutes, breathing unsteadily, not sure why she felt a mix of apprehension and delicious anticipation. Then it struck her – the woman was still singing. Kat sat up. She went to the window and pushed it open – and the woman's voice soared into the room. Kat stood mesmerised. It was as though the woman were singing about her as well as to her, about lost love and betrayal, the dissolution of dreams. Then the singing changed, and although she couldn't understand the words – she would have said there were no words at all although the only instrument was the woman's voice – she understood that now the song was about betrayal, and fury, and revenge. It was so beautiful and so terrible that she found herself trembling.

And then suddenly it was morning, and Kat was awake, the sun beaming. *What a weird dream.* The window was open. It had not been open when she went to bed because although it was May, there had been a chill on the night air. She made a mental note to ask Hannah about the singing, but of course, Hannah didn't come home from work that evening; she was away. Kat walked to an unassuming little restaurant she'd noticed while dragging her suitcase through the streets and had schnitzel and fries and two ridiculously large glasses of beer for dinner and as she walked back to Hannah's enveloped in a pleasant buzz, it occurred to her that for the first time she felt like she was finally doing this travel thing right.

Voices, not singing, woke her. And laughter. It was coming from downstairs. Kat reassured herself that burglars probably didn't chatter away and laugh while they robbed you, and went downstairs herself. A young man and woman, maybe in their early twenties, were in the kitchen devouring doner kebabs, the Turkish wraps that seemed to be wildly popular all over Europe. They looked up with surprised expressions, and the man said something to her in German.

'I'm sorry,' Kat said. 'I don't speak German.' She actually knew how to say that *in* German, but not at two am after having just been woken up.

'Ah, sorry,' said the man. 'I'm Christian. You must be my mother's guest?'

Kat nodded. 'She's away for the weekend.' She had wondered why Hannah had called it a 'family home' on the listing when she seemed to be the only one living there but it had seemed rude to ask. This explained it.

The woman spoke then. She had a stronger accent than Christian. 'Did we frighten you? We thought she would be home.'

'And we didn't know anyone was staying here this weekend,' Christian added.

Kat shook her head. 'No, it's all right. I'm Kat.'

'I'm sorry if we disturb you,' the woman said.

'No, you didn't,' Kat said, which was dumb because they obviously had. She stifled a yawn. 'I'm going back up to bed now though.'

The woman smiled at her. 'We are going swimming at the lake tomorrow. You can join us if you like.'

Kat made a noncommittal noise and smiled back, but the next day she was surprised to find she felt eager to accept their invitation. She'd slept late, but they slept later, and it was well past noon when they straggled into the kitchen where she sat drinking a cup of coffee and reading, waiting so that she didn't miss them.

They took her to the lake that had been described as a ten-minute walk away on Hannah's Airbnb listing although Kat thought they walked for at least fifteen minutes. It turned out to be the blue circle she could see from the window. On the way, Christian told her that there were thousands of lakes throughout Berlin and Brandenburg, that the area was known for them. 'Ancient lakes,' he added. 'From the –' He paused, clearly translating in his head. 'Would you say Ice Age?' Kat nodded. 'Tens of thousands of years old!' Christian went on. 'We are here in only an eyelash blink!'

'Blink of an eye?' Kat said, and Christian grinned. 'Yes, that.'

Blink of an eye. Kat thought about everything she'd seen on her walking tour two days ago, about her dad saying *We won*, about tens of thousands of years stacked up against a couple of centuries. About her own broken life and its insignificance against such a scale. *Is this perspective? Is this what I came looking for?* And: *Now that I've found it, can I go home again?* Two short months to enlightenment: she could write a book about it. People liked their epiphanies as efficient as possible these days. Do this, get that result, job done.

No home to go to, she reminded herself again, but any temptation to sink back into self-pity was forgotten as they emerged from the copse of trees they'd been walking through and suddenly there was the lake, impossibly blue, *ancient indeed*, Kat thought, such an old lake would be so wise and hold so many secrets. Christian and his girlfriend – her name was Ania, she'd told Kat, and she was from Krakow – went ahead of her, chatting to one another in German, but Kat held back. Years ago, she'd developed a temporary case of tinnitus, and what was happening now, very suddenly, felt similar to that. The difference was that instead of a ringing, it was reminiscent of the song she'd dreamed about.

Kat looked all around – surely someone somewhere was playing music from their phone or something – but the lake was deserted save for the three of them. She caught up with Ania and Christian and Christian commented on it over his shoulder to her. 'It's very strange there is no one here on such a beautiful day. Germans love to be outdoors in the sun.' It was as though his voice had interrupted the music, which just as suddenly as it had begun, she could no longer hear. At the lakeshore they all dropped the towels they'd brought and Kat fumbled with her clothes, feeling slightly self-conscious about her bathing suit. Months of stress eating and drinking had done a number on her body image not to mention her actual body. But when she looked up, Christian and Ania were splashing into the lake wearing nothing at all, their clothes crumpled next to their towels.

'I'll just be over here with my American inhibitions,' Kat said, too quietly for them to hear, and then she laughed – out loud, at herself, and tried to remember the last time something had made her laugh.

This is a good place, she thought. *This place is good for me.*

They were there for hours. Swimming, dozing, chatting in a desultory way. Kat regretted she hadn't brought a book to read at first and then gave herself up utterly to the languor of the afternoon. The sun moved across the sky. A few other people did eventually drift over to the lake as well, swim for a while, and drift away. Kat could not remember the last time she had felt so relaxed. It wasn't a question of months or even years. It was more like decades. It was, she thought, the kind of relaxation she had only ever felt as a child, a calm so lost to her that she'd been unaware of its absence. It was the kind of tranquillity that as an adult you took drugs to try and achieve, and yet there was something bright and expectant about it, not drug-like at all. 'Christian,' she said, watching a fat bee bumble through the air, 'I think your ancient lake has restorative powers. You should bottle this stuff and sell it.'

'Spoken like a capitalist!' Christian said, and she heard Ania laughing along with him.

Kat, lying on her stomach, propped her head up on her chin and looked at them. They were teasing her, of course, but she thought: they're too young to remember it, any of it – the Wall, the ominous phrase 'The Iron Curtain,' the quotidian fear of nuclear annihilation. *She* was too young to remember any of it, really, but they hadn't even been alive. It was her father for whom it had been a big deal, who'd wrecked his life fighting against everything the division of Germany represented and came to understand he'd been nothing more than a pawn in the plans of powerful men. Brandenburg would have been part of the East. Hannah would remember it well. She might have been one of the young people herself there at the Wall when it came down. Kat made a mental note to ask her about it.

'Do you think it was better then?' she said. 'For people?'

Christian shrugged. 'For some. Of course. Not for others.' She was really curious about what both of them genuinely thought, but she sensed a hesitation on their parts. They clearly didn't want to talk about politics, which was fair enough, she thought, especially these days, but she still wished that wasn't the case. She wondered what the world looked like to them, these people half her age, products of an entirely new millennium. She wanted to tell them what she'd thought about portals, back in the Mauerpark, and see if they thought it was strange or stupid or interesting. She wanted to thank them for the portal they'd brought her to here, on this ancient landscape. She imagined the great glaciers that Christian said would have formed the lakebed, imagined them receding, imagined a woman born of the ice, or perhaps hiding in the ice, left behind, singing the wrenching song she had heard in her dream.

But she had, somehow, broken the spell of the afternoon as well, spoiled it. Everything felt different. A cloud passed before the sun. Kat could still feel the pleasant heaviness of the day in her bones, but the peaceful somnambulant feel of it was gone. They gathered their things and headed back. Kat took a shower and lay down and started awake after what she thought was just a few minutes although the night sky beyond her window suggested otherwise. A glance at her phone told her it was one in the morning. Her stomach was growling and no wonder – she hadn't eaten anything after midday. She went down to the kitchen where she was surprised to find Christian and Ania clearly dressed for a night out, all black vinyl and attitude. Ania's outfit showed more skin than Kat's bathing suit had. 'Isn't it late?' she said, and Ania laughed.

'Welcome to Berlin,' she said. 'The party is not even started yet.'

Kat rummaged in the refrigerator for some bread and salami Hannah had insisted she help herself to. 'Oh, God,' she said to them. 'I feel as ancient as that lake.'

Christian said, 'You should join us sometime. Techno's not just for people of a certain age. Sven at Berghain is probably sixty. It's an amazing experience.'

Kat didn't know who Sven was or what Berghain was and was shaking her head as she lifted her head above the fridge. 'I can't remember the last time I was up this late on purpose,' she said.

'You like music?' Christian asked.

'I do,' she said, 'but you know, like live music. Not techno.'

'It's all music though, isn't it? It takes us someplace else. It's like a magic spell,' Christian insisted, and she said she guessed so. After they left, she found she was restless. She went back upstairs, tried to read, and returned to the kitchen, where she opened a bottle of white wine she found in the fridge. She'd replace it before Hannah got back, she thought. She poured herself a glass and was surprised at how fast it went down. She poured herself another and found a playlist on Spotify, started to dance around the kitchen with her glass, humming to herself. *Maybe I* am *the kind of person who goes to a trendy nightclub in Berlin.* Then she caught of her reflection in the window and felt foolish. Still the same old Kat. Who else would she be? She put down her glass and paused Spotify.

And then she heard it.

This time she definitely wasn't dreaming.

Kat was no musician like her husband had once been but she often wished she was. Music could grab you in a raw, unfiltered way that no piece of writing ever could. And no matter how many writers tried to be experimental, no matter how many Burroughs-style cutups or bizarro fictions or novels like *House of Leaves* were out there, it remained a fundamentally rational art, passing through your brain's word processing centres before entering your nervous system. Music, on the other hand, went straight into the blood and the bones. Language was manmade; music was woven into the structure of the very universe. Hadn't philosophers and even astronomers once believed that the Sun, the Moon, the planets, glided through their orbits to the strains of a celestial symphony? That's what Kat felt like she was hearing that very moment, what they'd called the music of the spheres, passing through the vocal cords of a woman.

It was not beautiful. It was wild and discordant. It was spiked with rage. It was both human and inhuman all at once, in the way that people are themselves with all their messy emotions and pettiness and at the same time are made from stars.

Kat thought, I have to find this singer.

It was past two am when she let herself out of Hannah's house. The woman's voice was so stark and clear as it soared through the night that she could not imagine that no one else heard it and could not understand why they were not all outside their homes as well. At first Kat couldn't discern the direction that the singing was coming from. It seemed to be everywhere all at once, and so she followed her instincts and walked back toward the lake they'd visited. With every footstep her confidence grew that she was drawing nearer to the source of the singing.

But by the time she arrived at the lake, it had stopped. The warm night was quiet, and the surface of the lake was still in the moonlight.

Kat whispered, 'Hello?' and then, a little louder, 'Is anyone there?'

No one was.

Kat sat down on the edge of the lake. She took off her sandals and put her feet in the water. It was cool, as was the night air, but it was also so inviting. She wished she'd brought her bathing suit, and then she remembered that people thought little of swimming in the nude here. Why not? There was no one around. Kat shrugged out of her clothes and gasped a little at the feeling of the air against her naked body, the unaccustomed intimacy of it. She gasped more loudly as she waded into the cold lake. It took some determination to carry on, but determined she was, and before long she was swimming strong strokes across the middle to the other side and back. She grew used to the cold. She dove beneath the surface, searching for the bottom although she couldn't get deep enough to find it. She floated on her back, performed a sloppy breaststroke, did a little dogpaddling. Within a couple of hours the sun was rising, golden through the trees. Kat swam to shore and sat there until she couldn't ignore the goosebumps pimpling her skin any longer, got dressed, and headed back to Hannah's.

She fell into a dreamless sleep, and when she woke several hours later, she could tell the house was still empty. She needed to do some work – she had a Zoom meeting with her editor the next day – but she felt foggy and disoriented. She showered, scrambled some eggs, and took the coffee upstairs to her desk, where she opened her laptop and sat staring at the blue lake in the distance. She heard someone come in downstairs, but no voices, so she supposed it was Hannah. Her eye fell on the computer's clock and she realised that several more hours had passed. She had forgotten to replace the bottle of wine that she'd opened the night before, and she'd also left the kitchen in general disarray. She hurried downstairs to see Hannah standing in the middle of the room looking nonplussed. 'I'm so sorry!' she said as she burst in, and Hannah turned.

'Oh,' she said. 'No, *I'm* very sorry. I didn't know my son was coming this weekend! Did you get the message I sent you? On the Airbnb app?'

Kat shook her head and realised that she hadn't so much as looked at her phone since she was up in the middle of the night on Friday.

'Never mind,' Hannah said. 'I was just apologising and hoping they didn't disturb you!'

'Not at all. The opposite, really, they were absolutely lovely.' Kat frowned, remembering. 'They haven't come back though. They were going out last night.'

Hannah laughed. 'They probably won't be back until sometime tomorrow morning. Berlin,' she added, as though that explained it.

'I'm so sorry,' Kat said again. 'I left a mess down here, I meant to come down and clean it up and replace your wine and – my sleep has been –' She stopped and took a deep breath. 'Is there a singer around here?'

Hannah looked surprised. 'A singer?'

Kat moved around her, picking up dishes to stack in the dishwasher, putting things away. 'Yes, I've heard a woman singing. Every night since I've been here actually.' It occurred to her that Hannah might think she was complaining, even making some kind of covert threat about her Airbnb rating, and hastened to add, 'Her voice is beautiful. I'd just love to know who she is.'

Now she couldn't read the look on Hannah's face, or she could but didn't want to. It was the look, she thought, of a woman who was genuinely puzzled and who was perhaps wondering whether there was something wrong with the guest she'd invited into her home, whether there was something *off* about Kat, whether she ought to be alarmed by this strange American claiming that there was some woman singing in the night. Kat very much wished that she hadn't said anything at all, but she wasn't sure how to take it back.

'That is really very strange,' Hannah said at last. 'I don't know what you heard.'

Kat remembered reading that Germans tended to be very direct, and this seemed an example; there was none of the embarrassed effort to gloss over the awkwardness that Kat would have done in her place.

Hannah smiled then. 'I finished your book,' she said. 'I read the whole thing on the train to Munich, and then I loaned it to my sister when I got there. I thought I was very clever, thought I had solved it and that Daphne had done it. But it was Greg all along! I could see it, once I got to the end, you know, where you had planted all the little clues, just enough that you saw them when you looked back.'

Kat tried to smile back, and she stretched her mouth into a smiling shape, but it felt strange and finally she said, 'I'm so glad you enjoyed it.' Her voice sounded odd and hollow and formal. The warmth that had sprung up between them when she arrived was gone. Kat finished loading the dishwasher and turned it on and Hannah said she was going to go and do something, Kat didn't hear what, and Hannah left the room.

That night was silent. Kat lay awake for hours. When she awoke the following morning, her face and pillow were damp. She had been crying in her sleep.

She waited until she heard Hannah leave for work before she went downstairs. She was making coffee when Christian and Ania stumbled in, eyes bloodshot, giggling. They looked exhausted and happy.

'Christian,' she said, as the two of them were preparing to go sleep it off. 'Um, weird question. Do you ever hear anyone singing around here?'

He frowned. 'Such as singing in the shower?'

'No, no. Like a professional singer. A woman. It's, I guess you would call it experimental. Avant-garde.'

Christian betrayed something in the single beat that passed before he answered. 'No. There is no one like that around here at all,' he said firmly.

A surge of exhilaration seized Kat. She didn't know why Christian was lying to her, but his hesitation had told her everything she needed to know. She had not imagined any of it.

But why had the singer fallen silent? Perhaps she needed to be asleep first, but that wasn't right; on the Saturday night she'd been awake downstairs when she heard it, and anyway what would sleeping or not sleeping have to do with it? Kat was suddenly aware that she was pacing back and forth there in the kitchen, and then her phone buzzed. It was her editor, asking if she'd got the meeting time wrong. Kat dashed upstairs to her laptop and launched Zoom and stumbled through the meeting without having prepared at all. Where had the morning gone anyway? Sophie, her editor, stopped halfway through and asked if she were okay, if she were sick, if she wanted to reschedule. Kat said no to everything but she could see Sophie looking at her the same way Hannah had in the kitchen earlier.

Hannah. No sooner had she finished the meeting with Sophie – and everything they discussed left her head immediately as soon as she exited the Zoom – than she remembered she still hadn't replaced the bottle of wine. She didn't even think Hannah would care, but she felt like she'd fallen from her good graces, and wanted to get back in. It had begun to rain, and she pulled on her raincoat and headed out to the supermarket she'd seen when she took the bus from the train station.

She didn't have much of an appetite, but along with two bottles of wine, she also bought a couple of seeded bread rolls and some cheese and an apple. Standing in the checkout line, she almost convinced herself that the tinny music coming from the earbuds of the girl in front of her was exactly the sort of thing she'd been hearing, but of course it wasn't. Bored, Kat took out her phone and scrolled through her email. There was a message with multiple attachments from her husband's lawyer. Kat felt her face flush and put the phone away. *Bastards.*

Back at Hannah's, Kat put the wine in the fridge, resisted the urge to write a note apologising *again*, and took some bread and cheese and cut-up apple slices back upstairs with her, where she sat trying to make sense of her notes from the meeting and ignoring her food. Sophie had said, in not so many words, that the book still had some real problems. Kat looked from the screen to her scribbled notes to the screen again. She felt distinctly as though she were pretending to work, like she was under the eye of a micromanaging boss.

As the only micromanaging boss in sight was her, she

pushed the laptop away, put the raincoat back on, took it back off again when she noted the rain had stopped and the sky was clearing, and headed out for a walk. She often took walks when she was trying to work out a book problem. Yet her mind wasn't on the book at all. It worried instead at various worn and familiar grooves: grief, despair, numbness. She surfaced from somewhere deep in thought and found that her feet were carrying her back to the lake.

She stood once more on the shore. It wasn't a particularly warm day, but she remembered the pleasurable shock of the cold water when she'd swum here in the night. All at once she was tearing at her clothes, plunging into the lake before she'd got them off properly, and leaving them sodden at the water's edge as she pushed out toward the middle, taking long shuddering breaths to stave off angry tears.

She could hear someone shouting from the shore, and she turned, treading water, and saw Christian there, waving his arms at her, but she couldn't understand what he was saying, and then she couldn't hear him at all. His mouth was still moving, but the only sound she could hear now was the song: the beautiful, terrible song that was rising from her own throat, a song of fury, a song to both warn and seduce, a song more ancient than human utterances. She dove, still singing.

She thrust herself up toward the surface again. As she broke into the daylight, she could see Christian still on the shore. He wasn't shouting any longer. A look of relief passed over his face as he spotted her, and he made a move as if, she thought, to head into the water himself. *To save her.* She threw back her head and laughed and when she looked at him again his expression had transformed from relief into terror.

Her pain could split universes open.

He stumbled backwards. His mouth was still working, but she didn't think words were coming out any longer. She knew then she could draw him down into the lake and that unlike her, he would not breathe, he would not sing. She could watch the life drain out of him, if she wished.

She let him run away. There would, she thought, be others.

Her mercy could set the stars askew.

There were others here with her as well. Sisters, and they sang together now. Together, they dove far beneath the surface, down deep where the ice had once scraped craters into the earth and birthed all manner of things.

It's happened to me, she thought. *The thing I wanted most has happened to me at last.*

I am different now.

Her want was bottomless. Her rage was sacred. The dark of the lake was the dark of the womb, the dark beneath a glacier, the dark of the universe, and she sang about it all, and she would go on singing it with her sisters until someday the earth itself cracked apart and died, until all time stopped.

ORGANISM 46-B

In 2016, a story emerged from Russia that was, frankly, completely terrifying.

Before we get into the details, try to picture what is surely one of the most nightmarish environments on Earth: the cavernous darkness of an immense subterranean sea. How did it come to be? How far down does it go? What might live there?

It's no surprise that much mythology has been woven around this concept.

Underground seas and lakes have played key roles in such major works of nerve-shredding fiction as Jules Verne's Journey to the Centre of the Earth *(1864) and Greig Beck's* Fathomless *(2018). But such localities are not purely the inventions of fantasy writers. Several enormous bodies of subterranean water are known to exist and have even been surveyed: Dragon's Breath Cave in Namibia, the Lost Sea under Tennessee's Smoky Mountains, Kow Ata in Turkmenistan. But there are others even deeper down, virtual oceans trapped far under the Earth's mantle, never seen by man, ice cold, eternally pitch-black, seemingly bottomless, and of course, containing … what?*

That latter question is now asked regularly of Lake Vostok, a near incomprehensibly vast subglacial lake (160 miles long by 30 miles wide, and over 1,000 feet deep), which lies under millions of tons of ice at the Pole of Cold in central Antarctica.

Which brings us neatly back to the main subject of this story: how in 2016, one Anton Padalka, an eminent Russian scientist, finally broke his silence regarding a 2012 mission he'd been involved with to Vostok Station, a Russian research base located directly above (by a distance of two miles!) that soon-to-be-infamous, water-filled abyss.

It may come as a surprise, but the glacier-covered lake was named after the base rather than it being the other way round, Vostok Station having been established in 1957, at the height of the Soviet era, while the presence of the lake itself was only discovered in 1974.

Most of the world's true subterranean seas are unreachable because they are entombed by rock. But that clearly wasn't the case with Lake Vostok, and so it wasn't long after it was located that Russian scientists, realising they were sitting on a gold mine of potential new discoveries, delved downward. The obvious hope was that Lake Vostok, locked away from the surface world for an estimated 15 million years, might well have preserved a prehistoric ecosystem. Anticipation was high that a wealth of relict lifeforms, mostly microbial, might be discovered still flourishing.

The road to Hell is often paved with good intentions, and on this occasion, the road to Hell was literally opened. And to such an extent that human personnel could descend through it.

According to Padalka's account (because he has consistently claimed that he was personally involved), by 2012 a traversable passage had been bored down to an air pocket sitting on the lake's surface, wherein an ice shelf proved sufficiently stable for the exploration team to set up a sub-glacial camp. Delicate water tests had already revealed that Lake Vostok was in a near pristine state. The next step was thus unavoidable, a manned dive into the lightless depths, the divers in heated wetsuits and equipped with strong lamps. How many were set to take this plunge is unrecorded, but Padalka himself went with them. It was only a couple of hours later, the team having descended to about 400 feet, when they encountered what would later be named Organism 46-B. In Padalka's words, it was simply waiting in the blackness, having already detected their presence.

The organism Padalka described was like something from the deepest recesses of H P Lovecraft's imagination. In short, a colossal, multi-limbed monstrosity, far larger than any known oceanic squid, equipped with many more appendages, and completely different in appearance in terms of its biological structure in that it appeared to be gelatinous.

Padalka described the diving team first becoming aware of the thing as it hovered in the water about 150 metres away, observing them with huge, bioluminescent eyes and then, without warning, releasing a cloud of murky venom, which according to Padalka, seemed to seek out targets at its own whim, engulfing one particular scientist, who immediately was rendered semi-unconscious. To the utter horror of Padalka and the other divers, the beast then seized the dazed man with its tentacles, drew him in and devoured him while he was still alive.

How long Padalka's team remained underwater is unclear – it would surely have been a miracle if it had been more than one second longer – but by the sounds of it, even the ice shelf was no protection, the monster attacking again and again, pulling their equipment and makeshift tents into the night-black water. Several times during these battles, the thing is said to have displayed intelligence and even changed shape, while on other occasions, its limbs were severed but continued to thrash about as if each one possessed its own independent lifeforce. Two other fatalities are recorded in Padalka's account, one of them a female scientist, who was throttled, and another, one of the men, who was torn to shreds, before reinforcements came down from the upper world, helping to kill the monster and enclose its corpse in a steel tank, which was then hoisted to the surface and later transported back to Russia and out of the scientists' control. Needless to say, the Russian authorities have never had anything to say on the matter.

Thus goes the story of Organism 46-B, which is repeated ad infinitum across the internet.

The question remains as always, how much truth does it contain?

To start with, since these accounts were published, Padalka, though a renowned academic in his homeland, has become a frustratingly elusive fellow. No one from the western world has been able to track him down in order to verify this tale. In addition to that, all the usual caveats must be considered before one takes at face value the existence of a gigantic predator in a location where there is very little prey. What did it feed on normally? Where were the others of its kind, because it could only have survived as part of a breeding population, yet there are no references to any other such creatures. People have also queried how the Russian team could possibly have descended to the lake in the first place; two miles is a phenomenal distance to tunnel down, even when you're talking ice rather than rock. Today, water samples from the lake have been collected through extensive ice core drilling, but that in itself is a difficult and costly procedure even though the boreholes are usually no more than a *couple of inches in diameter.*

Does Doctor Padalka even exist? There's no clear answer to that either, though some researchers maintain that he does and is now in hiding for fear that his publicisation of the event went against the wishes of the Russian regime. Unfortunately, the most damning evidence against the existence of Organism 46-B can be found in the work of American science fiction author, C Michael Forsyth, who wrote a completely fictional story about an expedition below the ice sheet on Lake Vostok, and an encounter with a terrifying, multi-tentacled monster. So, in this case was fiction stranger than truth?

Perhaps the most interesting aspect of this tale is how the most unlikely sounding events, even those with their origins self-evidently based in fiction, can assume the dimension of urban myth if enough people want them to be true. Because despite the many doubts now stacked against this story, it kindles memories of the so-called Angels of Mons, which many World War One veterans attested to, even though the miraculous battlefield visitation only actually occurred in Arthur Machen's 1914 ghost story, The Bowmen, *and the emergence in recent years of Slenderman, the child-killing demon of American schoolyard rumour, who actually started life in 2009 as a creepypasta meme, and was entirely the work of one Eric Knudsen.*

Such is the need and desire to find stranger things in this world that, despite C Michael Forsyth's fiendish inventiveness, cryptid-hunters the world over still persevere in their quest to find Organism 46-B.

MEDUSA
C C Adams

The soul that has conceived one wickedness
can nurse no good thereafter.
Sophocles

Dion's, St Paul's, East Central London
21:41, 22/11/24

'Citrus and alcohol, that's the ticket,' she thinks to herself. 'You've already had that ticket once tonight and still you want to get up in Madison's. Do you really want to spend precious time and money here?'

But as she looks around the group, she realises that she might be outvoted. Charlene has already downed her shot, glancing over her shoulder in the direction of the bar to see if she can get the attention of bar staff. Dee has just downed hers, nodding in approval. Sandra's lips are pursed as her tongue runs a slow trail across her teeth, savouring the aftertaste. Elisha can't blame her. Kamikaze, after all. Lime juice setting off the vodka perfectly. And, Kim? Kim is watching her expectantly – the same way a dog might watch you as if expecting scraps from your plate and instead you hand it a fork. Elisha's attention drifts back to Sandra, her tongue still checking her teeth and, unconsciously, Elisha now does the same.

The longer the remaining shot goes undowned, the more it attracts attention from the gathering. Somewhere overhead from the unseen speakers, Sabrina Claudio hits the high notes in warning a lover that they'll never unravel her, while the rest of the bar's patrons make chatter that serves as a counterpoint to the crooning. Elisha almost wishes they would shut up for a minute – she always loved this song, ever since the last Tyler Perry film she saw.

But her tongue is also distracting her, checking one tooth in *particular. Incisor. Upper jaw. The tooth on the left hand side, next to the canine. The canine is sore, but not like the incisor is. That's sore. Loose, too.*

Tongue tip testing this tooth, tentatively at first, rocking it gently back and forth in the gum. But of course, there's no way of knowing how sore or how loose it is without pushing the boundary. Elisha now applies more force.

All of her girlfriends are watching her now. Kim lays a hand on her shoulder, smooth cool fingers reassuring through the fabric of her jacket.

Sandra gestures at the shot. 'Are you gonna do it?'

Indecision in Charlene's eyes and Elisha knows that where this friend is concerned, the same friend won't willingly let this shot go to waste

... and her tongue pushed harder against the battered incisor. This time it fell out of her mouth and clattered into the sink, with what appeared to be bloody pulp around the root.

He did it. He really did it.

Elisha turned her attention back to the mirror. Saddened, her reflection stared back, the right eye heavy at the lid, half-swollen shut. A trickle of blood from her nostril and sneering her lip back revealed, next to a canine, a fresh cavity from where a tooth was punched out.

Are you gonna do it?

Fingers splayed, she braced her hands against the sink on either side of the taps. Leaned forward a little. The highest patch of psoriasis on her body sat under the jaw, so it wasn't immediately visible – but then, that didn't mean it wasn't there. Ugly raised flesh, rough to the touch; scaly, as if from the body of a reptile. Some areas darker than her own skin, some of it purpled. Itching like mad, and only the threat of it looking worse if she started to scratch it stopped her – all the E45 cream in the world wouldn't abate that rubbish. As for the other patches? One on the back of her neck, toward the right-hand side. Others here and there, the lowest just above her left knee. Even as she leaned toward the mirror, denim dress pooled behind her on the bathroom floor, she saw how hideous her body had become, although her bare breasts, small and firm, were free of the condition.

GP appointment number one had been nearly a year ago, after soaping her neck in the bath had revealed a change in her skin. And it had taken the better part of a month to *get* that appointment, all for the GP to tell her it was a mild case of stress-induced psoriasis, and that trying some E45 for the next month should do the trick and if not, to come back and then other options could be reviewed. None of those other options did a lick of good, with more patches of psoriasis setting up shop in her body.

A breath shuddered out of her, as her forehead flushed with heat. Turning her attention back to the mirror, Elisha appraised her reflection. It had been beautiful before (*like butter wouldn't melt in your mouth, bitch*, Kim had once said and Elisha had laughed at that). Small face and large catlike eyes framed by lashes that curved perfectly, even without mascara.

Albeit with one of those eyelids swollen thick now.

Faint beauty spot above the left corner of her mouth, lips now bereft of Rimmel London's Bordeaux, but still a faint shade of purple. A drying line of blood from her nostril to her lip.

Are you gonna do it?

You're ugly now; you're so ugly. Once upon a time, you were ... you were pretty, you were beautiful; most of all, you were HAPPY. Look at you now. This is hideous.

Thoughts of beauty turned grotesque made her think of the Gorgon Medusa – once a beautiful woman, made monstrous as a consequence of her choices in love. Elisha remembered enough of the story in school to question why it was only the woman made into a monster, to which the teacher in question had shared her own idea that it was jealousy from another, and then invited Elisha to tell the class what she herself thought.

But, now, *seeing* her own eyes brimming with tears made her think of arrogance, that other people thought they were above reproach.

Repercussions.

But, had she really expected anything different or anything else? Just like the saying went: same shit, different day – and with *these* days, they had bled into one depressing cycle of fostering resolve, fearing repercussions, anxiety over police intervention, recriminations. Day after day after day.

'I'm going to do it,' she whispered.

Hands balling into fists, the knife handle clutched tightly in her right, she walked from the bathroom with each step enunciated in the language of stealth, the flooring underfoot morphing from linoleum to carpet. Cool and rough against the soles of her bare feet.

Mental monologues of rationale hissing around her head like a nest of snakes.

Is this … is this what you are now? An evil thing, a monster?

That's fairytale rubbish. It's … karma. Nothing else.

It's not my fault.

Really? How do you come to that conclusion, then? Because it sure looks like you.

Yes it looks like me, but it wasn't my choice – I've got no choice. I've been forced into a corner; sometimes literally, and the only thing I can do

– is do this.

Her gaze fell to her right arm, where tendons stood out in stark relief at the base of her fist. In her periphery below, slim legs – the psoriasis still evident in darker patches.

It's not my fault.

You keep saying that and yet I don't see anyone forcing you. Why? Because no one is forcing you – no one but you … and the truth is, you don't want to stop.

Shaking her head, Elisha rested a hand against the bedroom door.

'I can't stop,' she mouthed.

With the door ajar, she gently eased it inward, allowing a shaft of light from the landing to fall across the threshold, as did the hypnotic regularity of slumbered breathing.

Enough to quicken Elisha's heartbeat.

The rest of the bedroom lay in darkness, but already her eyes had adjusted to the gloom. Sean lay on his right side facing the doorway as he often did, eyes closed in a frown as if waiting on a dream that would never come (and Elisha knew this from having once asked him what he dreamed about, only be told that he never bloody had any). One hand by his face, fingers loosely curled into the palm as if ready to stroke the goatee, with the duvet snugly tucked under his left armpit.

Closing the distance to the bed now brought the sickening gravity with it. After days, weeks; months, even – the moment was here and yet it wasn't complete. Because when all was said and done, you never wanted to win or defeat anyone on a technicality. You wanted to look the monster in the eye and show them they were powerless, and that you were anything but. Monsters weren't exempt from fear; something that Elisha had told herself time and again over recent months. The notion of a fearless monster was propaganda, perpetuated by the monsters themselves, along with most of their prey.

A groan from beneath her and Sean's eyelids, although closed, fluttered as he rolled onto his back. The human body was a remarkable thing, fashioned in flesh, blood and bone and yet *some* elements appeared to fall beyond the realms of normalcy or the everyday; like the subconscious reaction to your partner. Whatever it was (and Elisha had prayed for the gift of stealth and she was *sure* that her prayers were answered), it eased another groan from Sean and lifted his other arm from beneath the duvet to rest on top of it.

Then his eyes opened.

It took less than a minute for Sean to wake, and a matter of moments to register the knife and spring into action. And then another minute, in which the duvet was left twisted in the maelstrom, hanging over the edge of the bed like a padded corkscrew, and with Elisha landed at the bottom of the stairs in a crumpled heap.

The same knife landing beside her a moment later after the hilt rapped her in the head.

From the top of the stairs, a muttered, 'Put that shit back when you're done, yeah?'

Retreating footsteps.

And then, silence.

At least, for now.

Allowing her to gather at least some degree of strength.

Sensory awareness creeping out like roaches in darkened rooms.

Silence both in the house and beyond it.

The smell of blood in the air.

Her head already throbbing, Elisha lifted it anyway, her cheek scraping along the carpet as she did so – and immediately she realised the roughness on her hip was not only due to psoriasis, but also a fresh carpet burn from where she had been flung down the stairs naked. The damage became clear in a synchronisation of the senses: the blood from her nose almost sticky as it trailed to her lip, the dull thudding at the back of her head at one with that in her left eye *and* jaw. It felt like another loose tooth, too.

Bracing herself, fingers digging claw-like into the carpet, only for her right wrist to flare in a bracelet of pain from where an iron grip had seized her – and the resulting gasp? A sliver of agony through her ribs, where maybe one or two were broken. Mammoth soreness at the back of her thigh where Sean's bare foot had slammed into her hamstring.

Resigned to resting on her elbows and stomach, Elisha hung her head, blood flow and gravity fattening her bruises.

I hate this. Oh God, I can't take this, please don't let me take any more of this.

Take any more of what? Aren't you Medusa, the one and only? The monstrous Medusa making … mockeries of men?

Look who's the mockery now. Do you think that if you were so monstrous you would be lying here like a sack of … shit? No.

Some threat YOU are. See how he gave the bloody knife back?

Please, no.

Oh, please, nothing. Your begging and pleading is what makes you weak. If you weren't so weak, do you think that you'd be in this position now? No. Do you think that he'd raise his hand to you? No. Could he even raise his voice to you? No. So, why does he?

Because I let him.

No. You let him because you WANT him to.

– and *that* was enough to clamp her teeth on her bottom lip with such force to keep the scream in that she drew blood; anything to keep the tormentor from upstairs returning.

On her elbows, stomach and knees, Elisha pivoted, her body a discordant chorus of pain. At least now, she could see the kitchen ahead, the door ajar, as it always was when the slightest breeze wafted through the cracks of the doorframe. From here on out, it was crawling like a soldier across enemy territory. Her bare stomach tightening as she made the graduation from the carpet to the carpet protector that ran the length of the hall (because you had to keep the walkway clean from everyone's dirty-ass feet, Sean had said. She had agreed). Teeth gritted, her pace grew slower now. More than ever, stealth was needed.

Wait a minute, wait a minute, wait a minute.

Exhausted, Elisha leaned to one side and looked up, having now stopped by the cupboard under the stairs. The cupboard door was held shut by a spring-loaded latch that, if she were standing, would have come up to her chin.

You can hide.

Better yet, you can escape. You'd like that, wouldn't you?

A hopeful nod, her eyes wet with tears.

Bracing one hand against the wall, Elisha pulled herself up to a kneeling position. As she reached up, the pain in her ribs stabbed at her and she winced, turning away from the discomfort as if slapped. Moving slower still, she finally reached the latch, and pulled slowly, surely.

It sprung open with a small click. Beyond the cupboard door, various junk. First, the smell of rubber from an assorted stack of coated Olympic weight plates (and having bought them on a whim during the pandemic, Sean hadn't used them since, but had kept up his Jamaican patty intake). One long handle of a Flymo (which, at least, he *did* put to good use). Mop and bucket, rubber gloves, an old can of Dulux emulsion on the little shelf next to the gas meter. A thick rubber torch hanging from a nail on the back wall.

The plates on top of the pile were twenty kilos each, but

Elisha could only guess that the two beneath were heavier, since they were bigger. She hauled herself on top of them and sat cross-legged. Fingernails digging into the wood of the door, she brought it in, shutting it as softly as possible.

And, there in the darkness, let her head rest against the wall.

Fingers groping upward, she found the barrel of the torch and thumbed the switch. A cone of light appeared, falling over one side of her body as she sat cross-legged, patches of psoriasis still looking harsh and ugly on her skin. In front of her, the handle of the Flymo and a tool bag rested on other garden implements, including a rake and a pitchfork. The tool bag that sat on top of them hung open; there were so many tools. An old bag, from the look of it: dirty but heavy-duty brown canvas with a deeper brown leather for the handles and piping. Dragging the bag closer toward her answered with a wooden clink as she pulled aside garden shears, a hammer, a Ouija board, a saw, a pair of chisels, one bigger than the other, and a crowbar.

She frowned, and in doing so, her cheek throbbed harder. Gingerly, she touched the flesh there; still puffy and tender. Running her fingers across the base of her nose, they came away streaked with blood, bright red in the torch's glare.

Scoffing, she returned her attention back to the matter at hand. Of all things to put in the cupboard, Sean had left a Ouija board. But she remembered it now: he'd been to watch *Late Night with the Devil* with friends last year and, off the back of that outing, one of them had made a bet with Sean. Elisha couldn't remember the details and she didn't care to, but she knew that Sean had been given the board as a booby prize and, not wanting to cause offence by throwing the board away, he simply tossed it in the cupboard instead. Which is where other items also found their final resting place: spools of washing line that were too short or too weak for the garden, heavy duty rubberised black bags for moving rubble (which were great if you were an actual builder rather than an account manager), and assorted lengths and widths of wood; off cuts from home repair jobs in years past. So many of the tools were wooden handled, and she marvelled at how old they must be to have been made with one.

Easing out the Ouija board, she placed it in her lap, where it lay slick and cool against her thighs. The board surface was roughly the same size as the lid of a shoebox with the wood around an inch thick. Smooth to the touch with the surface creases of age and wrinkled black inking on each of the four corners. At the top of the board, OUIJA in a slight arc imprinted on the wood in bold black font, sat above two arcs of capital letters: ABCDEFGHIJKLM on the first row and NOPQRSTUVWXYZ on the second. A sun symbol and YES in the top left-hand corner, with a moon symbol and NO in the top right. A straight line of 1234567890 above a simple GOOD BYE at the bottom of the board, making Elisha ponder why a board that looked so old had a spelling mistake; *surely* people could spell 'goodbye' back then, couldn't they?

But Elisha knew that the board by itself wouldn't be enough, so she dug through the deeper recesses of the bag, groping over slick handles and cool hard metal (the secateurs for those rare instances she had given Sean a hand in the garden), and finally found the other part of the board. She couldn't remember the name, but knew that you had to use a … *pointer* of some sort, and now, here it was. About the size of a cigarette pack, the wooden pointer was heart shaped, with a modest glass lens in its centre.

That's not what you came here for.

Isn't it? The knife is still outside.

But, I've got peace and quiet now.

So, you don't want to escape after all, then. Remember what I said about why you let this happen?

Elisha sniffed and touched her nose. Again her fingertips came away bloody and she turned her attention back to the pointer. The lens was curved, like that of a magnifying glass and when Elisha held it up the contents of the tool bag were magnified, as was the smear of blood on the underside of the lens.

Maybe this is what you came for.

No. I know what I came for, and it wasn't this.

Oh, no, of course not – you came to escape. And a very good job you're doing of it, too. Some monster you are. That pudgy bastard upstairs has gone back to sleep. Nothing like getting your second wind, right?

She slammed the pointer down on the board. '*Then why don't you* help *me stop him?*'

Silence.

Nothing but the smell of rubber and the musty air for an answer.

'*I. Said. Fucking. Help me!*' she hissed, jabbing the pointer at H-E-L-P-M-E.

Again, silence.

Moments stretched into minutes.

Resigned, Elisha tossed the pointer back in the bag, followed by shoving the Ouija board in to join it. All she had gotten for her troubles was a head pounding now with an added headache and a prolonged nosebleed. Sniffling did nothing to abate the flow and when she wiped her finger across the nose, it came away with enough blood to form a rivulet.

'Fuck off,' she muttered, flicking the droplets in the direction of the bag.

I thought you wanted to escape. So why are you still here?

Her mouth fell open as she pondered the question, eyes filling with tears. Some crested the brink, spilling onto her cheeks.

I like it here.

Do you? Because this sounds a lot like you want what that man has to offer. Too much respect on your hands? Any more teeth you want to lose?

Breath shuddered out of her, more tears falling as she reached for the garden shears. Each blade was over a foot long, blackened with oil, time and use, and yet, the edges were plainly sharp.

Reaching up for the torch, she thumbed the switch off, plunging the cupboard into darkness.

I like it here.

You're really going to do it. You're finally going to escape.

Thank God.

He has nothing to do with this.

No, I do.

No you don't; you don't have the guts. You're weak. You've always been weak and you'll –

Pushing her limb against the blade, Elisha swiped her wrist along its length, quickly doing the same on the other arm. Stinging lines scored her and she reflexively flung her hands under her armpits, wincing as she hugged her ribs.

Pain, like so many things, if continued for long enough becomes the norm and so, can prompt a body to acclimatise to a catalogue of abuse and injury.

Now I can escape.

Looks like it. He'll never find you.

There in the darkness, Elisha leaned her head against the wall, and let her arms fall by her sides, waiting for the darkness outside to creep in.

Letting peace fall over her.

Smother her.

Naked flesh now accustomed to the absence of clothing.

Skin desensitised to the junk that she sat on.

Cramp settled into her hips, those muscles contracting with almost painful force.

Invisible trickling down her wrists, like lost spiders. And while there were no doubt spiders in this cupboard, even though cobwebs were evident, creepy crawlies were the least of her worries now. Having reached rock bottom the only way was up, no matter how slow or small the steps would be

… but, top of the list was the *whispering*.

She sat forward with the slow deliberation of a snake alerted to distant but evident prey. Head lifting in the darkness, senses pulling taut, which only made her head throb even more.

It didn't make any sense. That whispering seemed diffuse like smoke, with the voice coming from *somewhere* outside the cupboard. It wasn't Sean, since the voice wasn't deep enough and, no doubt, Sean was still in bed, sleeping.

Her hand feeling along the panels of the door, stretching up to where the latch would be, slowly applying pressure – and then it occurred to her it was probably a fool's errand: the door latched from the outside. Being spring-loaded, it would have to be opened from the outside

… unless you break the latch.
You realise if you break it, he'll come running again.

andwhyisthatbad?

More force against the door, and wood creaked, groaning in response. But the whispering was maddening enough to cloud Elisha's reasoning so she pushed harder, oblivious to what would happen.

The latch popped, and slammed the door wide open against the side of the staircase, the impact loud within the confines of the cupboard.

Shit, you've done it now.
Really? Done what?
You know what?

fuckthatworthlessdonkeyIdon'tcare.

I'm sure you'll care when he comes charging after you, screaming bloody murder for disturbing his beauty sleep. What are the chances that he'll let you off with a warning?

One hand gripping the doorway, Elisha hauled herself up and out of the cupboard, concrete flooring and rubber plates underfoot now yielding to the carpet and its plastic protector that ran the length of the hallway. For a multitude of injuries from loose teeth to a broken rib, the whispering – now seemingly coming from the kitchen – took hold of her senses.

There's someone here.
there'sdefinitelysomethingelsehere.

Syrupy slow, her gaze fell to her forearms. Ugly gashes across the inside of both wrists, the wound longer across the left than the right. Each injury a darkened valley running through a rise of puckered flesh, with dried blood on her palms in haphazard streaks.

No more bleeding.

From cuts that she had hoped were deep enough to stop... everything. She had hoped they were deep enough but apparently they weren't – either that or she had miraculously healed in a matter of moments, but there was probably a simpler explanation.

Something else you couldn't do right.

Up ahead from somewhere in the kitchen, the voice; still whispering, muttering.

The trick to stealth was patience, the idea that you could move at a glacial pace as if you had all the time in the world, regardless of what your objective was. Step by step: planting her heel, slowly laying her foot flat then peeling it off the floor, one foot after the other until she reached the kitchen.

Nothing but the fridge, drawers, oven and hobs, cupboards and washing machine, orderly as always under the worktop's granite finish. Two saucepans on the back hobs. Electric kettle plugged into one of the twin sockets. Beyond the window in the back door of the kitchen, nothing but darkness of night.

Her heartbeat louder now, a pulse of distraction beating in her ears.

But I'm the only one here.

Are you?

youhopeyouare.

Her breath shuddering out of her.

A cursory look to the ceiling; nothing there but the grey fluorescent disc of the overhead light, currently switched off, and the dull metallic gleam of the extractor hood in the gloom. Whoever or *whatever* was whispering, they weren't here – but it sounded like they weren't far away either.

Which made no sense.

Opening the fridge, a swathe of light fell at her feet. Clinking in the fridge door, a bottle of semi-skimmed milk, one of Thousand Island dressing, a bottle of Lucozoade, a litre carton of Tesco's pulp-free orange juice, and a bottle of *Château d'Yquem* that was down by about a third.

No.

Footsteps; coming down the stairs, before scuffing their way along the hall. A moment later, slowing mid-way. Then picking up pace until Sean's head appeared around the kitchen door, the fridge light picking out his look of disdain.

'What happened to the cupboard door?'

She met his gaze, sidelong. 'I wanted to be alone.'

Immediate confusion on Sean's face now: brow furrowing as he cast a quick look back to the hallway as if that would fill in the proverbial blanks. Then, back to her, mouth falling open as he frowned. 'You mean,' – and here, he shook his head as if that would shake the words loose – 'that you sat in there? Are you mad?'

Elisha pursed her lips, weighing the question. 'You know, I don't think I am.' When Sean didn't answer, she continued. 'I'm guessing, to an outsider, they might question why –'

Sean's hand swung up and slapped her, the snap of skin against skin loud, sharp and ugly.

'– I've stayed here, or decided to stay here, or even why I *wanted* to stay …' Her voice tailing off now.

Comprehension dawning on both of them.

Until, finally, Elisha gave a small whispery laugh.

'You know? I'm surprised that it's taken this long to see the truth.' Bewilderment on her face. 'You're … *weak*. You're really weak.'

In a blur of speed, Sean's fist swung up to her face – and in a smack of flesh, landed promptly in Elisha's grip. His mouth a grim line, he yanked his hand back but apart from the briefest movement, Elisha's hand remained.

Holding him in place.

'All the abuse, the beatings. Wondering what the reason was. That if you had that much hatred for someone, why you would still spend so much time with them. Now, I understand. It's that weakness. You lash out because you can't admit that you're weak.'

No longer struggling, Sean stood there wide-eyed in dawning horror, there in the light from the fridge door in the gloom, his gaze following Elisha's … which almost slithered over his fist.

Her other hand came up to meet it, caressing the back of his knuckles. 'This, for instance. Pain and suffering from … just a bunch of fingers.'

Reaching into his fist, she gently uncurled his little finger.

Tears of fright now leaking from Sean's eyes

until the finger was held straight

and then bent beyond

until bone cracked unseen in that digit and Sean screeched in agony, his knees buckling.

'See?' she scoffed. 'It's nothing to be afraid of. You're just weak.'

But Sean couldn't see. Not when he was struggling to stand up, his face an ugly grimace, with his eyes screwed shut and tears on his cheeks.

Until that soft caress returned to the next finger – and Sean's eyes flicked open in terror.

Then confusion.

Whimpering now.

I never realised just how small he really is. It … used to be like I could feel him everywhere in the house.

Look at this coward now, realising that he's lost his power.

I'm surprised that he held on to it for so long. Honestly.

ifindthisweaknessdisGUSTing.

All of this simpering frailty from someone that had the audacity to lay hands on her earlier. 'You truly irritate me.'

His gaze flitting between her face and her hand.

'What?'

Sean swallowed, backing up to the wall as her grasp followed with him. *'What* are *you?!'*

'What am I what?'

Frantic now, licking his lips as he shook his head, a gasp here and there in response to his ruined finger. His eyes searching her face as if that would be answer enough. 'You look … you look –'

She flung her face into his, noses almost touching. *'Shut up, or I'll shut you up.'*

Snarling, she let go, turning away. All of that fawning was contemptible; sickening, and the nausea that churned in her stomach was something she could taste now. Hot, sour, and acidic. Gritting her teeth, her gaze fell to the worktop and then the kettle. Its reflective surface distorted her image as a funhouse mirror would but

something looked different.

Odd.

Taking it by the handle, her attention on the kettle's body, she stepped back into the light from the fridge.

And faltered.

According to the improvised mirror, her face was long, sunken-cheeked with additional patches of psoriasis, but most striking of all were her eyes.

Amber now.

Slitted black pupils, like those of a snake, staring coldly back at her.

She returned her attention to Sean.

Who stood rigid against the wall, his mouth agape and eyes so wide they appeared to bulge past their lids. Even when she shifted to meet his gaze, that frozen stare passed through her, sightless.

Elisha raised a hand to her face, unblinking, and stroked one of the new patches of scaly skin, rasping under her fingers.

Answering it with her whispery laugh.

NUCKELAVEE

For a relatively small clutter of sea-begirt rocks, the British Isles boast a very ancient and multilayered folklore in which numerous servants of chaos are to be found. From club-wielding giants like Cormoran and Blunderbore to hounds of Hell like Striker and Black Shuck, from lake-dwelling saurians like Nessie and Morag to misty mountain horrors like the Big Grey Man, the Barguest and the Ceffyl Dwr, all the home countries of Britain tell tales of monstrous beings that seemingly lurk with a two-in-one purpose: the destruction of mankind and the ruin of his civilisation.

But of all the monsters that bestride the myths and legends of the lands now called the United Kingdom, surely the scariest is to be found in one of its remotest corners, where the population it preys upon is extraordinarily small and isolated.

It may be that the numerous aquatic beasts said to haunt the roaring seas around the outer rim of the Scottish isles are among the most horrible in all British folklore because those seas themselves can be terrifying, rolling and exploding with volcanic force, the rocky pinnacles they beat upon looking more like petrified titans than geological formations. Alternately, these legends may stem from the various real-life monstrosities that have washed up on the outer isles' shores. In 1808, for example, the horrifying Stronsay Beast, an unidentified carcass some 55ft in length, wallowed onto an Orkney beach, and was said to have paws as well as fins. In 1860 meanwhile, the rotted hulk of what appeared to be a giant squid floated ashore at Scalloway on Shetland. There is no doubt that around those distant rugged outposts, genuine ocean life is intimidating enough, while the North Atlantic storms can be cataclysmic. And yet, one still must wonder what in the imaginations of those hardly islanders conjured up a ghastly and fantastical creature like the Nuckelavee.

Unless, of course, it didn't come from their imagination at all.

Originating exclusively in Orcadian myth, ie the folklore of Orkney, one of Britain's northernmost archipelagos, the Nuckelavee

– according to one 19th Century journal, 'the most cruel and malignant of all uncanny beings that trouble mankind' – is a sea monster, yet it commits most of its atrocities on land and announces its arrival in the most dramatic way.

Picture yourself on a scenic Orcadian beach: white sand littered with shells and seaweed, a blue sky overarching, an equally blue sea running inshore in the form of heavy breakers. And then, above the normal crash and rumble of the elements, you hear something much more distinctive: a tremendous, blood-chilling howl, which, if it wasn't sounding from beneath fathoms of surging, swirling seawater, would likely blast your eardrums. It is then followed by an approaching thunder of hooves pounding along the seabed, again muffled by the heaving waves above, yet growing steadily louder, and then, as it gallops up onto the shore, you see the Nuckelavee in all its glory, glittering wet, towering over you.

It is unimaginably grotesque to look at.

Skinless, all muscle and veins, it is at first glance an immense human/horse hybrid. Yet there is nothing elegant about it. This isn't a centaur. The human portion grows out of its back, and has excessively long, very strong arms with diabolical barbed claws on the ends of them. Both its heads, the horse and the human, are single-eyed and equipped with powerful jaws and rows of serrated teeth, while the legs are equipped with fins and gills.

According to tradition, and maybe unsurprisingly, many victims of the Nuckelavee (or 'Devil of the Sea', as it is known in Orkney) died from fright. Others were so paralysed with terror that they were easy meat for it, while the ones who managed to run, were overhauled with ease. The Nuckelavee has four legs, remember. Even if you stayed and fought, you'd also fail, because this monster has many ways to kill you. Aside from its claws and teeth, which are its most commonly used weapons, the horse part is said to possess toxic breath, emitting vapours so foul that humans and animals will succumb straight away and even crops will wilt and rot in the fields. Its mere presence, the folklorists say, can be fatal, as it carries many infectious diseases, including – in the past – the Black Death.

However, despite this, and unlikely as it may seem, there have been reports of individuals who survived their encounters with this Devil of the Sea. Invariably, those local folk said to have escaped the

Nuckelavee were either saved by sudden cloudbursts and pouring rain, which events always drive it back into the ocean, or because they had the sense to leap over streams or burns. Like many demons of age-old Scottish myth, the Nuckelavee cannot cross fresh water.

One might have thought that in the far northern reaches of Scotland, any beast's vulnerability to rainwater and fast-flowing streams might have put it at a considerable disadvantage, but such were these ancient belief systems that God, it was said, would only allow these hellish creations of his to dwell upon the Earth after he had first inflicted some weakness upon them. Or, if not the Judeo-Christian God, maybe it was the creator lords of earlier pantheons: the Dagda perhaps, the 'Mither of the Sea' (a powerful Celtic sea spirit often said to restrain the Nuckelavee during the summer months), or maybe the Viking 'allfather', Odin. In fact, Odin is probably the most relevant celestial power to reference in this case, because in ancient Orcadian documents, the monster was referred to as the knoggelvi, and if that sounds distinctly Norse, it's easily understandable because the Orkney Islands were a Norwegian settlement through from the 8th Century to the 15th.

The equine factor, which is visible in several other Northern Scottish monsters, may also be important here. It's a common misconception that the Vikings primarily pillaged Britain's coastlines, when in fact, their longships were so designed that they could navigate inland waterways, and when those waterways gave out, they used horses. Thus, during the full-on Viking conquests of the later Dark Ages, their armies rode to battle, or from village to village and hillfort to hillfort, ravaging all in their path.

Were horses so rare in those faraway reaches of early Britain that their use as deliverers of death and terror was wildly misunderstood? Was the human part of the Nuckelavee representative of the Northmen themselves, who were fearsome enough when you met them face to face, but when they came at you on horseback were all but invincible?

For all these perhaps rather pat explanations, the Nuckelavee continues to fascinate students of folklore, who consider it the archetypal polyglot monster, its constituent parts symbolic of the various trials and tribulations suffered by the Orkney islanders in distant times. It would seem possible that the crop-destroying breath is a race memory of the horror that fungi and other forms of blight could wreak in a society totally dependent on agriculture, while the infectious nature of the monster definitely hints at the dangers of pestilence in a world unguarded by medicine.

So fabulously nightmarish is the Nuckelavee that it almost seems a shame it probably never existed, though Orcadians themselves would doubtless disagree. Until as recently as the 19th Century, many islanders couldn't even hear the beast mentioned without crossing themselves, whispering prayers or even rushing to chapel.

DOPPELGÄNGER
David Barnett

It was not what you might call a usual Friday. I had my hair cut short, which is a bigger deal than you might think, as I've had it shoulder-length since I was fourteen. I fell out with my best friend, who I've also had since I was fourteen. I saw a kidnapping in broad daylight. And I met my doppelgänger. The first three things were sort of related.

The fourth was out there on its own, that's for sure.

So, my name is Brad Pope, and I'm thirty-three years old. I work in what they call a fulfilment centre, but it's really just a big warehouse where all the books and gadgets and general stuff you buy from a certain online retailer gets gathered off the shelves and parcelled up and slapped with a label so it can get sent to you and left beside someone's bins three streets away from your actual house. I do the gathering and parcelling and labelling; the delivery stuff isn't my fault, so don't complain to me.

I generally work three twelve-hour shifts a week, hence me being off on a Friday and spending the morning with Geoff, who is – was – my best friend. People often thought Geoff and I were brothers. We were into the same stuff; rock music, comics, sci-fi and anime movies, video games, fantasy books. We also looked a lot the same. We both had long hair, both were what you might call of a sturdy physique, without being overly tall, and we had a similar sartorial style … that is, jeans and a black T-shirt, which was usually related to one of our shared interests. That Friday morning it was actually identical T-shirts, with an image of Catbus from *My Neighbour Totoro*.

I think that's what caused this whole problem, to be quite honest. As Geoff and I sat in our usual table by the window in

Brenda's Cafe, both drinking a latte, the T-shirts thing was really, really bugging me.

'Don't you have another T-shirt?' I muttered.

Geoff paused stirring his latte, and looked at me. 'Don't you?'

'You know I have loads of T-shirts. So do you. Why did you have to wear that one?'

Geoff considered this for a long moment. 'What time did you get dressed?'

I frowned at him and looked at my watch. 'Dunno. Nine-ish, maybe?'

He sat back with a satisfied smile. 'I got dressed at half-eight. So I was wearing it first.'

As you can imagine, this infuriated me. 'When did you *buy* it, though, Geoff?'

He paled a little, a not inconsiderable feat given that he had the complexion of a lump of dough. As, I suppose, so did I. He knew I had him. I'd bought the T-shirt first and after seeing me in it he'd ordered one too. Quick as a flash, though, he recovered and said with a smirk, 'But who bought *Totoro* on DVD first?'

'You. One day before me. But who watched it *first*, Geoffrey?'

Normally, this sort of good-natured verbal sparring was the sort of thing we both immensely enjoyed. Not that Friday. It was, to be quite frank, getting right on my tits. As was Geoff. In fact, it was worse than that. As I sat across from him, staring at him, I began to loathe him. And it doesn't take a genius to realise that was because, deep down, I loathed myself. Geoff was me, and everything I didn't want to be.

And that was partly because of the email I'd received that morning from FamilyHistoryUncovered.

Yeah, FamilyHistoryUncovered, FHU. You know it. Everybody's mad for it. You sign up, they send you a little plastic test-tube which you have to spit in and send back to their labs somewhere in the wilds of Lancashire, and six weeks later they've analysed your DNA, and sent you the results. You're hoping to find out that you have a really exotic lineage but you open the email and you're ninety-eight per cent English, one per cent Scottish, and one percent Danish, which I think they throw into everyone's results so even if you're as boring as me you can at least fantasise that you've got traces of Viking in you. Every so often you get an email from FHU saying they think they've found birth records about your great-great-grandfather, and sometimes that you might have a fourth cousin in Slough because you share two percent DNA. And then you send a message to the fourth cousin in Slough through the app saying it's lovely to meet extended family, and they never reply. Though that might just be me.

So, I'd woken up to an email from FHU. They'd apparently enrolled me in a brand new feature that was in the beta-testing phase, and it wouldn't cost me any money. I wouldn't have normally even opened the email, let alone read it, but for some reason, I did. And I think that was down to the subject line:

Don't you think you could be a better you?

Well, yes, as it happened. I had been thinking about that for a while. I had a dead-end, zero-hours contract job, I was living in a smelly bedsit, I had exactly zero girlfriends and exactly one friend, who most of the time got on my nerves. I was unfit and my clothes were rubbish and there was only so far in life you could get by having an encyclopaedic knowledge of *Attack on Titan*, the back-catalogue of Rush, and Alan Moore's comics oeuvre. I was a little foggy on the details about just how I could be a better me, but FHU helpfully supplied a photograph of my maternal great-grandfather Fred at the top of the email. Mum always said I had a look of her grandad, and I had to admit that in the grainy, sepia picture I could sort of see myself in his features. There the similarity ended. Fred was in uniform, just about to take part in the Normandy landings on D-Day. He was smart and slim and handsome and tidy and looked precisely like the sort of person he was, which was someone who could go off to war and survive and still look presentable after it, which was probably precisely the sort of person I wasn't.

Be more Fred, the photograph seemed to say. I'd stood up and tried to adopt Fred's striking pose in the dusty full-length mirror by my bed, pushing my shoulders back and sucking in my stomach, which needed help from both my hands to get to the place where Fred's approximately was on his torso. Then I'd let my belly flop out, with relief. I wasn't great-grandad Fred, and I'd never be. And besides, I had no great desire to go to war. Unless it was to take part in *Attack on Titan*. And even then, if I volunteered to bravely leave the walled cities protecting the remnants of humanity to wage war on the gigantic creatures threatening the world, they'd probably tell me they'd get back to me.

The rest of the email was about a new project that FHU was running with a few carefully-selected members. They had gathered my various data together, everything from health records to financial reports, academic qualifications, job applications, the works. I vaguely wondered as I read it if that was all strictly legal, but they did point out that I had given tacit approval for any such data sifting when I signed the terms and conditions upon first signing up to them. The exciting bit, though, was that they had cross-referenced all this with information gained from my DNA sample to put together a programme of possibilities, probabilities and projections which, they were absolutely certain, would make me a better me. They would be in touch, they promised. And very soon.

I was thinking about all of this while I watched Geoff slurp his latte. He sounded like a pig at the trough. I took a drink of my own latte and realised I sounded exactly the same.

Geoff said, 'Do you want to come back to mine to watch *Andor*?'

'I've already watched it,' I said.

Geoff looked at me as though I'd said the sky was green. 'So?'

'So I don't want to watch it again.'

Geoff shrugged. 'What do you want to watch, then? *The Mandalorian*?'

I stood up abruptly, shaking the table. 'Nothing,' I decided suddenly. 'I'm going to get my hair cut.'

This was more earth-shattering news than the revelation that I didn't want to watch *Andor* again. Geoff stared at me, aghast. 'You had your hair cut at Christmas.'

'Proper cut,' I said. 'Short.'

'What's wrong with you?' said Geoff, anguished.

'And I'm going to buy some new clothes,' I said, relishing his discomfort and confusion. 'And I'm going to join a gym.'

'Are you ill? Are you on drugs?'

I walked to the door. 'I just want to be a better me,' I said, thinking of great-grandad Fred. Then I held my head up high, put my shoulders back, and pulled hard on the door, ready to march out to my new life.

'You have to push it, love,' called Brenda from behind the counter as the door rattled in its frame but didn't budge. I knew that, of course.

'Right,' I said, and slunk out, avoiding Geoff's stare as I walked past the cafe where he sat, for the last time, in our usual table by the window.

Half an hour later I walked out of a Turkish barber shop feeling the breeze on my neck for the first time in about twenty years. I'd gone in because it was empty, but the guy sitting on one of the plastic chairs with his feet up had seemed a bit surprised to see me.

'You want a haircut?' he said, as though I'd gone in and asked for a piece of haddock.

I looked around. 'Erm. Yeah. It's a barber's, isn't it?'

He shrugged. 'I suppose.' He looked around and dropped his voice to a whisper. 'Be quite honest with you, mate, it's really a money-laundering front. We don't actually get many real customers in. I get my brother to come and sit in the chair a couple of times a week and faff with his hair a bit.'

'Oh,' I said with a sage nod. I pulled out my phone and showed him the photo of great-grandad Fred. 'But you cut hair, right? Can you do this?'

It turned out he could, well, near as damn it, anyway. He was OK with cutting off most of my hair and shaving it up at the back and sides with the clippers, but his scissor-work on the top left a bit to be desired. 'Fine with a bit of product on,' he muttered, slathering my unevenly chopped fringe down with some sort of gel. Still, he only charged me a tenner.

As I stood in the street, admiring my new look in my reflection in the window, I thought I might pop down to Primark and buy some clothes. Proper clothes that fit. Maybe even a suit. And some working-out gear. I was just googling 'cheap gyms no subscription fees near me' on my phone when something caught my eye further down the street, outside Brenda's Cafe.

It was Geoff, talking with two guys in grey suits. They chatted for a bit, then they led him to a black car parked on the road, and opened the rear door for him. Geoff hauled his bulk inside, then the two men glanced around and got in the front seats, and the car pulled away.

I texted him immediately: *What are you up to?*

Wudnt you like to no, he replied. That was another thing I loathed about Geoff. He was dead thick on the texts. Immediately another one came through: *Hows being a better u working out*

I waited a bit, the car now disappeared from view, knowing that whatever it was he wouldn't be able to resist telling me. My phone pinged.

So these guys came to Brendas asking for u & said u might be interested in some original star wars action figs. Goin 2 see em at a lockup now. Reckon they've got a rocket firing boba fett and telescoping lightsaber Vader in ORIGINAL PACKAGING

I felt light-headed. They were the holy grail of *Star Wars* action figures. Then I frowned and tapped at my phone. Why was Geoff going with them?

I told em I was Brad Pope, he replied, followed by a string of laughing emojis.

'Bastard!' I said out loud, and an old woman being pulled along by a sausage dog glowered at me. Suddenly I didn't feel like I wanted a Primark suit, or to join a gym. I wanted to be taken to a lock-up to see a rocket-firing Boba Fett in original packaging. 'Bastard,' I said again, more weakly, and went to find a pie-shop and my bus home.

I bought three pies and was just worrying the third one when I heard a scratching noise from my door. I turned down the record player (*No Mean City* by Nazareth on vinyl). Probably the smackhead from upstairs confused as to which floor he was on again. But then I heard a key slide in and the lock click. I put down my pie and stood up. Must be the landlord, though he wasn't meant to turn up unannounced. I was just heading to the door when it opened and swung inwards. Geoff, I groaned inwardly as the figure filled the door frame. I'd given him a key ages ago so he could crash at mine while I was at work when his mum was doing his head in, before she died a couple of years back. Come to gloat about the action figures, no doubt. He was still wearing the Catbus T-shirt and the same jeans and …

… and it was then I got the sort of feeling you get when you nod off to sleep on the sofa and dream that you're falling off a kerb and jerk awake. It wasn't Geoff. It was me. The absolute spitting image of me, before I had my hair cut. My mouth went dry and my eyes bulged and I just stared at the other me, who stopped one step into the bedsit and stared back at me.

'Well,' said me, the other me. 'This is awkward.'

Which is exactly what I would have said in his position.

'You're not supposed to be here,' said Me. With a capital M. Which I'll call him to differentiate from, well, me. Was my voice really so … nasal?

I worked some spit around my mouth and managed to say, 'Actually, I could say the same about you.' I swallowed. 'In fact, I'd go as far as to say … you're not supposed to exist.' I glanced down at the half-eaten pie. '*Do* you exist? Or have I got food poisoning? Am I hallucinating?'

'You may be an undigested bit of beef, a blot of mustard, a crumb of cheese, a fragment of underdone potato …' said Me.

'There's more of gravy than of grave about you, whatever you are!' I finished, on autopilot. '*A Christmas Carol.*'

'Our favourite,' said Me.

Which was true. But none the less discombobulating for it. I felt suddenly weak, and steadied myself on the back of the moth-eaten sofa. 'What are you?' I said in a small voice.

'I appreciate this must be a bit confusing,' said Me. He peered at me curiously. 'You've had your hair cut.'

'Just this afternoon,' I said, running my hand through the gloopy mess the barber had slapped on top. I had no idea why I was talking about personal grooming with a –

'Doppelgänger!' I suddenly shouted, pointing to him, my other hand going to my mouth in horror. 'Oh my God. I'm being haunted by my double!'

'Well,' said Me. 'It wasn't strictly supposed to happen like this. I'm not really sure what went wrong. The outreach team was supposed to pick you up earlier. I didn't get any messages to say anything had gone amiss.'

I backed away, though my double stayed where he was in the doorway. 'Outreach team?'

Me smiled. 'Yeah, they were supposed to draw you in with some rare *Star Wars* action figures. Meant to be irresistible.'

'Geoff!' I shouted. 'I saw Geoff getting into a car with two men. He texted me about action figures. He said he'd told them he was me.'

Me sighed, putting his hand over his mouth and shaking his head. 'Oh. Oh dear. Geoff. Yeah, I can see why they might have thought … you two do look alike and … oh, oh dear.' Me moved further into the room and shut the door behind him.

I looked around wildly for a weapon and grabbed the plastic fork the pie shop had given me, brandishing it out at the other me. 'Don't take another step towards me! Who were those men Geoff went with?'

'I told you,' Me said. 'The outreach team.'

'And what have they done with him? Where's Geoff now?'

'Well, right about now ...' Me glanced at his watch. It was exactly the same model as mine. Well, of course it was. 'Right about now, he's probably mulch.'

'Mulch?' I thought of all the things that *mulch* could be, and none of them were the sort of fate I'd wish on anyone, even Geoff. '*Mulch*?'

'Mulch,' agreed Me. 'It's sort of how it works. How it *should* work, anyway. You get taken off to be mulch, I take your place and be a better you. It normally works very well. Except they took Geoff instead.'

'But what do you mean by mul –' I began, then stopped. 'Wait. What did you just say? *Be a better you*? That's like that email I got ...' I scrabbled in my jeans pocket for my phone but my hands were sweaty and I dropped it. It bounced off the threadbare carpet and landed by Me's feet. He bent and picked it up.

'I think I'd better have that, thank you.' He stuffed it into his pocket – the same one I used for my phone – and nodded. 'Yeah. FamilyHistoryUncovered. FHU. That's where I'm from. Sort of.'

'I don't understand any of this,' I moaned. I was starting to feel unwell, a little feverish. This must be a dream, surely. Me seemed to consider for a moment.

'OK, well, it's all gone tits up now, so I don't suppose there's any reason not to fill you in. Shall we sit down? Have you got any beer?'

'There's some in the fridge,' I said miserably. 'It's Neck –'

'– Oil,' finished Me. 'I know. Our favourite. Why don't you go and get us a couple of tins and I'll tell you all about it. And don't try to squeeze out of that kitchen window. It's too small anyway and we're four storeys up. No shouting to anyone.'

'What would I say anyway?' I said weakly. 'I'm being held prisoner by myself?'

'Always the way, isn't it?' said Me, flopping down on the

sofa. In my spot. 'People always say you're your own worst enemy, Brad.'

That was true, actually. People did say that about me. Teachers, family, bosses. I self-sabotage. I carry on making the same mistakes time and time again, which they say is the definition of madness. If a job's worth doing, it's worth doing in a desultory, half-arsed fashion, according to me. I had potential. I was clever at school. I could have gone to university, made something of myself. Instead, I just ... slobbed. And once you start slobbing, it's a downhill slope you're skiing down, in Val d'Slob. It's a fast train you're on, all the way to Slobville. You've booked your ticket in slob-class on Air Slob and you're strapped in for the long-haul. It didn't have to be that way, but it was. And as I sat there on my sofa, drinking beer and staring at myself, also sitting on my sofa and drinking beer, I wondered if I could have made things turn out differently by, well, not being a slob.

'Why is this happening to me?' I said as levelly as I could.

Me shrugged. 'Essentially, Brad, because you're a slob.'

Ah, well, that answered that one, then. But it raised many, many more questions.

Me cracked open another beer. 'OK.' He seemed to gather his thoughts. 'So. You probably want to know what I am.'

'Are you a robot?' I guessed. 'Artificial intelligence?'

'No.'

'A clone, then.'

'No. Well. Sort of, but no.'

'How can you be sort-of a clone but not?'

Me took a deep breath. 'I was grown in a laboratory. From the DNA sample you provided to FHU. In mulch.'

I considered this. 'Mulch like what Geoff is right about now?'

'Exactly. But it's not science ... well, it is science, obviously, but there's other stuff going on as well. Older stuff.'

'Older stuff than science,' I said. I looked at Me. 'So you mean, magic?'

Me said, 'The place where all this happens is called Homogenous Organic Bioengineering.'

'That sounds more science-y than magic-y,' I pointed out. I'm not sure why, but it helped to try to focus on all this being science-y rather than magic-y. The sudden suggestion of magic added a whole new dimension to something I was already finding difficult to process.

'To be honest, it's just words,' admitted Me. 'The initials spell HOB.'

'Ah,' I said, as though that explained everything. I shook my head. 'That explains nothing.'

'There are … spirits of place,' Me said. 'Genius loci. Old gods that haunt forgotten corners of the world. Owd Hob is one of them. And he is on a mission of revenge against the modern world that has abandoned him.'

I took it all in. 'If this was the blurb for a video game I'd be, yep, I'll have that. But you're telling me this is … real? But why does this …'

'Owd Hob.'

'Why does this Owd Hob want revenge against me?'

Me laughed. We showed too many teeth when we laughed. 'He doesn't. You aren't the target of his revenge, but rather the tool of it. Or, I suppose, I am. Supposed to be. HOB set up FHU to find people like you. Who could be duplicated, through science and magic. Exact copies, with all the same personality traits and memories. Just better.'

'Define *better*,' I said.

Me began to count off on his fingers. 'You're lazy. You're a slob. You never do anything to help anyone else. You're selfish. You never fulfilled your potential. You drift through life barely interacting with anyone else. You don't speak to your family, you have no friends …'

'Not now I don't,' I said. 'Thanks to the *mulching* and all that. But, yeah, thanks.'

Me shrugged. 'It's true. You know it's true. That's why you were chosen. You make no impact on society, one way or the other. You're already mulch, Brad, or about as much use as mulch. Who would miss you when you're gone? You just consume, and give nothing back.'

'And you'll be a better me, then? That's the idea, is it?'

Me nodded. 'That's the idea. I'll get a haircut – a proper haircut. Lose weight. Get fit.' He tapped the side of his head. 'Use this brain to do something useful. Something helpful. Get a proper job. Be a constructive member of society. And further Owd Hob's beliefs and teachings of a oneness with the world, a connection with the earth, a symbiosis with the environment. And his glory days shall return once more.'

'And what happens to me while you're off being Cthulhu's Greta Thunberg?' I said, reaching behind me to casually but exaggeratedly scratch my arse.

'I think we both know,' said Me, smiling. 'Mulch.'

I nodded, as though it all made perfect sense. Then I yelled, 'Han shot first!' and pulled out the small knife I'd secreted down the back of my jeans when I went to get the beers. I roared and brought it down, hard, right into his shoulder, feeling the blade scrape against bone and sink into his soft flesh up to the handle.

Then I jumped up off the sofa and ran.

Well, I say 'ran'. I haven't run properly since I was at school. I made it as far as the door before I heard Me grunt and the knife clatter to the floor. I was already out of breath when I turned and saw him, standing up, one hand over his shoulder to stanch the flow of blood where I'd stuck him. The sight of the blood actually made me feel quite queasy. I can watch a dozen horror films in a row and not be bothered by the gore, but if I get a paper cut I almost faint. Of course, I'd be getting far worse than a paper cut if Me caught me.

'That's not a knife,' said Me, glancing down at the little kitchen blade on the floor. He reached behind him and pulled out of the back of his jeans what I can only describe as a machete. I've no idea how he sat down comfortably with that down there. Of course, I knew what was coming next as he brandished the weapon. *'That's* a knife.'

Casting wildly about I grabbed the nearest thing to hand: A completed Lego Death Star mounted on a stand on the chest of drawers near the door, and held it up with both hands. 'Stay back!' I commanded.

Me really must have been imbued with my memories and personality because he drew back with a sharp intake of breath. He knew, deep down, how much these things cost and how much time and effort I'd put into building it. I took advantage of his momentary confusion and, with hardly any regret – it was the Death Star or me – hurled it at him. Me put his hands up to fend it off and as it shattered into a thousand bricks on his arms I turned round, tore open the door, and pelted out into the hallway.

As Me had pointed out, we were four storeys up, with another three on top. My instinct was to go down, which was what he would be expecting. There'd be no point knocking on anyone's door on this floor – there were two other flats, one empty and one lived in by a deaf old Polish woman. Running down there'd be more chance of meeting someone and I could get to the street and scream blue murder.

So I went up.

The lights on the stairway were out and I crouched in the dark, half-way up to the next floor, trying to stop breathing so hard. Me had obviously paused to put something on the wound, what looked like a folded up tea-towel tied on with a strip of what appeared to be material torn off the curtains. I held my breath as he looked to the left and right, then over the bannister, listening. He couldn't hear footfalls but started to go down the stairs, then stopped, looked up and changed his mind. He'd second guessed me. I hauled myself to my feet with a grunt and began to run up, hearing him huffing and puffing on the landing.

When I got to the next floor I hammered as hard as I could on the first door. It was the smackhead's flat. I'd lived here for four years and never thought to find out his name. I could hear Me stepping heavily on the stairs and was just about to give up when the door opened a crack, and a yellow eye appeared, sunk deep into a lined, thin face.

'Yeah?'

'Oh God, smackhead, help me!'

'Fuck off.'

'Let me in!'

'Fuck off.'

'I'm being chased!'

This seemed to interest him, and he opened the door a little wider. He was bald and gaunt and barely had any teeth. 'Who by?'

'Me!' I said, trying to push past him. He stood his ground, wiry and stronger than he looked.

'Fuck off.'

I heard heavy breathing behind me and turned to see Me standing at the top of the stairs, chest wobbling with the effort of the chase, holding the machete. 'I really need ... to get ... fit,' he said.

'See!' I said triumphantly to the smackhead. 'He's got a knife!'

The smackhead peered at Me, then looked at me. 'Oh, yeah,' he said.

'Sorry if my friend's bothering you, Robin,' said Me, to the smackhead.

I stared from one to the other. 'How do you know he's called Robin?'

Me shrugged. 'Takes two seconds to show an interest in someone.'

The smackhead – Robin – did something I've never seen him do before. He smiled. 'Yeah, cheers, mate.' He stepped out of his doorway, standing between us. He peered at me again. 'Who are you, anyway?'

'Brad! From downstairs!' I gasped. 'We've seen each other loads of times.'

Robin frowned at me, and pointed at Me. 'No, he's the fat hippy from downstairs. I don't know you.'

'I had my hair cut!' I yelled shrilly. I patted my belly. 'Look,

I'm still fat! Please, he's going to kill me!'

Robin shrugged. 'Fair enough.' He turned to go back into his flat.

'Bollocks,' I said, and gave him a hard shove in the back, that caught him off guard and sent him crashing into Me, bringing both of them down on the landing in a tangle of limbs while I set off again up the next set of stairs.

On the next landing there was, I shit you not, a dead cat. It mustn't have been there long because it was still quite stiff. Scrunching up my face I gingerly grabbed it by the tail and held it like a club, leaning over the bannister. When Me came up the stairs I threw it at him. I heard him curse as the machete clattered out of his hand and bounced down the steps.

'You're a big lad but you're out of shape,' I shouted and ran to the next set of stairs.

This brought me up to the top floor. Me was gaining on me, the dead cat having barely slowed him down. I was so out of breath there were lights dancing in front of my eyes. I ran along the landing, banging on each of the three doors there, but nobody answered. I didn't even know if there was anyone living in these flats. At the end of the landing was another door, I presumed a cupboard or something. Maybe I could lock myself in there until help came. I wrenched it open, just as I heard Me climb the last of the stairs, and a sudden cold wind hit me in the face.

It was the door to the fire escape. It had got dark out, and the inviting lights of the town shone at me. This was it. My chance. If I could keep ahead of Me, make it down to the street, I'd be fine. I plunged forward on to the cold metal gantry, and felt a hand close around the neck of my T-shirt.

I pushed forward, feeling the fabric rip, and kept going. On to the small metal platform, my stomach hitting the balustrade. Then my feet were off the metal, and the lights were spinning, and I lurched forward into space, pivoting on the handrail, like some grotesque gymnast working the bars. The back street, seven storeys down, loomed at me. So this is it. I fall. I die. I wonder if I'll still be mulch? I wondered all those things, but most of all I wondered why I wasn't falling. Then I realised I was being held by my belt, by Me.

'I just have to let go,' said Me, the wind whipping past us. 'And it's all over.'

'I don't think that's a very good plan,' I said.

'Well, obviously, you wouldn't.'

'Think about it,' I said quickly, and I knew he was doing. 'You let me go and what happens? I fall all the way down there and make a mess on the pavement. Somebody will come out and see me lying there dead before you get down to the street. And that's going to be awkward for you, isn't it? How do you take my place if I'm very publicly dead?'

I could feel Me thinking about it. I was still balanced on the handrail, staring down at impending death many feet below, only his hand on my belt keeping me alive. He said, though a little uncertainly, 'Well, it doesn't matter, really. You were going to die anyway.'

I thought fast. 'Thing is, all this has been a bit of a balls-up, hasn't it? What with carting Geoff off to get mulched. I bet once you kill me and there's two bodies instead of one ... well, that's going to be a lot of paperwork for somebody, somewhere. Probably be better if everybody just let things be as they are, save all that hassle.'

There was silence from Me for a moment, then I yelled out as I pitched forward, him pushing me further over the handrail. 'It's the only way,' he said, though hesitated. 'I can't see ...'

I risked looking back over my shoulder at Me, standing on the fire escape, only his hand standing between me and a splattery death on the pavement far below. He was a monster, an unholy creature of science and magic, grown in an occult lab for nefarious purposes, whose entire existence was predicated on replacing me. But he was also me. I risked a smile, and said in my best Michael Caine, 'Hang on a minute, lads; I've got a great idea.'

Three months later, Geoff and I were sitting at our usual window table in Brenda's Cafe, enjoying the summer sunshine filtering through the dusty glass. Well, I say Geoff and I; Geoff was the artist formerly known as Me. And I was me.

I'd waited a tense minute hanging over the fire escape while Me thought about my plan and then hauled me back over. It had come to me in a flash of inspiration. Geoff was gone, mulch. I was very much still alive. Surely Me could still fulfil the terms of his existence by taking the place of *someone* out in the world? And with Geoff already gone, wouldn't it be easier to take his place rather than have to make some awkward phone calls to the people who'd created him to say they'd mulched the wrong guy?

Geoff had even fewer friends and family than I did, which is to say, none. And we'd always looked similar – like I said, people often thought we were brothers. So it was pretty easy for Me to slot into Geoff's life. I got to stay alive, and what's more, I'd got my friend back into the bargain. Except Me was *better* at being Geoff than Geoff was. Because, after all, Me was me.

There were conditions, of course. The new Geoff was going to make sure I lived a better life, and I was more than happy to do that. We joined a gym together; nothing too ridiculous, just tried to offset the potential of dying earlier than strictly necessary. And having had a very close brush with death, I suddenly felt like I wanted to live. I got myself on a degree course, starting in September, at university, studying Earth Sciences. Geoff had us volunteering for all kinds of charities. I kept my hair short, and grew a bit of a hipster beard to differentiate us just that bit more. Geoff kept his hair longer. I suspect he's had a bit of Botox, too, but I've never asked him about it.

Don't get me wrong, I'm not some kind of paragon of virtue or anything like that. But having had the experience I've had … well. It changes you. Am I *better* than I was? That's subjective.

But I'm no worse, which must count for something.

'There's one thing we have to bear in mind,' said Geoff as he stirred his latte. 'At some point – I don't know when, maybe tomorrow, maybe in twenty years – all the people like me, the *replacements* … we're going to be called upon. I don't know what for. But we will. And we'll have to enact Owd Hob's will.'

'I hope it's not tomorrow,' I said, sipping my latte. 'The new *Red Dead Redemption* is out.'

'Good point,' nodded Geoff. 'Want to come back to mine to watch *Andor*?'

'Only if we can get pies and Neck Oil,' I said.

Geoff smiled, and I grinned and reached over and clapped him on the shoulder. 'I love it when a plan comes together.'

NINGEN

In short, the ningen is a colossal, humanoid whale-like creature, currently unknown to science, but said to inhabit the Antarctic Ocean.

Yes, we actually said that: a colossal, humanoid whale.

Before anyone falls around laughing, some qualification needs to be added.

To start with, the ningen, which has never actually been measured because no specimens have ever been captured, is the subject of several purported photographs and poor-quality video excerpts, so some actual evidence, albeit poor, does exist. It is supposed to be white or very pale blue in colour, a common trait among sea-dwelling organisms, and reportedly has human facial characteristics, as in two frontward-looking eyes and a small, slit-like mouth, which again is not unknown among inhabitants of deep water; check out the anglerfish, the blobfish and the Koi carp. At the same time, certain sea-going mammals that very decidedly have few human features can still occasionally 'look human,' such as the dolphin and the manatee. Even the ningen's arms, which witnesses have described as being roughly the same shape and length (in proportion) as human arms and sometimes end in articulated digits, ie fingers, have a possible explanation in that extended pectoral fins are not uncommon among various species of ocean life.

But if all this makes the ningen sound like a possible genuine animal rather than a semi-mythical monster, one should consider that what we are essentially describing here is a gigantic, hairless merman.

If that in itself doesn't give cryptid-hunters reservations, the sheer size of the entity should, because lengths of 100 feet plus have been attributed to it, and it has even been likened in mass to a blue whale, the largest known animal on Earth. Surely, you might say, any aquatic creature of such prodigious size would already be known about and probably the subject of much intensive study. The response most often given to this is that the location, the Southern Ocean and the Antarctic Sea, are two of the least sailed maritime regions of the globe, while the sheer depth of the world's oceans has ensured that other deep-sea giants have eluded mankind for many centuries. The colossal squid was only filmed in its native environment for the first time in 2004, while the blue whale itself was only established as a real animal in 1874.

Sadly though, for those who are keen to believe that there is substance to this mystery, the history of ningen sightings is somewhat sketchy.

To begin with, it first appears to have been mentioned during an anonymous internet post in 2007, the originator of which claimed to have been on board a Japanese whaling vessel at the time. Initially, or so the story went, the ningen, which was spotted shortly before nightfall in an unspecified Antarctic location, was mistaken for a large but curiously coloured submarine, which suddenly, on the whaler's approach, made an immediate and very unsubmarine-like dive into the cobalt blue depths.

Colourful as this story and others like it are – the ningen has most often, or so the witnesses say, been mistaken initially for an overlarge, unusually smooth iceberg – none of it counts for much without corroborating evidence. But the footage itself is rarely convincing.

A grainy Google Earth image dated to 2005 supposedly depicts a ningen swimming in the Southern Ocean, but it could easily be that this particular object is a genuine iceberg. Likewise, one very famous piece of film, first published by the Enoshima Aquarium in Kanagawa, Japan, in 2010, appears to show a large, humped, smooth-skinned creature lying motionless on an undisclosed part of the seabed, ignoring the silt swimming around it and smiling benignly at the camera, its eyes shimmering with eerie bioluminescence. At first glance, it induces a prickle of unease. As often may be the case with this kind of footage, if you're actively looking for a ningen, you can easily think that you've found one. However, after much discussion at fairly respectable levels in the marine expert community, this picture has now been dismissed as a rock formation with two crabs where the eyes should be. (It must also be pointed out that, in return, ningen believers have themselves dismissed this explanation, calling it convoluted, contrived and 'a bit of a reach').

Other so-called photographs have probably done the case more harm than good, portraying only the faintest images, objects that are almost certainly undersea bergs, and in one case, the comical cartoon-like figure of an immense white blob walking across a floating fragment of sheet ice on a pair of tiny matchstick legs.

But if nothing else, at least the ningen serves as a continuation of an age-old Japanese tradition because it isn't as if that country's sea-going folklore isn't already filled with strange, bizarre and often petrifying sea monsters, many with a vaguely human appearance.

The umibōzu, for example, are demonic sea giants, near enough featureless but human in shape, who often emerge from the waves as great shadow forms, and whose sole purpose is the sinking of ships. Likewise, there are the ningyo, a uniquely Japanese species of giant predatory mer-people, and then the appalling Nure-onna, a colossal sea snake with the head of a shrieking woman. Less humanoid to look at, but no less unnerving is Akkorokamui, a gargantuan octopus said to inhabit the volcanic depths of Uchiura Bay, the Bake-kujira, the skeleton of a whale that supposedly drifts along Japan's western coast, looking to sink the vessels of all those hunting its kin, and then the isonade, a colossal megalodon-type shark, which tears out ships' bottoms with its spiked tail.

Of course, most of these tales date to olden times, but there are sea monster stories almost unique to Japanese tradition that come to us from much more recently. In 1958, the Japanese captain and crew of an Antarctic research vessel named **Sōya Maru** sensationally attested to having encountered a truly gigantic animal, of a species unknown but equipped with both reptilian and mammalian features – fur, for example, but also saw-like ridges on its back – which they nicknamed 'the Antarctic Godzilla'.

Whether or not that latter sighting is in any way connected to the impact made by the original movie, Godzilla, released to huge acclaim four years earlier in 1954, or even to special effects maestro Ray Harryhausen's debut feature, The Beast from 20,000 Fathoms, released one year before that, and in which a fictional dinosaur, a Rhedosaurus, escapes its tomb of ice high in the Arctic and goes on a wild rampage, it shows that a sea-going nation like the Japanese has a great awareness of potential ocean-dwelling monstrosities.

In regard to the matter of the ningen, that could mean one of two things. Either they know an unnatural beast lurking in the deep sea when they see one. Or they have very fertile imaginations.

ECHIDNA
Mark Morris

There was a time when Ben would have felt so alive on a day like this. The combination of elements was damn near perfect: the sun blazing from a breath-takingly blue sky; the warm breeze whipping through his hair; the green blur of the trees racing by on his right; the wake of dust kicking up from the wheels of his Harley as it devoured the miles.

It was life-affirming, all of it. A day like today could make a man feel invincible, immortal.

Yet all Ben could think about as he focused through his shades on the hard-baked road ahead was Death. With a capital D.

Death had become a way of life in recent times, of course. Not that it hadn't always been there, lurking in the background, but these past three and a half years it had stepped right up, front and centre, and introduced itself. Even so, if you were careful, you could still hold it at arm's length, and not only build a life, but convince yourself it was one worth living. And after the terrible traumas of the early days, this past year, in particular, had been a fine one. The old world may have gone, but the new one he and his group had built from the ground up, although unbelievably tough, was simple and pure and, yes, *good*.

Because their new world was so much smaller than the old one, there was room to breathe, to think, to take stock. Room to identify and focus on the most fundamental aspect of life – namely, survival – and to prioritise all the elements that facilitated it: security, self-protection, community.

Ben was one of the lucky ones – *had been* one of the lucky ones – and he knew it. So many people had lost partners, children, parents, friends to Hybrid-One that he felt almost embarrassed, even ashamed, to have helped establish Haven in the company of his sister, Jess, and both his parents. Obviously, the situation hadn't been idyllic – *nothing* associated with Hybrid-One and its aftermath could be described as idyllic, and like everyone else, they had lost a great deal – but under the circumstances, it was the best he could have hoped for.

But now it was gone. Just like that. Snatched away, almost perfunctorily.

Before his crew had left on their scavenging mission two weeks ago, he had said his usual goodbyes to his family. The mood had been upbeat, but as was always the case in these situations, it had been an over-bright, over-casual kind of upbeat, a way of compensating for the anxiety that thrummed beneath the surface. Because everyone knew how dangerous it was out there, and how, every time you left the relative safety of Haven, you were putting your life on the line. But Jess had smiled and joked with him, as always. She had grabbed his lapels and said, 'I'm all out of Bombay Sapphire, so unless you bring me back at least a couple of bottles, I'm not letting you back in through those gates. You hear me?'

She might have said goodbye after that, amidst the hugs and kisses he had exchanged with her and their parents, but if she did, he couldn't remember. As far as Ben was concerned, those were the last words she had said to him before he'd left.

And those were the last words, it turned out now, that she would ever say to him.

Six of them had gone on the scavenging mission, and six of them had come back. And it had all gone pretty smoothly. Minimal trouble, and a good stash of stuff. They had returned in high spirits. Triumphant.

He should have known that life had a nasty way of kicking you in the balls just when things seemed to be going well.

As soon as the gates had swung open to admit the returning heroes, Ben had known that something was wrong. Neither Jess nor his parents were there to greet him. There was only Maya, Jess's partner, and she looked sick with tension. And as soon as she saw him her face crumbled into tears, and her body sagged, as if she was about to throw up or faint.

Alarmed, Ben had rushed forward and grabbed her arms, fearful she was about to collapse.

'Maya!' he had shouted almost angrily. 'What's happened? What's wrong?'

Still weeping, her voice clogged with snot and tears, she had moaned, 'Oh, Ben … I'm so sorry …'

'Sorry about what?' he said, and had to restrain himself from shaking her. 'Tell me! What's happened!'

'It's Jess, she … had an accident.'

'An accident? What do you mean? Where is she?'

But he already knew. He knew from Maya's face, her voice. He just didn't want to believe it.

'She died, Ben. I'm sorry, but … we couldn't save her. She was up on the store room roof … replacing some leaky tiles. And she … I don't know how it happened, but she slipped … fell …' She shook her head wildly from side to side, as if wishing she could reject her own words.

'No,' Ben moaned. 'Not after all this, after all we've been through …'

They'd all striven so hard to get this far, had beaten seemingly insurmountable odds. So to die by slipping off a roof, it was just so … so idiotic. So cruel. So *pointless*.

For a while he and Maya clung to one another, enveloped by misery, trying to give comfort to, and receive it from, the other.

Then Ben said, 'Mom and Dad must be heartbroken. I need to see them …'

But there was something in Maya's face that caused the cold fist of shock in his chest to clench again.

'What?' he snapped. 'Maya, tell me, what's –'

'They're not here,' she blurted.

'Not here? What do you mean?' He scowled, his voice rising. 'Where are they, Maya?'

Her tears, which had stopped a little, began flowing again. She gripped him hard, as though willing him to believe. Voice cracking, she said, 'I tried to stop them, Ben. I tried *so hard*, but they went anyway. They left in the middle of the night. Sneaked out past the guards. Even took the Firebolt.'

'The Firebolt? But Pops hasn't been on a bike for nearly ten years! Not since he smashed up his knee.'

Maya gave a defeated shrug. 'They must have figured it was preferable to walking.'

'But why did they go?' Then Ben realised there was a more pertinent question. '*Where* did they go?'

'Home. They went home.' That little shrug again. 'At least that's my guess. From what your Mom was saying ...'

'What do you mean?'

'I was sat with your folks after Jess ... after she had her accident. All of us grieving, crying, trying to come to terms ... y'know. And your Mom kept saying as how they didn't even have any pictures of Jess to remember her by, how no one could take photos of their loved ones anymore. Then she said there were plenty of photos in the old house. Albums full of them. Return tickets to the past, she called them. Then she said she and your dad should go get them. That they could take one of the bikes. That it wouldn't take them more than a few days, there and back.'

Ben was horrified. 'Don't tell me Pops thought that was a good idea?'

'Not at first. But she must have worn him down. I said that one of the scavenging crews could get them, next time they were over that way. But your mom ... she got this idea into her head that it needed to be done *now*. That otherwise the photos could be lost forever. Me and your dad, we managed to persuade her it wasn't a good idea ... at least, I *thought* we had. But then one morning I woke up, and they were gone. And the Firebolt was gone. They'd cut a hole in the fence by the side of the vegetable garden. Even repaired it behind them.'

Ben was incredulous. 'Who was on duty that night?'

'Glynn. Rochelle. Antonia. Couple of others. But your parents knew the routine. They knew how much time they had between patrols – which wasn't a lot, but it was enough. They knew where the warning systems were, and how to avoid them.' She shook her head. 'No one expects people to break out. Only in.'

'You said one morning,' Ben said. 'You said you woke up one morning and they were gone. How many mornings ago, Maya?'

Her eyes slid away from his. Quietly she said, 'Five.'

'*Five?*' he said, aghast. 'They've been gone five days? Why didn't anyone go after them?' But as soon as he asked the question, he raised his hand. 'No, don't answer that. I know why. No one to spare. They left of their own volition. Why should anyone risk their lives?'

'I wanted to go,' said Maya. 'I really did. But ...'

'I know,' he said. His voice was gruff, but he understood and he didn't blame her. 'Being on your own out there... it's a bad idea. You were right not to go. But ... *fuck!* Five days! The journey's ... what? Two days at most? Two days there, two days back. So they should have been back yesterday.'

'Maybe they decided to stay on a day or two. Old times sake.'

'What would they eat? Drink?'

'We know they took some supplies ...'

'Some? How much?'

She paused. 'Truthfully? Not much. Probably not enough. Minimum rations for four days. You know how diligent your dad is. He wouldn't take advantage ...'

Ben rubbed his face. His hand was shaking badly. 'So where are they? Why aren't they back?'

She had no answer. Had nothing but a grimace of sympathy.

'Fuck,' he said again, and then more vehemently: 'Fuck! *Fuck!*' The briefest of pauses, as he thought furiously. Then he shook his head. 'I've got to go after them.'

'You can't!' Maya said. 'Not alone.'

'I *have* to.'

'Then I'll come too.'

'No, you won't. You're not risking your neck just because my folks did something ... *stupid*. You're needed here.'

'But you can't go alone,' she said again.

'I'll take the Harley. It's fast. I'll be fine.'

Before she could speak again, he held up a hand. 'That's an end to it. No more discussion. I'm going.'

He'd set off pretty much straight away. Had hung around just long enough to see Balen, get his permission to take the bike. He'd thought Balen might throw up objections, but the older man had been full of sympathy. Ben had grabbed the bare essentials, and had been back out on the road not thirty minutes after arriving back at Haven. Heading south this time instead of north. Full of dread. Full of thoughts of Death.

But he was thirty-six hours into the ride now, and so far so good. He'd seen a few hybrids, but nothing to bother him. Nothing fast enough to give chase. There'd been what looked like a pig-dog thing that had burst from a field to his left and shocked him into swerving a little, his tyres cutting an S into the dust. But the thing had been in a bad way. Too many legs in the wrong places, too much bulk, eruptions all down its left side suggesting it had absorbed far too many organs to accommodate. It had been a truly monstrous fucker, stinking of death, and squealing like something way beyond crazed, but it had been slow and stumbling, its many eyes staring off in a multitude of directions. After the initial surprise, Ben had been able to steady the bike and shoot past it easily, leaving it shrieking in frustration behind him.

The paucity of hybrid activity had given him an increasing sense of hope. He allowed himself to think his mom and dad might have made it back to the old place unscathed, after all. It was farming country out here, or had used to be, so the buildings, and therefore the people, had been pretty few and far between, even before Hybrid-One. This meant there was not much reason for the hybrids to hang around here, which *further* meant that most of them had probably died out or moved on to highly populated areas, driven by the twin desire of the infection within them to feed and multiply.

Something else that gave Ben hope was that he had not come across the wreckage of the Firebolt since he'd left Haven. If his parents *had* fallen prey to hybrids, the bike would be *somewhere* en route, having either come to grief or been abandoned.

But no. There was no sign of it. Which Ben told himself was good news. On the other hand, he wasn't dumb or stubborn enough to think that just because there was no evidence of a hybrid attack, that automatically meant his folks were fine. He knew that not all the monsters out roaming these days were non-human. There were plenty of bandits, thieves and murderers out here in the wildlands. People who survived not through hard work and fortitude, but by preying on others. If his folks *had* come across such a group, or even such an individual, they wouldn't have stood a chance. These human predators were usually armed, and entirely ruthless. As the Harley sped through miles of thick forest, or past numerous acres of overgrown farmland, Ben was all too aware of how easy it would be to conceal a pair of bodies out here. At pretty much any moment he might be passing the place where his parents' corpses had been dumped in the undergrowth.

Last night he'd taken shelter in an abandoned farmhouse. One that didn't look as if it had been tampered with since its owners had either fled or died elsewhere. He'd had to break in, and inside he'd found the place in pretty good repair. There had even been a few cans of food left in the larder. He'd slept, fully-clothed and fitfully, in an armchair, the rifle that he normally carried in a sling on his back resting across his knees. He'd heard sounds in the night – strange, distant shrieks and snortings, and once a scrabbling that sounded pretty close, maybe even out in the yard, just beyond the front window. But nothing had tried to get in, and when he looked out the next morning, there was no sign of life, hybrid or otherwise.

Another six hours of riding, and his heart started to thump harder, his guts to churn with apprehension. He was close enough now to the home where he'd spent the first eighteen years of his life with his mom, dad and Jess, to recognise the meadows and woods he'd played in as a kid with his best friends Dougie and Rick. They were wildly overgrown now, and the road he'd travelled along a million times, either in his dad's truck or in the bright yellow bus that had taken him and his friends to school in Almonville fifteen miles away, was rutted and crumbling, weeds pushing up through cracks in the asphalt. But for all that, the area was still imprinted so indelibly on his memory that it sparked off a kind of sick and yearning nostalgia within him. A nostalgia laced with an almost overriding sense of desperate and terrible loss.

He tried to push that feeling down, to not dwell on it. In the early days it had been hard. That sickening feeling of grief, of mourning not only for people but for an entire way of life, had been with him constantly; he'd carried it like a sack of rocks on his back. But by moving forward, concentrating not so much on the future but on the here and now, he'd been able to relieve himself of the burden, to some extent at least. One small rock at a time.

As he powered on, passing the long-neglected farmhouse where Dougie had lived with his parents and his twin sisters, Tam and Jenny, he took a bunch of deep, slow breaths. He registered the building on his left, set way back at the end of a long track, beyond fields that had once been neat with crops and were now wild and tangled, only in his peripheral vision. He didn't dare look at it too closely for fear the past would rush up on him and disarm him completely. As he left the farmhouse in his wake, he tightened his grip on the handlebars of the Harley and tried mentally to brace himself. He felt sweat running down his face, and down his chest, beneath his T-shirt and his beat-up leather vest. The sweat of apprehension. Of dread.

Past a thick stand of bull pines; past a field that had been yellow with wheat the last time he had seen it; round a long bend in the road ...

And suddenly there it was, at the top of a slight rise on his left, the startling blue sky behind it.

He cruised to a halt and just stared at it for a while, trying to regulate his breathing, as the bike idled beneath him. From afar it looked just as it always had – white-painted wood, green trim around the windows, tall stone chimney on the right, wraparound porch which threw the entire lower floor into shadow.

Another couple of hundred metres along this road he'd come to the fence that bordered the property, the one he and his dad had used to paint white every other summer. He'd see the mailbox by the turnoff, the curving track that led between the gateposts up to the front yard. If he parked the Harley in front of the house and walked around the right side of it, there would be the basketball hoop, and the cavernous barn where his dad used to keep his truck and his farming vehicles, and all his tools. And if he walked round the back and looked up at the far left-hand window, there would be his bedroom, and the windowsill he used to perch on during the long summer nights, as he watched the fireflies hovering and darting above the pond, or stared up at the millions of glittering stars scattered across the night sky.

It was another life, and he closed his eyes briefly, as if that might help break his connection to his memories. As he did so, he heard a heavy slithering in the overgrown field to his left, the rustle of foliage as something passed through it. His eyes snapped open, but even before he turned his head, the sound had ceased, and he saw no sign of anything moving.

It was a reminder, though, that he shouldn't make himself an easy target by simply sitting here, and so he started rolling again. A few seconds later, he saw the white fence, paint flaking from it now, the mailbox, still intact but similarly weather-beaten. The track leading up to the house was narrowed by chest-high foliage that encroached on both sides, and there were weeds pushing up through the once-bare earth. He tried to ignore the sadness that nudged at him as he tore up the track on his Harley.

It was no more than a ten-second ride to the front yard, but he felt vulnerable through every moment of the short journey, aware that anything could dart out of the undergrowth that whipped and clawed at him on either side. He was relieved when he left the mini-jungle behind and burst out into the front yard.

His relief, though, was short-lived, quickly twisting into

anxiety when he saw the bright-blue Firebolt. It was sprawled on its side half a dozen metres in front of the porch steps, and the screen door to the house was hanging open.

He cut the Harley's engine, leaped from it and ran towards the house, his backpack dragging at his shoulders, the rifle in its sling slapping at his sweaty back. As he ran, his eyes darted everywhere, simultaneously taking in details and hyper-alert for danger. He saw marks on the dusty ground – tyre tracks, a jumble of footprints, a long wavy line that came out of the field to his left. All of these marks seemed to coalesce in front of the porch steps, and smeared and scattered among them were a number of dark stains.

Glancing up the wooden steps to the porch, Ben saw more stains. In the sunlight they appeared black, but was there a maroon tinge to them? Pulse hammering in his throat, he leaped up the steps and crashed through the screen door, into the house. The kitchen beyond was dark and cool after the brightness of the day, and smelt of must and neglect.

'Mom! Dad!' he shouted, his heart aching with bitter nostalgia as his eyes alighted on familiar items. On the worktop beside the dusty coffee maker was the brown ceramic hen with the chipped beak his Mom had bought from Pottery Barn years ago. Hanging on the back of the pantry door was the green apron she used to wear, with the slogan 'I Cook As Good As I Look' stencilled across the front. On the floor, smashed, was what had once been the tall 'daffodil jug' they'd used to serve iced lemonade in the summer. On the fridge, attached by a magnet depicting Bart Simpson on a skateboard, was a drawing, curled up like an old leaf now, of 'My Family' that Jess had done in third grade.

Each reminder of his previous life was like a body blow that left him reeling. But Ben knew he had to hold himself together, stay focused.

He moved out of the kitchen, into the living room. 'Mom!' he shouted again, raw desperation in his voice. 'Dad!' Trying to block out the equally poignant reminders here, he looked across at the stairs on the back wall.

As if aware of his attention, something on the floor above produced a series of scuffling thumps.

In his mind, Ben construed the sounds as clumsy, blundering movement. It made him think of someone half-asleep, stumbling to the bathroom in the dark. He thought of the marks outside again, the dark stains, which even now his mind shied away from fully acknowledging. Nevertheless, he wondered whether one or both of his parents might be injured. Had they retreated upstairs to escape from a hybrid attack and were too scared or hurt to emerge?

He crossed to the bottom of the stairs, looked up. Sunlight teeming with dust motes slanted in from the window at the top.

'Mom? Dad?' he called again. 'It's me, Ben. You up there?'

More blundering movement, and this time there seemed to be an urgency to it, as if something was reacting to his voice. Ben pushed his long, sweaty fringe back from his forehead, then reached over his shoulder and slid his rifle from its sling. He didn't want to point it up the stairs, didn't want that to be the first thing his parents saw if they peered timidly over the banister. So, for the time being, he held it loosely, its barrel angled towards the floor. He waited a minute, ninety seconds, but although the stumbling, thumping sounds continued, he heard neither a door opening nor footsteps approaching along the landing overhead.

Foreboding gnawed at him, but even now he convinced himself there were numerous reasons why his parents might not emerge from hiding. That was assuming, of course, that it *was* his parents up there.

Only one way to find out.

Pulse thumping so hard in his throat he could barely swallow, Ben started up the stairs. Although he had already announced his presence, he ascended on tiptoe, rifle now raised, his back sliding along the wall. The instant his head came level with the upper landing, he stretched his neck to peer through the wooden uprights of the balustrade, and was relieved to see there was nothing and no one lurking there. Keeping an eye on the six doors on this level, three of which were closed, three slightly ajar, he ran lightly up the remaining stairs until he was standing with his back to the window at the top.

The spill of sunlight which illuminated the landing was now bisected by his shadow, which stretched along the floor, a spindly giant. As soon as his shadow-head nudged the bottom of the closed door at the end of the landing, a soft flurry of scuffling movement came from behind it, as if whatever was in there was responding to a knock. Ben didn't know whether to feel alarmed or encouraged by the fact that this was the door to his parents' bedroom.

Creeping along the landing, he ignored the closed doors, but pushed the three that were ajar further open with his foot; the rooms behind were all empty. One of them was Jess's old room, and even though she had moved out years before, and had been living in Missoula at the time of the first Hybrid-One outbreak, even seeing the layout of this room, and skimming his gaze over the few things their Mom and Dad had kept from her childhood – the wardrobe she'd painted with a vine leaf design; the noticeboard plastered with photos; the display case of gymnastics medals she'd won – sent a sharp, nauseous twist of grief spiralling through his gut.

Reaching his parents' bedroom door, he rested his sweaty forehead against it for a moment. From within he could still hear movement, softer now, though no less blundering than before. The apparent purposelessness of the sounds made him feel peculiarly distressed. It brought to mind childhood games of stumbling around with a blindfold on, waving his arms in front of him and bumping into furniture.

He opened his mouth to repeat his parents' names, then closed it without speaking. Now that he was this close to whoever or whatever was behind the door, he felt reluctant to attract its attention. He listened again, and once he had established that the sounds were coming from over to his right, roughly where his parents' bed was located, he pushed the door quickly open and stepped through it, raising his rifle.

Had he been half-expecting the sight that met his eyes? Perhaps so, given the evidence. But he'd pushed the possibility so far down into his subconscious that his initial reaction was a blast of horror, shock, revulsion, distress, grief.

The strength went out of him; the rifle sagged in his hands; he tottered on unsteady legs, certain he was about to pass out. He opened his mouth, to scream, to wail, to make *some* kind of sound, but his vocal cords felt paralysed.

His parents had indeed come home, but the thing swaying and pulsing beside their bed was no longer them. It had used to be, that was evident – but their bodies were now fused together, at the torso and the head. Their clothes, shredded in parts, stained with transformative juices, had been pulled in as they had merged, becoming part of their conjoined form. This had created, across their chests and hips, a mass of twisted flesh and cloth, resulting in weeping rents, infected sores, tumorous conglomerations of incompatible material. Ben saw that his father's left arm had been almost completely absorbed, only a trio of twitching fingers protruding from the 'stomach' area of the bodily mass like monstrous teats. His mother's right arm, by contrast, had been twisted behind her, and now sprouted from the thing's back, bones bent and broken by the pressure of the transformation.

Monstrous though this was, however, most hideous of all was the thing's head. Almost twice as wide as an average human head, and hideously misshapen, the features looked as if they had been moulded in clay and then slammed together by a crazed sculptor. The face, a confusion of features, consisted of four eyes – two of which were crammed together into one over-stretched socket – a bulbous nose studded with four nostrils, and a wide, zigzagging mouth, overstocked with teeth.

As soon as Ben stepped into the room, all four of his parents' eyes swivelled to regard him. And having sighted him, the hybrid – little more than a fleshy manifestation of an infection, an *appetite* – opened its mangled gash of a mouth and let loose a hideous, gurgling screech.

That sound, though, wasn't *all* that spilled from between the contorted lips. With it came a thick, pale-greenish drool, that surged over the bottom row of teeth and spattered to the ground in strings and clumps.

Venom, Ben thought. *That's venom. Which means one of them was bitten by a venomous hybrid.*

What had happened was so gut-wrenchingly awful that he could hardly bear to think about it. Even so, he couldn't stop the probable scenario from playing in his head. Arriving at the house, his folks must have been attacked, and one of them bitten. The other – probably his dad, given the strength required – had then maybe fought off the hybrid, and dragged his wife into the house. Ben pictured him carrying her upstairs, laying her on the bed, trying to look after her, even whilst knowing she was doomed. And then, inevitably, the infection must have taken hold, and no longer herself, his mom had bitten his dad, infecting him too.

And now they're together, he thought, and a strangled sound escaped him; something between a sob and a cry of revulsion.

As if enraged by the sound, the quivering, pulsing hybrid let out another screech, accompanied by another gout of pus-green drool. Then, with a speed that belied its bulk, it launched itself across the room at him.

Traumatised as he was, Ben's reaction was immediate, instinctive. He jerked up the barrel of the rifle and pulled the trigger.

If he had had time to set his sights, his aim might not have been so true. As it was, the bullet hit the hybrid in the dead centre of its wide forehead, its head snapping back as though jerked from behind. Its arms – the right one still very much his father's, down to the oil-encrusted fingernails, the wiry black hairs on its knuckles, and the vintage Seiko watch on its wrist – flew up in the air. All four of its legs, the central two of which had fused together into a gnarled, trunk-like column, simply folded at what now passed for knee joints, and it collapsed backwards, smashing into the wall and sliding to the ground.

The thing's body twitched and thrashed for several seconds, as if something inside it was trying frantically to escape … and then it settled, and became still.

Ben dropped to his knees and began to sob. He knew he had

not killed his parents, knew the infection had done that; yet blasting the life from their physical bodies was hard to take, all the same.

He stayed there, slumped on his knees, for several minutes. Throughout that time, he stared at the floor, at his hands, anywhere but at the thing he had killed. He felt overwhelmed by a sense of exhaustion so acute he had to battle hard to resist the urge to simply curl up and go to sleep. The only thing that kept him awake was the knowledge that whatever had infected his parents was still out there, possibly close by, in which case it might be aware of him, aware he was here, inside the house.

At last, groaning like an old man, he rose to his feet. Still averting his eyes from the fallen hybrid, he exited the room and pulled the door closed behind him. Standing on the upper landing, he listened hard, but received no indication that anything had entered the house. One good thing about hybrids was that they were not subtle. They didn't sneak, they didn't hide, they didn't lie in wait, or set traps. If a hybrid *had* forced its way inside, he would know about it.

Even so, he remained cautious as he crept downstairs. He had his gun, but was aware that some hybrids were very fast, and also strong enough that it required several well-placed bullets to bring them down. Reaching the living room, he crossed to the big sideboard to the right of the kitchen door, leaned his rifle against it, and tugged open the upper left-hand drawer. Inside were several photograph albums, which he lifted out. Shrugging off his backpack, he stuffed the albums inside, then pulled open the bottom left-hand drawer. Here were packets of more recent photos, which his mom had never got around to sorting through. He grabbed these and stuffed them in with the albums, by which time his backpack was bulging. He adjusted the shoulder straps and shrugged on the pack, grunting at the extra weight. It hurt him that these pictures – what was it Maya had said his mom called them? Return tickets to the past? – were all that remained of his family. Hurt him so much, in fact, that he felt an almost overwhelming compulsion to rip them to shreds, enraged that these stupid little bits of paper had resulted in his parents' deaths.

But even now, hurting as he was, he knew that if he gave in to his rage, he would spend the rest of his life regretting it. Yes, for a while looking at these photos would be almost unbearable, but in time he would be grateful he had them. Grateful that when his memories of his loved ones' faces became blurred in his mind, there would be these 'return tickets' to remind him of happier times. It might never be enough, but it was far more than most people had.

With the straps of his backpack cutting into his shoulders, he grabbed his rifle and entered the kitchen. He crossed to the screen door and peered out into the front yard.

All was quiet. His Harley was still there, perched upright on its kickstand, and there were no new markings in the dust to suggest anything had emerged from the surrounding fields.

Even so, he remained cautious. Pushing open the door, and wincing at the faint creak it made, he stepped out onto the porch, crossed to the top step, and peered in every direction.

Silence. Heat. The only movement the occasional languid nodding of chest-high grasses as a gentle wind passed through them. It could be that the hybrid that had infected his parents had moved on. If it was still close, wouldn't he have seen it by now? Wouldn't it have attacked him when he was riding his bike up the overgrown track between the walls of foliage?

On the other hand, he still recalled the slithering he had heard coming from the field a few hundred metres down the road, when he had briefly stopped his bike earlier. Could it be that the hybrid *had* been moving away until his arrival? But then, sensing new prey, had followed him back to the house and was now, once again, lurking close by?

Although hybrids didn't set traps, Ben knew they *were* attracted by movement and noise. He knew too that they often became dormant when those attractors ceased, only to reactivate when the attractors resumed, or when a fresh stimulus alerted them.

Knowing the only way to find out if the hybrid was still in the vicinity was to flush it out, Ben took a deep breath, then clumped loudly down the wooden steps of the porch. At the bottom, he raised his rifle and fired a shot into the air, the crack seeming to echo in the stillness, as if he was standing in a vast, empty building whose walls bounced the sound back at him.

A flock of birds – normal birds, not hybrids – erupted from a line of treetops several hundred metres away, and rose like a flurry of ash into the piercingly blue sky, squawking in alarm. Ben tried to block out their cries and to concentrate on the dense foliage surrounding the house. He counted slowly to ten, and was on the verge of concluding that maybe there were no hybrids in the vicinity, after all, when, with the faintest of rustles, a dark shape emerged from the field almost directly opposite him.

Ben's immediate thought upon seeing it was that this was not a hybrid, but the victim of a hybrid. He saw a pair of hands emerge from the long grass, clawing at the dry ground, followed by a pair of slender arms, with a head between them.

The head was lowered, and all he could see of it at first was a curtain of long, dark hair, the ends brushing the dusty ground. Did he gasp at the sight? Make some sound? If so, he wasn't aware of it. But suddenly the head snapped up, causing the curtains of hair to swing back, revealing the face.

This time, Ben definitely *did* make a sound – a sort of strangled grunt. He also took an involuntary step back, almost tripping over the bottom step of the porch and landing on his ass.

The lower half of the figure's face was human and female – neatly pointed chin, plump red lips, snub nose. But above the cheeks the consistency of the flesh changed, becoming a greyish mass of overlapping scales. And the eyes that scrutinised him were not human eyes. Set so wide apart they were almost on opposite sides of the skull, they were gleaming black orbs, like globules of oil.

There was no doubt now that this was a hybrid. Without warning, it reared up. Now Ben could see that although the creature's torso was mostly human, and quite definitely female, below the waist the genitals, legs and feet had been absorbed into the thick, tensile body of a vast greyish-green snake. The snake woman's scales shimmered in the sunlight as the upper body swayed from side to side. Then the plump red lips of the creature parted – the mouth unhinging, yawning open, as though the jaw was splitting in two, revealing a ridged, pink gullet and a pair of sharp, curved fangs, each as long as Ben's index finger.

The snake woman let out a hiss, which sounded like pressurised steam escaping from an air vent, and then, with terrifying speed, she came slithering across the yard towards him.

Once again, Ben raised his rifle and fired – though whether he hit the thing, he wasn't sure; if he did, it didn't slow the creature down. With no time to fire again, he turned, hampered a little by the weight of the backpack, scrambled up the porch steps and hurled himself through the screen door into the house. He slammed the door behind him, then dived under the kitchen table, half-expecting the snake woman to come crashing through in his wake.

She didn't, though. There was not even a thud of impact. Even so, still lying under the table, Ben flipped around, the backpack now between him and the floor, like a turtle's shell, his rifle aimed at the outer door. For maybe thirty seconds he remained there, heart crashing in his chest. Then, when it became obvious the hybrid was not imminently about to enter the house, he scrambled awkwardly out from under the table, crossed to the kitchen window and peered into the yard.

He half-expected the snake woman to be gone, but she was still there, staring up at the house with her expressionless black eyes. Perched upright on her 'tail', she was a formidable creature. In terms of how snake and human had amalgamated, she was, without doubt, one of the most successful hybrids Ben had ever seen. At least seven metres long from the top of her black-haired head to the tip of her reptilian tail, her upper body was raised a good three metres from the ground. In her former life, Ben guessed the woman must have been no older than late twenties, early thirties. He wondered who she had been.

He wondered too how much she retained of her human instincts and thought-processes. Although the prime function of all hybrids was to feed and infect, the part-human hybrids had sometimes been known to display more intelligent and considered behaviour patterns than their non-human counterparts.

The questions to consider here, then, were: did the snake woman know he was inside the house and would have to emerge eventually? And was she aware that the Harley parked in the front yard was his only means of escape?

If so, he guessed she might try to damage the bike, though she was showing no immediate signs of that. Maybe she simply considered it not worth the effort, because she *knew* she was faster and more agile than he was, and there was therefore no way he could reach the machine.

For the next ten, fifteen minutes, he simply watched the hybrid, during which time it barely moved, except to occasionally sway hypnotically from side to side. He was reluctant to tear his eyes from it – he felt safer knowing where the thing was – but knew that he'd have to eventually, especially if he was to get out of here.

But *how* could he get past it? Should he try sniping at it out of the window? Maybe even go out shooting, and hope for the best? The thing was so fast he reckoned he'd get no more than two or three shots off before it was on him.

Would that be enough? Maybe. If he was lucky. If not, he'd become dinner, or a hybrid himself.

He thought of the mass of mindless, pustulating flesh upstairs that had once been his parents, and shuddered.

No. It was too risky. He needed a plan that would give him more of a fighting chance.

But what plan? What resources did he have, here in the house, that he could use against that thing?

He thought long and hard. It had been some years since he had last set foot in this house, but he tried to visualise every room, and what was in them.

Eventually, sighing, he left his place by the window and

crossed to a set of wall cupboards. Opening one, he found what he was looking for – candles and a box of matches, both of which seemed dry. Lifting down the matches, he opened the box, extracted a match and struck it; it ignited immediately. He blew it out, placed the box on the kitchen table, then moved to the opposite corner of the kitchen.

He had an inkling of an idea, but whether it would work or not would depend on split-second timing and dumb luck. Next to the dust-coated cooker against the far wall was a wooden door, which led down to the basement. It was a big basement, running pretty much the length of the house, and when he and Jess were kids, their dad had talked about converting it into a games room, where the two of them could chill out with their friends. But that particular plan had never come to fruition, and so later, during their teen years, their dad got it into his head to turn the space into a movie room, where they would show movies every Saturday night, invite friends and family along. Ben still remembered his dad speaking with enthusiasm about how he'd source some real cinema seats, and a projector, and a screen that covered the entire back wall.

Even as a teen, though, Ben knew how costly and time-consuming such a project would be, and sure enough, his dad had never had either the time or the funds to make it happen. And so the basement had remained as it was: part utility room (home to the boiler, the washer-dryer and the chest freezer), part storage area (cluttered with bikes, old furniture, half-empty paint cans, and a thousand and one other household items), and partly the place where the hardly ever used back-up generator was located.

It was the generator Ben was interested in now, or rather the fuel it ran on – though opening the door and starting down the concrete steps, he wasn't even sure there would still be any fuel down here. As he descended, the smell of the basement rose to meet him: old concrete, the mustiness of damp furniture, and something funky and organic, but thankfully faint. He listened, but there was nothing to suggest the place was occupied by rodents or hybrids – no scrabblings, no skitterings. Peering across at the generator, which he could make out via streams of milky light, which trickled in through a row of narrow windows set high on the outside wall, he saw, standing on the floor next to its dark, blocky shape, a couple of gallon cans with 'Gasoline' emblazoned in red across their fronts.

'Hallelujah,' he whispered, and slipped his rifle into the sling that lay snug alongside his backpack. Crossing the room, he grabbed the cans and jiggled them in his hands. From the weight, he could tell that one was full, the other quarter-full at best. Leaving the emptier one, he crossed back to the steps and placed the full one at the bottom, then rooted around in various boxes of odds and ends until he found a length of thin, strong rope. Rolling the rope up and stuffing it into his jacket pocket, he headed back upstairs, grabbing the fuel can en route.

He put the can and the rope on the kitchen table, next to the matches, peeked out of the window to check the hybrid was still there – it was – and then, taking a deep breath, he went back upstairs. Outside his parents' bedroom, he paused a moment – he hadn't intended to set foot in this room again, and was not relishing it one bit – and then he shoved the door open and stepped inside.

Last time he had been in here, not thirty minutes ago, the sense that, for him, had overwhelmed all others had been sight; he had been wholly occupied, and appalled, by what his parents had become. On that occasion he had hardly noticed the smell – but he noticed it now. It was a rank and visceral odour of sickness, of infection. Feeling his gorge rise, he clapped a hand across his mouth and nose, trying to suppress the urge to puke. In truth, it wouldn't have made much difference if he *had* upchucked on his parents' bedroom carpet, and yet it mattered to him. Even now, despite everything, it seemed somehow … disrespectful.

He was relieved, therefore, when, after a minute or so, the urge to throw up began to subside. Removing his hand from his mouth, he moved deeper into the room, crossing to his dad's side of the bed – which, fortunately, was not the side where the hybrid had been standing, and where it had met its end.

The hybrid was still there, of course, a mass of mostly shapeless, dead flesh, slumped in the gap between his mom's side of the bed and the built-in wardrobe with the louvered doors. Ben kept his eyes averted from it, was aware of it only as a vague shape in his peripheral vision. What he was interested in was the old-fashioned alarm clock on his dad's bedside table. It was the kind you wound up with a little key, and the alarm itself was on the top of the clock, above the face, a vibrating hammer set between two metal clappers, that Ben remembered from his childhood made a hell of a noise.

For his plan to have any chance of working, several things had to fall into place. The first had been that there were still usable matches in the cupboard – *tick*. The second was that there was some generator fuel left in the basement – *tick*. The third was that his dad still owned the alarm clock he'd been using forever – *tick*. The fourth was that the clock still worked, and Ben said a silent prayer as he picked it up and examined it.

The clock had stopped, of course – at 4.24, God only knew how long ago – and was coated with a layer of sticky dust. Using his thumb, Ben scraped as much of the stickiness off as he could, and then, hoping that the innards of the clock were not as gummed up as the outside of it was, he began to twist the little key in the back.

After half a dozen turns, he whispered, 'Please,' and then let the key go. It seemed to him there was a pause, as if the clock was deliberately milking the tension of the moment … and then it began to tick. Through the murk on the glass face, Ben saw the second hand moving steadily round the dial. He huffed out a chuckle of relief. 'They sure don't make 'em like you anymore,' he muttered.

It wasn't just the clock he needed for his plan to work, though, it was the alarm. Laying the clock on the bed, he set the alarm for a minute hence, grabbed a pillow off his parents' bed, and waited. Sure enough, as soon as the minute hand had performed another revolution, the alarm went off, the little hammer bashing away at the metal bells on either side with ferocious energy.

Instantly Ben dropped the pillow on the clock, muffling the sound. The alarm was loud, but with the pillow over it he doubted anyone standing further away than the bottom of the stairs would hear it. Even so, he glanced towards the door of his parents' room, knowing not only that hybrids reacted to sound and movement, but also that snakes were able to pick up airborne vibrations, so who knew how acute the snake woman's hearing might be? He waited anxiously, holding his breath, until the clock's alarm had wound down, and only then did he breathe a sigh of relief.

Satisfied he now had everything he needed, he picked up the clock and exited his parents' room for the second – and he hoped final – time. His heart was thumping as he paused at the top of the stairs and gave the clock a few more winds. The hands circling the dial now stood at 4.27. The time didn't need to be accurate for Ben's plan to work, but he did have to give himself enough time to set it up.

Would three minutes be enough? He hesitated, then set the alarm for 4.31. Placing the clock on the top step, he hurried downstairs.

Now that he was *literally* up against the clock, he felt all fingers and thumbs. Grabbing the loop of rope off the kitchen table, he shook it out, then rushed across to the outer door and tied one end around the door handle. He trailed the rope from the door to the walk-in pantry, which was on the left-hand wall when entering the kitchen from outside, then crossed back to the table and grabbed the gasoline can. He had a moment of panic when he thought rust had sealed the screw-cap shut, but after a few seconds of effort it came free with a gritty crunch. Running back into the living room, he poured gasoline over the wooden floor, splashing it up the first few steps of the staircase and trailing it back into the kitchen.

The stink of the gasoline made him feel sick and heady, but he did his best to ignore it. Hoping the smell wouldn't repel the snake woman, or make her suspicious, he gently turned the handle of the outside door and disengaged the catch. Terrified that a summer breeze would nudge the door open before he was ready, alerting the hybrid, he hurried across to the walk-in pantry, picked the trailing end of the rope up off the floor, and tried to squeeze inside.

But between the pantry shelves and the door there was barely any space, and with a hot rush of panic Ben suddenly realised there was no way he'd fit into the pantry wearing his bulky backpack. Fighting to stay calm, he dropped the rope, shrugged the backpack off his shoulders, dumped it on the kitchen table, then picked up the trailing rope, and tried again.

But no! He still couldn't fit. Not with the rifle slung across his back. *Fuck!* He scrabbled at the sling, trying to lift it over his head, but only succeeded in tightening the loop of cloth beneath his armpit. Acutely aware that time was running out, and he *still* couldn't fit into his hidey hole, his thoughts began to race. Come on! *Come on!*

He took a breath, trying to organise his thoughts.

And then, from the upper landing, and sounding horribly loud in the empty house, the alarm went off.

For a split-second, Ben was overcome with panic; his mind froze. Then self-preservation kicked in, and with it came an almost preternatural presence of mind. And all at once he realised he didn't *need* to remove the sling. He just needed to remove the gun.

Reaching over his shoulder, he did so, sliding the rifle from the sling and tossing it onto the kitchen table. Bending at the knees, he grabbed the end of the rope, soaked now in gasoline from the floor, then backed into the walk-in pantry, the edges of the shelves pressing against his spine. As soon as he was inside, he tugged hard on the rope, causing it to go taut and to yank on the handle of the outer door, which jerked open, an obvious invitation to enter. He dropped the rope, and even before it had hit the kitchen floor, was pulling the pantry door fully closed behind him, sealing himself in with the darkness and the sickly stench of gasoline.

Upstairs, the alarm was still yammering away, and now it was accompanied by a new sound, one that came from outside. It was the sound of something very large, very heavy and very powerful, slithering towards the house.

The slithering grew louder, came closer. Inside the pantry, Ben felt sweat breaking out all over his body. He gripped the inside handle of the pantry door as if his life depended upon it, hoping against hope that the snake woman would not be able to smell the steaming reek of his adrenaline, his fear.

There was a series of rapid thumps as the snake woman hauled herself up the porch steps. Then the half-open door of the house crashed back on its hinges, and suddenly the hybrid was in the kitchen, the slithering scrape of its huge body moving across the floor. The darkness inside the pantry turned even blacker as the vast bulk of the hybrid squeezed between the pantry door and the kitchen table. Would it see the backpack and the gun on the table and guess where he was? Would it smell him? Would it sense him? Would it hear his galloping heart?

As the pantry door creaked beneath the weight of the thing's body, Ben expected at any moment for the thin wooden barrier to burst inwards, for the creature to suddenly *be* there, to lunge at him, all fangs and claws, venom and fury.

The pressure on the door increased. The wood began not merely to creak, but to crack and splinter …

And then the darkness beyond the door became a little less dense. The sound of slithering moved away. And Ben realised that the hybrid had bypassed his hiding place; that it was heading from the kitchen, into the living room.

It had taken the bait!

As soon as he heard its vast body squeezing up the stairs, the steps groaning in protest beneath its weight, Ben opened the pantry door and stepped out into the kitchen. With the creature still in the house, his instinctive reaction was to remain in hiding, but he knew if he was going to get out of here, he had to be bold, and more importantly, he had to *hurry*.

Trying not to think about the monster upstairs, and what it would do in a few seconds' time when it realised its 'prey' was nothing but an old alarm clock, he stepped across to the kitchen table, lifted up his backpack and shrugged it onto his back.

Then he grabbed his rifle and slid it into the sling alongside. Aware his hands were shaking, and trying through sheer willpower to keep them as steady as possible, he picked up the box of matches, opened them, and grabbed half a dozen. He crossed quickly to the open screen door, through which sunlight was pouring, and stepped out on to the porch. From upstairs, he heard a metallic crunch and the alarm clock abruptly ceased its yammering.

Trying not to picture the hybrid twisting round on the upper landing and streaking back down the stairs, he dragged the six matchheads simultaneously along the striking surface at the side of the box. All six flared into life. Leaning forward, he tossed the burning matches on to the gasoline-soaked kitchen floor.

Then he turned and ran for his life.

Even as he leaped down the porch steps, he was aware of the sudden flare of light and heat behind him. Did he hear a *whoomph* as the gasoline ignited? Maybe. But maybe that sound was only in his head.

Hitting the hard-packed ground so hard that dust kicked up in a cloud around his boots, he sprinted for his Harley. Behind him, he now heard the roar of fire taking hold; things cracking and bursting; his past going up in flames.

Reaching the bike, he swung his leg over the seat, careful not to unbalance himself with the weighty pack on his back, and flicked up the kick stand with his heel. Starting the Harley was normally second nature to him, but with his mind racing he found he had to concentrate hard to remember what to do.

Turn the key – thank God he had left it dangling from the ignition, and didn't have to root through his pockets; turn on the fuel pump; check the bike was in neutral; press the starter button.

There was nothing to suggest the machine had been tampered with, but even so, he felt such an incredible rush of relief when the engine came alive, with its familiar throbbing growl, that he let out a cry of triumph.

As if in answer, from the direction of the house, there came a sudden splintering crash, followed by an inhuman screech. The sound was so chilling, so full of fury, that the goosebump-ripple that scrabbled up Ben's back and across his scalp felt like an electric shock.

Twisting his head to look over his shoulder, he saw the snake woman emerge from the inferno that the house had already become. She was on fire. Her flesh black and curling away into ashes, her hair aflame, she looked like the Devil itself.

Loath though he was to look away from her, Ben turned back to face front and twisted the throttle on his bike. The engine roared, drowning out the sound of the hybrid descending the porch steps, sidewinding across the yard towards him. Then the Harley leaped forward, slewing a little from side to side in Ben's haste to get away. For a split-second he thought he was about to lose control, take a spill. Then he thought of the precious cargo he was carrying on his back, those return tickets to the past that would sustain him over the years ahead. Thinking of his family, and of the happy times encapsulated in those pictures, both steadied and galvanised him, and he leaned forward, using the extra weight of the pack to balance both himself and the bike. Immediately, the Harley righted itself beneath him, then shot forward like an arrow.

In his wake, the burning hybrid let out a scream of rage and frustration. Even above the roar of the engine, the scream seemed to go on and on, to echo across the fields.

But the snake woman's rage couldn't hurt him now. He was away. He was safe. Or at least, in this terrifying new world, as safe as he could be.

Carrying all that was left of his past, of his family, on his back, Ben rode into his future.

SPRING-HEELED JACK

On a misty night in August 1877, a soldier was on sentry duty outside the front gates of one of the military camps at Aldershot, Hampshire, when he was approached out of the vapour by a bizarre figure: a tall, thin outline of a man, wearing what appeared to be a heavy cloak. More alarming though, the figure appeared to have glowing eyes and devil horns. Ignoring the soldier's challenge, the thing launched a violent physical attack, striking him with hands that seemed to be clawed. The soldier fought his assailant off and opened fire from close range. Other sentries, attracted by the noise, also opened fire. Several, the first man included, claimed to have struck their target cleanly ... to no apparent effect, other than to see him leap prodigiously away into the fog.

'Like a man-sized grasshopper,' as one said, but shrieking with hysterical laughter.

This would be a frightening incident in almost any circumstances, but it especially was in 19th Century England, as the fiend that had attacked the sentry was already well-known. So well-known in fact that the press had given him his own nickname: Spring-Heeled Jack.

It's difficult to be sure whether or not the Bouncing Devil or Leaping Madman, as he was also occasionally referred to, had by this time passed into British urban folklore, but by 1877, Spring-Heeled Jack's depredations had been reported many times, most commonly in London, but also in locations as far apart as Sheffield, Northamptonshire, Brighton and Devon. The incidents often followed the same pattern. An unaccompanied person, usually a female – the attack upon a squad of armed soldiers was unique! – suddenly encountering a terrifying figure, tall, lean, cloaked and with a genuinely demonic aspect, which would rake at their clothes and flesh with fingers that were more like knives. And these weren't just rumours. Many victims reported the assaults to the police, and/or were taken to hospital with severe wounds. A couple were even said to have lost their minds as a result.

Several times, there was more than one witness to the attack, all of them describing the same tall, horned figure with crazily glowing eyes. On some occasions, such as in Lincolnshire in 1877, hue and cry was raised and a mob pursued the miscreant, though he always escaped them with ease. Even now, in possession of all this information, it's tempting to blame the crime-wave on some dangerous lunatic or straightforward sex offender, but that would be to discount his apparent supernatural powers.

Numerous times, for example, he was said to have breathed out clouds of blue flame, but more spectacularly still, to have eluded his pursuers by leaping over high fences or walls, and sometimes even over the roofs of houses. Witnesses to the latter always asserted that these astonishing feats were way beyond the ability of the most skilled gymnast or acrobat. It seems even less likely that an ordinary person could be responsible when you consider that the first recorded attack was in 1837, when Spring-Heeled Jack accosted a young housemaid in Clapham, and the last one in 1904 in Liverpool, when he leapt onto the roof of a church; a crime spree lasting 67 years!

(It is even longer if we link Spring-Heeled Jack to the equally mysterious but not dissimilar 'Perak, the Spring Man', who terrorised Prague between 1939 and 1945).

If all these fantastical details – the horns, the glowing eyes, the inhuman athleticism, the astounding longevity – seem like embellishments added for effect in a later era, the facts would disagree. From a very early stage, the weird assailant was known on Britain's nighttime streets as Spring-Heeled Jack. The case was widely discussed in Victorian London at all levels of society. The theories put forward regarding his apparent paranormal abilities included spring-loaded boots, or some kind of primitive flying apparatus concealed under his cloak (though the first manned flight would not occur until the Wright Brothers made themselves famous in 1903, one year before the end of Jack's reign).

Early horror magazines, such as the 'penny dreadfuls', had an absolute field-day, speculating even more wildly, proposing that the offender was either a mad scientist, a ghost, or even a demon marooned on Earth after a black magic ceremony (for a brief time, during the 1870s, he was referred to in South London pamphlets as the 'Peckham Ghost' and in Yorkshire as the 'Park Ghost').

Less imaginative observations were made by the various police forces in those areas where Spring-Heeled Jack was reported, but they nevertheless took their investigations seriously. They noted that the figure was sometimes described as wearing a helmet and oilskin clothing, which perhaps to their minds (and maybe to ours) hints at there being something mechanical about his abilities. They also received confessions and made arrests. A certain Thomas Millbank, taken into custody in 1838, seemingly wearing a partial costume, was considered a viable suspect, especially as he willingly admitted his guilt, but on sterner interrogation he was unable to produce Spring-Heeled Jack's fiery breath and so eventually was released.

No matter how one looks at it, the case of Spring-Heeled Jack is utterly mystifying. This wasn't some fairy tale from a distant era. It was reported on extensively in The Illustrated Police News, *and perhaps more respectably, in* The Times.

Crime historians give credence to early theories that the Bouncing Devil's antics were performed by some upper-class rake or perhaps a group of such, who were simply drunk and bored. They, it's been argued, would likely have had the time and resources to finance such an escapade. In this regard, one particular name has been put forward: Henry Beresford, 3rd Marquess of Waterford, a hell-raising eccentric, who even without the use of elaborate disguises, was said to have found fun in waylaying late-night pedestrians.

Of course, none of these sensible conjectures can explain the felon's apparent superhuman prowess, though modern analysis looks further back than those recorded cases, to other similar series of violent or sexual attacks on random victims.

The London Monster for example, a London sex offender and knife attacker of the 1780s; Whipping Tom, also a London criminal, who between 1672 and 1712, overpowered dozens of woman and girls, and brutally flogged them with a cat-o-nine tails; and even the Ratcliffe Highway Murderer, who in 1811, broke into two different homes and savagely killed all seven occupants. This latter case may be especially relevant, given that several of Spring-Heeled Jack's attacks had allegedly taken place in upstairs bedrooms, which he had jumped into through supposedly secure windows.

If nothing else, these crimewaves indicate that there was a precedent for random predatory violence, often sexual in nature, in Britain's fogbound industrial cities. Was the case of Spring-Heeled Jack simply part of that phenomenon. Were all his recorded attacks the work of one man, or were several twisted individuals at work over several decades? Would it really have been that difficult to create theatrical effects so impressive that they could deceive the eyes? One thinks of actor Richard Mansfield's extraordinary transformation in Thomas Sullivan's version of Dr Jekyll and Mr Hyde *at the Madison Square Theatre in 1888, which literally had audience members running for the exits and put the famous actor in the frame, at least for a brief time, as a Jack the Ripper suspect.*

It is also possible that there was much exaggeration by witnesses. Was Spring-Heeled Jack a reasonable athlete rather than an exceptional one? Perhaps just a very fast runner, whom embarrassed pursuers needed to find reasons for failing to catch?

Sadly, we'll likely never know. It's another of those unsolved mysteries and terrors from a seeming golden age of such, the answers to which lie hidden behind blanket-thick veils of sulphurous London fog.

TUPILAQ
Simon Kurt Unsworth

They got on at one of those small, faceless and almost nameless towns that were scattered infrequently along the branchline.

Colley didn't think anyone was going to enter the carriage at all. The boy and girl in the nearly-but-not-quite-matching outfits got off and the doors stood open for a long moment, the air in carriage dancing and swirling because of the storm brewing around them.

Outside, the sky flickered and twitched with distant lightning and clouds, grey and heavy, scudded against a backdrop the colour of old bruises. The wind rushing into the carriage brought with it the smell of electrical discharges and earth and baked iron. Leaves danced and fell, litter zephyred and, as the doors started to close, they burst in.

There were two of them. They were similar looking enough for Colley to think they might be sisters, in their early teens maybe, and they arrived in a babble of chatter and noise and made straight for the rear of the carriage. Straight towards Colley.

Thankfully, they didn't sit in the seats facing him but on the other side of the aisle from him, in the rearmost twin seat. It was an old train and it had no tables, only seats worn threadbare and thin by countless buttocks and thighs and backs and arms rubbing against them, the exposed leather tired and drab. Colley tried not to look at the girls but couldn't help it, watching as they fussed and got comfortable, watching them not because he was interested but because, God help him, he was intimidated by them.

They weren't dirty, not exactly, but there was a roughness about them, some kind of grittiness worn into them by upbringing or economics or hopelessness, and their eyes were older than the rest of them, older and flatter and harder, as though they had lived two or three or four or five years for each of the years he had lived. In his sideways glances those eyes were almost ancient.

They were loud. And they talked *constantly*.

The younger of the two was sitting in the aisle seat, nearest to Colley and she had a box on her knees. It was the size of a large shoebox, the sort of thing he thought might once have contained a pair of child's boots. Her arms, which were freckled and skinny, pressed firmly on it, jamming its lid down, pinning it to her bony legs.

Colley deliberately looked away, turning instead to his reflection in the window pasted across the rangy, streaked sky beyond. In the reflection was a man he barely knew any longer, older and fatter and wearier than the one he expected to see and that he had never planned to become. How had he come to this place, to this train on his near forgotten line, travelling to the middle of God's own nowhere to a cheap hotel so that tomorrow he could teach IT to a hardware company back-office staff, IT so simple a dim monkey could master it in moments? By taking every wrong decision, of course, especially when those wrong decisions were to remain sedentary, to avoid, to shy away. By clawing his way onto a slope that was not so much downwards as it was endless and hopeless, angled gradually further and further towards all the things below.

Colley's reflection scratched its cheek and he heard the sound of a finger roughing against stubble. He took a long, slow breath and felt the waistband of his pants cut uncomfortably into the gut. Letting the breath out eased the discomfort but there was always another breath to hurt, wasn't there? And then another, and then another until all the lights went out.

He had been doing a good job of blotting out the girls' inane conversations, the volume of his own self-pity useful for that at least, but they broke back in on his attention when they both laughed together, loud and piercing. He looked around to see the box on the girl's knee jerk.

At first, Colley thought she'd simply bounced her leg but then it happened again and this time the box's lid snapped up a centimetre or so before she pinned it back down with those thin, bare arms. He had a glimpse of something in the box, something grey and patched with mottled darker areas, before the lid clapped back down over it. Both girls giggled.

Did they have something alive in there? Jesus, really? Despite himself Colley turned more fully towards the girls to try and work out what was going on. Something alive in the box? It seemed cruel. Was it a cat? A pigeon? God, was it a rat, all teeth and claws and a long, hairless tail, with an appetite unfettered by mercy or morals? He shuddered.

The box jerked again, this time not just up but also sideways. It shifted, slipping along slightly and starting to tilt off the girl's knee before she retained her grip on it and steadied it.

'Stop it, you,' she said mildly to the box, as though scolding an exasperating friend. Colley saw there were no air holes in the box.

'Here, let me take it,' said the older girl. The younger one slid it along, keeping the lid firmly down as she did so, and the other took it. She laid her arms over it as the other girl had, but also clamped her hands around the lid for extra security. She looked over quickly and, seeing Colley looking at her, said, 'It's okay, it won't get out.'

Colley opened his mouth, got torn between protesting that he wasn't worried even though he was – God, a rat and its teeth, a pigeon and its flapping and shitting and panic – and saying something about not carrying things on trains in boxes, and ended up making a non-committal grunt and closing his mouth again. The younger girl giggled again, this time clearly laughing at Colley, as the elder said, in a clear, oddly condescending voice, 'The thing in the box, don't worry. It won't get out. We've got it safe here.'

'Yes,' said Colley and then, because he felt something else was called for, added 'Is it a pet?'

Both girls giggled then, and the younger said, 'Oh no, not a pet,' but didn't elaborate further. The older girl simply looked at him.

'Not a pet? So what is it then? It seems agitated. Maybe it can't breathe and you should cut holes in the lid?'

'It doesn't need air,' said the younger girl and the elder elbowed her in the side, hard. The younger glowered at the elder for a moment and then turned back to Colley, who realised that now he was engaged in a conversation whether he wanted to be or not.

'Well, everything needs air, doesn't it?' Colley said, trying not to sound too stuffy, too pompous. Too adult. 'Even if it's not a pet, if it's something you're keeping in a box because it's injured or because you're taking it somewhere, it needs to breathe, surely?' The box, as if in agreement, gave another jump on the girl's knee but her hold was firmer and lid rose little more than a couple of millimetres before she forced it back down. Outside the landscape flickered past and a lightning bolt cracked across the sky. In moments, they left the thunder behind.

'I said, it doesn't need air,' said the girl loudly, insistent.

'Well, what kind of animal doesn't need air?'

'It's not an animal.'

'It's moving,' said Colley as the box gave another jerk. The girl slapped at the lid in irritation. Colley wondered how he'd been sucked into this, and how it might look from the outside, a fat man in a too-tight suit going shiny with age and a coat draped over his knee talking to two unaccompanied young girls. At the far end of the carriage was a teenager, lost deep in a pair of oversize headphones, head bobbing to a beat Colley would never hear. Closer was an older woman, feet surrounded by shopping bags that bulged and strained with her purchases. Other than them, Colley and the girls, the carriage was empty and neither the teen nor the woman was paying anyone else the slightest attention.

The box jumped again, more fiercely this time. Rain slashed down against the train windows then, the storm finally catching them. The younger girl jumped, although whether from the rain or the box's movement Colley couldn't tell, and the elder girl put a reassuring hand on her arm for a second before returning it to the box.

'It might be moving but it's not an animal,' she said, her tone still insistent and now slightly hectoring.

'But if it's not an animal, what is it?'

'It's Daddy's soul,' said the younger girl, and smiled brightly at him.

Colley's mouth fell open. For the second time in as many minutes, he had no idea what to say but, unable to say nothing, managed to push out a confused, 'His soul?'

'His soul,' the older girl confirmed. 'It's in this box.' The box gave another savage jerk, upwards, knocking against the girl's arms and lifting off her knees. When she slammed it back down something in the box scrabbled violently and the box shook. The younger girls gave a little shriek as it did so.

'Now look,' said Colley, trying to sound stern rather than schoolmarmish, 'this has gone far enough. Whatever's in the box isn't happy, clearly, so at the next station you should let it go.'

'No,' said the older girl as a look of fear passed over the younger one's face.

'We can't do that,' said the younger one. 'Not at all. No.'

'I don't,' started Colley and stopped, *I don't believe you* warring with *I don't want to know* warring with *I don't understand*. He wanted this to stop, wished he'd never looked at the girls or spoken to them because everything felt wrong, felt off-kilter now: from the subject of the conversation to the looks on their faces of something like animal triumph to the colour of the sky outside, a storm-lashed purple shot through with streaks of black and sunset orange. He wanted to be at his cheap hotel eating his cheap hotel meal planning his next day's cheap training and most of all, he wanted to not be talking to these two girls.

Unbidden, his traitorous mouth asked, 'Why have you got his soul in a box?'

'Because we wanted him to stop.' The older girl.

'Stop? Stop what?'

'The magic. All the magic.' The younger this time, and now her face seemed to catch the shadows and become serious. 'Using his thing on us for some types of magic, putting it in us while we had to lie all still and quiet, taking bits of our hair and blood and nails for other types of magic, never asking, just taking and hurting and being mean if we said anything. We wanted him to stop so we listened and listened and one day we heard him talking about how to bring something out to do things for you, and I've got a good memory so I remembered and remembered and then we waited 'til he was asleep and we put our coats on backwards and we said the right words and we got a toopey lack to take his soul for us. It caught it in this box, like we told it too, and now it's all okay. It stopped the magic. *We* stopped the magic.'

'Toopey lack?' He gave up trying to fight it. Better to pretend everything was normal, keep things calm, and simply walk away when he could.

'Tuppilackey?' said the older girl but it was more a question than a correction. 'We never heard Daddy say it out, we found written in a book that we managed to get a look at. A tuppilackey, toopey lack, chewpillack, it doesn't matter, it's a thing we could use, so we did.'

'It comes from somewhere very cold,' said the young girl, her voice serious. 'I think it probably likes it better here where it's warmer, do you think so?'

'Yes, I suppose it does,' replied Colley weakly.

'We had to use hair and skin and string and sticks and we made it and we said the words and it did our bidden.'

'Bidding,' corrected Colley without thinking. 'Bidding,' repeated the girl, enunciating very precisely. She looked down at the box and said, almost to herself, 'No more magic from you, Daddy. We'll put you somewhere far away and make sure you can't get out and then you won't do no more magic on us. On anybody.'

Colley was swept over by sadness. Whatever was in the box, how damaged must these two girls be, to make up such an outlandish and depressing story? What abuse had they suffered to be able to talk about it so glibly? Daddy's thing, hair and nails and blood? *And*, he thought, *what can I do about it?*

Could he do anything about it? Did he want to?

'Once we bury the soul, we're going to live with Mummy,' said the younger girl. 'We couldn't before because Daddy did magic that makes her hate us and think we're nasty but now he's gone it'll be okay.'

'Yes,' said the older girl and smiled and looked, perhaps for the first time since she alighted on the train, the age she actually was. Her smile was bright and cheery and it made Colley want to cry, that she couldn't look like that all the time.

'Where are you taking the soul?' and could he believe he'd just asked that? *No, I can't. Just humouring them, just 'til they get off or I get off.*

'There's a beach,' said the elder girl. 'Daddy liked the beach so we thought we'd bury him there so that he's somewhere nice.

'That's thoughtful of you,' said Colley and was oddly touched when the girl beamed back at him. Outside the rain intensified, casting moving, crawling shadows around them.

Whatever was in the box had been quieting over the previous few minutes, its scrabbles and jumps growing less. It gave a last burst of energy and then fell entirely silent. Everything was quiet except for the sound of the train itself and the rain pocking and prying against the windows. Colley, who didn't like silence between people, wondered how to start them talking again and wondered more at his own weakness for needing them to talk, for being intimidated by the girls and the silence and really, the whole fucking world.

'I really think –' began Colley and then the train jolted and, almost as though it had been waiting for right moment, the box spasmed violently and slid out from under the girl's relaxing arms, dropping to the floor. It slithered under the bottom of the seat in front of her, disappearing from view. Immediately she followed it, falling to her knees and lowering her head to look under the seat, thrusting her arms into the space after the box. The younger girl, as though in counterpoint, shrieked and drew her feet up off the floor, pulling her legs into a tight clench before her and wrapping her arms around them. From behind the legs came a long wail that resolved in a cry of 'No, no, no, no, no, nooooooo.'

'Shut up,' shouted the older girl, her voice muffled. Colley saw that her entire head was under the seat now, her backside up in the air as she tried to manoeuvre in far enough to grab the box. There was the faint sound of scrabbling and of cardboard tearing and Colley thought again of a rat, its claws and teeth shredding the walls of its prison as it prepared to burst forth in a feral temper, and he shuddered.

'No, no, no, no,' the younger one was saying over and over, her voice rising in pitch and volume and the woman with the shopping bags was looking around now, seeing what? Colley and an upset young girl and he turned away from the girl to look out of the window and realised only after that his action probably made him look even guiltier, breaking a contact when the contact was observed. How had he got into this? How had things gone so badly on the train, this shabby carriage taking him to some shitty seaside town to do a job he hated for people whose names he would know for only six or seven hours?

The woman was staring at him with open interest. 'I think she's upset because her sister dropped something,' said Colley in an act of desperate appeasement but then, again, a realisation, that if the girl had dropped something and the other girl was upset surely he should be helping rather than sitting there doing nothing, because what kind of monster sat and did nothing while a child was upset? He glanced to his side. The older girl had crawled under the seat to the middle of her back now, he legs bent up against the seat front she had previously been sitting on. The box must have gotten very jammed because she was wriggling a lot, jerking back and forth, almost thrashing, presumably trying to free it.

The woman along the carriage half-rose, the rain struck the train harder and harder, thunder crashed overhead and was cast behind them as lightning filled the train with harsh, flat streaks of light and dark.

Another glance and now the girl was under the seat to her waist and when Colley looked in front of the seat expecting to see her emerge from its front there was no sign of her. Even as he watched the girl crawled further and further in, pale thighs and knock-knees vanishing from view which was surely impossible because she should be emerging from the front now, dusty and dirty and holding the box but she *wasn't*, she just *wasn't* and that was impossible.

I'm done, thought Colley and stood. He lifted his coat, took his bag from the rack above him and, ignoring the shrieking girl and her vanishing sister, started for the carriage door. The train was slowing down, a station on the line ahead waiting to gather travellers into its concrete embrace. He had made his choice. He had walked away, chosen not to get any more involved. *I'm a coward,* he thought, and then, *so be it. I'm a coward then. I am what I am.*

The younger girl's cries rose in pitch again. The woman along the carriage stood properly, a look of concern upon her face. A last glance and the older girl was gone under the seat to her ankles, just her socks and trainers showing and Colley stepped into the aisle and then the younger girl's shriek's became wordless and out of the corner of his eye he saw her point along the carriage, pointing at something and simply *howling*, howling in something like complete and absolute terror.

There was a figure at the end of the carriage.

Despite the fact that it was in the carriage, it seemed to Colley to be hundreds of yards away, a thing seen close up but at a distance and it made no sense, must have been a trick like the girl vanishing under the seat, a trick played by two rough little children from rough little background, played upon Colley because he was weak and gullible and too frightened to say anything but 'Yes' when they bated the hook and first drew him in.

A trick that walked along the carriage with a splintered, ragged gait.

It grew cold then, not just chilly but a bitter, freezing cold and then by God it started to *snow*, inside the carriage, *inside*! Fat flakes plunged through the air around them all, another impossible thing. The teenager in the headphones simply pulled his coat around him as the figure passed and the woman, when it reached her, sat back in her seat, fell really, and her head rolled back and her eyes closed.

The figure reached Colley.

It was standing next to him, was a tall as he was and yet so far away as a storm blew outside and snow fell between them and around them. The figure was leathern, brown and dry-looking, its face angular, the leather stretching between deep set eyes and a jaw that was more of a muzzle jutting forward, and its teeth were yellowing and huge and there were too many of them for that small space and they were uneven, doubling and tripling on themselves like a shark's teeth. Something that might have been feathers swept back over its head, low to its scalp which showed through in dry, flaking patches.

'I thank you for the distraction,' it said, and its voice was rasping and low as though unused to making words, used more to howls and groans and shrieks. Colley couldn't speak. He shivered, his hair wet from the snow. The figure nodded and went on, to where the remaining girl was sitting.

'You should be congratulated, I suppose,' it said, and the rasp in its voice was easing as it used it, an old engine gradually lubricating itself with oil. 'It is no small feat to summon me, especially as you are so young and have had no instruction in these matters. You must be powerful shaman. Not powerful enough, though, but powerful nonetheless. It is a shame. He could have used you if you had simply waited and been patient and obeyed.' It bent, its upper body remaining absolutely straight, its legs folding, and a long, spindly arm reached to the floor and brought up the box. It straightened, brushing something that looked like long, flayed cobwebs from the edges of it, and then unfolded part of itself, a flap of skin or cloak or some fucking thing that Colley couldn't understand and he wanted to scream but he couldn't, and placed the box inside so that it vanished when the flap closed. Colley wanted to scream, to run, but it was as though the snow had frozen him in place and all he could do was watch, be witness.

'I am *tupilaq*,' it said, 'I am the walker of the snows and ice, and I serve whosoever is most powerful. That, child, is not you but the person you cast me against. That was your error.' It reached out then, long fingers spreading into claws and wrapping around the younger girl's face, pinching together at the back of her head and muffling her screams. 'I take back what you have removed. I take back what you have stolen. I take you now and there is no escape for you. Your confession is not enough to appease me because your sibling did not confess and she was equally involved in this wickedness with you, and one fellow traveller on a train is not a public confession but merely private discourse. You have not completed the steps to salvation, only those to damnation.' It took a step back, pulling the girl from the seat and into a loose standing position. Her arms hung motionless by her side, her feet dragging and Colley realised she wasn't standing but being held upright by the thing, the *tupilaq*.

Had she fainted?

Was she dead?

The train slowed, and now the landscape outside was passing by at a speed that allowed him to make it out, storm-swept and battered by rain, leaves and detritus stripping past the windows as the wind tore it all along. Inside, the snow continued to fall, settling on his head and shoulders and hands, numbing them, soaking his suit. He staggered before the thing and reached the carriage door, reaching out and, despite the fact the train was still moving, stabbing at the door open button, knocking clumps of snow off the plastic nub to do so.

'Be not afraid, man,' said the thing, as it drew alongside Colley and for the first time he heard an accent hidden in its words, something clipped and short and hard-edged. 'You are not my quest, and you will not be harmed. These two are punished enough now, and the soul is back where it belongs. Go in peace.'

The girl's toes made long dragging sounds as the *tupilaq*

progressed along the carriage, each step seemed to cover yards, and it dwindled into a black spot before, as the train finally, *thankfully* slowed to a halt, vanishing entirely, taking the girl with it. Colley glanced back but the older girl was gone too. All that remained were those long strings of dusty cobweb-like material shifting in the air currents that played across the floor.

Beyond him, the woman rolled her head forward and opened her eyes. She looked confused for a second, then blinked and stood, collecting her bags. She went to the far door, looking out of the windows at the foul weather beyond and grimacing. The boy carried on nodding along to the beat in his ears.

The doors opened and Colley stepped out into the storm in a swirl of snow that no one else could see.

GOBLIN

There is a small, rather picturesque valley in Somerset called Goblin Comb. At first glance, there is much scenic weirdness to be had here: mysterious clumps of vegetation, eerily twisted trees. Whether these are the reasons for the valley's curious name, or whether local folktales are responsible is uncertain. It's not exactly a forbidding place, but Goblin Comb definitely has a mystical aura. And those previously mentioned tales contribute.

Though little known in the wider world, the mysteries of Goblin Comb come down to us in tantalising snippets from long-ago published collections of Somerset folklore. One tells how in the late 19th Century, a small group of children were busy collecting flowers there. One child, a little girl, was separated from the others and started crying. In response to this, a nearby boulder split open and she was taken through it by strange but kindly beings into a pleasant realm, where, because she was carrying primroses, which were accepted as a gift, she was rewarded with a golden ball and then sent safely home. Eager to have a golden ball of his own, a scheming village man made the same journey, also carrying primroses. The boulder opened again, but waiting inside this time was a far more malignant creature, who dragged him in. The boulder then closed, and the village man was never seen again.

A typical fairy story, you might think. Not uncommon in the chronicles of Old England.

But there is more.

A curious individual with the stature of a small boy but strange facial features was several times reported in Goblin Comb, always refusing to answer questions, but beckoning folk to follow him, though no one, it seems, was willing to take the chance.

It's difficult to trace the origins of these stories, but they first seem to have emerged in the early 20th Century. Around the same time, it was reported that a signpost had been put up in Goblin Comb, presumably by the authorities, advising travellers that there was NO footpath through the valley. Supposedly, this was in response to the regular appearance of a mysterious path, which if you followed it, would supposedly lead you to who knew where.

Again, it's familiar stuff. In fact, we're all well accustomed to the concept of the goblin.

While the faerie folk in general, or fae, have a reputation of their own for being untrustworthy, alternating from story to story between goodliness and villainy, their woodland-dwelling cousin, the goblin, is much more commonly associated with wickedness.

Our mental image of the goblin is of an ugly, stunted creature, often small in size but with exaggeratedly creepy features: pointy ears, an overlarge nose, snaggle-teeth, serpent-like eyes, and though much of this undoubtedly owes to the way such beings were illustrated in Victorian nursery books, again they're indicative of how devilish the goblin was long perceived to be. In fact, our culture is so fixed on this image that we've never been able to shake it off. The scariness of goblins is referred to in several of Shakespeare's plays, most notably A Winter's Tale and Hamlet, though counterbalanced by their playfulness in A Midsummer Night's Dream and Romeo and Juliet. But much more recently, in some of the greatest works of modern fantasy fiction, they have come to play an out-and-out darker role. In the writings of J R R Tolkien, for example, the goblins, or 'orcs', are an aggressive, cannibalistic species, who share none of the other races' values and plot constantly to conquer Middle Earth, while in J K Rowling's Harry Potter novels, they are intelligent rather than violent, but supremely devious and deceptive.

There aren't many folk today who believe in the existence of goblins, yet in past times that wasn't the case at all. They are probably most strongly associated with Western Europe, where the word itself was first written down in medieval times. The 'Gobelinus,' mentioned by Orderic Vitalis in a document of 1141, referred to an evil entity living in the woods close to Evreux in Normandy, while Ambroise of Normandy's 1195 Guerre Sainte, ostensibly relating the adventures of Richard the Lionheart, also describes 'gobelins' causing chaos.

Despite this strong Anglo-Norman connection, fear of these strange beings once extended across the whole world. You'll have heard of the Kobolds of Germany, the Puca of Ireland and the Bogles of Scotland, but what about the Dokkaebi of Korea, the Tengu of Japan, the Ifrit of the Middle East, the Pudgie-Wudgies in the wilderness of New England, and perhaps much more infamously, the little green men of Mammoth Cave in Kentucky, a tribe of diminutive but malign creatures so widely believed in that they even appear on Kentucky postcards and road-signs. In so many ways, all these mythical but adversarial beings are a close match for the goblin in terms both of magical ability and rampant ill will. And it's that latter issue, the goblin's malevolent nature, that made earlier societies take them so seriously.

To anyone thinking that goblins are nothing more than harmless tricksters, look at some of their more spectacular appearances in myth and legend.

In one of the most famous goblin myths of all, this one from medieval Germany, the evil and stunted Rumpelstiltskin offers to spin straw into gold to save a miller's daughter from execution, but in return demands she hand over her firstborn (for what terrible purpose, we can't imagine), and when denied, goes insane with anger. In Northumberland, the Hedley Know was not a cow at all, but a shapeshifting goblin, its existence reported as recently as the 18th Century, who delighted in interfering with midwives while they were attempting to assist birth, beating lone travellers with a club, and calling to village girls in the voices of their sweethearts, thus luring them alone into high risk situations. The Erlking meanwhile, a forest goblin who appears in old Scandinavian tales, was associated with burial mounds, where he could strike humans, usually children, with a fatal illness simply by touching them.

'Stories read to me at school,' I hear you say. 'Nuggets of romantic fable collated by such treasurers of childhood esoterica as Hans Christian Andersen and Ruth Manning-Sanders. Well-loved tales rather than warnings from history.'

You think so, eh?

Interestingly enough, even now in the boringly rational 21st Century, the internet is filled with video snippets allegedly depicting glimpses of the unexplained. There's the usual plethora of Bigfoot sightings, of ghosts, UFOs and long-necked lake monsters, but there are still a remarkable number purportedly showing minuscule *humanoid creatures scampering out of sight into the woods, or across someone's back yard or even around corners inside their house, often, or so the original posters tell us, at a time when paranormal activity was rife.*

I'd challenge anyone, preferably when they're alone at night, to view any of these modern goblin encounters, and not feel at least a faint stirring of age-old discomfort.

HARPY
Stephen Laws

'So why now?' asked the reporter. 'After all this time?'

'Because you were the one who seemed more interested. Obsessed even.'

It was true. Jerry Fortnum had been obsessed, and had remained so with this apparently stable, happily married man; retired early after running a small business – not what you would call a rich man but successful enough to have a nice, detached house in the suburbs. No children. A beautiful wife, with whom he appeared to be besotted and who, it seemed, was very much in love with her husband.

A wife who he had killed, for apparently no reason, with a pitchfork. Rammed into her chest while she was sleeping next to him in bed.

'But now you've decided to tell your story.'

'Yes.'

'On the day before her funeral. And when I say, "Tell your story" I'm working on the assumption that it differs from the story – or non-story – that you told in court?'

'I began to tell the full story at the time. To the police, I mean. But they clearly thought that I was insane, believed that I was aiming for the "guilty but insane" plea. That's certainly what the psychiatric team believed. So I stopped ... telling everything, I mean. But now. Well, now – it's all over. I'm in here. And tomorrow they're putting her in the ground. So now I want to tell.'

'Why me?'

'I read what you wrote in the newspapers and magazines at the time about what happened. You said that you always felt that there must be more to the story.'

'I did.'

'There was.'

To say that Fortnum was surprised to hear from him was a massive understatement. They were in an interview room in His Majesty's Prison Gallow, NW and the interview was taking place at the murderer's request, said murderer being one Terence Moran, forty-seven years old. Found sitting on the edge of the marital bed, having telephoned the police, he had meekly held out his hands for the cuffs. He had considerately unlocked the front door in advance to allow the police easy access before rejoining his wife in the bedroom. The bed was drenched in blood, the pitchfork still protruding from his wife's chest. He had volunteered his confession immediately but steadfastly refused to give any reason or motive for his act. After post-mortem investigation and forensic details had conclusively proved that he was responsible for the act, he was tried, found guilty and sentenced to life imprisonment. When all avenues on the mystery appeared to have been closed, Fortnum had received a 'message' that Moran wanted to talk – without a solicitor – about why he'd done what he'd done. The means by which the request had been channelled had been torturous. The Prison Governor and system itself had been resolutely against it, but Fortnum had an Ace up his sleeve that had never failed him yet: a PR agent by the name of Anna Moss, who had an uncanny knack of calling in favours and exerting pressure to sensitive 'points'. She hadn't let him down in the past and had secured the interview in ways that she was 'not prepared to discuss', adding 'Don't fuck it up, Jerry.' Her voice was distinctly husky because she smoked far too much. 'Moran has no friends; no relatives and his wife's funeral is on the following day. All very bleak, really. But perhaps he's had enough time to think and wants to get things off his chest.'

'That's almost a joke, Anna. Given what he did to his wife.'

'That's not funny. I've really had to go out on a limb for you hear darling, particularly with the Prison Governor, and there are enough tag lines in this story for good copy so I'm hoping even you couldn't bugger it up.'

Now, here was Fortnum – and Moran, in a secure interview room. While the interviewer was judging how to move the interview on, Moran started to speak.

'My wife was very attached to me.' He looked down at the hands clasped in his lap. 'Very *attached*.'

Fortnum noticed the curious way that he emphasised that word. There was a long pause and it seemed as if that one word had so much *import* that Moran wasn't quite sure how to proceed.

'Are you going to tell me why you killed her?'

'Yes.'

'You don't want the police here, or a solicitor?'

'No.'

'Why?'

'Because they won't believe me. But I think that you will.'

'I don't know how I should feel about that. But I'd be a liar if I said that I wasn't intrigued. Please. Go on.'

'My wife was … is … very beautiful …'

Is?

'But when anyone looks at her – and I mean *anyone* – that's not the way she is, in real life. She doesn't look like that, at all.' The look that he gave Fortnum was both pitiful but also, it seemed, edged with a contained kind of terror.

'So if I were to look at her,' ventured Fortnum, 'She would be beautiful.'

'Because that's the way she *chooses* to look.'

'And how does she really look?'

'*Terrible.*' The word seemed to shudder out of his weak, apparently malnourished frame.

'Doesn't sound possible.'

'No it doesn't, does it?'

'Sounds … inhuman?'

'Yes, she was.'

Fortnum had been waiting for this to happen for so long. There was something – *something* – that had obsessed him about this case from the very start, and it was vital to keep Moran 'on track' if he was to get anything close to the truth that he felt in his gut was hiding inside his story.

'But human enough for you to fall in love with her, to marry her, and to have a life with her?'

'Yes, I fell in love with her. On that holiday island in Greece. Or rather, I fell in love with the person she said she was.'

'Melina Marcouris.'

'No, the thing that I married made itself *look* like Melina Marcouris. It found her there first. Killed her. Consumed her. Took her likeness. And her passport.'

'And the … *thing* … as you call it … was clever enough to do that, because …?'

'It was time to leave the island. It wanted new blood. New torment. It was so very clever, you see? It found Melina – a single woman on holiday, single like me and with no relatives. What could have been better? It took her. Took her place. And then, it found me. I fell in love with something that only looked like Melina.'

'So, a whirlwind romance on a Greek island. You return together to England. That's very clever of her – of *it* – to be able to organise the passport, not to mention complicated personal affairs back here in the UK.'

'The passport wasn't hard. But being clever isn't even close,' continued Moran. Beads of sweat had appeared, marbling his white face. 'It's cleverer than you could possibly imagine.'

'Why you? Why should she – it – pick you?'

'A single man. A tourist alone on holiday. I said that she could "*attach*".'

That word again.

'Yes, but I mean – why "attach" to you? No offence, but couldn't Melina – I mean "it" – "attach" to all kinds of other single tourists? Again – why you?'

'Because,' Moran dry gulped. 'It liked the taste of my fear.'

The light strip in the interview room fizzed for a second.

'So – the thing you married wasn't Melina Marcouris. What was it?'

'A harpy,' replied Moran.

The psychiatric evaluation and report came instantly to

mind. An evaluation and paperwork that Fortnum should not have had access to but whose PR agent Anna had been able to access in a less than legal manner: *'An insecure man with extremely low self-esteem problems. It appears that his wife has been the one and only significant female relationship in his life (apart from his mother, which appears problematic in itself) and it's likely that the misogynistic fantasy that has become so real for him lies in a deep-rooted fear and abhorrence of all women as "harpies".'*

'She was abusive, then? Perhaps she ...?'

'Abusive?' Moran's eyes sparked anger, two flashes of pinpoint ice in that face of dough. He looked down, clearly trying to pull himself together. 'Abusive?' He began again, fighting to remain calm. 'No ... you don't understand. And I know you're thinking about that psychiatric evaluation. About how I did what I did because I'm a woman hater. That I hate all women. But that's *not* – what I mean. When I tell you that she was a harpy, that's exactly what I mean.' He paused then, this time with an expression of yearning on his face. He wanted me to understand and was waiting for my dawning realisation, which just wasn't arriving.

Angrily again but aware of the attendant guard and the very real possibility that this interview could easily be ended, he took a breath, closed his eyes and continued.

'I'm telling you that she wasn't human. Not that she was human and behaved inhumanly, but that she was *in fact* inhuman. She was not a flesh and blood, human woman. She was a *harpy.'*

'Like the creature of legend?'

'Yes!' Now pathetically grateful that I seemed to be 'getting it' at last, something like a shuddering gasp escaped his lips. 'Exactly that. A tormentor. Created to prey on human misery. Getting its strength from torment and pain – and terror.'

'You said that she "attached" to you. Because, you said, it – *liked* – your fear?'

'She was drawn to my misery and she loved the particular taste of my fear and terror. She could create it, work with it, and she *fed* on it.'

'So – let's get this straight. You were on what they call a "singles" holiday in Greece. Right?'

Moran swallowed and nodded.

'Let's just have a straight talk through of what happened. There was a woman. The real Melina … not the harpy thing that looked like Melina. She wasn't part of the holiday package that you were on.' Moran shook his head. 'She – Melina – was there already, separately, on holiday alone. But the harpy killed her and took her place, which is when you met her – it – the harpy – when you were out walking alone on the beach. She told you that she was also a tourist, from the UK researching her family roots. That much I got from the original reporting.'

'Yes. Later, she joked that she had been born in a cave there. I know now that she wasn't joking with me, because I think it was true. She said something else. It didn't make any sense. She said it then and she'd say it again sometimes – like she was in a trance.' Moran paused, as if he'd gone into some sort of daze himself at the memory. 'And she said – apart from "being born in a cave" … that she was also born out of fire. That fire had been her "life giver" and friend.' Moran's eyes were still glazed. 'She said that fire had given her life.'

I waited.

Moran seemed to 'unglaze'.

'And you fell instantly in love?'

'She cast a spell on me. She could do that. I don't mean magic and mumbo jumbo, all that stuff. I mean she could just *do it*. By being herself, by just – even standing next to you.'

'Pheromones.'

'I don't know what that means.'

'It doesn't matter. So there was a whirlwind romance. She *attached* to you, as you put it.'

'Yes, to feed from me. But probably more importantly, to make me take her back home to England.'

'Why more importantly?'

'I've told you. New territory, new hunting grounds, more victims. She took the greatest pleasure from me – doing the thing she did, making me *share* …' Moran steeled himself as if he was going to throw up, then continued: 'She'd go out at night. Hunting. Finding victims. Do what she always did. One-night stands. Killing and *consuming*. Sometimes – bringing *things* back to our home, like mementos of what she'd done.'

'You lived together for a year.'

'A year in Hell.'

'And you killed her.'

Moran paused. Fortnum feared that he'd killed the conversation with that last statement.

'Let me tell you,' he continued at last. 'She could have killed me at any time. And in the most unimaginably horrible way that I don't think you'd ever be able to understand. But she didn't, because she still had "use" of me, feeding from the terror she could create in me. But … if something, an animal, a human, is terrorised constantly to a point beyond despair, I think that it'll just – shut down. I think it will either kill itself because of the torment or just shrivel up and die. I realised at one point – one *awful* point …' Fortnum sat back in his chair, this time truly believing that Moran was about to throw up at the table. Moran gulped and managed to contain himself. 'Then one day, one terrible day, I think she knew I was getting close to the end of my usefulness as *food*. We both knew it, I think. It brought extra surges of fear and terror to me as I was reaching burn-out that I knew she found pleasing.'

Fortnum struggled not to prompt him again, feeling that he was getting close to something important, and so proved to be the case.

'The solution to my problem came from the most banal setting. Well, I say "banal", but there's a sick irony here as well. The Greek restaurant we were in was not, I'm sure, "banal". I'm sure it was a very nice restaurant. I really couldn't say.'

'Wait a moment. Are you telling me that you dined there with that "thing" – this harpy – this creature from Greek legend, in a *Greek* restaurant?'

Moran glared at Fortnum, who reined himself in, trying to remain stoic and blank faced. After what seemed a long time, Moran's expression softened and he continued.

'She took me. Suddenly. It amused her. She said she wanted to see what it would look like. Insisted that it be a restaurant that employed Greek waiters. It took some time to find one but, you know, terror can be quite an "inspiration".' Moran grinned and looked sick. 'When we arrived, just as we walked through the door – *she changed her face.* I didn't look, but I knew that she was doing it. Making herself more "glamorous", perhaps?' There was a rictus on Moran's face, a ghastly attempt at a smile. 'She got the attention she wanted. They were falling over themselves to please her. The waiters, the staff, the customers. You could see it on their faces. And the way they looked at me? What on earth is this wonderful creature doing with this sickly, wizened specimen? Must have loads of money or something. But – a funny thing. There was an old guy, sitting apart at a table by himself, drinking wine. The only person in that restaurant not paying any attention to us. And all the time, she's looking around at the décor of the place, the attempts at old Greek design, old Greek cultural references – and beneath that mask of a face, a face that I couldn't bear to look at – a cold wave of contempt. I felt sick to my stomach.'

'So you didn't eat?'

'Oh, yes. She saw me trying to keep down my bile. But then when the food came, she would just say – command – "*Eat*" – and I'd eat. I had no choice other than to eat and keep it down.'

'And she could eat the food, as well? I mean, you say she fed on "fear" and … other things.'

Moran gave me a look of contempt. 'Of course she ate! She ate the food; she ate the attention and the lust and the desire and the envy of everyone in that restaurant!'

'There must be something more to this incident. Otherwise you wouldn't be telling me this …'

'This banal story?'

'You used the word, not me'.

'At one point, when it seemed that I might pass out at the table …'

'Pass out?'

'She told me to eat when I was sick to my stomach. I told

you. So I ate, and I kept on with the pretence because she'd ordered me to and I could only do what she wanted. You must understand. I had no choice. But my body started to rebel. I couldn't help it. She could see what was happening.'

'And so?'

'She ordered me to go to the rest room.'

Fortnum raised his eyebrows, still staying stoic.

'To throw up.' Moran sneered at me. 'What else?'

'Which you did?'

'And on my way back – I'd just opened the rest room door – and there was someone waiting for me. It was the older man I mentioned, the one sitting at the table by himself. Well to do, very respectable. I think he might have been the owner of the restaurant. I believe he was Greek. He had a heavy accent.'

'Okay …'

'He looked … concerned. Well no, actually … he looked frightened. We were in an anteroom sort-of-thing between the restaurant and the rest room. He took me by the arm, kept looking back over his shoulder towards the restaurant. Actually, he looked as frightened and sick as I felt. He told me … told me … that he knew what was happening. He was from the "old country". He could *see*. He could see the real her, knew what she was and what she could do.' Moran shuddered to a halt. 'I need some water.'

Fortnum looked up at the guard. He looked back. Fortnum looked at Moran.

No water.

'"Three times," the old man said. "Three blades. All strike at same time. All *stab* at same time. You understand? You have two friends? You three, with three knives. All stab same time together her. Must be three. Then you be free."'

Moran loosened his collar and licked his lips. The guard refused to take the hint.

'Suddenly,' Moran continued. 'She was there. In the anteroom, with the old man and I. Good God, it was as if she'd somehow come through the wall. I've never seen so much hate on anyone or anything's face. It was *animal*. Worse than that!

Not the face of anything I've seen in my life. Good God – there was *smoke*. Around her face, I mean. The old man fell back against the wall, terrified. *"We're leaving!"* she hissed at me, like a snake. *"No pay!"* gibbered the old man. *"No pay!"'*

Moran cleared his throat, glared first at Fortnum and then at the guard, as if daring them to sneer or dispute what he was saying.

'And then we were gone.'

Moran didn't speak again for a full minute, his head down. Fortnum was convinced that this was the end of the conversation. A horror fantasy ending with a weird confrontation in a bloody Greek restaurant. Banal, indeed.

'I don't know how I managed to drive us home. I could barely function. My hands were shaking so badly on that steering wheel. But she ordered, and I – somehow – obeyed. I really believed that these were my last moments on earth and that something beyond terrible was going to happen to me when we got home. Had she heard what the old man had said? It hadn't made much sense to me, and I couldn't be sure she'd heard – but it was clear that he knew *what* she was. I only knew that she was *luxuriating* in my fear as I drove. It might have been one of the best and most satisfying *feasts* I'd ever given her, perhaps both of us also knowing that it would be the last. And that satisfaction seemed to calm her down. When we returned home, I stood in the living room and waited. She pointed to the bedroom. I entered, and she left.

'She was gone for two hours. When she returned, she carried something under her arm, wrapped in newspaper, something I couldn't see. She took it into the kitchen and I heard her unwrap it. And then she called to me. She said: "I have something here that you might recognise." Oh God … I knew what she'd done. "Come here, Terence." When she called me by my name, it always sounded like snakes hissing. I had no choice. I went in there to join her and …'

'And?'

'She showed me, and asked: "Do you recognise an old man's face? Someone who knew – but should have known better."'

'The old man from the restaurant? She killed him?'

'Yes. She brought home his face to show me.'

'His *face?*'

'Yes. And ...'

'And?'

'She made me wear it for a while.'

Not finding the right words to respond, I could only look at his sick, sweat beaded white face. After a while, he continued again.

'That seemed to amuse her. And then she made me watch – and join in – with the other things that she always did after a killing.'

The sound of impatient shuffling drew Fortnum's attention to the prison guard in attendance, who was now making a great show of looking at his watch.

'It was bad when we – did things together. Then we would just sit together at night afterwards and she would talk to me about things that made no sense. English words, you know? Not Greek words or what might have been Greek words, but those *looks* of hers – her eyes – you've no idea. But then there'd be the silences, where she'd just sit and look at me and I'd weep. Because those silences would always end with ... oh God ...'

Fortnum felt a sudden, terrible coldness.

'Because then she'd say – she'd know I was dreading that she'd say to me, finally –'

Moran suppressed a sob.

'Come to bed.'

Fortnum shuffled uneasily, looking at the guard. 'I don't know how much time we have left. Or whether I'll be allowed to interview you again. But after everything you've said, if I believe everything you've said, I don't understand Terence how you would be able to kill something so terrible, something that had so much of a hold and power over you, and with the – abilities and powers you say she had.'

'I've told you that I sensed she realised that I was coming to the end of my usefulness, of my ability to feed her the way she needed to be fed. That night, after what … happened … in the kitchen, and then in the bedroom …' Moran paused, searching for more strength to continue. 'I just wasn't sure that she had heard what the old man said. If she'd just come out and asked me, I would have been forced to tell her. But she didn't and … I was afraid and confused. There was so much that she *knew* without asking. Did she know and was torturing me with her silence? But if she'd known then I couldn't have been able to do what I did. So confused. Don't you understand?'

'What *did* you do?'

'After what happened in the bedroom – what *always* happened in the bedroom, she'd go into what seemed to be some kind …'

Fortnum waited for him to find the right word.

'Some kind of trance. Very brief. It wouldn't last long, but I could never tell whether she was asleep or awake, because her eyes were always open. But she'd be very *still*. I lay next to her as I always did after she'd fed, waiting, afraid to move or to speak – but this time believing that I was going to die. God help me, I think a part of me welcomed it and wanted to get it over and done. But some other part of me, and I swear I don't know where it came from, made me get up off that bed. When she hadn't *turned* and killed me there and then, I left the bedroom and walked quietly and carefully out of the house and into the garden. The previous, more human, younger man that I'd been had loved that garden. Now overgrown and wild, just a tangle of bushes. I went to the garden shed, with the old Greek man's frightened words in my head about three friends striking at the same time to make three wounds. Hah! Me, with friends? Even *before* she came into my life, I had no friends. I believed she sensed that when we met and it was one of the things that made me her target. It made my feeding potential even more attractive.'

The guard added a cough to his shuffling.

'I went into the garden shed. I took out what I knew was in there. Unused since she had come into my life. At every step, I expected her to come screeching at me out of the night. Every step back to the house and to that bedroom felt like my last. She was still in that trance, still lying on her back with her eyes open. At the bedside I tried not to look at those eyes. Asleep or awake, there was no way of knowing. I raised my arms above her, not believing I'd get that far.

'"*Three separate knife blows delivered at the same time*", the old man had said.' Moran's face was now dripping with sweat, his eyes closed as he relived the memory. '*By three friends*. But as I've said, I had no friends. But I'd loved my garden. Once, I'd tended and loved it when I had nothing in my life and no friends. Was this enough? Did that weird and terrified advice extend to the garden tools?

'I brought the three-pronged pitchfork down with all the strength that I could find and drove it into her chest.

'There was screaming. I don't know whether it was her, or me. They were sounds that I had never heard before and never want to hear again. I kept my eyes squeezed tightly shut because I could not bear to see and leaned heavily with all of my body weight on the shaft of that pitchfork. Everything below and around me *erupted as* the bedsheets flapped and flailed and the mattress bounced and juddered and ...

'It was like she was there and *not there*. There was something screeching and clawing at me from below and those flapping bedsheets had become something else. They felt like ... *wings*. Like they'd come out of her shoulders and were frantically flapping and gigantic and enormous and all around me as I kept my weight there, pinning that thing that she'd now completely become down on the bed. With each second, I expected that those hands turned to claws would pierce my arms and drag me down into her embrace. I screamed on and on, along with that other screeching below me. I think I passed out. Believed that I was dead.'

'Time's up,' said the guard.

'It was morning when I "came around" again. I was sitting in a chair at the bedside but I have no memory of pulling it there and sitting down. I was covered in blood, of course. The bedsheets were shredded and soaked. And Melina – well, she was lying dead in our bed, the pillows rent and split with feathers all over the bed and bedroom, some in her hair. Her face looked – human, just like Melina in the passport photo, not staring open eyed and agonised, but with her eyes closed and her face beautiful, still and peaceful. And that pitchfork was still in her.'

'Okay, enough,' said the guard. 'I was told you only had an hour.'

'I called the police. The rest you know.'

'So you killed a monster – a harpy – not a woman?'

'That's right,'

'And you want me to believe that?'

'Because it's the truth,'

I began to collect my papers, not sure just what kind of article I was going to write here. The police, psychiatric team and court had agreed that Moran was delusional and a murderer, but just how delusional seemed unclear until he had decided to tell me his 'true story'. Where the hell was I going to go with this?

'Thank you, Terence.'

'No – thank you. At last, I've had the chance to tell what really happened.'

The guard moved to a side wall, lifted a telephone from its bracket next to the door and began to speak to someone beyond the room. Moran stood up meekly, waiting to be told what to do. I cleared my papers into a folder and also stood.

'One last thing,' I said.

'Yes.'

'There was obviously a post-mortem.'

'Yes.'

'Don't you think that a coroner might have noticed something at least slightly unusual if, as you say, Melina was not a human being?'

Moran's smile looked ghostly.

'You have no idea of my wife's abilities in life – and in death. At least by tomorrow, the thing that called itself Melina will be put into the ground.' Moran sighed with a sound like the last of his soul escaping.

'Put into the ground?' I asked.

'Her funeral tomorrow.'

'Yes, it's her funeral tomorrow. I guess that's why you've asked me here today. But presumably you know about the funeral arrangements? They must have been discussed with you.'

'What do you mean? She's dead, and she's going to be buried.'

'Dead, yes. But she's not being buried.'

'What the hell are you talking about?'

'You must know this, Terence. The prison authorities must have discussed this with you.'

'I was asked if I wanted to attend the funeral. It shouldn't surprise you to learn that I said no. After everything I've told you, can you see me standing by a graveside, mourning that monster?'

'Terence, Melina left a will.'

Moran looked at Fortnum with a blank face.

'You wouldn't be standing at a graveside. Because she's being cremated tomorrow.'

'*What?*' Moran's expression changed to one of sick horror.

'It's all in her will, Terence. What she wanted if something should happen, if she should pass away.'

'*What do you mean, a will?*'

The prison guard at the telephone was moving quickly back to them now. 'Moran!'

'Her will.' Fortnum continued. 'All the paperwork is in order, Terence. I've studied it. She isn't being buried tomorrow.'

'*Not* buried …?'

'No. She's being cremated.'

Fortnum took an involuntary step back as Moran's face turned in mere moments from that pasty, dough white and sweaty complexion to a mask of crimson rage.

'*Cremated?*'

'Yes, at Mount Lawn Crematorium. All the arrangements have been made.'

'You fool! *You complete bloody fools!* Didn't you hear what I said? What she told me?'

'Stand back, Moran!' snapped the guard, pushing me behind him as the prisoner slammed his hands down on the table.

'She told me that she was *born in fire!* Don't you think I've had time to think about that? She's got to go in the ground, *not in the fire!* That's what she wants. Because if she goes in the fire, there'll be no way of stopping her from …'

Bewildered, Fortnum shrugged, holding his arms wide, and something about that gesture – not intended to illicit any kind response from Moran's outburst – seemed to infuriate the prisoner. Moran roared and came straight across the table at him.

'You've got to stop them! You've got to stop it before it's too late!'

The table went over as Moran's clutching hands reached for Fortnum's throat, just before the guard body-slammed the prisoner and brought him down hard to the ground. Klaxons began to sound, bearing witness to the fact that the interview had also been observed by others beyond the room, since within seconds other guards and security personnel had flooded the space. Fortnum watched, dazed, as Moran was dragged from the room.

'You can't put her in the fire!'

They were the last words that Fortnum heard as the interview room door slammed shut.

On the next day, driving to the crematorium, Fortnum experienced a mixture of self-doubt, uncertainty, shame, anger, unprofessionalism and, indeed, self-loathing. His mind returned to the first reporting of Moran's crime, the news coverage (some of it his own), the weirdly blank non-reasons that he had given for the murder of his wife. Now that he had managed, with Anna's help to get the interview with Moran – only to hear the detailed horror fantasy that this pathetic and deranged individual so clearly believed – Fortnum could just not shake off a sickening feeling that perhaps he had somehow become obsessed with this case *against his will*. As he drove through an autumnal wind that scattered clouds of papery brown leaves against the car's windshield, he recalled Moran saying how the woman he claimed to be a monster could *attach*. Ludicrous though the thought was, he could not shake that alien idea out of his head. What if this thing that Moran believed had made itself into the image of the murdered Melinda had somehow – through him, and without even meeting him or knowing who he was – *called out to him*, siren-like and made him become obsessed with the case and with a view to some horribly pre-planned and fatalistic outcome? In ways that it was impossible to understand, had Fortnum already in some way been snared into some horrible purpose?

Why the hell am I thinking like this? The man's a lunatic, and I'm behaving like I believe what he told me. Is craziness infectious? I've got to shake off this insanity. The simple fact is that I obsessively sought a hidden purpose and truth in the murder and somehow hadn't expected what I finally got – the ranting of a deluded madman. The monster hadn't been his wife. It had been Moran all along.

After this last journey to the crematorium, this last gesture towards something that might still make for an interesting and lucrative magazine feature (*'How I was deluded by a delusionist'*) he hoped to let this whole crazy self-assignment business go.

Ahead of him, on the other side of the motorway's central reservation boundary, Fortnum saw a white van heading towards him suddenly shoot across lanes, hit the central barrier and then flip end-over-end onto the motorway on which he was travelling. There were two cars ahead of him. The first was clipped by the van in a cloud of dust as it passed and span screeching across the three lanes. The car immediately in front of Fortnum careered onto the grass verge, smoke billowing from its rear tyres. Slamming on his brakes, Fortnum saw the white van finally disintegrate in a blur of smoke, dust and tangled metal. Car horns began to blare.

Fortnum's car had screeched to a halt but his anxious glance in the rear-view mirror revealed that the cars behind had also come safely to a halt. In shock, he jammed on the emergency lights, steered the car into the verge and then jumped out onto the grass. Using his mobile phone to ring police and ambulance he looked back to see that other drivers were doing the same. He had no idea that the motorway crash had probably saved his life.

By the time the police and ambulances arrived, medics and support staff had made their initial investigations, taken names and addresses and finally cleared one lane for traffic to pass the accident scene, Fortnum was two hours late at the crematorium. But why rush? Was there any real need for him to be there for the final act in this grim business? Melina's will had been blunt and straightforward. Her remains were to be cremated, not buried and there was to be no religious or humanitarian service at all. The body was to be burned and the ashes disposed of in the most perfunctory way possible. It only seemed important to Fortnum if he was going to write up any kind of story at all to have this last act attended to provide some sort of coda.

Eventually entering through the main gates, Fortnum followed a long drive to find the designated car park. By then, it was late afternoon and there were clearly no other services that day. Up ahead, he could see the crematorium. Just beyond, a garden of remembrance and then – hidden by trees – another low, concrete building masked by trees from which a thin trail of smoke was spiralling into the sky. Was this where the final act took place?

The chill autumn wind continued to blow, sweeping a carpet of leaves before him as he started towards the main building. Weirdly, it made Fortnum wonder whether these were the same leaves that had swirled earlier that day against his car windscreen. Were they following him around, and why was he again having such peculiar thoughts? Just as he was castigating himself for these ridiculous musings, a deafening blast of sound froze him in his tracks and seemed to scatter the leaves, making them fly like living things.

On the tree line ahead, from which the thin smoke had been crawling and rising, a great blossoming cloud of oily black-orange fire and smoke had suddenly erupted into the sky, now drawing in upon itself and exploding outwards into an even greater and louder explosion of flame. Flocks of birds joined the scattering leaves and Fortnum flinched back as the great fireball cloud yet again gathered in upon itself as if trying to contain its own power, before flaring and billowing out and upwards into the sky.

Fortnum pulled out his mobile phone as he ran towards the source of the explosions, seeing as he drew nearer through the screen of trees the blasted remains of the building beyond wreathed in flame. Urgently asking for police, fire brigade and potentially ambulance attendance, he reached the trees and picked his way through undergrowth to take a closer look at the ruins and the flame. Moran's words seemed to ring in his ears.

'You can't put her into the fire!'

'It's happened before,' said Anna Moss. 'A crematorium blowing up, I mean'.

'You can't be serious.'

'I'm always serious. You pay me to be serious. I'm part of that clever secret system that you've got of pulling wires behind the scenes and calling in the favours. Particularly when you don't want to get your hands dirty.'

'Explain to me then, darling. Why a crematorium can suddenly explode like that.'

'A pacemaker,' continued Anna.

'Explain.'

'As I say, it's happened in the past. Someone offs it. The family or the surviving relatives or the medical profession, whoever that might be, forgets to mention that the deceased has a pacemaker. The body goes into the burner. They turn on the taps. Boom. A big bang.'

'So that's what happened here?'

'No.'

'What do you mean, "*no*"?'

'Melina Marcouris as was – didn't have a pacemaker. The coroner's report confirmed it and the funeral director and crematorium people were advised. I just mention it because it's something I found out when I was making enquiries.'

'Anna! That's not helpful!'

'It's a bloody big mystery. They're still investigating but they haven't got a clue. Anyway, in the meantime, something else is going on that I can't get to the bottom of yet.'

'What's that?' Fortnum flinched from the telephone when Anna had one of her explosive and usual coughing fits. He waited impatiently for her to finish. 'Anna, you've got to pack in the cigarettes. They're going to kill you. What are you trying to tell me?'

'Something's going on at HM Prison Gallow,' replied Anna, recovering. 'Your interview with Terence Moran seems to have caused more than a stir. You told me that he had "lost the plot" when he found out about Melina's funeral?'

'Yes.'

'Well, he's had to be constantly restrained since then. And I mean *constantly*. They've had to sedate him. Keeps ranting on that his wife is coming back. That she's going to find him. Really off his head. You got your interview – and I'm the one who did the hard graft there darling, don't forget it. But you might want to keep your head down for a bit. When I make sure … wait … wait a minute …'

Fortnum heard another telephone ringing somewhere at her end and waited while she took the call. There was a clipped and urgent edge to her voice as she responded to whatever was being said, even though he couldn't hear a word.

'I'll ring you back,' she said on return, followed by more coughing.

'Why? What's going on?'

'Something's happening with your Terence Moran. I'll have to find out and get back to you.'

'Try to make it soon.'

Something deep in Fortnum's gut had become cold. Very cold, indeed.

Fortum worked on his notes, going over the interview and the incident at the crematorium. But Anna's last words preyed on his mind, again adding to his worry about why he had become so obsessed with the case. How on earth could he find the right angle and conclusion without finding out what the hell was now going on? Moran had revealed himself to be insane, weirdly and confusingly convincing in his belief of his tale, and he seemed to have taken Fortnum into a world of chaos. Moran's sudden meltdown about the funeral arrangements. The crack up on the motorway that had delayed his attendance at the crematorium, the explosion – underlying all of this was a nagging *something else* inside Fortnum that he just could not pin down. It would not leave him alone, but deep down, he knew that it was something *dangerous* – but dangerous in a way that refused to be analysed.

When the phone rang again, Fortnum knew that it could only be Anna.

'Yes?'

'What did you say to Moran?'

'What do you mean? I told you everything about that interview. He went batshit crazy and they had to restrain him, take him away.'

'But what did you *say*? Tell me again.'

'Look, Anna – when I told him that his late wife wasn't going to be buried on the next day, that she was going to be cremated, he just lost the plot and came at me. Something about her being put in the fire, that she had been born out of the fire.'

'And that's why he freaked out? Just because you told him that?'

'Yes. He did most of the talking. I never egged him on. He was crazy – and then he blew up.'

'Nothing else?'

'For God's sake, Anna! What's happened?'

'Moran is dead.'

'*What?*'

'There's hell on at HM Gallow. They're already organising a cover-up.'

'Cover up? What the hell ...?'

'They're going to try and fix it as a suicide. But I don't know how they'll pull that one off. It seems that someone *broke into his cell*. They heard him screaming. By the time they got inside ... well, at first they thought he'd done some kind of "dirty protest". You know, smearing his own excrement all over the walls. But then they realised that it wasn't excrement on the walls. It was blood. His blood. And he was very dead.'

'Wait! Wait a moment. You said, "someone broke into his cell" and then "by the time they opened the door, he was dead" ...'

'Whoever it was didn't break in through the cell door. They broke in through the window.'

'The *window?* Wait a moment, I did my research on this, Anna. Weren't there iron bars on that window and a plexiglass window with mesh on the inside?'

'Yes, I know. So do they. The bars were torn off and the Plexiglas yanked out with the mesh. And, by the way, that cell window is eighty feet from the ground, looking out over the recreation area. They found the remains of the bars and the glass down there afterwards.'

'None of this makes sense.'

'You're telling me? Look, I've got most of our tracks covered here, but they're going to come to you for a statement – and soon. Are you sure there isn't something else that you haven't told me?'

'No.'

You've got to stop them! You've got to stop it before it's too late.

'I told you what we talked about.'

She was born in fire. She's got to go into the ground, not the fire!

'Then hang on. Just wait. They may get to you before I can get back with more information. This is crazy stuff. Doesn't make sense.'

'Crazy ...'

'Just wait. I'll get straight back to you when I can.'

Anna hung up.

Fortnum had been told before he met with Moran that he would not be able to use a tape recorder, so had to rely on his notes – to which he turned yet again as soon as he had finished speaking to Anna. Moran's story was insane, but it all made sense on its own terms. He had 'fallen foul' of some hideous thing from Greece, a 'harpy' in his own words – and it had 'attached' to him because it enjoyed feasting on his terror and bringing him torment just as the creatures of ancient Greek legend were said to have done. In the knowledge that he would soon be 'used up' and have served his purpose, he had somehow turned the tables and – he thought – killed his tormentor. But now? Following the insane logic of his story, the harpy had already provided for just such an eventuality. Fortnum threw down the pen. Was he going insane? On one mad level, it all made sense. But he refused to accept it. Was he somehow being sucked into this insanity against his will? For a long time, he sat, trying to find a way of unravelling the madness and finding a loose thread in the whole thing that would make sense of his ridiculous obsession. Fortnum punched the table in frustration and stood up angrily as the front doorbell rang.

This had to be the visit from the police that Anna had warned him would be happening. Fortnum 'straightened' himself. He'd needed a drink of something strong but hadn't taken one since he wanted to be fully compos mentis when the police called. Clearing his throat and forcing upon himself a composure that he didn't feel, he opened the door.

But it was not the police.

It was Anna.

'Bloody hell, Anna. I thought it was going to be ...'

'The police,' she replied, blank faced. 'I know.'

'Come on in. Fix yourself a drink if you want. I'm staying off the booze until after the police have been.'

Anna came into the room and headed for the kitchen.

'Any more developments?' Fortnum asked.

'Not yet. But I came.'

Fortum paced the living room, heard Anna settling in the kitchen and then strode to join her.

'So how are we going to handle the ... Anna! For God's sake, I've told you before. Smoke as much as you want, but not in my place!'

Cigarette smoke was crawling around Anna's face.

Fortnum stopped, mesmerised at the way that smoke was obscuring and masking the PR agent's features.

Until he realised that it was not cigarette smoke.

'Do you recognise this face?' asked Anna, holding up her bloodied hands and revealing what they contained.

A sound came out of Fortnum's mouth. He didn't recognise it as his voice.

'Why don't you wear it for a while?'

'*Anna ...?*'

'And then afterwards, Jerry ...'

'*Afterwards?*'

'Come to bed.'

YATEVEO

The explorers have penetrated deeply into the equatorial jungle. Invariably, they are white men, Americans or Europeans, perhaps with one woman along to provide moral support (and love interest), while their guides and bearers are natives, and increasingly nervous because they know the legends of this place and are tired of giving warnings to their employers, who thus far have ignored all of them. But the dauntless explorers are themselves wilting. The heat and humidity are tremendous, and they are swarmed by stinging insects, while danger threatens not just from the savage carnivores that roam this region, but hostile tribesman too, and all this when they don't even know if their objective, an elephant graveyard or some fabulous lost city, even exists. And then suddenly, they fall into the grip of a new peril. A monstrous plant, initially blended in with the rest of the lush green flora, explodes upon them in a mass of writhing, spiny tentacles, which immediately wrap themselves around one or two unfortunates. Already draining their life fluids, the cellulose horror drags the hapless, screaming victims into the depths of its leafage, from where they can never be retrieved no matter how hard the rest of the expedition go at it with machetes or rifles.

The brave, or perhaps foolish, intruders have fallen foul of one of the most feared denizens of steamy jungles the world over: the man-eating plant.

A not atypical scenario in the minds of pulp fiction readers in the late 19th Century and early 20th. As the colonialist age came to its zenith and vast regions of Earth previously unknown in the Anglosphere but automatically assumed to be dangerous wildernesses, were opened up to westerners, authors like H Rider Haggard, Edgar Rice Burroughs and Arthur Conan Doyle popularised tales of derring-do in semi-alien, usually tropical environments that were teeming with deadly threats. In truth, in those long-ago days when imperialist pluck often overrode common sense, and wisdom, experience and careful prep might be sacrificed on the altar of schoolboy adventurousness, these unmapped jungles probably were extremely risky places to visit. But there were huge exaggerations as well. Volcanoes were often woven into the fictional mix, even in areas where there was no known volcanic activity. Dinosaurs and giant apes were still in existence. And then, of course, there was the idea that even the vegetation, given half a chance, would make a meal of you.

Of course, readers weren't stupid. Just because they'd read The Lost World (1912), that didn't mean they thought tyrannosaurs were still romping around the Amazon, or because they'd been stunned by the concepts in Tarzan and the Lost Empire (1928), they believed a form of Ancient Roman culture secretly thrived in parts of central Africa. And yet strangely, the concept of the man-eating plant was commonly accepted. No one ever seemed to question it. Most likely, this is because stories were circulating from the 1870s onward, purportedly the outcome of detailed scientific studies, which made repeated reference to such ghastly aberrations of nature as the infamous 'vampire vine', more generally known as the 'yateveo'.

It seems to have begun in 1874 with a report made to the New York World newspaper by a German botanist called Karl Leche, who related an horrific experience that he and his companions had while seeking out new plant species in a little-known region of Madagascar. Already in some degree of danger, as the Mkodo people were very hostile to outsiders, they suddenly came upon an astonishing scene. An immense unknown plant, more of a tree in truth, sat in the midst of an unnatural jungle clearing. Leche described as it as huge in stature, but of grotesque appearance, a colossal mass of thick, thorny foliage erupting outward from a trunk so horribly swollen that it resembled an immense, mutated pineapple. But it was what followed next that really shocked him. The Mkodo, possibly in an effort to intimidate the unwelcome trespassers, but maybe also because it was a regular sacrificial ritual in their lives, threw a bound female captive into the heart of its vast mesh of vines, all of which promptly coiled around the screaming woman, their innumerable barbs ripping deeply into her flesh, the blood literally raining down, until she'd been completely torn to shreds. The subsequent succulent parts were then drained of blood and eventually consumed by a range of voracious palps and suction cups.

The newspaper article, which was penned by a well-regarded journalist called Ed Spencer, named the monstrosity *Crinoida Dajeeana*, and it made an immediate and massive sensation, so much so that, by the end of that year, it had been reprinted in magazines across the world from London to South Australia. Very rapidly after this, similar tales began to appear elsewhere, naming other monstrous plants in different but equally inhospitable localities.

In his 1889 book, Sea and Land, self-styled 'naturalist' J W Buel, presented us with the name 'yateveo' as a kind of umbrella term for these species of killer plants, claiming that they didn't just occupy Madagascar, but also parts of central Africa and the Guiana Highlands, a heavily forested region at the junction between Venezuela and Brazil (where the same cliffs and plateaux that inspired The Lost World are also to be found). 'Yateveo' itself supposedly translates as 'I-See-You', indicating that these flesh-eating horrors didn't just wait until some unfortunate prey blundered into them or was thrown into their clutches, but were secretly watching, and easily capable of lashing out and snagging anyone who happened to be walking past. In Buel's account, the South American version of the monster initially presented itself as a comfortable seat, so to lure weary travellers, while another spectacularly named abomination, the 'Devil's snare', grew in remote parts of Nicaragua, and adopted a similar strategy. An article in the scientific journal, Lucifer Magazine, told how a New Orleans explorer known simply as Mr Dunstan, lost his dog to the latter of these two monsters.

It was the mid-1920s before the first doubts about these tales seem to have appeared in writing. By this time, a number of follow-up expeditions had been held, to no effect (though further expeditions were being planned as late as the 1930s). It was politician and travel writer, Chase Osborn, in his 1924 booklet, Madagascar, Land of the Man-Eating Tree, who first suggested that the whole thing might be a myth. By the 1950s, thanks to continued explorations, none of which returned with any specimens, it was more or less confirmed that the original articles had been hoaxes and that even the Mkodo tribe were an invention. Whether those who'd experienced the ghastliness for themselves, like Mr Dunstan and Karl Leche, had ever even existed was open to conjecture.

We now know for a scientific fact that, while some plants can damage animal tissue with poisonous substances, sometimes fatally, the physical structure of plant-life would make it impossible for any known species of plant to overpower any animal significantly larger than an insect. It was the thinking of the time that made western society assume otherwise.

We've already mentioned the plethora of imaginative jungle-bound adventure fiction so prevalent in that era. In addition, the choice of Madagascar as the wellspring of the horror was rather clever. Most Europeans and Americans of the day couldn't have pointed to it on a map, and yet it held status as a place of mystery. Thanks to the growing popularity of public zoos in the western world, it was known to be the home of a number of rare and exotic animals. In addition, it figured frequently in such well-known myths as the Sinbad stories, and was supposedly the birthplace of, among other legendary monsters, the giant, two-headed bird known as the Roc. The existence of thinking, predatory plants also seemed plausible thanks to the researches of Charles Darwin; in the mid-19th Century, it had come as amazing news that some plants could capture and devour flies and wasps.

Despite the yateveo having been thoroughly debunked by the mid-20th Century, the seed had been planted (ouch). And later authors, telling what might be considered more sophisticated stories, continued the tradition. Obvious examples include John Wyndham's Day of the Triffids, *in which the plant antagonists arrive on Earth from outer space, and Old Man Willow in J R R Tolkien's* Lord of the Rings, *wherein the adversary is a magical tree spirit. One perhaps needs look no further than Alan Menken and Herman Ashman's comedy musical* Little Shop of Horrors *to understand how seriously we should take the yateveo. But one final word of advice. If you're ever in the jungle, and you spot a comfortable-looking, couch-like assemblage of greenery, it's probably best not to recline on it.*

JORŌGUMO
S L Howe

A breeze whispered through the cherry blossoms as Archie sank into the deep hot water in his *furo*. From his bath, he looked out of the open window onto the beautiful garden. Surrounding the foliage were three high walls, ensuring his complete privacy from any potential onlooker, as the house had been designed to give its occupants a traditional sense of Japanese culture.

Even after several months, Japan remained a fascinating place to Archie, and the modern *machiya* he had rented for a few weeks in Kyōto offered many comforts. The house was built high on a hill, over two floors, just above the town, but accessible to the friendly streets via steep, wide stone steps that led all the way down into the heart of the city.

Archie's general opinion of the Japanese people had been reconfirmed during his stay in Tokyo. They were hard-working, loyal, dedicated and yet so in touch with the world around them. They loved their simple luxuries and wanted to preserve their standards, even as they fought to be more westernised. But his coworkers also had a great deal of respect for their superiors, one of whom Archie now was.

Their women were off limits to him, of course, but Archie didn't worry too much about that. He wasn't in Japan looking for any hook-ups and certainly not love: he was there for business and his firm had sent him to learn all he could about the running of operations in their Tokyo offices, with an aim to see how they could cut costs there.

Now, having a small break away, and on the recommendation of one of his colleagues, Hinata Sato, he'd come along to this much sought-after tourist destination, and former capital, to replenish his energy reserves after a bad virus had taken him down for a few weeks. He'd tried to work through it, but failed until he realised that a break from the gruelling long days might be what he needed.

Already a few days in the cleaner air of Kyōto, away from the bustle and industry of Tokyo, made Archie feel better. The hacking cough had finally disappeared, and the heavy feeling in his limbs was eased by the soothing hot water. Now his strength had returned he was considering taking a walk out to eat at one of the restaurants his landlady had recommended to him when he arrived.

After the bath, wrapped in a kimono, Archie picked up the stack of leaflets Mrs Tachibana had left for him in the small kitchen. He flicked through the menus – all of which had been printed in what he thought was Japanese but could have been a local dialect. It was fortunate that most of the restaurants also had the menu on the back page in English. What appealed the most were the restaurants that boasted of being *obanzai*, which Mrs Tachibana had said was specific to Kyōto and which she'd assured him was the best homecooked food that would give him the true taste of the region – food that only used homegrown products directly from Kyōto.

Archie was always interested in experiences, especially culinary ones, but he had been neglecting himself since he'd arrived in Japan, eating sporadically, and he'd lost a good stone or more without really trying to. With the return of his health came a resurgence of appetite and he found himself feeling hunger pangs for the first time in weeks.

Once he was dressed, Archie took the leaflet for the closest restaurant and stepped outside of the *machiya* and began the slow descent into the town.

A long walk found him on Shijo Street in downtown Kyōto. Looking at the map on the leaflet, he noticed he wasn't far from the restaurant he wanted but was surprised to find it off the main road in the outskirts of town, away from the well-lit tourist areas.

He paused before plunging down the back alley the map

indicated.

If his landlady hadn't given him the leaflet he might have thought it some kind of trap for tourists, possibly a point where he might be attacked and robbed, but a leap of faith made him move forward and soon found him in a beautiful courtyard, looking up at some stone steps to the well-lit frontage of Jorōgumo-Kyōto.

Colourful painted screen doors parted as Archie approached and a mature but beautiful woman in a royal blue kimono came forward, smiling and bowing.

'Jorōgumo Kyōto e yōkoso,' she said which Archie recognised as 'Welcome to Jorōgumo-Kyōto'.

He hadn't heard the name Jorōgumo before and wasn't sure what it meant, but accepted it may well be a family name for a family restaurant.

After removing his shoes, and stowing them on a rack outside the restaurant, he was led inside and asked if he preferred to sit western style or on *zaisu* and *chabudai*, which was a high-backed legless chair with a short-legged table traditionally used in Japanese homes and restaurants.

'I think I'd prefer a western table,' he said thinking of his still aching limbs and the many uncomfortable dining experiences he'd had with Japanese colleagues. He still marvelled how they sat on their knees so easily and at all ages when he found it so difficult to do and he was only in his thirties and generally fit – at least he had been until recently.

'This way, sir,' the hostess said immediately dropping all use of *Nihongo* and switching completely to English with barely a trace of accent.

She led him into a private room that held a regular table and chairs set for four people.

'There are no other English people tonight to join you but we will provide entertainment for you,' she said before bowing and leaving.

Now alone, Archie looked around at the highly decorated room and the shōji walls, all of which were capable of opening in any direction. The walls were fascinating and covered with paintings of beautiful women and an array of local insects and spiders crawling over depictions of local plant life. The pictures gave an idyllic view of humans and nature living as one and it went well with the silence around him, for he could hear nothing beyond them. He wondered what groups of people were on the other side. Were they dining on the local food, because they were all completely quiet? Surely he couldn't be the only patron in the restaurant that evening?

A waitress in a dark blue kimono came in with a jug of *umeshu*, a plum wine that Archie had tasted before. He sipped at the wine and nodded politely to the girl, asking her to bring him the chef's choice of local foods he might enjoy rather than struggling with a menu. She bowed and left without a word or any acknowledgement that she understood, but a few moments later, food arrived and Archie found himself eating with relish the purest, cleanest food he'd ever tasted, and which was seasoned so well, you tasted the produce more than the seasoning.

As the end of the meal approached the wall he was facing opened and there was a beautiful young woman in red and gold who Archie realised was a traditional Geisha because her white painted face and bright red lips. She was playing a *shamisen* which was a three stringed instrument like a guitar but with a much longer and thinner neck. The girl began to sing with the most beautiful clear voice and Archie found himself captivated. He paused eating, chopsticks held in midair between his mouth and the bowl. After her haunting song finished, the girl put aside the *shamisen* and began to dance to otherwordly music that seemed to come from nowhere but floated around the air with every movement she made.

Archie was swept away with the romance of the situation. All his knowledge of the art of these amazing artist-hostesses came from westernised views of Japan. Of course, he knew that Geisha were rarer in Tokyo. They could be found in the capital, even though Archie had never sought the company of one as he saw them purely as a tourist attraction. But he was in the old capital of Kyōto now and this was where Geisha were founded all those centuries ago. An ancient art, a tradition, a fantasy for many men.

The music stopped. Archie remained frozen, in a trance almost and unable to react as the last echoes of the music lingered in the air. She had stopped moving and stared at him now with equal fascination.

'*Anata wa juyō-tekidesu,*' she said and then repeated her words in English when he didn't understand. 'You are receptive.'

Archie's limbs began to work again and he placed his bowl and chopsticks down on the table in front of him. They stared at each other.

The spell was broken when the woman who'd welcomed him into the restaurant initially arrived in the room.

'*Akikosan, mō ikimashou,*' she said to the girl who gathered up her instrument and left the room without argument. The hostess then turned to Archie and said, 'Mr Archie, we are closing now.'

'How much do I owe you ...?' Archie said, scrambling for his wallet.

He experienced an odd feeling close to embarrassment, as though the hostess had known his thoughts all along and saw him as a bad person now, lusting after a young woman, who was only doing her job to entertain him with her voice and dance.

'You owe us nothing,' said the hostess bowing. 'It is our pleasure to serve you.'

She bundled him out into the courtyard before he could protest further and Archie was left outside as the restaurant lights switched off and the building was plunged into darkness.

Somehow he found his way back to the main high street and stumbled up the steps to his rented townhouse. Even though he didn't remember having more than one glass of the plum wine, the drink had gone to his head.

Back in the *machiya*, Archie collapsed down onto the futon

bed and slept, but his dreams were confused and full of violent scenes. He found himself running through the Kyōto streets pursued by something while around him the life was sucked out of innocent passersby. Even when he turned his head to look, he couldn't make out what this awful creature was, but despite his feet feeling like lead weights, he somehow remained slightly beyond its reach.

The next day, Archie woke feeling sick again. The harsh virus that had affected him in Tokyo had returned and his temperature soared, until he was hallucinating. In his vision, he imagined the Geisha girl in his room, feeding him a sweet spicy liquid, which he swallowed down as though it were nectar. He felt her cool hand on his brow along with the soft touch of the sleeve of the gold and red kimono.

By nightfall his fever broke and he woke, finding a jug of fresh water by his bedside, along with a bowl of still steaming sweet miso soup.

He sat up, sweat dripping from his brow, but the hunger pangs drove him to pick up the small bowl and drink down the soup without stopping. Once he'd finished, he felt a little better. It was as though the soup contained some healing property for whatever was ailing him. Looking around the townhouse he could see that the landlady had been in to do her usual tidying that day. He realised that on some level his fevered brain had confused the elderly woman's ministrations with the girl he'd seen at the restaurant.

Mrs Tachibana lived next door in a smaller townhouse. Archie showered and dressed and went to thank her for the soup and the water.

'Mr Archie,' she said bowing when she saw him at her front door. 'You feel better today?'

'Yes. Thank you for the soup.'

Mrs Tachibana bowed again. 'Your *friend* tell me you sick. I think soup good for you.'

'Friend?' asked Archie. 'I don't know anyone in Kyōto.'

'The girl … She tell me she help you home.'

Mrs Tachibana flushed as she mentioned 'the girl' and

Archie now remembered someone by his side as he'd stumbled up the steps to the townhouse. A figure wearing a black cloak, with a hood that covered their head so that he couldn't see their face. He wondered how he could have forgotten such a detail.

'Oh yes, someone helped me home ...'

'I must go now. Work to be done,' Mrs Tachibana said and with a final bow she closed the door.

Archie looked down the hill and the challenging steps he'd traversed the night before in search of local cuisine. He began to wonder if he'd found more than food on his jaunt after all.

Standing in the courtyard before Jorōgumo-Kyōto, Archie was surprised to find the restaurant in complete darkness. His stomach roiled and hurt with a growing hunger that wouldn't leave. He thought of going back to the main street and finding somewhere else to eat but what he craved was inside this location and he was sure he wouldn't find it anywhere else.

Just as he was about to give up, the lights inside switched on and the doors slid open. Standing at the door was the young Geisha who had entertained him. She was dressed in a plain pale blue kimono now and she was not wearing the *oshiroi* make-up, leaving her skin natural and fresh.

'*Anata wa koko ni irubekide wa arimasen,*' she said.

Although he didn't speak any Japanese Archie knew she'd said he shouldn't be there.

'Last night ...' he said. 'She called you Akiko.'

Akiko looked around as though fearful that they would be seen together.

'Come inside,' she said, stepping back.

Archie entered and instead of taking him into the seating area he'd been placed in the night before she led him through the kitchen and out of the back of the restaurant.

Behind the restaurant lay another larger courtyard with several one-level structures in a horseshoe around the edges. Akiko crossed the courtyard to the one farthest away and then opened the panelled doors ushering him inside.

The dwelling turned out to be a bedroom. By the light of a small lamp on the floor, Archie saw the contents of the room, which was sparse but for a dressing table and chair, an open canvas wardrobe that held a few simple kimonos and a low futon bed. Hanging from a railing at the back of the room was the red and gold kimono she'd worn the night before.

'Izumi should not have sent you away so soon last night. Especially when you were affected ...' she said.

'I had a strange dream, that someone cared for me and I was sick,' Archie said.

Akiko bowed her head, 'I was afraid for you.'

'The wine was strong,' he said. 'I was a little drunk.'

She met his eyes for the first time and he saw they were pale blue which was unusual. She looked away soon after.

His stomach made a loud growl then.

'I apologise!' he said.

'You must eat,' she said. 'It is crucial to keep your strength up at this time.'

Opening the panels again, Akiko looked outside and seeing that they were not observed, she hurried him back through the courtyard and into the restaurant.

'Wait here,' Akiko said.

Leaving him in the reception area, she disappeared back through the kitchens.

Confused, Archie waited for Akiko to return, but it was Izumi, the restaurant hostess, who appeared from behind the reception desk.

'Mr Archie you have returned! Your table awaits.'

Archie found himself back in the room he'd occupied the previous night and all manner of food was brought in. After that the evening passed by in a confused blur and Archie ate all that was brought to him, until his stomach was distended. He'd felt such awful hunger before he'd arrived and found Akiko, and now he was replete with food, but still hollow inside.

The panel doors opened then and Akiko began to play and

sing once more. Archie fell deep into a trance watching her. He had no resistance at all to the power of her hypnotic charms.

His evenings followed this same pattern night after night until it was the penultimate day of his trip. Although Archie wasn't thinking at all about his return to Tokyo. All he thought about was Akiko and food.

That day, Mrs Tachibana arrived to tidy the townhouse. Archie hadn't seen her for over a week as he'd been sleeping late and she hadn't disturbed him.

She took a shocked breath when she saw her guest. 'Mr Archiesan! You feeling much better? You been eating very good since you arrive in Kyōto!'

Archie caught sight of himself in the glass window she was polishing and saw his much more rotund shape but although he understood he'd gained significant weight, he wasn't too concerned as his illness had shaken too much from him in the first place. He also knew that once back at work the weight would stabilise.

The thought of leaving Kyōto and Akiko struck him for the first time. Such a thought was inconceivable.

'I may stay a little longer, Mrs Tachibana. If that is possible?' he said.

'Of course, Mr Archiesan. Mr Sato had booked you in for a month should you need it.'

Archie was pleased. Hinata Sato was the person who'd recommended Mrs Tachibana's townhouse, but he was also the one person that Archie had been sent to monitor at the Tokyo offices. Sato had been nothing but professional the whole time and had proven to be a good friend to Archie. His report back to head office would be filled with praise for the man as he couldn't fault him.

For the first time since arriving at this beautiful former capital, Archie opened his work laptop. He then spent the afternoon writing up his report. Head office had wanted him to find ways to cut costs, and that usually meant cutting employees, but Archie was feeling more than generous towards the man who'd led him to Akiko and therefore his report was positive and strongly recommending increasing the staff, rather than depleting it, as he had also observed how hard everyone had to work to stay on top of the excessive workload. All of this happened without complaint in Tokyo and he told his bosses in very clear terms how grateful they should be. He pointed out that if only they would take a leaf out of the Japanese model, then improvements in the London office might be made.

Archie felt a perverse pleasure at telling them all these hard-hitting home truths, something he never usually did, even though he knew the deadweight was always at the top and never in the general workforce. He'd reached a point in his life where he no longer wanted to destroy but wanted to build, and on some level it was all because of his blossoming relationship with Akiko.

He sent the report in and then shut down his laptop. His work for the company was done now. But he'd spend the next two weeks getting to know Akiko. Rather than just watching her dance and sing, he would talk to her.

He left the *machiya* that evening determined to ask her out on a date, away from the restaurant but when he reached Jorōgumo-Kyōto the restaurant was buzzing with activity and was now surrounded with decorative pines and flowers that suggested a private party was taking place.

'Archiesan!' Izumi said greeting him more casually than she had previously. 'We celebrate tonight the coming of age of Akiko.'

'Coming of age?' Archie said.

He was shocked by this for although she was a young and beautiful woman, in Japanese culture a woman 'comes of age' when she is in her twentieth year, and Archie had thought Akiko older.

'You are invited as her personal guest, Archiesan,' Izumi continued. 'Come and meet our family.'

Archie followed Izumi inside, finding the entire restaurant was now opened into one large room as the *shōji* walls had either been removed or, where possible, slid open. The room was set out with the traditional low tables and chairs and Archie was taken to the one at the front, and given pride of place.

As though he was someone important, Archie was introduced to a variety of cousins, and distant relatives of Izumi or Akiko: he wasn't sure which. He didn't quite understand the relationship Akiko had with Izumi for sometimes it appeared that Izumi answered to Akiko, even though custom dictated this would not be the case as Izumi was much older and deserving of respect.

The room fell silent when Akiko came in, wearing the most ornate purple kimono that Archie had ever seen. It was decorated with tiny insects, like those he'd seen on the screen walls – spider-like. The images were beautiful because they were silver and woven with care into the purple silk robe, but Archie did find the choice of pictures to be strange and thought it had to be one of those cultural images that remained a mystery to him but had significance to the locals. He made a mental note to find out what it meant and then promptly forgot about it as Akiko sat down beside him.

A tea ceremony ensued, which Archie recognised because it was a favourite with Sato who had taken him many times to a local teahouse in Tokyo that specialised in the ritual.

There was one significant difference though: the otherworldly music that Archie had grown accustomed to hearing when Akiko danced was now absent and none of the occupants of the room spoke or moved as Akiko served tea to Archie.

Archie experienced a pang of nerves at the weirdness of the situation. It was as though he was being courted by Akiko, and he wasn't sure how he felt about that, even though he'd come to ask her to go on a date with him.

Akiko pressed the hot tea cup into his hands and, automatically, Archie took the cup and sipped. He enjoyed the flavour and, soothed by the liquid and as if he'd been passed a strong sedative, began to feel relaxed and stress free.

'I wanted to talk to you,' Archie said. 'But I didn't realise just how young you are. I'm thirty-five and ...'

'There is no need to concern yourself Archiesan. I'm much more mature than I seem,' Akiko said.

With that a round of food was delivered to the table. Archie began to eat but became aware that Akiko did not join him.

'This is for you,' Akiko said with a respectful bow of her head.

'But this is your celebration,' he said.

'Indeed. And it pleases me to see you eat and be restored to your full strength.'

Despite the tea, Archie began to feel anxious again. The party was not what he expected and despite it being a 'coming of age' for Akiko, all of the guests, the hostess and Akiko herself were all focused on his happiness instead.

'It is time,' Izumi said. She clapped her hands and the entire room of visitors stood and left the restaurant, collecting their shoes on the way out.

Archie struggled to his feet without the ease of the others and found himself face to face with Akiko.

'I'm hungry,' Akiko said.

'But the food ... you should have eaten ...'

'Perhaps you will help me?' Akiko said.

'Of course.'

Akiko took Archie's hand and she led him out into the back courtyard once more. There Archie saw party-goers gathered in a small circle around a huge table made of stone. He didn't recall seeing the table when he'd passed through before, but now Akiko led him there, and she lay on top of the table.

Archie now knew what this ceremony really signified – or at least thought he did. Geisha's had started their careers traditionally as prostitutes. Only later had it become an honourable job, one which involved entertaining clients with their music skills, serving tea and hosting with light-hearted repartee. But Archie had heard that wealthy business men kept some of these girls as their mistresses too.

Akiko was being offered to him now in such a capacity and because it was being witnessed by her family, it would be a contract between them, something in which he was supposed to uphold and agree to – a bond to take care of Akiko. After today she would travel with him. He was expected to give her a good life. Like a wife, but leaving him free to still take one. It was not the western way and he had far too much respect for Akiko to do this to her. It was, he thought, utterly disgusting that this girl was being offered to him like a piece of meat.

'No!' he said. 'I can't. This isn't ...'

Izumi rushed forward and begged his silence.

'If you refuse, Akiko is shamed ...' Izumi said.

Archie glanced around at the now murmuring crowd, he thought he saw Mrs Tachibana amongst them, along with a man that resembled Hinata Soto.

'Please?' Akiko said. Her blue eyes looked more purple now as they reflected the colour of the kimono and her beauty sucked him in. She pulled him into her arms as his resistance failed him.

Archie did as any man might when offered the perfect body of a woman he'd been falling for, but the interaction left him feeling sullied and sick to his stomach because it should have been private and between them. Despite all of this, Archie performed admirably, shutting out the quiet murmurs from the onlookers. When it was over, Akiko pulled her robe over her exposed limbs and, even as he straightened his own clothing, she took his hand and led him into her private room, away from the prying eyes of the witnesses.

Alone, she led him on to consummate their partnership again. This time he went to her more willingly, and like the start of an addiction, Archie found himself scared of the power she had over him but was driven on with some morbid fascination that he knew, on some level, would not end well.

Several more couplings took place throughout the night until, exhausted both in strength and virility, Archie slept.

He woke at dawn, when Akiko, beside him cried out with pain. She was doubled up holding her stomach.

'What's wrong?' he asked. 'Did I hurt you?'

'I must eat,' she said.

'I'm sorry. I forgot you didn't eat at all last night. I'll go into the restaurant and find something for you,' Archie said.

Her eyes showed her gratitude even as she appeared to be unable to speak with the discomfort she had.

He stood and pulled on a kimono that someone, at some point, had left for him. Barefoot he left her simple dwelling and hurried across to the back door of the kitchen.

Inside he foraged through the fridges where he found a bowl of cold rice and some fried chicken pieces. On the stove was some clear miso soup. He lit the gas and warmed the pot before pouring some of it into a cup. Then he turned everything off, wary of causing a fire and juggling the cup and a bowl in which he'd put the rice and chicken, Archie took them back to Akiko.

When he reached her room she was sitting up in bed looking frail. He held out the soup to her, pressing it into her hands as she had with the teacup just the previous night. She looked down into the cup and sipped at the soup as though trying to please him.

'Drink it all now, and then try some of this chicken and rice,' he said. 'It's cold, but should still be good.'

Akiko tried, but within seconds of consuming the barest mouthful, she leapt from the bed, opened another panel beside the bed and ran through it. Archie followed and discovered that the hidden chamber held a private bathroom. Akiko now had her head over the toilet bowl.

Such an extreme reaction to the food made Archie concerned that the girl had some kind of eating disorder. He had never seen her eat. Perhaps this was why her relatives were so keen to find her a benefactor?

Akiko stood, and then ran some water into the sink, swilling her face.

She looked at Archie with round sad eyes and her

expression showed him she was still in pain.

'I must eat,' she said.

'You must … but perhaps just the soup for now until we get you back on solids,' Archie said.

His heart was broken for her. What had driven her to such lengths of starvation? Was it Izumi, keeping the girl barely fed, even as she entertained her patrons as they gorged themselves? Archie had so many questions that he wanted to ask Akiko, but he was afraid of the answers she'd give him. After all, despite how he felt for her, he couldn't really take her on, could he? He'd been caught up in the moment, falling into a holiday romance without looking for it. But all this had to end – he would be back in England in a matter of weeks, and taking Akiko with him was not really an option. Aside from the obvious visa requirements, Archie also didn't know where the firm would send him next. He was more likely to be in Rome, London or Washington than to be returning to Japan – which wasn't likely now that his report had been submitted.

Even as he remembered doing the report, a part of him understood that it made no difference. Whatever his findings, London had concluded already that cuts would be made, and Archie's presence had been the formality to justify that decision. He hadn't given them the bullets to fire though, and that meant executing the order would be much harder. It also meant that he may well receive some kind of reprimand, or worse still, his marching orders. With this thought now sinking in, the severity of the situation highlighted just how much he'd been carried away in the moment. He had lost his mind. What was he thinking?

Archie helped Akiko back to bed, wondering how to extricate himself with as much grace as possible. The girl seemed to have aged overnight. Gone was the rose-blossom hue in her cheeks and the subtle cherry pink of her lips. Her irises looked whitened, as though cataracts had covered the pale blue. Her cheeks looked sunken, and this made her eyes too deep-set. There was a soft scent he'd never noticed before, and it wafted from her skin, reminding him of old age, neglect and decay.

A terrible thought struck him. What if he had caught some awful disease from the girl too?

Akiko was staring at him now.

'I didn't want to,' she said. 'I told them …'

Archie pulled the covers up over her and tucked her into the small bed.

'Sleep,' he said. 'I have to … I'll be back … later.'

The plane to Tokyo took off on time and Archie breathed a sigh of relief as it lifted into the air. He planned to go back to his small, rented flat, pack the rest of his things and be on his way back to London within two days.

After receiving the report from him, Archie's bosses had ordered his immediate return. This gave him the perfect excuse to send Akiko a message saying he had to leave Japan, but like a coward he made promises to be back and with her again as soon as he could. The note wished her well and a return to full strength, but it also voiced concerns about her relationship with food, all of which was well meant, even though he had no intention of seeing her again.

Archie closed his eyes and drifted into sleep with the purring of the plane's engine. When he finally woke, the plane had landed and people around him were taking hand luggage from the compartments above his head.

'What? We here already?' he said, pulling himself round. He reached for his holdall underneath the seat in front of him, then followed the murmuring and disgruntled passengers as they exited. He did not understand that the plane had landed back in Kyōto until he saw the signs within the airport.

As he reached Customs, he removed his passport, but the man facing him was familiar. The officer took his arm and he was led away, through a door off the passport control area and down a long corridor. There he was placed in a holding cell which contained nothing but a long bunk bed.

'Please … I don't speak Japanese,' he told the man. 'Why

am I here?'

'I'm uncle to Akiko,' the officer said. 'You did not do right by her.'

'You have no right to hold me. I need to speak to someone from the British Embassy,' Archie said.

Akiko's customs officer uncle gave him a sly smile, 'Of course you do,' he said.

With that the man left, slamming and locking the cell door behind him.

Archie had fallen asleep on the bunk and when he woke, the cell was in darkness. He moved and tried to stretch his limbs but the bunk blanket had tangled itself around him.

A shaft of light came into the room as a *shoji* door opened in the wall. Archie saw Akiko standing before him. She was restored and more beautiful than he'd ever seen her but there was something off about the way she moved into the room, with a gait that was less dainty and smooth than usual.

He had a slight pain in his leg, which he assumed was from lying in a bad position on the uncomfortable bunk. But it occurred to him then that he was no longer in the airport, but back at the restaurant. After all there had been only solid walls in the holding cell.

Maybe I'm still on the plane, he thought.

'I loved you Archiesan,' she said.

'I *am* dreaming ...' he said aloud.

'All I wanted was for you to stay with me until the end,' Akiko said. 'I was ready to turn away from my destiny.'

He tried to move again and then he felt a peculiar sensation, rippling through his leg and up to his thigh as though a million insects were crawling across his skin at once and each touch tiny legs brought about shock waves of white-hot pain.

'I'm hungry, Archiesan,' Akiko said. 'Feed me.'

And then Archie discovered what it was that ailed the four-hundred-year-old *Jorōgumo* who he knew as Akiko, and what it was that she was supposed to do on her most important birthday.

As she devoured him feet first, Archie was witness to the transformation as the creature came into her powers: from beautiful human Geisha to half woman, half spider and at last to a large, monstrous arachnid, whose web he'd fallen into and from which he would never escape.

GERYON

In the great work of late medieval literature, Inferno, *the third part of* The Divine Comedy, *a lengthy narrative poem composed around 1321 by Italian philosopher, Dante Alighieri, we are treated to the ultimate descent into the Underworld. It is a work of metaphysical and metaphorical instruction and is regarded as one of the great books of Christian fiction.*

In it, Dante himself is guided by the ghost of the Roman poet, Virgil (who made his own trip to the Underworld in The Aeneid) *down through the nine circles of Hell, so that he can witness for himself the final destinations of all those on Earth who eschew the paths of righteousness. The circles, which are basically nine concentric levels, each one of them harsher than the one above, are filled with the tortured and the damned. Perhaps inevitably, Dante sees many familiar faces: historical persons who are deemed to have done evil in their lives, such as Julius Caesar and Judas Iscariot, mythical beings such as Helen of Troy and Prince Paris ... and many recognisable monsters, evil chaotic beings who are not just there to be punished but who also have their own demi-demonic role to play.*

For example, Medusa and the Furies dwell in the Fifth Circle of Hell but have guard duties on the gates of its capital city, Dis, while down in the Seventh Circle, the harpies hold court in the Wood of Suicides, where they continually peck and claw at those whose self-destruction on Earth has turned them here into helpless man-tree hybrids. We soon see that all of these monsters have become prisoners of their own foul natures, the harpies' cruel attacks on mankind, usually on the orders of pagan gods, having earned them a place on the level of Hell where violence is punished, while Medusa's sentence is to be served among those who are damned because of the wrath that overtook their lives (in her case, vengeance).

Perhaps it's confusing therefore that one other famous monster, whom Dante encounters even further down in the pits of Hell, in the

Eighth Circle, whose crimes are deemed so evil that he must spend eternity among fraudsters, deceivers and scam artists, is Geryon.

You may recall that Geryon was one of those many monsters defeated by Hercules during the course of his Twelve Labours. In appearance alone, Geryon certainly sounds as if he belongs in Hell. Of enormous stature, he had one pair of tree trunk-like legs, but three conjoined upper bodies, three heads and three pairs of arms. Inferno also sees him equipped with wings and a scorpion's tail, though neither of those attributes figure in the original Greek stories. Even minus the wings and tail, Geryon was so horrifying to look at that men were said to have died from fright the moment they beheld him. And that was before they experienced his homicidal temper and astonishing combat skills (he would attack with three spears and three swords all at the same time). So fearsome an opponent was he that it's difficult to work out how he ever finished up in Hell. How is it possible that he was ever even killed?

The answer of course lies with that greatest of all heroes, Hercules.

The story of the Son of Zeus's Twelve Labours is one of the most celebrated legends to emerge from the Ancient Greek canon. They were laid on him by King Eurystheus of Mycenae in atonement for Hercules's killing of his own wife and children during a fit of madness. The hero's trials became progressively more challenging as he proceeded through them, but at first glance, the Tenth Labour, even to a lionskin-wearing superhuman, must have seemed utterly impossible. It was to obtain the beautiful red cattle that lived on the Red Isle, Erytheia, which lay far to the west of the Mediterranean Sea.

This part of the story at least rings true.

In the early days of the Ancient World – and Hercules's journey to Erytheia is said to have taken place several centuries before the Trojan War, which occurred around the 13th Century BC – almost no one had the guts to sail out into the Atlantic Ocean. Its unexplored vastness of mountainous waves and howling storms was believed to be the last obstacle before the edge of the world. The Pillars of Hercules, the two cliffs that now stand one to either side of the Straits of Gibraltar, were named in testimony to the courage the hero showed in simply venturing beyond them. It was an even more heroic feat when one considers that the isle of Erytheia could only supposedly be found at the point where the setting sun descended into the ocean. In other words, it was one of those mythical lands that can never actually be reached.

Even Hercules only made it because, as always, he had divine assistance, the sun god Helios providing him with a golden vessel, which would take him straight there. On arrival in Erytheia, an unspoiled land of fast flowing rivers and immense, forested mountains, Hercules knew that he wouldn't be able to negotiate for the red cattle. Firstly, he had nothing to trade. Secondly, they were the most prized possession of the nightmarish entity called Geryon. This meant that he would have to steal them, but initially he needed to defeat the herdsman, Eurytion, and his dog, Orthrus.

Eurytion was reputedly another fearsome being, possibly a centaur, while Orthrus was the ferocious older brother of Cerberus, the three-headed guardian of the gates to the Greek Underworld. As soon as Hercules arrived, he was attacked by Orthrus, and then by Eurytion, both of whom he slew. The third protector of the cattle was of course their owner, and the unofficial king of this land.

Hercules subsequently fought a protracted battle with Geryon on a river called Anthemus and eventually was so exhausted that he had to withdraw, leaving the island's ruler laughing and jeering. Never having met his match in combat before, Hercules became suspicious that this monster of monsters was also the recipient of divine assistance. Detecting the hand of the goddess Hera, whose wiles had lain behind the deaths of his wife and children, Hercules also opted to cheat. When he returned to the fray, he did so wielding neither club, sword nor spear, but his bow, now fitted with arrows dipped in the toxic blood of the Lernaean Hydra, another beast of almost unimaginable horror. Raining these missiles down on Geryon, he eventually scored a direct hit on the monster's middle forehead, piercing him to the brain and killing him instantly.

A typical Greek legend, you might say. A ghastly monster, which defies all the rules of nature, felled by a mighty hero.

Later investigators, seeking some kernel of truth, sought to place Erytheia on the Iberian peninsular, while Renaissance era excavators of huge prehistoric bones wondered if they might have uncovered Geryon's actual remains, though in the end the tale has remained too *outlandish to ever be taken seriously as a misinterpretation of real history. Even Geryon's presence in* The Divine Comedy *hints at the author having cherry-picked a terrifying monster, most likely because Virgil utilised the same being in* The Aeneid, *as there is nothing in the original legend to associate Geryon with fraud. If anything, he died nobly, protecting his property against a rampaging thief.*

As is often the case in Greek mythology, there is a degree of ambiguity in the story of Hercules v Geryon. Who was the hero and who was the monster?

KRAKEN
Tim Lebbon

'Are you sure about this?' Kelly asked. 'I mean, it looks freezing.'

'That's sort of the point,' Nick said. 'And how can something *look* freezing?'

'Well, you know ...' She shrugged and hugged her thick coat around her. 'The waves.'

'Cold waves,' Nick said.

'It's cold here on the beach. It'll be even colder in there.'

Nick looked back and forth along the beach at half a dozen others from last night's party who'd drunkenly agreed to take the plunge. They all looked equally as hungover as him. *I feel terrible*, he thought for the tenth time that morning. He'd heard legends about New Year's Eve in Scotland, and yesterday had revealed most of those legends as true. It was the second bottle of Scotch that had done it. That, and the third. He, Kelly and their group of friends had polished off the first – after a hearty meal with plenty of beer and free-flowing wine – an hour before midnight, and their host Nathan had announced that there was no way they could see in the new year without a toast. By one in the morning the second bottle was empty and Nathan had produced a third. Nick couldn't recall going to bed. He could barely remember his name. *I feel terrible.*

'Like I said ... cold is the point.'

Nick took a deep breath and stripped off the dryrobe he'd brought to Scotland 'just in case'. Some of the others – Kelly included – had placed bets that these six brave souls wouldn't get up before noon in time for the New Year beach dash, or if they did they'd bail. Proving them wrong was the main reason he was doing this. Nathan was a good mate, but also a bit of a piss-taking dick. Nick wouldn't give him any ammunition.

Clad only in bathing trunks he shivered, hugged himself, stepped from foot to foot, and then someone screamed a war-cry and they started running for the sea. Their pace soon slowed to a painful hobble across pebbles and uneven stones. Still, Nick's competitive spirit kicked in, and he didn't want to be last.

'Be careful!' Kelly called after him, and he waved one hand without turning around. He used his arms to keep balance as he negotiated his way down to the sea, and then a wave came in and broke around his shins.

He gasped in a breath. *Holy fuck it's freezing!* The North Sea was so cold that for an instant it felt hot, a white heat scorching his skin and flesh and reaching down to his bones. His head pounded even more as his heart rate increased and blood thumped around his body. He kept walking, accompanied by the shouts and whoops and cries of the others, and a sudden sense of utter delight settled over him. He let out a joyous shout. His hangover throbbed and his heartbeat was that of the land, waves pulsing in, water flowing back and forth around him. When it reached his balls his sense of balance failed, and he stumbled and fell forwards.

Water closed around him, and he grinned beneath the waves. The taste was almost overpowering, and when he stood and balanced again he was gasping, heart stuttering, spitting water, and then shouting out as loud and long as he could, 'Whoo-hooooooooo!' He looked around and caught Silvia's eye, and they smiled at each other as the low swell nursed them. Something niggled at him about her, some deep alcohol-swamped guilt. A flirt, last night? Surely nothing more. He and Kelly had their problems, and 'new year, new beginnings' seemed to ring truer than ever right now, with Nick thinking maybe the distance between them had grown too wide. But he wasn't a dickhead; he wouldn't have done anything with someone else. Would he?

Silvia broke their gaze and spread her arms, falling forward as if giving herself to the sea. Others were jumping around and splashing, and then diving through the breaking waves and taking a few strokes.

Online the water temperature was announced as close to freezing, and he knew he shouldn't be in for more than a handful of minutes, but he felt a rush of freedom as he dived beneath the surface once more. The others' delighted shouting and laughing disappeared and he heard only the ocean, an intimate roar as pebbles were rolled and water surged and ebbed. He kept his eyes closed and took a few powerful strokes beneath the surface, stirred sand abrading his skin. The cold embraced him and squeezed tight, his hangover throbbed and combined with the cold-burn pain behind his forehead. He gasped and took in a mouthful of water, spat it out, turned, struck for the surface –

And the water was all around. Up and down became confused. The surface boiled beneath him, the smoothed sea bed was above, and as he reached for air with one hand and sand with the other, the ocean seemed to expand. Surrounding him was a darkness deeper than he had ever thought possible; the deepness of infinity, the darkness of nothing. That sense of vastness struck him so hard that he stopped swimming and struggling. He simply floated as the sea buoyed him up.

There was something close by. Something huge and dense, unknown and unknowable, drowning out his history and sense of the world. He felt observed. He felt *examined*, and the depths and distances defied logic.

I am smaller than a grain of sand, he thought, and as his breath began to bubble out from his nose he imagined the beach he'd just left filled with everyone in the world, one person for each stone or pebble. Even those billions of people were nothing compared to this boundless ocean.

The water seemed thick and heavy, and then suddenly more comfortable as a surge of strange warmth nudged him into a slow spin. Nick was an experienced swimmer so he went with it, knowing that fighting a strange turn in the tide would tire him quickly. He opened his eyes but everything was too blurred. The sea was heavy with sediment, so thickly loaded that it felt more like a sickly treacle than water. He pulled again for the light and opened his mouth to cry out, gasping for air as subtle panic turned deeper, darker.

Something forced into his mouth, a slick, thick intrusion. He panicked at the idea that he'd inhaled a jellyfish. A memory blinked at him from the blacked-out depths – a face close to his, a breath whose taste he did not know, lips pressed and tongue questing in urgent betrayal. He almost retched, then he broke surface again and the strange feeling was gone.

He stood on the shifting sea bed, took in a deep breath –

– *something swallowed, something slicking down my throat* –

– and looked around at the other bathers. Some of them were thrashing a little, struggling to stand and coughing, spitting, wiping at their mouths in surprise, even fear. Silvia was twenty metres to his left, staring down at her hands and turning them back and forth as if searching for something.

A surge of sediment, Nick thought. He spat again. He felt sick but didn't quite puke. No one was puking. The shouting and whooping had ceased, and the others were making their way back up onto the beach. Yet there was no sense that a fun, healthy event had ended in a negative way; it was more that they had come, it had happened, and now it was time to go. Shivering and flushed with water beading across skin, the cold dippers left the sea with an air of quiet satisfaction.

Kelly waved and he waved back, and she held up the dryrobe. He nodded, but remained where he was for a few seconds as the waves broke around his waist, swaying him this way and that. The sea swaddled and nursed him, and for a final calming moment he welcomed its powerful caress.

'You're so rosy red!' Kelly said as he finally walked up the beach towards her. 'Here, chuck this on.' She held the dryrobe open, and he stepped into her embrace as she wrapped him up. He pecked her on the lips and it felt hollow. 'Euch, you taste of the sea,' she said.

Nick licked his lips a few times. His hangover was gone. He was ready for the day ahead, and the changes this year would bring.

'It feels like such a sad ending,' Kelly said on their long drive home.

'Not really,' he replied. 'As long as we're both sure about it. That makes it easier.'

'But it's still sad. And it's not that there's anything bad. But …'

The word hung for a while, and silence fell. Somewhere around the Lake District Nick said, 'But it's just not good enough.'

Lips pressed against his. Silvia's tongue probing his mouth, insistent, almost violent. It was barely a memory. Those strange moments beneath the waves replayed with far more clarity.

It took almost twelve hours to drive from Ayr to his place on Pembrokeshire's south coast, and by the time they arrived it was nine p.m. and dark. Nick had taken the last four hours down through Wales while Kelly napped, and although he was exhausted he still felt a draw to the water.

'Just stretch our legs on the beach?' he suggested as they finished emptying the car. 'We can sort all this shite tomorrow.'

'And everything else?' she asked.

After a pause he said, 'No rush?' The statement hung unanswered, an ellipsis into their future.

'I'm knackered,' Kelly said. 'Not up for a walk. And it's dark and cold, you really want to go down there now?'

Yeah I do, Nick thought, but he knew she was talking sense. It was only a fifteen minute walk to the beach, but it had started drizzling, a cold wet mist that had already soaked them as they'd unpacked the car.

'Maybe tomorrow,' he said.

'Maybe. I'll put the kettle on.'

They slept together in his double bed but were still miles apart. She was on her side facing away from him, and Nick lay for a long time unable to nod off. He imagined he could almost hear the sea in the distance, the constant breath of the world drawing and releasing, drawing and releasing, utterly indifferent to the people who listened and watched and lived their lives to its constant rhythm. His stomach rumbled and turned, and he considered going to the toilet. Nick liked looking after himself with exercise, good food and attention to his mental health, and in all regards it hadn't been an easy week. The growing distance between him and Kelly had been difficult, especially as even without discussing it they'd both tried to keep it to themselves. They'd drank a lot, and too much booze never sat well with him. *Alky blues*, Nathan would say, but Nick knew it was something more fundamental. Drink took him further from the world he wanted to inhabit.

He lay with his eyes closed, frustrated at not being able to sleep, and then he jerked awake from what could only have been a dream. His stomach felt distended and something had been moving within, squirming and twisting and stroking his insides. It was as if his centre had come to life with its own mind, striving to turn this way and that as it attempted to leave and cast out on its own. He turned on his side and curled his legs up to hug away the discomfort. His stomach rumbled again.

He got up, still dozy and dopey from the sleep he'd feared would never come, and went into the bathroom. He sat for a while but nothing happened, and when he returned to bed his stomach felt normal.

Maybe I dreamt it all, he thought.

He smelled the scent of the sea, salt and dead things. He felt the ocean so close, exuding a shattering sense of scale and time. He stared into the endless dark, and when dawn came and Kelly put a cup of tea on his bedside table, he couldn't tell whether he'd slept at all.

'You smell,' she said.

'I'm going to the beach,' he said. He stretched, joints clicking. 'Wow, you really are obsessed. It's raining and cold.'

Nick groaned and propped himself up against the

headboard so he could sip the tea. 'You said.'

'I said maybe.' She turned and walked from the room. 'I'm showering. I texted my sister in Cardiff, I'm going to stay with her later for a bit.'

As the sound of the shower came on and Kelly started humming beneath the water, Nick searched for a pang of sadness. He could barely find it. They'd been fun together for a few months, with great sex and a shared love of rock music, but a hollow growing at their centre had pushed them apart. There had been few arguments, and that had persuaded them both that there wasn't anything worth arguing about. The realisation made it a lot easier.

Instead of sadness, he felt a blooming excitement for the future.

He threw on his clothes from the previous day, grabbed his tea and went downstairs. He opened the back door and looked out onto his small garden. It faced south towards the sea but the coast was a mile away, frustratingly out of view. A soft rain fell. It wasn't early-January cold, but still chilly enough for him to start shivering.

He closed the door and picked up his phone, turning it on and scrolling to the weather app. It was due to rain like this all day, with the next few days depressingly similar.

He spotted a message waiting for him. He opened the app and saw it was from Silvia. His stomach roiled with nervousness and guilt. He still couldn't remember, and he hated that. A kiss, that was all. He was sure there had been nothing more.

His thumb hovered, then he opened the message. 'Come join with me in Portsmouth', was all it said. *Weird wording.* He closed the app without responding. Maybe he'd reply later.

As he went to put his phone down a news app pushed a notification, and the name 'Aberystwyth' caught his attention. It was where he'd gone to university, and though he'd only been back a few times since, he felt a close affinity to the town.

The end of the pier had collapsed into a stormy ocean the previous night.

Shocked, Nick opened the news app and read more. There wasn't much detail, but it appeared that storms had battered several coastlines overnight, resulting in the loss of a small fishing boat off the Dorset coast and damage to the famous pier in Aberystwyth. Buried in the middle of the article as if through embarrassment, an eye witness had mentioned 'several waterspouts that looked like tentacles' which had whipped down and smashed the end of the old pier to pieces.

Nick's stomach rumbled and rolled, and when he burped the memory of the sea rose in him. His tongue felt swollen and slick, and he opened his mouth and grabbed at it. It was wet and slimy. He spat into the sink, his spittle thicker than it should have been. His stomach rolled again, as if something within was trying to get out. He didn't feel sick. Leaning on the edge of the sink, he poured a glass of water and was distracted by its bubbles and swirls. He held it up to the light to watch it settle.

But it didn't settle. The water in the glass kept spinning and spiralling. He was drawn in by the diamond bubbles and shimmering patterns.

'Still tired from new year?' Kelly asked as she entered the kitchen. She was wrapped in a bathrobe, hair held up in a towel.

'Nah, I'm good. So, I'm going down to the beach?' It was a question, but he hoped she hadn't changed her mind about coming.

'I'm packing my things.' She waited for a moment as if hoping he'd say something more, but he could only smile. She smiled back as she turned away.

'Aberystwyth pier collapsed last night,' he said.

'Oh?' She made her way to the stairs.

He frowned and said, 'Aberystwyth,' again, and he remembered that Nathan's friend Alain came from there. He and Alain had sat together for a while at the party, drinking whisky and sharing their love of the sea. Alain had sailed around the world and said the sea was his lover, strong but never judgemental. He lectured in the university in

Aberystwyth. He'd been one of those cold-dipping on New Year's Day.

Nick shrugged on a coat and his walking boots and closed the door behind him.

He rushed down to the beach, and as he walked across the dunes and onto the sand his stomach settled, and his heart calmed. Kelly already felt far away.

The sea was rough from the storms that had apparently rolled in overnight. It had been grim when they were driving home, and it had rained a few times, but nothing that he'd have called a storm. Maybe the main violence had happened out at sea and along the coasts.

He breathed in familiar scents, tasted sea mist on the air, and strolled down to the water's edge. There were a few other people walking alone or with their dogs, and he'd probably know some of them from his regular mornings on the sand. Right now, he wanted to be on his own.

On his own with the sea.

He considered continuing forward, walking into the breaking waves and further, allowing them to swallow him down. *I swallowed something,* he thought as he remembered the sea plunge off the Scottish coast. Yet that did not feel quite right. He felt like two people occupying the same space, muscles flexing against each other, spines entwined. It was disconcerting, but not uncomfortable.

I won't be able to breathe in there, he thought, and another voice answered, *You won't need to.*

He stood, stared, waited, and when a waved broke around his feet he was startled back to reality. He glanced at his watch and saw that it was almost midday. He'd been standing there for two hours, at least.

He glanced at his phone and saw a couple of missed calls from Kelly. She'd messaged him instead, and told him that she was going. She'd be back for the rest of her things, if that was OK. 'Of course' he messaged back. 'Take care'.

Another message came through – 'Portsmouth. Fucked up.'

Nick's heart skipped. *Oh fuck what did I do what does she know?* He hated the idea of acting like a prick, however over their relationship had already been when they'd agreed to go to Scotland to Nathan's place for a few days over New Year. He and Kelly liked each other, but they both wanted love. Whatever had happened between him and Silvia had been a stupid accident, and he felt nothing for her, not now and not potentially in the future. He hated the idea that Kelly would leave with the knowledge of that stupid drunken kiss. It was shameful. Demeaning.

He looked at the message again, and frowned. It didn't feel quite right. He typed 'Portsmouth' in a search engine, and the first few hits were breaking news.

'Seventeen missing in yacht tragedy'.

'Fuck,' Nick said. He read on. A yacht had been smashed against neighbouring boats in a sheltered harbour just this morning, and there was no indication that there had been inclement weather at the time. Some blamed a water spout. Other eyewitnesses were talking about a 'monster with long tentacles'.

Nick started back across the dunes, but then he paused and turned around again, looking at the sea. It rolled and beat, surged and withdrew, breathe, breathe.

Aberystwyth, where Alain lives, he thought. *Portsmouth, Silvia's home.* He tried to remember who else had run into the sea with them. Nathan's friends, not really his. He wasn't sure where they came from, but …

'Close to the sea,' he said, and he walked back down the dunes and onto the beach. It was quieter now, the dog walkers gone home, and a wind had whipped up. It drove sand and sea mist through the air, and he inhaled the smell that made him feel so at home.

The phone rang in Nick's hand and he dropped it into his coat pocket, then shrugged off the coat. He left it on the beach. He kept walking, pulling off his sweatshirt and tee shirt, unclipping his belt, and he paused only to kick off his boots and pull off his jeans and underwear. Naked and free, he raised his arms to either side as he walked on. Soon the water broke around his ankles and it was beautiful.

His insides rumbled and squirmed, flexing and wet, but there was no pain. It felt like poetry of blood and flesh. He laughed aloud and his booming voice joined the roar of waves coming ashore.

The water reached his waist and then his chest, and he fell forward and let the sea enclose him and pull him down.

That huge distance crashed around him once more, an incredible depth that was no longer terrifying but comforting. Its smothering weight crushed him down, but he did not feel the need to breathe. He rolled with the waves and swam and revelled, as whatever had been implanted inside him –

– *I was impregnated* –

– started to break free.

His limbs grew, stretched, reaching for infinity. Four limbs, and then more, more. He thought of the past, but all he could recall was the sea. Words failed him. The dark music of the mysterious ocean played in his soul and he sang along with it, feeling his voice travel far and wide to others like him.

A while later, different voices welcomed him in.

He was no longer afraid of the vastness.

He *was* the vastness.

GHOUL

When the Christianised Eastern Roman Empire, or Byzantium as it later became known, held sway over the Middle East, beliefs were rife that once the great conversion from paganism was complete, many of those devils and demons formerly revered as gods in the various cities of that region were driven out by the arrival of the true faith, and forced to dwell in the vast, arid wilderness beyond. This made travelling through those realms, which was difficult enough at the best of times, extraordinarily dangerous. Even those beloved of God were at risk out there. We think perhaps of St Anthony the Great, who while living as a desert hermit during the 3rd Century, was constantly tormented by evil supernatural beings.

But a range of monstrosities was always said to have haunted these sun-burned wastes: the implacably evil gallu, the mysterious karkadann, and El Nadaha, a faceless siren who lured men to their doom with her angelic singing voice. But perhaps most frightening of all was a soulless entity who is just as familiar today: the notorious 'ghūl', or as we refer to it in the West, the ghoul.

Perhaps one of the best examples of a folktale concerning this creature comes to us from ancient Syria. It tells how a poor woodcutter who lived with his wife and two daughters was one day overjoyed to receive a visit from his long-lost sister, who now came to him as a princess and invited him and his family to spend the rest of their days in her opulent palace.

Immediately, the woodcutter's wife became suspicious. Her husband had never once mentioned that he had a sister, lost or otherwise, and she couldn't help but think that this wealthy woman was mistaken and her husband taking advantage of it. Nevertheless, the palace they were accommodated in was easily as glorious as they had been led to expect, and once they were settled there, every comfort was provided. Despite this, the wife continued to watch her husband and his so-called sister, seeing no sign that they really knew each other at all. Indeed, she now fancied there was a feral gleam in the sister's eye, while an aura of dread pervaded every room she entered. When she whispered these fears to her spouse, he called her foolish and bade her hold her tongue. Thus, under cover of night, the wife took her young daughters, and they stole away from the palace. For several days, they roamed in a trackless desert, lost and hungry, until they encountered a passing caravan, which took them in. When the woman explained where they had come from, her hosts insisted that no such palace existed. Eventually, the woman returned in the company of others, and where the palace had been, found only a wasteland, and in the middle of it, the bleached bones of her husband.

Without doubt, the storytellers would conclude, he had fallen under a glamour cast by a ghoul, and as sure proof of this, the addendum was usually added that wherever the wife went afterwards, she kept a keen eye open for any person who resembled her husband, for in keeping with the lore of the ghouls, this would be that same monster that had snared him and it would now be hunting for her.

On the surface, this old and chilling folktale may not marry up with the stories about ghouls that we know today. In the 21st Century, the word 'ghoul' is commonly used to describe a particularly fiendish person, the adjective 'ghoulish' meaning much more than something that is merely distasteful. A modern-day ghoul might be a sadist, a serial killer, a cannibal or necrophile, though thanks to innumerable horror novels, stories and movies, we also have an understanding of the supernatural ghoul. To present-day folk, the ghoul is traditionally an eater of corpses, a non-human scavenger, which lurks in the vicinity of crypts and graveyards, particularly those where mortal remains have been laid in unhallowed ground. This modern interpretation has at least partly been shaped by fiction; one viewpoint holds that the prototype of the modern ghoul owes much to Edgar Allan Poe, HP Lovecraft and Clark Ashton-Smith. Such hellish depictions of the creature could surely only come from the imaginations of true masters of terror, but there are versions of these kinds of ghouls to be found in old world mythology as well.

They appear in this form in One Thousand and one Nights, the medieval-era collection of Arabic folktales first translated into English as The Arabian Nights in the 18th Century, while another *myth describes a particularly fearsome ghoul, Ghul-e Biyaban, who was said to have depredated widely over what is now modern-day Afghanistan. While the ghoul as a real creature is not mentioned in the Quran, several Islamic writers have addressed the matter, drawing similarities between the ghoul and another enemy of mankind, the djinn, an earthbound demon with many malevolent powers at its command, though this again implies that in distant times, the ghoul was much more than just a subhuman predator with a taste for carrion.*

Of course, at the end of the day, as with many of the grotesque creatures in this book, its origins will be less important to the average person than the inevitability, once it has latched onto you and your family, that nothing will ultimately protect you from its rending teeth and claws. Not even death.

BAOBHAN SITH
Carly Holmes

The first time I saw my love he was sitting on a rock, straight backed and poised as a god, so high among the crags there was nothing but heaven around him. He was singing something in an ardent, sweet tenor; something stirring and sad that cut into the marrow of my bones. It was his voice and that song, more than the blood that trickled from a shallow cut on his leg, that led me to him. I'd already eaten, had followed the fresh stink of entrails to a poacher a few miles away and dropped to my knees before him, pushed my face into the doughy yield of his stomach – my mouth landing a little higher than he'd envisaged – and feasted. I'd laid him out beside the deer he'd slaughtered, both bodies torn and glistening, a pleasing pink against the soft purple blur of heather. I'd arranged them like art, hoof tucked into hand, hollowed middles spilling shiny loops of intestines, and I'd left them there for the eagles. We've all got to eat.

If I hadn't already been sated then I don't know whether that particular appetite would have won out, whether I'd have seduced the man I loved and then fed from him, but I really believe not. Even if I'd been starving, half dead from malnutrition, I don't think I could have compromised my heart and severed it from my chest, exchanged it for that most basic function, the need for flesh.

He used the sleeve of his shirt to wipe the smears of blood from his shin, pausing his singing for a moment to bend his head and examine the small wound. Then he raised his face to the sky, exposing the pure cream slide of his throat, and filled his lungs. His chest swelled, became a bellows. As I watched he flung his arms out in wild, desperate gestures and *roared*. It was a duet, I knew it had to be, and I gasped and wept, wished that I knew the words for my part and could give them to him. Ravens pitched themselves from a gnarled little copse above us and joined in, circling and rasping. I could tell that they were annoyed at the disturbance but he didn't understand their language so he just laughed and tipped a hand to them in salute, then heaved his rucksack onto his shoulder and stood.

There was a moment when I could have stepped out from behind the boulder that hid me and made myself known, used my glamour to bring him close and then undressed him, pushed him down to lie beneath me. The sight of his fragile neck, that vast slab of chest, those muscled calves below the shorts, dried my mouth. But I was suddenly shy, self-conscious about my appearance. The once bright green of my dress was stained brown with viscera; my breath was sour, and my teeth trellised with the chewy gristle of my last meal; my furred legs sturdy but not shapely. I followed him as he picked his way down the mountain using the narrow tracks generations of sheep had driven into the ground. I hung back when he reached a car parked on the side of the road, and then once he'd driven away, I stepped onto the warm sticky tarmac – the rough base of my hooves cringing from the shock of a manmade surface – and followed his scent.

We'd never left the mountains; we'd never had need to in all these years. The hunters had always come to us, and then the modern fashion for hiking brought us further choice. Children as well as adults, females among the men. They were all equally mesmerised when they saw us. The meat of the younger ones was more tender but somehow less satisfying on the palate, though they were always little champions when we played games with them before the meal.

I thought I could hear the howls of my estranged sisters – distant and desperate – as I trotted away from them and towards the city none of us had ever seen, though its scorched smell had coated the hair and skin of day-trippers. Fumes and decay gritty as ash on their eyelashes, clogging their blood. I'd found images of this vast prison of concrete and glass on cameras they left behind after I seduced them: grey landscapes with no sky; mountains made from brick. Our collective shock and repulsion had bound us sisters together for decades, until the day I found a recording on a tiny plastic box and, fumbling with the buttons of this new toy, had collapsed speechless and besotted as human voices, legions of voices, wailed and trilled and *exploded* into my ears. They beseeched each other through song, broke each other's hearts, mended them and then broke them again. I played the little box over and over until it stopped working, learned the sounds but couldn't understand the words. I copied them as best I could as I walked the Highlands and Lowlands through days and seasons and years. I was first one voice and then another, finding my way into their characters and their stories, until I could imagine myself on a stage in that dreaded city. Until I couldn't imagine anything else. Clutched to a man's chest as he begged me to run away with him. Leading a chorus of courtesans at a masquerade or a mob of rioters through a ruined castle. I perfected a curtsey and caught invisible bouquets of roses.

My sisters were scornful at first, mocking and mimicking my shaky soprano, my gruff baritone. But as time went on and my obsession showed no sign of waning, they became frightened. This infatuation with humans and their hobbies was dangerous. Once they stopped being simply prey the door was opened to comparison, to kinship. The sisters knew, even if I didn't, that I was ripe for that ultimate human failing: falling in love. And then my downfall would be theirs too. So they shunned me, left a glade in a swirl of skirts when I entered it, packed up and moved from our winter dwelling before the first frosts. Without realising, they'd exposed me to that other human failing: loneliness.

And now, as I neared the larger, busier roads that tangled around the city, following the scent of the man I loved and humming the song he'd sung until it sunk into the sponge of my vocal cords as memory, I knew they would be scattering in panic across the ridges of our mountain, fleeing our ancestral home before the inevitable tragedy, the final act of my foolish fascination, reached them.

The city would have been bewildering, terrifying, if I'd let it overwhelm me, but I wasn't bred to feel fear of this kind. I simply followed my lover's scent trail to a small, terraced house, set back from a quiet side road and perched atop a flight of stone steps. I hovered there for a few moments, listening and sniffing the air, and then returned to the busier streets I'd passed. I had a shopping list to fulfil before presenting myself to him.

The staff in the first three shops I tried weren't helpful when I stood beside the counter and demanded a new green dress – a silk one with lace trim, floor-length – and another music box to replace the one I used to have. I sang the song to passing customers and asked them what it was called. Girls younger than I had ever been stared and giggled, rearranged displays of lipstick or turned away in confusion.

Once more on the street, I spotted a pretty young man with black curls and leather trench coat, heavy boots shiny with buckles. He leaned against the wall, smoking a cigarette, eyeing me. Hunger stirred; the walk had been long. I strode up to him and told him to take me to a shop that had dresses and music. My gaze held his until I felt that minute *click* and his expression glazed into rapture. The cigarette burned through the flesh of his drooping fingers until I plucked it away and gently licked the wound. We walked slowly, my wrist resting on the crook of his arm, until we reached a small winding street as narrow as an alley.

'Here,' he said, pointing at a row of shops that leaned haphazardly in every direction. 'You'll find what you need in these.' He kissed my hand and held it against his heart. My stomach growled and I told him to wait where he was until I returned.

The first shop smelled of damp cloth and stale skin. Ballgowns hung from racks; velvet cloaks were draped over mannequins and topped with high, brittle hats trailing feathers as long as my arm. False faces and wigs dangled in front of the window. I stripped off my ruined dress and called to the old man behind the counter, pointing at a green satin frock, all flounces and froth. He tottered across to me and dropped it over my head, stroked it down my naked body with trembling hands. The fit was perfect. I left him there, weeping and pawing at the air, and continued along the row of shops until I found one with musical instruments and records in the window.

When I emerged with bags filled with music and a new little box to play them on, I was giddy from excitement and faint from hunger. The boy was where I'd left him, frozen to the pavement. I hustled him into a deep doorway and told him to close his eyes, let him push his fingers into my hair as I knelt before him. That first bite through flesh and muscle, the pop of tendons against my tongue and the warm gush of blood into my mouth, made me shiver and strain. I used the hem of his coat as a bib to protect my dress and rode the spasms of his body as I tore into the tender lining of his gut and tasted the aftermath of his lunch. Beef. Why was it always beef with these young men?

I left what remained of him there for the foxes and rats and strode back along the darkening streets to my lover's home.

There were perhaps half a dozen houses in a row. They all had a flight of steps leading up to the front door, dusty cellar windows tucked below, and potted plants dotted around as decoration. Identical little homes for humans to live out their little lives, quaint in their prettiness. My shyness had returned now that I was back here, a bashful reluctance to expose myself and risk rejection. I could, of course, have thrown my glamour over him and made him mine, but I wanted him to love *me* without the tricks. I hesitated for a while in the glow of lamplight, fidgeting between pockets of shadow, and then moved along to the house next to my love's.

I knocked once, an imperious rap, and watched as a shape

wavered towards me through the frosted glass in the door. A middle-aged man with a rigid medicine ball for a stomach and an impatient expression that slackened into lust as soon as I smiled at him. I held his gaze for a second then tapped his chest and stepped past him and down the hallway, into the kitchen at the back. 'Close the door,' I said over my shoulder. I heard him shuffling after me as I opened the window and leaned out.

Next door's garden was all neat lawn edges and pastel flowerbeds. I felt an absurd pang of disappointment. Where was the wildness? A man who sang like him surely didn't like *this*? At the far end there was a shed and a trampoline. A swing set was tucked away beside the shed and rusting, listing to the side. Outgrown, probably. I considered it. That could be awkward.

A rich baritone reached me from an open window, somewhere close by and above my head, singing a song I now knew. A swelling of sound, a singing-in-the-shower lack of self-consciousness. I closed my eyes and listened, felt the blood surge and thump against the back of my eyeballs. My knees were weak. I was suddenly starving again.

I turned to the man who'd been standing behind me, close enough to push me out of the window if he'd wanted to. He had a thin stream of drool hanging from his bottom lip and his palms stuttered through the air, making shapes around my body. Desperate to touch but unsure of the response. I looked deep into his helpless, intoxicated face and touched him lightly on the cheek. 'Dinner?' I suggested.

I was still cleaning my face when I heard a door slam and a shouted farewell. Trotting to the lounge window, I watched my lover run down his front steps and pause to wave extravagantly at someone inside the house, then turn and walk quickly away. A child's high voice followed him down the street and he waved once more without breaking stride. Tossing down the stained towel I'd been using to wipe off the remains of my meal, I checked my appearance quickly in the hallway mirror and then swiped a jangle of keys from the cabinet by the door and rushed after him.

The night-time sounds of the city were distracting, exciting. Invisible people called to each other from nearby streets, shrieking and laughing. Cars hooted and revved engines. For a second my consciousness groped towards my sisters'; there was a brief flash of panic and recoil as they glimpsed what I was experiencing, a backwash of pine needles and damp soil in my nostrils. Then the connection was severed with a violent tear, as though they'd all thrown themselves from the highest mountain peak and snapped their necks rather than remain even vicariously linked to my existence in this alien, hostile place. I felt a brief nostalgic yearning for them and the fresh green paths of my old home, the crisp ceiling of unpolluted sky, but smothered it viciously in my new gown and trailed after my man.

The hall he went into was bright inside, buzzing with noise and hazy with cigarette smoke. I lingered in the entrance and peeked at the crowd of men and women circulating, calling greetings, holding mugs of tea aloft. There was a row of chairs, a piano, and a stage at the farthest end. A stage! I twitched towards it, longing to be up there and looking out at the enthralled audience, bathed in spotlights and rapturous applause. I sidled into the hall and busied myself at a table set against the wall, fiddling with a mug and teapot and flicking quick glances around. A woman passed me – grey hair wild and loose on her shoulders – and stumbled to a halt, staring. 'What a ... what a pretty dress,' she said breathlessly. 'Are you new here? Are you going to sing?'

I put down the mug and pivoted gracefully towards her so that the skirt of my dress swung out in a rustling arc. 'Yes,' I said, holding out my hand and dipping my knees in a small curtsey. 'I'm going to sing with *him*.' I tipped my head towards the figure at the other end of the hall, watching as he appeared and disappeared among the knots of people. He seemed to know everyone, and everyone wanted to shake his hand or slap his shoulder.

She followed my gaze and took my hand; wouldn't let it go. 'Joshua?' she asked, stroking my palm with the tips of her fingers. 'Gosh, your skin is so soft, like velvet. Are you going to be his Cressida then? I thought Anne had that role.' She leaned in, her lips close to mine, her eyes wide and wet. 'But you'd be perfect at it,' she whispered ardently. 'I can tell a star when I see one. Is that a smear of ketchup on your neck? Do you want me to …?' She plucked a tissue from her pocket and dabbed at the air.

I released myself from her trembling grip and smiled gently. 'Unfortunately, Anne will be indisposed,' I told her. 'But I'm just here to observe, this evening. I haven't learnt all the songs yet.' I turned and left her, wandered across the hall and tucked myself into a shadowy corner beside the stage. 'Joshua,' I whispered to myself. 'Joshua.' My cheeks were hot.

As if his name in my mouth had summoned him, he appeared on the stage above me and flung out his arms. 'Welcome,' he shouted. The gathered crowd cheered and hushed each other, surging towards him. His feet, encased in polished brown shoes, were inches from my face. I could throw my arms around his ankles right now, kiss those perfect toes. I could flip his feet out from under him and bring him down like prey, leap onto his fallen body and unbuckle his trousers, ride him right here, between these faded velvet curtains. My teeth were bared, my hands clawed. I shivered towards him and then flinched back when he glanced down and saw me – his expression momentarily disorientated, shocked – before I slunk deeper into the shadow and he blinked, lost sight of me, and remembered his role.

A woman seated herself at the piano close by and began to slide her fingertips up and down the keys. She frowned as she tinkered, thumping at the instrument with more vigour and drowning out what my Joshua was saying. The sound was strident, harsher than expected from what I'd previously heard on my music box. But then she settled into her seat and shook out her hands from the wrists, and she began to play the song I'd first experienced that very day on the top of the mountain. A lifetime ago. The crowd moved to the chairs and sat down as Joshua helped a young woman leap onto the stage and spun her into an embrace. He began to sing, rocking her against his chest and then twirling her away so that she was at arm's length, linked to him through their entwined fingers. She swayed back and forth, her free hand weaving through the air as she waited for her cue to start.

I strained towards them and listened as she began her part of the duet, trying to commit the words and tune to memory. I would need to be perfect when I took to the stage before a paying audience as Joshua's leading lady. The people behind me murmured and then stood and began to clap and whoop as the song built and increased in volume until both singers were thundering out their lines, flinging themselves away from and back towards their partner. My heart galloped along with them, my hooves stamping on the wooden floorboards of the old hall as I cheered and roared, brushing tears from my face. When they finally trailed into silence and offered little half bows around the room, panting and grinning, I tore the silk flower from the bodice of my dress and threw it up to them with blown kisses. This was everything I had dreamed of; such exquisite alchemy.

The woman – Anne, I assumed she must be – stooped to pick up the flower, laughing. She scanned the darkness beyond the spotlights and found me, raised the crumpled fabric in a salute. I stepped forward to the edge of the stage and let her *see* me properly, felt that *snap* in her psyche as she swooned into love. She stumbled and almost toppled from the stage, reaching for me. 'You must sing,' she whispered. Then, shrill: 'She must sing! This part was made for her!'

The tears were still damp on my skin, my blood surging with the thrill of all this. I had to be up there right now, taking my place by Joshua's side, wooing him with my songs. The grey-haired woman from earlier took up the cry and clutched my wrist to lead me to the steps at the side of the stage. People parted to let us through almost grudgingly, confused by who I was and what claim I could possibly have. I gifted each of them a long, smiling look as I passed them and the tide of faces glazed into one single mask of infatuation. But not him, not Joshua. I lowered my gaze when I stood beside him so that his searching eyes didn't meet mine. *He* would fall in love with me for no other reason but the fact that we were destined for each other. For him there would be no false glamour.

As the piano player began once more to obediently stroke the keys of the instrument and the crowd roared, I stood like a dancer with shoulders squared and back rigid as a statue. I stared past the lights and the people, into the shadows in the far corners of the hall, tasting every victorious second. My consciousness groped again towards my sisters, with a gleeful need for them to witness this triumph, but there was nothing but a vast blankness where the connection used to be. I conjured them with my imagination instead, placed them in a row at the back of the hall and gave them identical expressions of delight and pride.

When Joshua started tentatively singing his opening lines for the second time, scanning the cheering crowd in bewilderment, I closed my eyes and laid my palms gently on his chest. I could feel his body's warmth through the thin material of his shirt, sense the confusion he felt. I couldn't remember all the words for my part but I was sure I knew enough, and besides, it was the atmosphere that mattered, not the specifics. And atmosphere I could do.

I started out too low, too husky, so I took a breath and pitched the next lines of my part of the duet higher and louder, tipping my chin up to stretch my lungs. With my eyes squeezed closed I couldn't see anyone's reaction but there was a splintering second of collective silence before the cheering started again. Joshua flinched from me, wincing in spasms. I took a handful of his shirt to stop him from stepping away and sang into his face with all the gusto I had. He missed his cue to join me in the final verse, fumbled the words and then rallied for the finale. I risked the tiniest peek at him as we reached our crescendo; the expression on his face was excruciating, a tortured rigor mortis of horror and pain, as if he were being flayed by my singing rather than enchanted by it.

As the crowd yelled and surged forward, clambering over each other to be the first to reach me, I took his hand and dragged him forward into a low bow. This was a joy purer than any I'd ever known before. Even when he tugged his hand from mine and turned away, grabbing at Anne's arm to swing her into a huddle, I felt only the briefest pang of rejection, immediately dismissed.

People swarmed around me and kissed my cheeks, knelt at my feet and held onto fistfuls of my skirt, gazing up. 'Incredible!' they shouted. 'A star is born!' The few who hadn't yet got close enough to see me properly muttered in bemused little knots around the hall, shrugging and sneering. The pianist stood and pushed her stool back, strode to the edge of the stage with an air of outraged bewilderment. I leaned down and smiled at her and she stumbled to a halt, smiled back uncertainly, and then sank to her knees and began to clap. 'Bravo! Bravo!'

I waded through the jam of bodies to Joshua and Anne, needing to be close to him again, needing some kind of validation from the only person who mattered. His back was to me; I could see Anne's furious, vehement face over his shoulder. I knew she was telling him that the part of Cressida was now mine, handed over with pleasure and grace, but he didn't seem to be taking it as well as I'd imagined. I stepped right up to them, hovering discreetly behind.

'… explain to me how you couldn't *hear* that,' he was saying. Then, '*Honking*, Anne. She was honking in my face like a bloody goose. My eight-year-old, tone-deaf son could hold a tune better than her.'

I spun him around a fraction after Anne's slap landed like a slammed glass on his cheek. I held his chin and brought his face to mine. I watched him melt and whimper. Then I thrust him away and leapt from the stage, running through the besotted crowd, shoving people out of my path. I could barely see for the tears of rage, launching myself at the darkness beyond the lit hall, and then storming through the streets. I tripped over the long train of my dress again and again, paused to rip it at knee-length and discard it, not caring any longer that my furred legs, my cloven hooves, were exposed to anyone who saw me. Pain like nothing I'd ever experienced before cramped my stomach in acid spasms, doubling me over and bringing me to my knees to retch. Humiliation, I realised. That other human failing. And the humiliation consumed me.

The child answered the door; the tone-deaf, eight-year-old son. I crouched before him and stroked his arm. 'Hello, darling,' I whispered. 'I'm your daddy's friend.'

He threw himself into my arms and clung to me. 'I love you,' he told me.

I pushed my nose into the soft skin of his throat and breathed him in. There was something so delightfully pure and honest about children. They processed the glamour I threw over them as a gift; there was none of the cynicism of adult humans, for whom love was a bargaining chip that demanded more from the giver than it did from them. A child simply *loved*, and that alone made them happy. Even when my sisters and I used to play with the little ones, dressing them up like dollies or teddy bears and squabbling over them, tearing them apart in our determination to each have the biggest piece, they screamed and wailed but they never struck out.

Carrying him into the nearest room, I unwound his arms from my neck and deposited him on the sofa but allowed him to hold my hand. 'Where's Mummy?' I asked.

He pointed towards the wall behind his head. 'In the kitchen. Talking to her friend on the phone.'

I smiled down at him. At the soft, squirming body, flushed and rosy in his blue flannel pyjamas. 'Close your eyes,' I said.

There was just one single yelp, high and thin, but it brought the mother, Joshua's other woman, running into the room in a panicked scramble. She still had the phone in her hand. I held the child's body out to her, slumped across my outstretched arms like an offering. Blood shone black in the low light. She dropped the phone and began to keen, the sound almost identical in pitch to her son's, but when I hushed her and tipped him against her chest she slid to the floor and held him to her heart, gazing up at me. 'Why?' she asked. Her legs were stretched out in front of her like a stuffed doll propped on a shop shelf, ankles floppy.

I bent down to look searchingly into her face. She was pretty in a tired, faded way, or she would have been without the slick of grief and infatuation twisting her features. 'Revenge,' I said. 'Take it up with Joshua.'

She nodded and smiled dreamily at me, then hunched over her son, murmuring a lullaby. The nape of her neck, the fragile abacus of spine, gleamed in the lamplight. I put my lips to it and felt her sigh, push back against me slightly with desire as I tongued her skin. When I opened my mouth and set my sharp teeth around the bump of bone she moaned and whispered *yes*.

I'd thought, when I charged through the streets to get here, that I would rip them apart, decorate the house with their organs, but now, suddenly, I didn't feel the need for such drama. I bit through the spindle of spine and severed it neatly, allowing myself only a taste of her before laying her gently down on the carpet and arranging her boy so that he was curled within her arms, nuzzling at her collarbone. Then I moved to the sofa and sat down, and I waited.

The key thrusting into the front door lock jolted me from my reverie. I'd been thinking of home, of my sisters; yearning to be away from this dirty, cruel city and back where I belonged. The humiliation was still an arrow embedded deep inside my stomach, loosing rusty poison into my blood stream, and only the green-tinted air of the mountain could heal me now.

'Sue?' Joshua called from the hallway. I stood up. There was a muted metallic crash as his keys skittered down onto the table. 'I'm sorry I'm late. I hope I haven't ruined dinner.' His footsteps towards the lounge door were uneven and stumbling. He'd been drinking.

'You?' he gasped when he saw me. 'Oh, I thought I'd never see you again!' He stepped carefully over the fallen bodies of his wife and child and reached for me. I moved back and held up a hand to halt him.

'Look at them,' I told him. 'Look what you did.'

He saw them then, looked properly, and knew. He dropped to his knees, gathered them both up and began to rock them. The boy's arm hung to the side and swung like a snapped twig. 'Why?' he asked. 'I love you.'

'I know,' I said. I was suddenly weary: of him, of humans, of having to explain myself. I had miles to travel, and I just wanted to go.

'I honk like a *goose*,' I whispered. 'That's why.'

'No, no!' He was trying to keep them both in his arms whilst straining past them to touch me. His wife spilled out from his embrace and onto the floor, the back of her head knocking hard against the wood. He hauled her up and clutched her to his chest. His face was joyful, terrified. 'At first I thought that... But then I realised you were just unique. Perfectly unique. Oh God, *Sue*. Mikey. We can leave now, run away together. I'll take the blame if we're caught. It'll be days before they're found. Oh, his face. Look at his face. My sweet little boy.'

I stepped carefully past him to the door. 'My sisters were right,' I said. 'I should never have come here. But I fell in love with you.' My voice faltered and broke. I hated myself for that.

Self-hate: another human failing.

I turned and left him there, hobbled under the weight of his perished family and unable to summon the strength to rise from beneath them. Though he tried when he realised that I was abandoning him, rose to a crouch and then slumped back down and began to sob in hard, torn gulps.

I pushed the front door wide and stepped out into the greasy city air, set my face to the distant horizon where the glow of streetlamps ended and the true dark of night began, and I galloped towards home.

SPHINX

Surely one of the most enigmatic of all legendary monsters is the Sphinx, not least because it comes down through the ages as a mysterious, wise and hyper-intelligent entity and yet its purpose is confusing, because for all its intellect, encounters with the creature so often ended in violent death. But also because though Sphinx-like monsters feature in worldwide mythologies, particularly across Asia, there are two clear and yet opposing versions of it in western culture, where it earned the name we know it by today ('sphinx' deriving from the Greek word 'to crush'), one on either side of the Mediterranean.

The Ancient Greek and Ancient Egyptian worlds weren't just aware of each other, they interconnected at many levels, both through trade and war, marriage and travel, and of course through storytelling. Numerous Egyptian myths had made it into the Greek pantheon long before 305 BC, when the Macedonian general, Ptolemy, founded the Ptolemaic Kingdom of Egypt (from which Hellenic line, Cleopatra would descend). A whole range of Olympian gods appear to have prototypes in Egyptian culture, including Apollo (Horus?) and Hades (Osiris?). Then there is the existence of Atlantis, originally an Egyptian tradition. And of course, the story of one of history's most ancient monsters: the dreaded Sphinx. Except that it isn't strictly true to compare the Egyptian version of the Sphinx with the Greek version, because the two of them are very different indeed, and that in itself is a big mystery.

In the Greek tales, the Sphinx, a very beautiful woman but with the hindquarters of a lion and the wings of an eagle, was the last-but-one child of that mother of all monsters, Echidna.

The main thrust of the Greek version comes from a range of different sources, but mainly from the biography of the tragic hero, Oedipus, who is referenced numerous times in Ancient Greek literature – Homer, Hesiod and Euripides have all mentioned him – but most famously and fully by Sophocles, in his play, Oedipus

Rex. It tells how Oedipus, unknowingly the heir to the kingdom of Thebes, arrives at the gates of the city, which is ravaged by famine as a terrible monster, the Sphinx, has set up home on a rock overlooking the main gates. No one is allowed to leave or enter unless they are prepared to try and solve one of the Sphinx's riddles. If the intrepid traveller succeeds, he or she can pass unharmed, but if they fail, the Sphinx swoops down on them, kills them by strangulation, and then eats their corpse at her leisure. Fearless Oedipus accepts the challenge and in a scene that has influenced many dramatic moments in fantasy fiction ever since, not least Bilbo's first encounter with Gollum in J R R Tolkien's The Hobbit, *is presented with the famous riddle: Which creature walks on four feet in the morning, two in the afternoon, and three at night? When Oedipus answers successfully, naming the creature as Man himself – he crawls on all fours as an infant, walks on two legs as an adult, and on three in old age, as he has need of a stick – the Sphinx, distraught that its most ingenious riddle has been solved, flings itself from the rock and dies on impact with the ground.*

It's a strange one even then, because while the Oedipus melodrama is filled with prophecies, curses, family murders, incest and other domestic disasters, the appearance of the Sphinx is brief and near enough incidental. From the perspective of an amateur myth-hunter, the monster's mere presence is confusing. Why was it there? What role was it supposed to play? The dramatist is clearly using the monster, in this sequence at least, as the point in the story where Oedipus transforms from a windblown wanderer to a kingly saviour, and as a metaphor for the riddles the hero must solve about himself. But the actual legend predates the play, and according to that legend, the Sphinx besieged Thebes on the orders of either Hera or Ares, to punish the sins of the villainous King Laius.

Once again, it would seem, a mortal but monstrous being was used by the gods as a means of imposing divine retribution.

Thus goes the tale of the Greek Sphinx, but what of her Egyptian cousin?

It may come as a surprise to many that, though the Sphinx is probably most commonly associated with Ancient Egypt, the monster makes no actual appearance in any of Egypt's myths. What we do have, though, are countless visual representations of the beast in Egypt's age-old statuary and decorative art. In fact, it's probably true to say that the iconography of the Sphinx is almost entirely the handiwork of Egyptian architects and artisans.

The most famous sculpting of course is the limestone Sphinx of Giza, the world-famous guardian of the Pyramids of Giza, the colossal reclining figure of a lion with a man's head, the latter believed a depiction of the pharaoh Khafre, who died in 2532 BC (or perhaps his father, Khufu). There is a school of scholarly thought that the statue's head, which is out of proportion with the rest of the body, might have been a later addition, probably to celebrate Khafre's reign, and that the original image might date to much earlier, and might even simply have depicted a lion, or perhaps, who knows?, even the original female Sphinx.

Khafre or Khufu, it is argued, simply discovered this pre-existing monument buried in the desert sand, dug it out and adjusted the head to portray their own grandeur, though this is a theory that is hotly debated in archaeological circles.

One interesting and undeniable fact. The Great Sphinx of Giza seems to embody neither the fury nor malevolence of any kind of monster, and if anything, gazes eastward towards the rising sun, a solemn godlike symbol of a magnificent but antique civilisation now understood only through the marvel of hieroglyphics. But not every early culture regarded it this way. During the days of the Roman Empire – even then the pyramids and the Sphinx were a tourist destination – a range of different names were attributed to the immense figure: Hauron or Bethoron, originally a Canaanite god, whom in Hebrew writings was more of a demon, as he could be invoked by a curse; and Peor, another barbarous deity who was connected by early Christian writers to the arch devil, Belphegor.

Perhaps most telling of all was the name given to the Great Sphinx by another desert people, the Arabs, who in medieval times, referred to it simply as Abū il-Hawl, which translates into 'Father of Terror'.

WOODWOSE
James Brogden

'We're here!' Martin announced, and pulled the minibus over to the side of the road.

'Here?' said Josh, looking up from his phone to peer out of the window. 'Where the fuck is here?'

It was a potholed country lane with high hedges to either side overhung with trees, and grey sky above those. He couldn't see anything of the surrounding countryside, not that it would have made any difference; once they'd left Rednall he'd lost interest. It could have been Never Never Land for all he knew. Martin had parked by an old wooden farm gate set into the hedge, but there were no signs, not even a 'Do Not Enter'.

'Lesher's Wood,' he replied. 'Your home for the weekend. Going to need someone to get out and open that gate for me.'

Nobody said anything. Arjay had his headphones on and was pretending he couldn't hear. Rizz was pretending to be asleep.

'Fucksake,' Josh muttered. He slid back the minibus door and hopped out, slamming it shut behind him.

The gate was reluctant to let them in. For a start, the big metal hasp that swung over the top of the gatepost was rusted, and he had to haul on it hard to get it to shift at all. Then the actual gate had dropped so that its bottom bar was dragging in the mud, forcing him to pick it up and shuffle-shove it open; it creaked and wobbled, hinges wailing in protest, so rickety that he was afraid it would simply fall apart.

Martin babied the minibus through the gap. 'Top man,' he grinned through the driver's window as he passed.

'You sure this is the right place?' said Josh. 'Looks like it's just a field.' There was only a farm track past here, parallel muddy wheel ruts heading uphill towards a dark line of trees.

'I've been bringing groups here for years. Don't worry, we're not going to get shot by an angry farmer – though we might do if we leave his gate open. You good to shut that again?'

Josh sighed.

'Top man. Catch us up.'

As the minibus crept past, Arjay grinned at him from inside and gestured 'wanker'. Josh gave him the finger. He dragged the gate shut and trudged after the vehicle as it bumped and slewed up the track. Some kind of Land Rover thing would have been better, he reckoned, especially since there were only four of them, but the Centre probably couldn't afford anything else and anyway there were meant to be more than just him, Arjay and Rizz. Eight people had signed up for Martin's 'Wood Skills Weekender' but the other five just hadn't turned up, despite how they'd all been talking for weeks about how hard it was going to slap. Fair play to Arjay – he was a dick but at least he showed.

It looked like the minibus wasn't slowing down for him and he wasn't surprised; stop that thing here and it probably wouldn't get going again. Josh slogged along after it. He looked around. It was just a field: sheep shit and weeds. Up ahead the track disappeared into the thick trees of Lesher's Wood which covered the hillside for miles around. Emerging from it right on the very skyline was a high rocky outcrop, and as soon as he saw it Josh knew he had to climb it. He didn't know why. He'd never done anything like it before, never hiked, never even gone camping. He just knew that there was a view from that point, a way of seeing something *more*, even though he couldn't articulate to himself what that 'more' was, only that it tugged on his nerve endings like the need for a smoke.

He stepped up his pace and followed the minibus as it disappeared into the gloom beneath the trees.

There was a circle of log seats around a fire pit, damp and long-unused. Martin set them to clearing away the weeds and dead leaves from last year's autumn while he collected kindling and got a fire going. He struck sparks into a bundle of dry grass and bark curlings from a fire-steel using the back of a squat-bladed knife, and soon had a flame.

'You know we do have lighters,' Arjay pointed out.

'I know,' Martin replied, grinning. 'But this is more fun.'

Rizz's eyes lit up. 'Hey, do we get knives?'

Arjay snickered. 'Thought you carried one everywhere.'

Rizz chucked a stick at him.

'No,' said Martin. 'At least not to keep. I'll show you how to handle one safely, the way it's meant to be used. You're going to need one to build your shelter for the night.'

Rizz looked horrified. 'I thought we was having, like, tents or something.'

'Pfft, tents,' scoffed Arjay. 'Like you'd sleep in one of those. Did you even read the letter?'

'What letter? No, seriously man, is there not like an AirB&B somewhere?' He took out his phone. He'd lasted a whole five minutes without it, Josh thought, probably a personal record. But Rizz obviously wasn't happy with what he found.

'Shit man, there's like fuck all signal.'

'I know,' said Martin, smiling as he fed larger sticks to the fire. 'The bedrock here is solid granite. Reception is patchy because these hills and the woods that cover them are full of big outcrops.'

'Like the one right on top?' Josh asked. 'Can we go up there?'

'Later maybe, if there's time. You can see the caves. But you need somewhere to sleep first.'

Josh and Arjay looked at each other, eyes shining. *Caves.*

Matt went to the minibus and brought back a big old metal army-surplus ammunition box that was secured with a padlock so big it looked like belonged in a medieval dungeon. It thumped to the ground, heavy things rattling inside.

'Right lads, listen. The tools you need for this weekend are in here. Like I say, I'll show you how to use them safely. There are only two rules. One, things come back to me when you're finished with them. Two, do not mess around with them. All right? As you've seen, there's no phone signal, and we are an hour away from the nearest hospital. If you accidentally cut something off, you'd better get used to living without it.'

Arjay snickered again. 'Josh should cut his dick off right now in that case. It's getting fuck all use anyway.'

Josh gave him the finger. Rizz laughed. Martin was stony-eyed and expressionless.

'I am fucking serious,' he said, and they subsided immediately. For a youth worker he was a soft touch a lot of the time but the kids at the Centre knew that when he drew a line you didn't step over it because nobody wanted to be barred, and when he dropped the f-bomb you knew he was serious. 'If I see anything pointy in your hand that isn't doing a job you won't be building anything – you'll sleep on the ground in the open. You might think that a night under the stars wouldn't be so bad, but the forecast is for rain so don't try to be clever.' Then he shrugged. 'Or maybe I'll just send you out into the woods to be eaten by Bosky Tom.'

The three boys stared at him.

'Bosky what-the-fuck-did-you-just-say?' said Rizz.

'Oh, didn't I tell you about him? Sorry, it must have slipped my mind. Let's get a brew on, shall we?'

He refused to answer any of their questions until he'd set up over the fire a tripod of sticks from which he hung an old tin kettle of water. Josh produced a huge bottle of cola from his rucksack which the boys passed around. Another of the rules for this trip had been no booze and no drugs, but if Martin suspected that the cola was liberally spiked with vodka he didn't say anything. Only once he'd made himself a cup of tea did he sit back and look at them through the steam rising from his mug.

'Nobody knows who or what Bosky Tom really is,' he said. 'Only that he's hungry and he has a taste for human flesh. There are caves in the rocks high up where they say he makes his lair. There have been stories about him around these parts for hundreds of years, so it's either a copycat thing or a family tradition or, well, something else entirely. Stories about livestock going missing, and sometimes people too. During the Civil War a company of Royalists routed by Cromwell's forces at the battle of Worcester were said to have taken refuge in Lesher's Wood, and disappeared without a trace. The soldiers that went in after them found only blood and gnawed bones.' He paused to let that sink in. 'Local farmers make sure to lock their animals away securely at night and nobody travels the road that passes the bottom of the hill after dark if they can help it. Some people say that they've heard strange noises, like something calling from deep within the woods, only not using words that anyone can understand. I've been bringing groups here for years and I've never seen or heard anything. That said, I do like to make sure that the fire is kept burning all night.'

Rizz and Arjay scooted a little closer to the fire and Josh saw Martin trying to suppress a smile as he sipped his tea. The old man was loving this, but Josh didn't blame him. He had a campfire and a captive audience.

Later, he gave them a hatchet, a folding saw and a small knife each, and after showing them how to use them safely he sent the three of them off into the undergrowth to collect as much greenery as they could for their shelters.

'Get that nursery school bullshit about Bosky Tom,' Arjay said as they walked. 'Like we was little kids or something.'

'Big man,' Rizz teased. 'You were cacking yourself.'

'Piss off.'

'You want someone to tuck you in nice and safe tonight, don't ask me.'

'*Piss off!*'

'Guys,' said Josh, pointing. 'Look.'

In a small clearing ahead of them was a tall tipi-like structure of bone-pale logs propped up around a large dead tree. At its base a dark opening yawned like a cave between roots as thick as their thighs.

'The fuck is *that* thing?' breathed Arjay.

'Bosky Tom's home, innit?' grinned Rizz, and shoved him. 'Yo Tom!' he called. 'I've brought you a snack!'

'It's just an old shelter,' said Josh, walking up to it and peering into the opening. It was large enough for several people and its floor was sunken below ground level. There was leaf mould at the bottom and a crumpled crisp packet. No mystery there, he thought, feeling oddly disappointed.

'Ain't going to shelter you from much,' said Arjay, kicking at one of the logs, which collapsed with a loud crack that startled them all.

'Don't!' Rizz protested.

Arjay rounded on him. 'What the fuck is wrong with you, anyway? Why are you acting like such a pussy all of a sudden?'

'It's creepy, man! This whole fucking place!' He looked around, as if afraid that he'd been overheard by something that might have taken offence, and lowered his voice. 'There's … there's too many trees.'

'That's why they call it the woods,' Josh pointed out.

'I know we're in the fucking woods, man! I'm just telling you. It feels like you can't see where you are. Like you could be anywhere. Or, like, nowhere at all.'

'The only thing I feel is hungry,' said Arjay. 'Sooner we get these shelters built the sooner we get barbecue.'

'Yeah, we can use a lot of these bits,' said Josh. 'Come on.' The pair of them started to haul at one of the logs. After a little while Rizz joined in reluctantly and helped them carry it back to the campfire, while they did their best to ignore him glancing fearfully at the undergrowth and muttering, 'Just too many trees.'

There was no way that the three of them were going to sleep together in one shelter so they each made their own – a simple lean-to facing the fire, formed of a crossbar lashed between two trees with greenery piled against it at an angle. Martin gave them sleeping bags and plastic bivvy bags too. Josh wasn't sure that any of this was going to keep him dry, and decided that if it did rain he'd go and sleep in the minibus whatever Martin had to say about it. The blades went back into the ammo box but the hatchet stayed out for splitting firewood.

They cooked hamburgers and jacket spuds in the embers of the fire, and sat up smoking and telling crap jokes and trying not to check their phones every five minutes. If Martin noticed that they were getting steadily pissed on Josh's spiked cola then he didn't say anything, but when Rizz produced a bluetooth speaker he got about ten seconds of music out of it before Martin took it off him.

'If I hear that bloody thing again I'll kill you and eat you myself,' he said amiably.

Eventually he retired to his tent, and somewhere around one in the morning the three lads decided it was time to crash.

'What do we do about the fire?' asked Arjay. It was little more than a low red glow, painting their faces a ruddy orange. 'Martin said that we had to keep it going all night.'

'Yeah, to keep away Bosky Tom,' said Rizz. 'Who as we all know is just a bullshit kiddies' campfire story. Chill, yeah? Get some sleep.'

'I can't sleep in this! What if, like, bugs get into my sleeping bag?'

'Trust me, Arjay,' said Josh, 'nothing is going to want to sleep with you, not even a bug.'

But sleep he did, as did they all.

Until Josh awoke with the sense that something had moved past him.

His sleep had been restless anyway – the pile of bracken he'd collected for a mattress wasn't anywhere near thick enough and he might as well have been sleeping directly on the hard ground – so it didn't take much, just the sense that something large had momentarily blotted out the ember-light glowing through his eyelids.

Then the adrenalin kicked in and he was instantly wide awake. But he kept himself lying completely still, the way you did when you were little and afraid of the dark, a small prey mammal, maybe a shrew, hoping that the thing with teeth and claws wouldn't notice you. He opened his eyes a crack, and bit the inside of his cheek hard to suppress a whimper.

A tall, shaggy humanoid shape was looming over Rizz's lean-to. It was across the other side of the fire with its hairy back to Josh so he couldn't see his face, for which he was profoundly grateful.

Maybe it won't hurt him, he thought in that terrified shrew voice. *Maybe it's just curious. It's got no reason to hurt us. It'll smell the hamburger and go for that.* Hard on the heels of that thought came one which was colder, and had claws and teeth of its own: *Or, you can get to the minibus while it's distracted by ripping him apart.*

The creature roared, grabbed the long cross-piece of Rizz's shelter in two enormous furry hands and began to shake it.

In Josh's memory the next few moments were a blurred chaos of screaming, fire and blood.

Rizz woke, saw Bosky Tom leaning over him, and began to shriek in high-pitched yelps like a puppy being tortured. Arjay was soon screaming too, and thrashing like a maggot to escape his bivvy bag. The creature continued to shake Rizz's shelter while roaring something that sounded oddly like 'Booga-booga-booga!' but by that time Josh was moving, not thinking. The cold thing in him with claws and teeth shoved the shrew aside. He didn't even bother trying to struggle out of his bag; he only needed his arms free. He snatched up the hatchet from beside the fire and threw himself at the creature – pogo-ing straight through the embers in a way that would have been comical under other circumstances – and slammed the blade square between its shoulder blades. Its roars turned to screams. Its long arms flailed backwards, fingers grasping vainly for the weapon. Josh pulled it free and slammed it in again, this time at the junction of neck and shoulder. Its screams turned to gurgling as it lurched away, trying to escape, but Josh clung to the handle and bore it to the ground under his weight. Dimly he was aware of the smell of burning plastic, but ignored it. He yanked the hatchet free with difficulty – it had got lodged in some bone or other – and blood fountained (the cold voice in his head howling with glee at the salty spurt of it), then he brought the blade down a third and final time on the back of the Bosky Tom's skull with a crack like a watermelon being split open and a reverberation that numbed his hands. Still the creature did not die, but began to crawl, face down in the leaf-mould, making choking noises that sounded almost like slurred speech.

Then Arjay shouted, 'Shit, Josh, you're fucking burning!' and hands were tugging at his sleeping bag.

Its plastic outer shell had melted in the embers and caught fire. So far the flames hadn't made it through the down filling but it would only take moments; Arjay helped to peel the sleeping bag off him as he kicked free of it frantically, then they threw it onto the ground between two of the lean-tos and whacked it with the frying pan until it went out.

Acrid smoke drifted across the clearing. Rizz was curled in a foetal ball, his screams muffled by his own bag. The embers were a smeared and blackened ruin. Without their glow, everything had slumped back into shadow, including the shaggy shape that was feebly dragging itself by its arms through the dirt, its breath wet and rasping. The hatchet was still sticking out of the back of its skull.

'Fuck, Josh!' Arjay whispered. His eyes were wide and white. 'What the *fuck*?'

'Wake up Martin.'

'How is he fucking still *asleep*?'

'I don't know. Just do it.'

Arjay did as he was told while Josh went back to his shelter for his head-torch. He approached Bosky Tom cautiously. In the torch light he saw something weird by its head that hadn't been there before – something pale and oval-shaped, like a shallow bowl with indentations at the bottom. He reached for it, not really afraid that the creature would make a sudden grab for him as it sounded like it was close to death, and turned it over.

It was thin plastic, moulded into the visage of a snarling gorilla. The elastic string that should have held it across the back of a head was cut neatly in the middle as if severed by, say, a hatchet blow.

Arjay came running back. 'Martin's not in his tent!' he gasped. 'Where the fuck is he?'

Feeling like he was about to throw up, Josh crept to the face-down figure, heedless of Arjay's warnings, and rolled it on to its side. The fur of the gorilla costume was matted and sticky with blood.

Martin stared at him, one eye completely red, both roving over his face in confusion. He was trying to say something. Josh leaned closer.

'… just … a … joke …' he whispered. Blood bubbled from his mouth, he shuddered once, and then his eyes weren't staring at anything at all.

Josh did throw up then.

The three boys sat far apart from each other, staring in numb horror at the body. None of them had been brave enough to go near it, even though Arjay had said they should cover the face at least, so the glazed marble of Martin's eye stared back at them accusingly across the cold firepit. Arjay and Rizz were bundled up in their bedding again, but Josh wore only the t-shirt and jogging trousers that he'd slept in. He didn't mind the cold; it helped to clear his head so he could work out what needed to be done. His room at Werrington had been cold most of the time because of funding cuts; they only turned the central heating on when inspections were due.

No way was he going back there.

'We need to call an ambulance,' Rizz said.

'What for?' replied Arjay. 'Paramedic's going to fix that?'

'Then we need to call the police!'

'Fuck that!'

'Yeah, fuck that,' Josh agreed. 'We need to hide him. We can bury him – we've got the shit trowel. And these.' He held up the minibus keys that he'd taken from Martin's tent. 'We drive back to town and torch the minibus. If we cover for each other there's no way the police can prove anything.'

Arjay stared at him. 'You want to bury a full-sized human

being with a fucking *trowel*? Are you actually crazy?' He shook his head and uttered a hollow laugh. 'Oh Josh, bruv, you really did a number on him, didn't you?'

'It was an accident!' Josh protested. 'I was trying to help! I thought Rizz was being attacked by ... by ...'

'Bosky Tom?' Arjay scoffed. 'That's some defence. Sorry, your honour, I thought my friend was being attacked by fucking Bigfoot. You don't *accidentally* merk someone with a fucking axe to the skull! You going to tell the feds he, what, *fell backwards* onto the fucking thing? Fuck bruv, you couldn't just jook him with a sharpened toothbrush handle could you? Oh no, not mister I-done-six-months-in-juvie-how-hard-am-I.'

'Why are you talking like some kind of roadman all of a sudden? Your dad's a doctor.'

'Least I fucking got one!'

Josh stood up and walked over to him. To his credit, Arjay didn't back down. In fact he stood up, letting the sleeping bag fall away to reveal the frying pan that he raised in one fist. It was heavy, made of black cast iron and large enough to fry breakfasts for several people.

'Don't even fucking think about it,' Arjay growled, but beneath the bravado Josh could see that he was scared.

He laughed. 'What are you going to do – sauté me to death in self-defence?'

Rizz jumped up too. 'Guys, allow it! Arjay, what are you doing, man? Calm down! Of course it was an accident. We're all in bits.'

Arjay's mouth curled. 'Yeah, look how fucking upset Josh is about it,' he sneered with heavy sarcasm. 'About as upset as he was over stabbing that kid. 'Cept now we're all in the shit with him, fucking psycho.'

It was ridiculously easy for Josh to get the frying pan; he didn't know what Arjay was expecting him to do – hit or tackle him or something – not to simply reach out and take it. Arjay stared at his empty hand with comical surprise, then raised both of his hands in surrender.

'Wait –' he said, but the cold thing with teeth and claws in

Josh's mind that had capered at the smell of blood didn't want to wait. It swung the frying pan into Arjay's face. There was a muffled scream and a crunch as Arjay's nose broke, then he tripped over his own bedding and fell backwards.

'Guys!' yelled Rizz uselessly.

Josh stood over Arjay as he writhed, groaning. 'I can just as easily bury two if it comes to that,' he said.

Arjay roared, sat up and grabbed Josh around the knees, then twisted. Josh fell too, and Arjay was on him instantly, punching. Blood poured from his nose and sprayed into Josh's face as he accompanied each punch with a congested grunt of 'Fucking psycho!' His fist mashed Josh's lip against his teeth and it split, but it was a lucky hit. Arjay was just flailing wildly. You could get into a lot of fights during a six month stretch in a Youth Offender's Institution, and Josh knew how to end this quickly. He drove his knee up hard between Arjay's legs. The other boy fell away from him, clutching his crotch and retching.

Josh hunted around for the frying pan, found it, and raised it high.

'Josh, no!' Rizz shouted. 'You've won, okay? Look at him!'

Josh looked at Arjay, and saw someone who, despite the beating, would fuck him up at the first possible opportunity unless the lesson was made very, very clear. He brought the heavy pan down – not as hard as he could, but hard enough. Then he did it again, just to be sure.

Arjay stopped squirming and retching. He might even have stopped breathing, but there was nothing Josh could do about that now.

Then he heard the minibus door slam.

He looked for the keys. They had dropped to the ground when Arjay had tackled him but now they were gone.

The engine started up.

'Shit!'

Josh ran.

Rizz was hunched over the steering wheel in the dashboard glow, trying to figure out the controls. Josh tugged at the door, but it was locked, along with the two at the back, the big sliding door down the side, and the front passenger side. He ran around the front to the driver's side and banged on the glass. Rizz flinched but the window didn't break.

'Rizz, come on man! Think about this! The feds'll do you for accessory to murder!' He tried not to sound too much like he was pleading.

Rizz ignored him. The headlights came on and the engine roared louder as he found the accelerator.

'Rizz, don't make me smash that window and drag you out of there!' He thumped on the glass, panicking now. Rizz – on his own and outside – could easily be coerced into helping him hide the evidence of his crime. Rizz weeping and confessing all to the police, on the other hand, was a nightmare waiting to happen.

Sharpened toothbrushes, for fucksake. None of them had the first clue what it had been like. There were a lot worse things that could happen to you in a YOI than just getting into fights.

'RIZZ!' he bellowed, and punched the glass. Still it didn't break.

The minibus lurched forward, stalled, and started up again. Josh was hammering on the glass now, yelling and pleading for Rizz to stop, but the minibus lurched away again and this time it kept going. He gave chase but it easily outpaced him, out of the woods and slaloming down the farm track. At the bottom of the hill it crunched into one of the gate posts and stalled again. The door opened and Rizz leapt out, a spidery silhouette running off along the road, but by then he had so much of a head start that Josh wasn't sure he could catch him.

He looked back at the tree line, trunks just paler shadows in the night.

From somewhere in his memory – a fragment from some long-lost English lesson – words came to him unbidden:

The woods are lovely, dark and deep, but I have promises to keep, and many miles to go before I sleep.

He'd do it on his own, then, just like he'd had to do

everything else since he was a kid.

He turned back and retreated beneath their shelter.

He decided against using his head-torch as his eyes had become accustomed to the dark and he had a decent spatial memory – at least, according to the psychologist who had assessed him. Silver linings and all that. The first thing to do was check what state Arjay was in, but when Josh got back to the campsite he stopped in surprise.

Arjay was gone.

Josh whirled around, expecting an attack from behind.

Nothing there. Just the angular shadows of lean-tos and a tent.

'Arjay?' he ventured. 'You out there, man?' He shouldn't have been; he'd been clobbered pretty hard. Josh listened, opening his senses to the night-shrouded woodland. There was no sign of a torch, which meant that wherever Arjay was he'd be blundering around making a racket, but Josh heard nothing except the whisper of branches. Wherever Arjay had got to, he was either hiding or had passed out again. Either way he wasn't a threat for now. Josh could look for him when it was lighter, if there was time. He pictured Rizz stumbling into a farmhouse, blubbering and shouting his mouth off, a phone call to the feds, and then cars, helicopters, maybe even dogs. How much time did he have? Hopefully enough to get rid of as much evidence as he could, starting with Martin's body.

Josh froze in horror.

The corpse was gone too.

The hatchet was still there though, clotted with gore.

'No ...' he whispered.

It was impossible. Martin had been absolutely, definitely dead. Arjay had been too fucked up to drag it away, and in any case, why? Maybe he was concussed and thought somehow the man could still be alive? Josh shook himself. It didn't matter why, it only mattered *where*. Arjay was in no fit state to have dragged him very far.

He used the head-torch this time, searching the immediate area around their campsite with increasing frustration as he found nothing, not even any drag marks, which was really weird. Even on a good day, without having taken a cast-iron frying pan to the face, no way was Arjay strong enough to carry a body any distance.

'What the fuck is this?' he yelled, spinning around. 'Arjay what the fuck are you playing at?' The jerky light of his head-torch threw shadows from the tree trunks that swept and lurched like long fingers reaching out for him or figures darting into hiding, so he turned it off. Absolute blackness flooded into their place.

Lovely, dark and deep.

And then it occurred to him.

He has a taste for human flesh.

'Is … is there somebody out there?' he called. The woods swallowed his voice and returned not even echoes, only whispers.

He relit the fire – it didn't matter that a police helicopter's IR camera would pick up the heat since Rizz would probably lead them straight to the campsite anyway. No point trying to dismantle the shelters or hide the ashes; it would all be found sooner rather than later, and wouldn't stop them hunting him. Besides, there was something about the flickering circle of firelight that felt primal and protective, and Josh wasn't planning to stick around for very long.

He sat staring into it for a while, and when he roused himself was surprised to find that already the thin light of dawn was beginning to outline the trunks of trees and their canopies against the sky.

'Can't afford to zone out like that, dickhead,' he told himself. 'Get moving.'

He quickly packed a rucksack with whatever he could find that might be useful: a sleeping bag, a bottle of water, the hatchet, some of the snacks that were lying around. All the actual food, along with the strongbox of bush knives, was in the minibus, and he didn't want to risk going all the way back out there to salvage it. For all he knew the road was already crawling with feds.

When he thought he had everything, he stamped out the fire and set off – uphill, towards the big granite outcrop he'd seen yesterday and the caves where, it was said, Bosky Tom had his lair.

As he climbed, he became increasingly convinced that someone or something was following him. He tried to tell himself that it was just the after-effects of shock, but that cold thing in the bottom of his mind knew better. There was nothing so obvious as the cracking of a twig or the sway of a branch, but the indefinable sense of a presence kept pace with him – sometimes behind, sometimes to one side or the other. Strangely, he didn't feel threatened by it. Rather, it seemed like he was being escorted – guarded, even.

It disappeared when he came out of the trees on top of the hill and the world spread itself out around him, wreathed in dawn mist. From the road below it had looked like a single outcrop, but he saw now that it was instead a tumbled landscape of granite boulders. They piled against each other, some as large as houses, the gaps between them presenting multiple openings that weren't exactly caves but were definitely wide enough to crawl into and hide. Which was exactly what he did.

The space was barely high enough for him to crouch, formed by the haphazard jumble of several boulders, and he found that, just like with the old tree, someone had been here before him – but much longer ago. Old bones, cracked and splintered, littered the floor, and every inch of the interior was carved with whorls and spirals, dots and circles and wavy lines. He traced them with his fingers, feeling their smoothness. It reassured him that others had used this place as a refuge once upon a time, and the lack of anything like cigarette butts or chocolate wrappers told him that maybe modern people had forgotten about it.

Maybe here he could be forgotten too.

He swept aside the old bones, unrolled his sleeping bag and lay down, looking up at the carvings, wondering what ancient hands had worked them, and whether they were anything like his. It seemed impossible that he could rest, but his body knew its business after the shocks of the night and he was asleep in moments.

The distant barking of dogs awoke him.

He went to check the time, but he had no watch and his phone was long gone. He could have been asleep for moments, hours, days, or even years, like Rip van Winkle awakening as an old man with a long white beard. He stretched his cramped limbs and sat up, wondering how far away the police were. If they had a helicopter as well as dogs he stood no chance. Then he froze mid-yawn.

There was something white and curved at the entrance of the cave – something that hadn't been there before. At first he thought it was another bone.

Then he saw that it was the underside of a plastic gorilla mask.

He crept closer.

The elastic string had been carefully re-tied.

'If you think this is funny, Arjay, it fucking isn't!' he yelled.

Someone moved past the cave mouth; he saw their shadow against the daylight filtering through the cracks between the boulders, and heard their footsteps.

Josh snarled, snatched up the hatchet and ducked outside to confront whoever was trying to fuck with his head.

The hilltop was deserted. Below the encircling woodland (*dark and deep*), the morning mist had burnt off and the countryside was a patchwork of fields and hedgerows. There were many more boulders up here, and so most likely a lot more places to hide.

'*Who are you?*' he screamed. '*What the fuck do you want with me?*'

As if in response came the barking of dogs again, nearer, and the burring of a helicopter.

Before Josh could react, a single policeman stepped out from the trees little more than a hundred yards away. For a second they gaped at each other, then the fed's head dipped to his shoulder radio. The cold thing took over completely then and Josh's head swam as he stepped outside of himself and watched his body throw itself at the man, howling with feral abandon and striking with the hatchet in a blood-soaked frenzy. When he returned to himself he was standing over the policeman's body, panting, his arms aching and dripping red to the elbows.

The sound of dogs grew louder still. Into the sky on the other side of the hill rose the gleaming wasp-shape of a police helicopter. There was no point trying to hide now. Josh ran back to the cave, picked up the gorilla mask and put it on. Then he took off his clothes and painted his body in the dots and spirals all around him, using the blood of his enemy. If there really was anything out there in the woods watching him, it would know him for one of its own.

People would find out what it meant to fuck with Bosky Tom.

Moments later more men came out of the woods – four armed response officers in dark body armour and helmets, carrying rifles. An amplified voice from the sky squawked: 'Drop your weapon and lie face down on the ground, NOW!'

He raised his bloody hatchet to the sky with a roar of defiance and ran down the hill towards them.

BEHEMOTH

While the heavyweight title 'Most Terrifying Monster in History' must surely go to Typhon, the offspring and personal weapon of Kronos, Chief of the Titans, and a beast of such elemental size and ferocity that it took Zeus himself, King of Mount Olympus, to destroy it, there are several others in the upper echelons of mythical monstrousness who, if for no other reason than sheer gargantuan size, would certainly rival him for that crown. Three of these in particular were said to be so immensely powerful that they too would require an immortal – in this case God himself – to defeat them.

I'm referring to the three primordial chaos monsters of the Bible*: Leviathan, lord of the sea, Ziz, lord of the air, and Behemoth, lord of the land, and yet, if we take Behemoth as an example of this invincible trio, it can be seen that there is much misunderstanding about who and what he is, and what role he plays in the Cosmos, as planned for by the Creator.*

To begin with, most everyday folk are familiar with the name 'Behemoth', even if they've never studied the Old Testament*, which is a sure sign of the huge impression he made in those long-ago centuries. In his simplest form, they perceive him to be a vast and ferocious monster, maybe a dragon or perhaps something more mammalian, colossal and armour-plated, but with hooves instead of claws and tusks instead of horns, but either way someone who will cause the ground to shake when he approaches, who will rend the heavens when he roars, and who is invulnerable to all earthly weapons.*

This is pretty much how Behemoth is described in the Book of Job *(which, in fact, is the only appearance he makes in the whole of the Christian* Bible*, though he also is referred to in other texts that were composed later). However, at the same time, it's also possible that the passages mentioning Behemoth in* Job *have been misinterpreted, and that this horrific monster was actually so commonplace an animal that most folk, if they encountered him* today, would consider him an everyday sight.

In the Old Testament, God speaks to Job, describing Behemoth, a monster that he himself has created, emphasising its divine nature and indestructibility. But he also describes it as living off grass like an ox (which suddenly makes it seem a little less terrifying) and preferring to lie down amid the reeds and lily-pads of the river shallows. Could it be that the Behemoth God was talking about was actually a hippopotamus or an elephant? Such animals were widely known in the Ancient World. Is it possible that Behemoth, this most monumental of creatures, so indescribably immense that his shadow would blot out the sun, might in today's world more likely be seen in a zoo?

Academic assessment of the Book of Job, along with those appearances he makes in other ancient manuscripts would suggest not. According to the Book of Enoch, an apocalyptic Hebrew text, Behemoth, who is never recorded as having attacked any man or woman, is said to have lived far from human habitation in the desert of Duidain, to the east of the Garden of Eden, a wilderness region unknown in the modern world. The overall inference of this is that while God holds him at bay, mankind is safe, but if God were to let him off his leash, allow him to rampage under his own will, it would be the end of everything.

A metaphorical reading of the Behemoth story is no less unnerving, as it implies that the monster's sheer invincibility is a perfect illustration of God's power and the utter futility of challenging Him. Something of a frightening lesson considering that it came from the Judeo-Christian God, whose worshippers had always regarded him as an all-forgiving father.

Behemoth, or so the story tells, was born at the dawn of time and will only expire at the end of it. Jewish apocalyptic literature of the 1st Century asserts that as the end times approach, amid all the rest of the chaos, Leviathan, the sea monster will emerge from a boiling ocean intent upon destruction. At the same time, Behemoth will also be released and will charge across the land, seeking prey, and yet the daemonic duo will engage each other in battle rather than humanity. It will be an epic struggle, fought out amid ongoing storms and devastation, with neither side backing down until both are torn to pieces, though they will only expire when God comes down from his *high place and destroys the pair of them, using their hides to provide shelter for his surviving children, and their meat as food.*

The two unimaginable monsters will then be shown as having existed to serve mankind rather than terrorise him. And yet when it comes to Behemoth there is an interesting addendum, which has perhaps more sinister connotations.

Throughout Christian culture, as Behemoth was held to be a real entity, there was also a firm belief in devils and demons. But it still might have been a surprise to many in 1818 to learn that Behemoth, far from being a flesh and blood device created by God for the benefit of mankind, was in fact a denizen of the infernal pit... no less than Satan's Watchman.

This information was first offered in Dictionnaire Infernal, *a treatise on demons from the occultist, Jacques Collin de Plancy, the gigantic adversary in the* Book of Job *now listed among the apostate angels. Instead of shaping a monstrosity out of the Earth and letting it loose in the wild lands east of Eden, did God simply lift one of his former but now cursed followers from the darkness of the Underworld?*

Seeing as there is no evidence of any of this and it's all a matter of faith anyway, it's impossible to provide an answer. De Plancy was regarded by many of his contemporaries as eccentric and even possibly mad, but his book made an impact, because this is the way Behemoth is often portrayed these days, certainly by writers and movie makers. It seems that the original chaos monster of the Bible *has now become a permanent member of those legions of fallen deities trapped in Hell. His more instructive, less damaging incarnation has ebbed away in wisps of crimson smoke.*

KRAMPUS
Paul Finch

Grandpa Ludwig didn't usually participate on Christmas Day when we all gathered around the fire after dinner and urged the adults to tell ghost stories. Part of the time it was because he was asleep, but also, I think, it was because he didn't enjoy such things. We all knew he'd had a difficult time as a child. It's not everyone who can boast that his father was condemned in absentia to die by the guillotine, even if he did live to tell the tale, but Grandpa Ludwig was of such an age by this time – seventy-five at least – that he surely had no real memories of those dark and deadly days. In addition, his father had been a great storyteller, an author of children's fiction as famous in Germany at one time as Enid Blyton was in England, so it hardly seemed possible that Grandpa Ludwig had not inherited at least a smidgen of that talent.

As such, one year, when it was plain that Grandpa Ludwig was wide awake after dinner, laughing uproariously with the other adults, mince pie in hand, paper crown perched at a jaunty angle on his balding pate, we urged him to start off the annual ghost story game by telling us one of his own. Grandpa was very thoughtful for a moment or two. He took a sip of port wine, before nodding gravely and saying that, yes, it was time he told us all his ghost story.

His choice of phrase quite surprised me. The notion that, all along, he'd possessed a ghost story that was exclusively his own, and that for so many years he'd been withholding it – who knew for what reason? – was an eerie and mysterious concept.

I remember how we youngsters huddled together on the carpet in front of the fire, legs crossed, and how my mum turned the lights down, as she always did on this occasion, leaving only the faint glow of the candles on the Christmas cake and the orange embers in the hearth to reflect our rapt attention. Grandpa Ludwig took off his spectacles, polished them with his handkerchief, and then pinched the bridge of his nose, a sure sign I would later learn that the event he was about to recount came from memory, not imagination.

This is what he told us ...

Most of you will know that my father and his brother, Klaus, were not identical twins, but that they *were* twins and as children they were so alike that many people could not tell them apart. Of course, in terms of temperament and personality, they could not have been more different.

My own recollections of Uncle Klaus are that he was more physically imposing than my father; he was tall and athletically built, with shining blond hair and piercing blue eyes. A more idealised Aryan male there could not have been, though I didn't understand that philosophy at the time. Nor did I really notice how relations between my father and his brother, while not exactly hostile, were never better than cool. At least, that was always the case during my lifetime. Of course, I knew nothing about my father's refusal to join the Hitler Youth in 1927, which had meant that my family – Uncle Klaus's family, more to the point – was regarded with suspicion for a brief time.

The one thing about Uncle Klaus I didn't like was the scar on his left cheek. It was not a particularly awful one, little more than a horizontal white line, but even to my childhood eyes, it gave him a colder, crueller aspect. Apparently it had been caused when he'd run into a barbed wire fence while playing outdoors as a toddler, but he was always rather proud of it, or so my father would later say, telling anyone who asked that it was a duelling scar, as if he was the scion of a Prussian aristocrat rather than the son of a small-town Bavarian solicitor.

The last time I ever saw Uncle Klaus was in 1939, and though I was still very young, I had some vague notion that Germany was on the eve of war. He was wearing a uniform when he came to see us. Many times in the past he'd been in uniform – uniforms were quite commonplace in those days – but this one was jet black and it sported the SS Sig Runes on its collar and the *Totenkopf*, or Death's Head, as they would call it here in England, on its armband. I don't think Uncle Klaus had come with the express intention of warning my father that he was in imminent danger, but I was sent to my room while the adults discussed matters, and so fierce was the resulting argument that I heard it through the floorboards. Snatches of that dispute still remain in my memory.

'Will you continue writing fairy stories while the world burns, Eric?' my uncle demanded to know.

'What does it matter if I do?' my father replied.

'It matters if they call you "traitor" for it.'

'Never once have I written or spoken a word of treason.'

'Nor have you written against it. Is it not the case that, several times now, you have been invited to supply poems, ballads and books in honour of our cause, and have always refused? We stand on the brink of a great destiny, and yet you – a man of widespread influence – seem determined to disapprove of it.'

'Klaus, I am not a political writer.'

'Eric, not everyone agrees with that ...'

Before Uncle Klaus finally left, I came to the top of the stairs in tears. I might have been a child, but I was not a fool; I knew the sound of irreparable damage when I heard it. He glanced up as he pulled his hat down over his brow and climbed into his long leather coat; his expression was one of deep regret, but also bitter anger and betrayal. He spoke to me, but I was in too anguished a state at the time to make sense of his words.

We left our home the very next day, not just our house, but Germany itself. I have almost no memory of that rushed dawn departure as I apparently slept through most of it.

Grandpa Ludwig sipped his port.

The mood had turned rapidly and unexpectedly sombre. His

family's narrow escape from Nazi Germany had never been the easiest topic of conversation. His writer father, though he'd adopted England as his new abode, had been haunted to the end of his days by his inability to reconcile himself with a homeland whose history and culture he had loved but which had been subverted to such a ghastly degree that he no longer knew it when he left. Grandpa Ludwig, of course, had barely experienced Germany. He now had only the faintest discernible accent, and though his early days were undoubtedly difficult – a boy named Weidmann living in post-war Britain! – he soon adapted to his new home and in time became as English as Winston Churchill.

Perhaps this was why, after another contemplative sip or two, he was able to continue with his narrative. Though his mood was no lighter. Far from it …

We must move forward now, to the Christmas Eve of 1948.

To an eleven-year-old those pre-war days already seemed a receding memory, but the good times had not yet returned. Britain was a land of food rationing, bombed cities and bereaved families. Ironically, though my family were immigrants, our position was better than some. My father had learned to speak English, but never to a standard where he might write in that tongue, at least not with the same eloquence he'd shown when writing in German. However, he was able to teach, so we had regular money and a reasonably comfortable home in the suburbs. My two best friends at the time were Billy Flynn and Peter Osgood, boys from the same road in which I lived and fellow pupils at the Catholic school I attended. Both their fathers had fought in the war, and survived – one had even been present at the relief of Belsen – so to them any German who'd annoyed the Nazis to the point where they'd driven him into exile was someone to be admired. Hence, they never treated me like an outsider.

Hard though youngsters may find it to believe now, on the Christmas Eve in question we were required to attend school as if it were any normal day. We had a two-week holiday, but it only commenced the following morning on Christmas Day. For all that, our teachers were kind enough to release us at lunchtime, so Billy, Peter and I took the opportunity to divert through the town centre on our way home. There was a raw, wintry feel that afternoon. The snow that had fallen the previous week had thawed a little, but had later frozen again, and great, dirty mounds of it were now piled at the end of each pavement. The gutters and bus shelters sparkled with icicles; white frost covered every branch and blade of grass. We were well wrapped in our coats and scarves; we had our balaclavas and our woollen mittens. Even so, there is only so much one can do to fend off that depth of cold, but we were determined to endure it because a great treat awaited us.

The English version of our German Saint Nikolaus is of course Father Christmas. They share much in common. Both are fat, jolly men with white curls and white beards. They wear warm winter robes and dispense presents to good children. However, there are some differences. In Germany, Saint Nikolaus would visit homes on the eve of December 6, whereas in England, Father Christmas would visit on Christmas Eve itself. While Saint Nikolaus bore ecclesial accoutrements – for instance, he wore a mitre and carried a crosier – the English Father Christmas had a druidic air; there was something in his makeup of the old spirit of winter, which, looking on it as an adult, seems almost pagan to me. But even so, in England, as in Germany, children were taught that this benign figure was a saint, beloved of Christ, so his magical gifts were to be welcomed and adored. As a small side-matter … in Germany, St Nikolaus had a shadowy other-self, little known and an entirely dissimilar personality. But more about him later.

The purpose of our diversion into the centre of town that Christmas Eve afternoon was concerned neither with Saint Nikolaus nor Father Christmas, but in fact with Santa Claus, their American counterpart, newly introduced to the United Kingdom in the aftermath of the war. Santa Claus, though in many ways indistinguishable from his European brethren, had one very unique attribute: he could actually be spoken to. He would sit children on his knee, and they could request their presents face-to-face. I'm talking of course about the famous department store Santa Claus, who had been a fixture in American cities since the turn of the century, and now at last had come to Britain.

The department store in question was *Halley & Meredith's*, whose palatial residence was in the very centre of our town, in a space, if I recall correctly, which is now occupied by a wine bar, a Poundstretcher and a kebab shop. At the time we referred to *Halley & Meredith's* as 'posh', though in truth it would probably have seemed fairly second rate compared to Harrods in London or Kendals in Manchester. But it occupied a great baroque building, and its frontal canopy was hung with international flags. It even had its own taxi rank outside, the implication being that the sort of people who shopped at *Halley & Meredith's* could easily afford to take cabs rather than having to get the bus. One entered the premises through revolving doors, assuming that the concierge on duty – a dapper chap with a military air, wearing a shell grey overcoat with gold braid at its shoulders – would permit you access. Under normal circumstances it seemed highly possible that three schoolboys lacking the governance of their parents would be refused, but this was Christmas Eve, and everyone was excited and in a good mood, and in any case, Santa Claus was waiting inside.

Or was it Father Christmas or Saint Nikolaus? Or someone else?

Halley & Meredith's seemed vast and crowded that day; we trekked past *Scarves, Gloves And Hats*, past *Cosmetics*, past *Haberdashery*, past *Men's Tailoring*, past *Ladies' Shoes*, all locations which, when I'd been present with my mother, had signified hours of tedium. But now, to see them decked with tinsel and boughs of evergreen was almost too much for an eleven-year-old to take – our sense of thrill rose inexorably, and of course we still had the 'Christmas Grotto' at the end of it all. We finally found this hallowed place down at the basement level, a venue normally reserved for tools and gardening equipment, though now it had become a magical kingdom.

In hindsight, it had probably been done quite cheaply, but we walked along a side-aisle which we no longer recognised, passing under arches made of pine branches and hung with multi-coloured Chinese lanterns. Streamers and paper chains were looped across the ceiling. Christmas trees stood on each counter, decked with ornaments and fairy lights. Cotton wool had been laid over racks of goods to imitate snow. In the drab, grey Britain of those immediate post-war years, it was a delightful thing to behold. Even the shop assistants, those straight-backed ladies who always teetered around *Halley & Meredith's* in tight skirts and tall heels, looking beautiful but severe, seemed so much more human in green conical 'elf' hats, and also because they were smiling and chattering brightly.

Santa Claus himself was quite remarkable. A knee-high white picket fence woven with holly had closed off a small area, and he was in the middle of it, seated on a throne-like chair. He wore the traditional crimson robe trimmed with white fur, and it flowed out around him on all sides; it was far too large to be practical – one could never have walked around in such a garment. Beneath it, he wore a bottle-green waistcoat, crimson pantaloons and black boots, again trimmed with white fur. Of course, he had a capacious belly and a thick white beard, which fell almost to his belt-buckle. To complete the picture, there were oodles of gift-wrapped presents stacked behind him, as if he was ready right now to load his sleigh and depart on his goodly mission.

There was a hubbub of excitement from the queueing youngsters, most of whom were there with their mothers and grandmothers, or both. It may seem strange now, three eleven-year-olds waiting to see Santa Claus in a department store, but we weren't the eldest there. Other older children were also present, patiently waiting their turn, eyes fixed with wonder on the resplendent figure. World War Two, with its prolonged loss of life, property and innocence and then the drudgery and austerity that had followed, was entirely responsible for this. In some ways we were older than our age back then, but in others we were much younger.

Of course, when Santa's hearty laughter finally told us our turn had come, we older children didn't actually sit on the big man's knee. We advanced through the gate in the wicket fence and stood there politely, hands behind our backs, as he addressed us.

'And what do we have here?' he said, his blue eyes twinkling. In keeping with the myth that he hailed from some frozen Tyrolean land, he spoke with a central European accent. 'Three young men, in whose steady hands the future of the world must reside.'

Peter, always the boldest among us, answered first when we were asked what we were hoping to obtain at Christmas.

'I would like a new bicycle, sir,' he said soberly, as if he knew that he really was asking for quite a lot and that such an extravagant gift might be beyond even Santa Claus's ability to bestow.

'A new bicycle, hmmm,' our host rumbled. 'We'll have to see about that, but who knows? Anything is possible.' He switched his attention to Billy. 'And for you, young sir?'

'I would like a toy gun and holster, sir,' Billy said. 'Like you see on the cowboy films. Maybe a cowboy hat as well?'

'Hmmm ... well, a hat and a gun. Those are quite the sort of items a young man should possess, though you won't be meeting many Red Indians here in Lancashire, I shouldn't think.'

'No, sir,' Billy said in a tone which suggested he'd given this matter weighty consideration but was still set on his course.

'Hmmm ... well, this is all to the good, gentlemen. Such manly gifts will prepare you for the trials of adulthood.'

This conversation might have seemed a little more protracted than most of those Santa Claus had engaged in up until now, and yet he still didn't turn to me - and frankly I wasn't concerned in the least. Because from the moment I'd set eyes upon him up close, I was struck with the kind of horror that even back in the war-ravaged 1940s most people would experience only once in a lifetime.

It was Uncle Klaus.

That is all I can say.

Feel free not to believe me, but I swear to you it is the absolute truth.

He'd changed enormously. Beneath that thick, white beard and the rosy cheeks – the former of which was clearly real, the latter fake – he was as gaunt as a leper: his skin had a yellowish tinge; his eyes, which were neither as blue nor as twinkly as I'd first thought, were sunken in skullish cavities; his lips were thin and covered with cracks and sores. But there was no mistaking that horizontal scar on his left cheek, even though many other scars had appeared since. And now at last he turned to me, and he pointed with a long, bony finger, the nail at the end of which was sharp and twisting.

'And for you, Ludwig?' he said, though it wasn't really a question. 'Krampus ... ja?'

'I ... I just want to go home,' I stuttered.

'Nein!' he said harshly, wagging that terrible finger in admonition and fixing me with a stare so malevolent that it was all I could do not to faint. *'Krampus!'*

The next thing I knew, we were being ushered away down another aisle by one of the elf-ladies, and Peter and Billy were gossiping excitedly about whether or not they had increased their chances of receiving their much sought-for presents. In their eyes at least, nothing unusual had happened, and when I glanced back over my shoulder at the diminishing form of Santa Claus in his golden grotto, a little girl was positioned on his knee, shivering with delight as he cuddled her and crooned a carol, and the queue of other children awaiting their own turn had extended until it snaked down the entire length of the department store's basement.

When we emerged outside, it was turning dark and tiny spots of snow were spiralling down. There were many more people about, attending to their last-minute shopping, and the roads were a chaos of vans, wagons and cars. My two friends were still in a state of exhilaration as we commenced the long walk home, so it was difficult broaching the subject of whether or not they'd thought there was something strange about the man masquerading as Santa Claus in *Halley & Meredith's*. Clearly, neither had detected anything. Peter did acknowledge that I'd seemed a little tongue-tied when Santa Claus had spoken to me, though he hadn't noticed the man address me by my own name, and certainly recalled nothing about his use of the term 'Krampus'.

Not that they would have known what it meant, anyway. Not that anyone in this country would have known. You see, Krampus was the name given to that shadowy other-self of Saint Nikolaus, the one I referred to earlier. Whereas in English-speaking lands, Father Christmas and Santa Claus have always preferred to ignore naughty children, in Germanic countries Krampus actively punishes them. I had seen illustrations of him in children's books written by my father, and he is truly grotesque; a monster, a deformed devil with horns, hooves and a humped back. The sack he carries is not intended for the provision of gifts, but to abduct those misbehaving youths he encounters on his travels, and to carry them back to his lair where all manner of torments will be inflicted on them. You look shocked. Don't be. In the days of my youth, children were to be seen and not heard. Parents, while loving, were stern. There was a price to pay for transgression. Bad behaviour was never tolerated.

Even now, it pains me to recollect that journey home from the shops. I was so distressed by what had happened that I contributed almost nothing to my friends' joyous jabber. All of a sudden, Christmas – the culmination of so many weeks' eager anticipation, the date we had ached for since the onset of winter – meant nothing to me. The ruddy glow of Yule candles in passing windows, the falling snow – now a thickening, shimmering cascade – should have rendered a perfect setting. But my thoughts were in turmoil. More than once I glanced over my shoulder, especially after we left the town centre and entered the residential districts, where doors were closed, curtains drawn and fellow pedestrians little more than occasional muffled shadows. Though I never saw anything amiss, I was increasingly certain that someone was keeping pace with us just beyond the range of our vision.

At last the moment came when we were to go our different ways. We stopped beneath a corner streetlamp, Peter and Billy pumping my hand, clapping my shoulder, wishing me all the best for the season.

'A little touch of Germany for you tonight, Ludwig,' Peter said.

'What do you mean?' I demanded, even more unnerved.

'This!' he said, smiling, indicating the snow. 'We get this now and then at Christmas, but in Germany you get it every year, or so I'm told.'

'Not every year,' I replied, still shaken.

'Happy Christmas anyway, Ludwig!' they shouted as they walked away, leaving me alone in the lamplight, flakes swirling past. I looked again over my shoulder.

The street we had just walked along was lined down either side with terraced houses; a perfectly normal street in our part of the world, yet now an increasingly stiff breeze was whipping the snow in eddies; on some occasions I could see as far along it as the coal wagon parked at its distant end, on others no more than thirty yards. I remained there for several minutes, convinced there'd be something to fix on if only I could gaze into the murk hard enough. Intermittently down that street, curtains were only half-drawn, thus allowing rays of soft, warm lamplight to penetrate outward. Without warning, someone passed one of these. I blinked – and they'd gone again, hidden by renewed swirls of flakes. But it was someone headed in my direction. Someone wearing red.

It could have been any ordinary person walking home; there was absolutely no need to assume the worst. But briefly I was rooted in place. Only slowly, with great difficulty, was I able to retreat to the edge of the pavement, where again I waited. I don't know why; it makes no sense now – it was as if I had some inner urgent need to *know* I was in danger rather than simply fear it. But then something happened that leant genuine panic to my heels. I spied the figure again, much closer this time

– maybe forty yards away – crossing the street to the side on which I was waiting. It was only a silhouette, half-glimpsed as it passed through another shaft of flake-speckled lamplight, but it was bent forward in ungainly fashion, its back humped, its heavy robes trailing behind it.

There was no further debate in my mind. I spun around and raced blindly along the next street, and along the one after that, regardless of the treacherous footing. I must have covered half the distance home before I stopped to get my breath. I had seen no-one else that whole way, but likewise no-one was in sight behind me either, and now, the flakes having relented a little, I was able to see a good distance in every direction – and spied nothing but snow-covered road junctions, the red-brick gable walls of houses, the weak palls of light cast by streetlamps. Nothing advanced through them, so I felt a little better, though I had yet to cross Dalewood Brow. That place no longer exists today – a supermarket and offices have been built there instead, but in my childhood it consisted of several hundred yards of derelict colliery land, hummocky and deeply overgrown; a wonderful place for children to play in summer, but in wintry darkness a test of anyone's nerve. Especially on this occasion.

I didn't need to go over the Brow. If I turned left at this point, I could just as easily walk around it, making my way home via lamp-lit streets, passing more houses, more cars. Yet that would take much longer – maybe add half an hour to my journey, and all at once I wanted desperately to be home, if for no other reason than my fingers were frozen and my feet turning numb. So, I pushed open the creaky gate in the wrought iron fence that ran along the Brow's edge, and set off hurriedly up its winding, cindery path. Because the Brow was covered with snow, much more of it was visible to me than I'd expected, and somehow that was comforting. All the way I glanced nervously around, able to see a vast expanse of white, broken only by the occasional black skeletons of trees, or protruding twists of frosty underbrush.

I quickly lost sight of the wrought iron fence, but my

confidence was growing that I would soon be home. I was approaching the Hump, as we knew it; a great slagheap with a foot-tunnel driven through it. Beyond that I needed only to cross the canal bridge and ascend a footpath through thickets to the edge of the housing estate on which I lived. That was when I heard the distant *creak* of the gate.

Did I actually hear it? Was it possible to hear anything in that situation? The gate was dozens and dozens of yards behind me. My ears were muffled by the balaclava. Even if I had heard it, might it not have been shifted by a gust of wind? I couldn't see far enough back in this twilit snowy realm to be sure one way or the other, but then I heard something else – the steady *crunch* of approaching feet.

I didn't wait to hear more. I ran on up the remainder of the path and through the foot-tunnel. This in itself – a straight low corridor of damp brick, completely unlit, running for at least fifty yards – would be a nightmare in the modern age, but notions of 'stranger-danger' were almost unheard of in that long-ago era. I was nearly home; this foot-tunnel was part of my normal world; I had no fear of it – until this point. Because though I got through to the other side without hindrance, I stopped again, for no good reason I can think of now, and peered back, and to my utmost shock I beheld a figure entering the tunnel from the other side. Again it was nothing more than a silhouette framed on the moon-lit snow, but, as before, it was hunched forward – so much so that I couldn't see its head, and it moved with a heavy, shambling gait; immense, unwieldy robes dragged behind it. The clomping of its footfalls on the stony ground echoed along the passage towards me; those sounds were like no impacts of shoes or boots that I'd ever heard.

I simply fled. Raw terror drove me across the canal bridge at reckless speed – it had no safety barriers and was shod with ice, yet I careered over it like a madman. The path beyond led uphill through tangled, snow-clad thickets. There were any number of places where an assailant might lie in wait and leap out, but I bypassed them all without a glance. Even when I left the Brow and ran along the next street to my own, I was pursued by inexorable fear, which only intensified as I rounded the corner onto the final straight. I had a nagging certainty that I'd be grabbed at the death.

I wasn't, but worse was to follow.

With sobs of relief, I kicked open our garden gate and ran up the path. The front door was locked, so I veered left, running down the side alley past our allotment and coal bunker, to the kitchen door. To my disbelief, this was locked too. I fumbled wildly under the scullery window, found our spare key, and let myself in, slamming the door closed behind me. The next thing I noticed was the cold supper waiting on the kitchen table – some boiled bacon, bread and jam, a mug of milk – with a handwritten letter alongside it. Though the house was luxuriously warm, coals burning in both the kitchen stove and behind the fireguard on the grate in the living room, a new kind of chill struck me.

My parents were out.

I knew that before I even snatched up the note and began to read. It was from my father, and it explained that he and my mother had been invited round by neighbours for a Christmas Eve sherry. They would only be a couple of hours.

But which neighbours? He didn't specify.

And when had this couple of hours commenced? Was it shortly to expire or did it still stretch before me?

I yanked off my balaclava, my hair soaked with icy sweat – and heard a distinctive *clank* as the front gate banged open again. Incredulously, I listened to the progression of heavy misshapen feet along our snowy front path, and then into the alley beside the house, whereupon they abruptly stopped. I was now listening so intently that I fancied I could hear the whispering of the snowflakes outside, but apart from that there was only silence. Torturous, prolonged silence.

It is almost impossible to convey the horror and isolation I felt at that moment, even though I was ensconced in my own home. I stared fixedly at the kitchen door. For a time, there was nothing else in the world but that door – and what I suspected lurked just beyond it. I was unable to move; I didn't *dare* move, terrified that if my feet scuffed on the floor they would alert the thing to my presence, even though such thoughts were patently ludicrous – it had followed me all the way home. Even if it hadn't, it knew where I lived; according to our myths, it knew where every child lived.

There was a soft crunch of snow, this directly on the other side of the door, and then a further pause. Was it listening in through the planks as I was listening out? We had a telephone – I don't know why it never occurred to me to run and dial 999. I suspect I was simply too mesmerised by events. My nerves were taut as cello strings, my hair standing on end. But I quickly broke from this stupor when the door-handle started to turn.

I think I may have screamed aloud as I lurched forward and rammed home the upper bolt. Immediately, the handle ceased moving. There was another prolonged silence. I stood rigid, eyes goggling, awaiting the next move. Then the handle turned again, this time with violence, and there was a long, dull groan as a significant weight was pressed against the door from the other side. I was far from confident the single bolt would hold, especially when the weight was withdrawn and, instead, a heavy blow landed. Followed by another blow and another; loud, echoing reports, increasingly angry, which must have been heard all along our street. The kitchen door was solid oak, but it shook and shook, and I imagined that its screws would flirt from their moorings under such an assault.

It was a sure sign of how enthralled by fear I was that only now did it strike me to drive home the lower bolt as well. At first this was difficult: the assailant was hammering on the woodwork, not just with hands but with feet like iron clubs, and the lower section of the door vibrated so hard that it rarely lined up with the jamb – so hard that I thought it would shatter inward – but at last I managed to slide the bolt into its mount, and then ram my key into the lock and turn that too. All violence without instantly ceased.

The silence that followed this was perhaps the worst part

of it, for all I could do was hover there in a state of near-paralysis, unsure whether my unwanted visitor had slunk off into the night, or was still present, contemplating another means of ingress. When I suddenly heard a *clunk* of metal at the front of the house, I shrieked hoarsely and stumbled through into our entrance hall, but not without first taking my mother's rolling pin from one of the kitchen worktops. I still remember vividly how that hall seemed to elongate before me, to telescope out to inordinate length as I stood at the kitchen end and peered down it, past the evergreens draped over the stair banister, past the telephone table, past the wooden coat stand, to the front door itself, which, even as I watched, began to open.

I dashed down there with rolling pin raised, like some fearless warrior, screaming. But I was actually on my last legs, and I tripped on the rug before I got there and found myself pitching forward – into the arms of my astonished father.

Neither he nor my mother could speak they were so taken by surprise, but it soon became clear to them from my flow of semi-delirious gibberish that I was not playing some silly game. Despite my pleas that he lock all the doors and call for police assistance, my father went promptly down the side alley to the rear of the house. He found nobody lurking there, but with the aid of a candle, he noted extensive damage to our kitchen door. Afterwards, he listened again to the tale I had to tell him, and I left nothing out – but though he turned a trifle pale at my mention of the department store Santa Claus who'd appeared to know me and looked like Uncle Klaus, I don't think he really believed that part of it.

Though I was eleven years old, I spent that Christmas Eve in my parents' bed, alongside my mother. My father slept in the armchair downstairs, next to the fire, which he stoked up to a good blaze before switching off the lights. Apparently, he spent an uncomfortable but undisturbed night, and never once relinquished his grip on the poker. By morning, a fresh snowfall had obliterated all traces of footprints on our property. In a strange way, I was quite glad of that – I had no desire to see the shape of those left by our Christmas Eve intruder.

Grandpa Ludwig lapsed into distant memory as he sipped his port wine.

'Surely there was some kind of investigation?' my dad finally asked. Clearly, this was the first time he'd ever heard this particular story.

Grandpa Ludwig nodded. 'Absolutely. At the first opportunity my father sought out the general manager of *Halley & Meredith's* to officially complain that their Santa Claus had frightened me, and that he might well be the same person who had followed me home. Even the police became involved, and the Santa Claus in question – his name was William Harrison, and he was an out-of-work actor – was spoken to at length. Of course, Harrison denied any responsibility, and insisted that he was of good character. Others vouched for him, including fellow staff at *Halley & Meredith's*, who also provided an alibi, claiming to have shared a festive tipple with him once their work that Christmas Eve had finished. And indeed, when I was eventually shown a photograph of Harrison, it was a completely different man. This ended police enquiries at the store, for *Halley & Meredith's* had no other gentlemen employed in the role of Santa Claus.'

'That can't have been the end of the matter?' someone else asked.

'Far from it.' Grandpa Ludwig shifted to get comfortable in his armchair. 'The news had got out, and there was wide concern in our town that someone – nobody knew who – had followed a child home and tried to force entry to his house. The police continued to ask questions for quite some time. It was perhaps two years later when my father finally contacted them to say that he was sorry for all this trouble, but that he felt I had simply fallen asleep while alone in the house on Christmas Eve and had suffered a nightmare.'

'Did you?' my mum asked gently.

'Not a bit of it.'

'So, what brought your father to this conclusion?'

Grandpa Ludwig shrugged. 'It's anyone's guess, but it was quite a coincidence, I think, that around this time we learned the fate of Uncle Klaus. It seemed he'd been taken as a prisoner of war by the Soviets in 1944, and eventually, when hostilities were over, had been put on trial, accused of leading his unit in the massacres of civilians in Poland and Belarus. He was found guilty as charged and executed by hanging. I'm not sure of the exact date ... but it was some time in December 1948.'

Even my dad was speechless; evidently, he'd never heard this part of the story before either. The snapping and spitting of chestnut shells finally brought us round.

'Krampus,' my auntie said with distaste. 'What a horrible being to conjure up at Christmas time. The flipside of everything that is good and kind and forgiving.'

Grandpa Ludwig nodded. 'As Uncle Klaus said to me.'

'When did he say that?' my dad asked. 'If you never saw him again?'

Grandpa glanced up, his spectacles glinting with firelight. 'Why ... that final night before the war, after the argument with his twin brother, when he left our house in Mittenwald. At the time his exact words were lost on me, but since then I've remembered. He said: "Be warned, Ludwig ... there aren't just good fairies in your father's stories. There are bad ones too".'

ABOUT PAUL FINCH

Former police officer and journalist Paul Finch was a script-writer on *The Bill* and now, as a best-selling crime novelist, is the author of the very popular DS Mark 'Heck' Heckenburg and DC Lucy Clayburn novels (the first one of which made the *Sunday Times* Top 10 list). He is also widely published in the horror and fantasy fields, having written *Doctor Who* scripts for Big Finish and winning the British Fantasy Award twice for his short stories and novellas. He has also now edited 16 volumes of the *Terror Tales* series.

Paul is a native of Wigan, Lancashire, where he still lives with his wife and business partner, Cathy.

ALSO IN THE TERROR TALES SERIES: